Chet Hanson

The Buyer

ISBN 978-0-9861677-0-6

Printed in the United States of America

Portrait art by Steven Graber
Front cover layout by Roxann Graber

Cover design created by Ron Bell of AdVision Design Group
(www.advisiondesigngroup.com)

Edited by Skip Coryell

Published by Grateful Publishing ☺

Dedication

I would be taking undue credit if I did not say I owe all to my Lord and Savior, Jesus Christ. This includes life, both here and the hereafter, the talents I have and the wonderful inspirations in the form of that which He has created – especially the wonderful people with whom He has filled my life.

Of special note, my beautiful wife, Dr. Kathy Hanson, who inspires me with her presence and excellent ideas. My son, Chip, who expanded my life's tool box by introducing me to the computer. My son, Joshua, who gave me permission to write by doing so himself. My lovely sister, the late Bobby Hanson, for pointing out I was not a businessman, despite my success – I was an artist and would be much happier once I lived like one. She was right.

Prologue

ONE COULD NOT BE FAULTED FOR THINK-ing this might be a scene from Hemingway's Paris. It was not the Roaring 20's, nor was the room full of artists and those who chose to hang around artists.

But the long, narrow bar itself was certainly old enough to have accommodated the likes of Ernest Hemingway. The unmistakable fragrance of Gitanes cigarettes still hovered.

However, the year was 2010 and the cast had changed.

Off to the right, the larger half of the room, there was but one occupied table. Three young adults, one female and two males huddled, listening intently as their questions were answered by a fourth person. He was a somewhat short, powerfully built man, an old man of about seventy.

On the left side of the room, nearly hidden by the stairway, sat a lone figure. He was tall, even when sitting. He was thin with unkempt dark brown hair and a beard to match. His dress was simple: dark blue jeans, a black wool turtleneck and running shoes. He intensely hunkered over a laptop that sat on his table.

The owner was not present. He had inherited the place and kept it for sentimental reasons. He came in only to open up and to close.

There was only one waiter. He was very conscious of the needs of the disheveled figure, and obviously kept his distance so as not to intrude in any way.

This same scene had repeated itself day after day. It had gone on for weeks. On the right side of the room, the listeners of the old man changed frequently. The old man, himself, never changed save that sometimes he sat alone with his head bowed, as if in prayer.

The tall man on the left side of the room had changed only in that his hair and beard had become progressively longer. He worked on his laptop without ceasing.

Then, one day, shortly after noon, he closed his computer and sat back in his chair and closed his eyes.

He was satisfied that he had taken this methodology as far as he could when he became aware of a presence. Looking up, he found he was gazing into the bright, blue, but ancient, eyes of the old man from the other side of the room.

"Pardonnez-moi monsieur, did you want to speak with me?"

"Yes," said Leonard, without hesitation, "that would be nice."

"Bon," said the old man as he reached out his hand and gave his name.

"My friends call me Papa Chevalier."

Leonard rose briefly in a respectful gesture and said simply, "Leonard LaFrance."

"From the corner of my eye," began Papa Chevalier, "I have watched you very closely since your first day. I did not come over sooner, because I could see you working – how do you say, frantically?"

"Well," smiled Leonard, "not so much frantic as urgent."

"Let me see if I can understand," said Papa. "You were lost – then you were found – and now you are lost again – and that brings deeper pain than being lost the first time."

Leonard began to increase his smile.

"Papa, I can see you are very perceptive. You must have seen a lot over the years. Would you please, give me the honor of your life story? I need to know who you are if I am to seek your counsel."

"Heh, heh," laughed Papa. "And you are wise to understand that you must know who it is that is offering advice.

"There is not much to tell. I am the only son of a well-off family from the South of France. The source of our income was a family-owned company; my father and his brother were equal partners. They each had one child; each a son, me and my cousin Phillipe.

"My cousin and I, were and are, quite different. We were smart in different ways. He with money and me, well, perhaps with more ethereal things. Our fathers had expected us to continue to run the company in the fashion that had worked so well for them.

"My cousin was 21 and I was 19 when we sat down, just the two of us," continued Papa. "He was so full of enthusiasm. He had so many ideas for the family business that were excellent."

"I could not get excited about the business. I had been spending a lot of time at church. I would talk to Father Andrea and Father Dominic. Father Andrea was our Priest and Father Dominic had retired and was spending his last days in the place he loved most.

"It was so different," said Papa, in a manner that disclosed the notion that he could still see that time, place and people. "They spoke of things that other men never speak of. There was no talk of football or business or women, but the concepts they dealt with were on a different plane. Part of it was theoretical and part of it spiritual. But it challenged my thinking and it became like a drug.

"Just as my cousin Phillipe was addicted to the drug of business, I was addicted to the drug of spiritual thinking. I became a priest."

Leonard had a question at this point. "But you are not a priest now?"

"You are correct. I left the priesthood. I fell in love with a married woman. We never had anything beyond intense conversation, but adultery is a matter of the heart, even as it is a matter of the flesh. I had too much respect for the Church to ignore its rules."

"Are you," asked Leonard, "sad about leaving the priesthood?"

"You know, at first I could not breathe. It felt like I held my breath for two years. Then, one day, I came in here for a coffee, probably much like yourself.

"I heard a young couple at the next table arguing. I could not help myself. I listened closely. To me their problem was like a small wave in a calm sea. It was about nothing!

"I," said Papa, "as politely as I could, asked them if I might offer them a suggestion. They were polite and allowed me to counsel with them. It was wonderful to watch them as the steel plates that guarded their ego slid away and were replaced with a fabric of love and respect. They are now married – three beautiful children – mostly happy." Papa

3

ended with a small shrug.

"Papa, on a scale of one to ten, ten being very happy, how happy are you?"

"If," said Papa, "we are to use a scale, then I would have to include not only happy, but also satisfied, and grateful. On all of those I would rate them, on your scale, an eleven."

"So ... you think this is what you are supposed to be doing with your life?"

"For now, it is precisely what I am supposed to be doing. My passion is to do God's work. Let me tell you, because I was faithful and left the priesthood when I knew that I had sinned, I believe God gave me this.

"Leonard, do you know the priests I went through the seminary with are telling me that church attendance is down to rock bottom? Do you know very few younger people go to confession? Do you have any idea how freeing it is to confess your sins and get advice without agenda from some learned person who loves you in the name of Christ?"

Papa Chevalier stood up, stretching all of his 5-feet, 7-inch frame, and with his right hand up in the air with finger pointing around the room, he declared, "Leonard, this is my church. God brings me those who need me the most. I have no other job, but to listen, and then point out a simple truth. The one thing that will give them a true, rich smile – is to make God smile."

A proper silence followed.

Leonard digested the words, examined his memory, recalling the parade of people who had come to Papa's table. After due consideration, Leonard said, "Papa, I want to tell you my story."

And so, in a most objective, third-person telling, Leonard relived the roller-coaster life that had been his ... up to now.

Chapter 1

Leonard LaFrance was fully awake 8 minutes before his 4:30 AM wake-up call. His habit was to rise immediately upon waking and get into the shower, where his hands would go on autopilot, cleansing his hair and body, while his mind envisioned the one important thing he wanted to accomplish that day.

His father had taught him that.

But this morning he found it near impossible to get out of bed.

His father would not have been pleased.

"A man needs a solid 7 hours of sleep if he is going to compete at peak efficiency."

That was Part A, of one of the more constant, father-to-son lessons Leonard had been subjected to for 32 of his 51 years.

Part B, always came in tandem to it.

"By getting up and getting going a half hour or so before his competitors, a man will have a slight advantage all through the day. Leonard, for a man who has his mind on his business, and not distracted in any way, this is all the advantage he will need."

His father had been largely absent until Leonard's 11th birthday. It was on this day that his father became omnipresent, and the constant lessons that were the glue between them continued until his father's death 8 years ago.

Still, the task of getting out of bed seemed to be too great this morning. However, when the alarm did go off, Leonard literally leapt from the bed.

In the shower, his mind went to the La Crosse Instrument deal that was coming to a head. His father would not be at all pleased by this decision.

"We are in the real estate business." That was his motto. "We don't take the risk of building a business, leave that for those foolish enough to accept the risk. We buy distressed properties, in good locations, make them more attractive, get long-term, iron-clad leases, and let them take the risk of building something."

Say what you will, but Fred LaFrance, his father, started with a farm his uncle had left him. He moved in, renovated it with his own hands, leveraged it, then leased it out and bought 6 small houses in Watts. For about a decade his father was admittedly a slumlord, but little by little he improved the quality of his holdings and when he had a stroke and passed the reins on to Leonard the properties were valued in excess of 280 million dollars. Interestingly, he still owned the farm and the slums.

Fred LaFrance was a buyer, not a seller.

For a total of 11 years – 3 years after his father's stroke and 8 years since his death – Leonard had called the shots. Yes, the decisions were all exactly in line with the blueprints his father had drilled into him over the years, but the decision maker was Leonard. Under the son's watch the empire more than doubled, but up until now Leonard had precisely followed his father's formula, as was his habit.

Now, he was about to acquire La Crosse Instruments, a company that made something. It made a small number of high-quality medical products. Their problem, as Leonard saw it, was that they were scientists, and engineers, not salesmen. They put almost all their best assets, including their human capital, into R & D and precision manufacturing. They had all but ignored building a sales or marketing staff. As a result they were broke and had no income stream bountiful enough to save them.

However, the little company had one big hope; a device that promised the early detection of Alzheimer. It was not totally perfected, and it had yet to undergo all of the required, cost-intensive, testing, but it looked to Leonard like this little company could explode in profits.

La Crosse Instruments was literally on the verge – but – out of money. The nail in the coffin came when the one bank that had lent them money finally decided they too had better follow the new federal regulations to the "T," and they demanded payment.

It was very difficult for them, but the owners of La Crosse had no choice but to sell or simply close their doors.

Buying La Crosse was a move filled with trepidation for Leonard as well. However, in his own mind, he had no choice either. He was losing interest in everything. Maybe, this would give him back his edge.

At precisely 5:15 AM a very good-looking young man of 26 rang Leonard's front door bell. Shawn Davis was a very crisp fellow. He was lean, his height was almost exactly 6 feet, his dark brown hair was neatly trimmed and he was clean-shaven.

Shawn had worked as Leonard's personal assistant, just as Calvin Frost had been a personal assistant to Leonard's father, Fred LaFrance. Shawn took the job with the understanding it was a dead end, lifetime job that paid well; very, very well. The duties were not demanding. Loyalty, promptness, and sealed lips lead the job description.

There were also two other men waiting. They had names of course, Simpson and Shook, yet they were non-entities. Simpson, a formidable specimen at 6-feet, 5 inches and nearly 300 pounds, was standing on the curb. He was constantly looking up and down the street, watching the windows, shrubs and shadows of the adjacent homes and checking every perimeter.

Shook sat behind the wheel of an idling Mercedes-Benz S 600 Pullman Guard limousine, literally an armored car. He too was obviously watchful.

Mr. L, as all of his employees referred to him, emerged, perfectly tailored and neatly coiffed, as always, from his toney Beverly Hills home and quickly took refuge in the waiting limo. As was his habit.

How it was done

THE boardroom was large and opulent, but not overdone. The kind of room that made the visitor quite aware that every decision was final, and there was little to no wiggle room.

The Buyer

Three of the LaFrance attorneys along with two very sharp account-ants sat on the west side of the table. The four guests, the partners in La Crosse Instruments, sat on the east.

The blinds were open and the morning sun streamed directly into the eyes of those facing the window. That was of course, the La Crosse contingent.

Though to the casual eye it was not apparent, the seats of the chairs on the guest side of the table were one point five inches shorter than ones on the side where the LaFrance team always sat. The height difference was not immediately noticeable because, the chairs backs were all precisely the same height. Though not conscious as to why, the occupants of the shorter chairs were at a disadvantage.

The custom made chairs were expensive, but then again, Leonard's father would always pay a bit extra for an advantage. That is why he named his empire the Advantage Corporation.

Each attendee had a folder in front of them that had been drawn up by the Advantage Corporation team. The folder contained the terms of the deal they were about to enter, including: the price to be paid, the employment contracts along with strict non-compete agreements and pages and pages of fine-print particulars.

There was a most uncomfortable silence in the room as they waited for The Man. Nine minutes after the agreed start time Mr. L finally entered the room.

As was his habit, Leonard did not take a seat, but walked to stand directly in front of the sun-filled window. He liked closing deals in the early morning, because the sun screamed in behind his 6-feet, 1-inch frame causing an aura around his person that made him both imperial and nearly invisible.

Those who faced the window that morning could not see much in the way of detail about the man who held their economic fate in his hands. What they could see was the silhouette of a tall, impeccably tai-lored, broad-shouldered, slender man who carried himself in a manner that clearly supported his realization that he was the king of his domain.

The Advantage lead attorney, the Harvard educated Mr. Leon Hard-ing, started to read the contents of the folder line by line.

Mr. L allowed that for 14 minutes before he quietly coughed, as was his habit. The attorney stopped reading and gave Mr. L his full attention, as did the rest of the participants.

After noting the barely perceptible nod of Mr. L's head the lead attorney, started to speak again, but this time he was not reading.

"I should have asked if you have had time to peruse and understand the agreement and its particulars. Have you Mr. Blake?"

Mr. Blake, a smallish man with heavy glasses, thinning hair and a most intelligent face replied with a bit of frustration, "But of course."

"Have you any questions?" queried Leon Harding.

"Yes, I have one," answered Mr. Blake. "You are buying our company, paying each of us a mutually agreeable amount for our stock, paying off our debt that is about to bankrupt the company, additionally, you have promised an unspecified amount of operating capital, and all of that is a godsend. However, La Crosse Instruments is quite possibly on the verge of bringing a breakthrough product to market. You are demanding employment contracts for the four of us with a very strong 7-year non-compete clause, but there is no specific guarantee of how much we will have in the way of working capital.

"If," continued, Mr. Blake, "there is an insufficient infusion of cash the company will collapse and we will all be out of work with no path for us to earn income in the only field we are skilled in. I am surprised at this for two reasons: one, I do not think the non-compete is enforceable and two, the collapse of the company will leave Mr. L, as you like to call him, with very little for his money spent. What can you give us to ensure we will not be hung out to dry?"

Mr. Harding nodded his head as though he understood and had anticipated this question.

"Mr. Blake, as for your first point, had you and your partners in La Crosse Instruments been mere employees then indeed the non compete would be indefensible, however as owners in the company, the non-compete is fully applicable. As for your second point, Mr. L is not prone to losing money and will do whatever is necessary to bring your new Alzheimer testing equipment on line as we fully believe it will be profitable. You will notice that the four of you are in line for a generous profit sharing, if and when you bring in that product, in a timely and efficient manner. Any other questions?"

"We are at a loss," sighed Blake, "because we have exhausted every financial avenue. We know our innovation will be very valuable in the treatment of Alzheimer's; therefore, it will be widely used in what is likely the fastest-growing health problem worldwide, and therefore enormously profitable. If, and it's a big 'if' we are able to have access to sufficient working capital to bring it to market."

Mr. Blake continued, almost mumbling, as he finished with, "It seems like, even discussing this issue is off the table. So, how can we know we will have the resources to fully develop the device? And by the way, we are more passionate about seeing the success in the treatment than we are about profits. Can you understand that or is money your only metric?"

The lead lawyer started to answer, but Leonard spoke for the first time. His voice sounded more akin to an exhausted sigh than the commanding tone his people were accustomed to.

"Mr. Blake, I will only say that I have personal reasons for making this work. You can sign and trust – or – you can leave."

With that, Mr. L left the bright place in front of the East window. As he exited the La Crosse contingent realized, that except for the imperial impression and a glimpse of a rather good-looking face, no one ever really got a clear look at him.

Leonard was enormously good at reading people, especially when it came time to close a deal. It crossed his mind he was perhaps even better at it than his father had been.

Blake and his partners sighed, but signed.

The lead lawyer for Advantage now took over and made it clear that Bruce Saunders, one of the brightest young accountants at Advantage Corporation, would take over as Chief Financial Officer of La Crosse.

Just at that moment Shawn Davis, Leonard's assistant, came into the boardroom and handed Leon Harding a note. The lead lawyer then smiled for the first time and announced that when Mr. Saunders came in as their CFO of La Crosse Instruments, he would be bringing with him operating capitol in the amount of up to 10 million dollars – three times the amount Blake and his partners had assumed would be required.

La Crosse Instruments people were very happy; they also knew it was not a gift and that much would be expected of them. They looked at each other and silently agreed; they were ready and anxious to get started.

The reward

AFTER lunch in the office, which was his habit, Leonard decided he did not want to remain there. He would do the unthinkable and take the afternoon off. The limousine stopped with the rest of the traffic at the light on the corner of Rodeo Drive and Wilshire Boulevard. Leonard was looking out the window in an absent-minded manner. He saw something of interest.

She was very pretty, twentyish, shoulder-length, dark-brown hair, stood about 5-feet 7 inches tall and weighed about 120 pounds. She did not look like she belonged on Rodeo drive. Leonard looked over at Shawn Davis and then, back to the girl. Shawn was on it.

Shawn hated this part of the job; nonetheless, he leapt from the car before the light changed. The driver went around the block - twice. On the second lap Shawn and the girl were standing by the curb. The limousine swooped over and picked them up.

Chapter 2

THE FOLLOWING MORNING LEONARD LAF-rance woke at 4 AM. At 4:30 AM, the alarm went off. Leonard continued to lie there. At 5:15 AM Shawn Davis stood at the door for several minutes after ringing the door buzzer. The two security men became a bit nervous. Finally, Shawn's cell phone rang and Mr. L informed him, that he would not be going into the office today.

At 7:45 AM Leonard had to go to the toilet. Once up, he saw no advantage to going back to bed. Leonard did not shave. He stayed in his pajamas and a robe.

He had no housekeeper that lived in. The service that cleaned his office building had one of their most trusted employees come three times a week, but they always called to be sure that Mr. L was not in residence. Privacy was as important to Leonard as oxygen.

Breakfast and lunch were usually eaten at the office, rarely in a restaurant. Supper was usually brought in by a local bistro fully prepared. Therefore, he avoided any personal entanglement with a cook.

He was alone and very worried. He had no energy and no thirst for anything. He knew he had been slipping into depression over the past few months, but he had been functioning … but not today.

He had somehow anticipated, and hoped, that today would be different. This should have been a good day. The La Crosse deal had come together exactly as he had planned. A deal that broke one of his father's foremost rules.

Leonard had done something on his own, and hoped it would brighten his outlook. He thought that would lift his spirits. It didn't.

The girl who was out of place on Rodeo drive accepted the offered $10,000, just as did almost all of the girls Leonard picked out. This girl was nice, followed directions and asked no questions. This was usually the case with these girls who were too intimidated by vast wealth. Leonard did not allow himself many of these rewards. It was, indeed, a minor habit. Not nearly as often as his father, who had introduced him to this reward system, had allowed himself. Yet, Leonard had sent her home earlier than was his custom.

He did not want to be around people, yet by 10:15 AM he felt lonely. He reached for the remote and turned on the TV just to hear voices. This was all unprecedented. Leonard did not ever miss work. Leonard did not watch TV – not even sports. When he did watch, it was restricted to Bloomberg and random business reports.

After turning it on, he tried to interest himself in a local talk show. It was soon clear he could not focus on it, so he chose to ignore it. As he turned to leave the room he heard something that drew him back to watch. What he heard was a voice. A voice quite familiar, yet buried in a distant memory. He listened with greater intent and realized the voice was that of his mother. A voice he had not been privileged to hear since he was 11 years old.

It was, of course, not his mother. It was a local TV show with one goofball doctor interviewing another doctor. The interviewer was a hack, but there was a certain compassion and thoughtful intelligence to the interviewee.

Moreover – her voice was very reminiscent of his mother.

Leonard sat down in the club chair. She, the woman who sounded so much like his mother, did not shoot from the hip when asked a question. She did not try to appear to presume to have the answers to questions no one had ever asked before.

She thoughtfully gave a carefully reasoned answer. Leonard liked her immediately. Not as a potential "Reward", but just as a person. Her mannerisms also reminded Leonard of his mother; though that memory was dim.

Leonard made the call himself. The doctor's name, so the script below her image read, was Lillian Carroll, Doctor of Psychiatry. With strength and urgency he asked for an immediate appointment. The receptionist was caught off guard by the force of his demand and babbled something about she did not think the doctor was seeing patients this morning as she had scheduled the TV appearance and then had planned lunch with her daughter. She added that if this was an emergency he should hang up and call 911.

The show had been taped earlier and Dr. Carroll was just walking into her office when she picked up on her receptionist in a fluster and asked what was going on.

"Please hold," the cheerful receptionist directed Leonard.

Leonard almost hung up. He did not hold for anyone, but he also never made an appointment with a psychiatrist. In his moment of indecision the receptionist returned and apologized saying "The doctor will have no time for a new patient until November 26th."

Today was June 5th.

Always quick on his feet he hammered the receptionist with, "Did you not say you didn't expect her in, but I heard her ask what was going on. I want to see her now," he said with sufficient authority to cause the receptionist to once again put him on hold.

This time Leonard waited.

When the girl returned to the phone she asked Leonard, "How soon can you be here?" After finding out her office was but three blocks away he said, "fifteen minutes," and hung up.

After his hasty declaration of being there in 15 minutes, Leonard made several quick decisions. First, he did not have time to shave, shower or get into a suit and tie. He would wear a sport shirt and slacks (highly unusual he thought, but liberating). He would not call for Shawn or his driver and he would walk the 3 blocks. He also decided he would not be late.

How she got here

Dr. Lillian Carroll was 41, a widow and a mother of a 22-year-old daughter who was apparently going on 50.

Her father had been a petroleum engineer in East Texas, and that is where she did most of her growing up. When he was transferred to the home office in LA, the family moved to the storied land of Southern California. She felt a bit out of place. Her southern accent was quite pronounced and the difference between Kilgore, Texas and Santa Monica, California was a bit overwhelming.

On the first day at her new school she had been deflowered, culturally speaking, and learned firsthand what it meant to be uncool in the coolest place on earth. Or so it was locally assumed.

On the very first hour of the second day all that changed. There was a group of wanna-be-cools surrounding her before class. The chief object of their amusement was Lilly's southern accent. They were dissing her in the most uncertain terms when, quietly, their circle was enlarged by one more person.

He was taller by a head than any of the others and was breathtakingly handsome. He smiled at her over the heads of the small and undistinguished crowd. She saw kindness in his eyes and smiled back.

The chattering classes continued chattering, but Lilly did not seem to hear or see them. She saw only this young man, who extended his hand, and with assurance, he said to the others, "Excuse us please." And they walked away.

The two had no way of knowing how far their walk would take them.

Lilly would marry her high school sweetheart when she was younger than her daughter was now. He, Brian Carroll, was a prince, sweet, considerate, extraordinarily handsome, but not all that smart.

It was clear to both of them that it was Lilly who had the exceptional brain. Her parents were devastated when she ran off with Brian, because Lilly held such promise. The marriage was spurred on of course by the unplanned pregnancy.

Brian was no slouch. He jumped into the role of husband and provider. He had no skills and had just barely graduated high school. But he was in love, and took to the husband's role with a profound relish. His one major possession was a Ford F-150 pick-up truck. Brian's three minor possessions were a lawn mower, leaf blower and an edger. He had been mowing lawns since junior high school and had saved close to $900.00 from his efforts.

Once married, upon the advice from Mr. Wu, one of his wealthier customers, Brian's savings, along with a loan from mister Wu, were invested in more and better equipment. Also, in compliance with Mr. Wu's sage advice, he and Lilly created some snappy promotional material.

They both went door to door with his flyers and in 10 days had forty customers who wanted their lawns cut, some every week, others every 10 days and a few just twice a month. When the jobs were totaled up, Brian was fully booked.

But because they had put out so many flyers and talked to so many people the requests for service kept coming in. So Brian, while no genius, understood that getting the job was pretty easy, it was the quality of his work that would make people want to stay with his services.

There were many of his buddies, especially the guys he played football with, who were hard-working guys and wanted full time work. One by one he brought them on, trained them and then recruited more customers.

When he ran out of high school pals Brian put an ad in the paper and one of the first to respond was a guy who went to UC Davis and had a horticulture degree that lined up perfectly with the lawn, tree and shrub business Brian was building.

Still leaning on advice from the wealthy customer who got him started, Brian made very few mistakes. By the time Lilly gave birth to Sharon, Brian had eight trucks and eight teams that were all doing quality landscape work. Brian's Lawn and Tree was becoming well known and the income was more than enough to meet all obligations and keep Lilly in school.

She earned her Bachelor of Science, went on to get her MD and then did her residency in Psychiatry.

Her parents were very pleased when they retired and moved back to Kilgore.

It was the day after their 16th anniversary when Brian fell from the tree. It did not seem that great a fall, maybe 30 feet. Brian held on for three days, but the brain trauma was too great. The neurosurgeon spoke to Lillian, a doctor herself, as he would any other colleague. "It is probably a blessing," he said.

Lilly and Sharon were stunned and staggered by his loss. He was a life force for them both. So full of love, self-sacrifice and gentleness. And in a mere moment he was no more.

Had he survived with his cranial injuries ... the thought was more than Lilly could handle.

Sharon did better than her mother. Her mother faked it very well, but even after 5 years she felt an emptiness that could never, in her wildest imagination, be filled. She had her daughter and her work. Now, however, her daughter would be returning to Berkeley in the fall and that would leave Lilly with only her work. The upcoming loss worried Lilly, but, as always, Lilly went on.

Meeting mother

LEONARD was moving fast. He was walking at an unaccustomed pace. He hit Dr. Lillian Carroll's door with such momentum that he fairly sailed into the room and nearly collided with the receptionist's glassed-in booth.

Breathless, he voiced the fact that he had an appointment with 'Dr. Lilly', as he called her.

The receptionist slipped a clipboard with insurance forms and an H&P questionnaire under the glass partition.

Leonard looked at the device and repeated, "I have an appointment with Dr. Lilly."

"Yes sir," she said, "we just spoke on the phone, but I did not get your name and now we must fill out these forms for insurance and to get some health background information on you."

"Maybe later, but I don't fill out any forms and I'll pay cash."

"Sir, please, you must fill these out or the doctor can't see you."

"Can _you_ see me?" Leonard asked, slightly raising his voice. "Any-one can see me, I am right here, but I need to see Dr. Lilly right now or I will leave and I don't know what will happen after that. Please. Please. Please. Please, ask her if she will see me now."

The sounds of the conversation carried through the door and into her office. Dr. Lillian Carroll opened the door to see what was going on.

Her receptionist said, "Doctor, he won't fill out the forms. He won't even tell me his name."

In the same thoughtful way she addressed the interviewer on the TV show this morning she looked steadily at Leonard and asked with a clear, calm voice,

"What is your name, sir?"

To Leonard she looked, sounded and now, even smelled, like his mother. He was immediately calmed and yet he answered cautiously, "Mr. L."

"Won't you come in Mr. L?"

Lilly held the door open and Leonard meekly walked into her office. Lilly did not close the door.

Her receptionist dialed 911, but did not push send. She also removed the Taser from her desk drawer.

The doctor pointed to a chair directly in front of her desk. It was not a particularly comfortable chair. Not nearly as comfortable as the chair and sofa in the far corner that she usually ushered her patients to. The doctor did not care to make this agitated man comfortable enough to encourage a long stay.

"I must be candid and let you know I do not usually see patients on the spur of the moment like this, but Trisha said you sounded particularly desperate. What brings you in today Mr. L?" asked Lilly calmly.

"I saw you on the television show this morning and I thought you were someone I could talk to."

"Why did you think that?" asked Dr. Carroll.

"Because you thought before you spoke," he answered with a sudden calm.

"What did you want to talk about?"

"Can you tell me why I have lost all interest in everything even though I am doing all of the right things?" Leonard asked.

"What are the right things and who defined 'right'?" she asked.

"I keep my mind on my business. I get up at least a half hour before my competition. I do not allow distractions. I seek every advantage. I buy and never sell. I have followed every rule of my father since I was 11. Until yesterday, when I thought if I broke one rule and was successful my father would congratulate me. I'm talking like a fool and I don't know why."

The doctor ignored the last part but inquired, "By that, am I to assume it was your father who set the rules as to what is 'right'?"

"Yes."

"Did your father approve of your breaking the rules yesterday?" asked the doctor.

"I have no way of knowing," responded Leonard. "He has been dead for eight years."

Dr. Carroll tried to hide any discomfort that answer brought, but she did adjust her posture a bit.

She then said, "I am a bit uncomfortable calling you Mr. L. Is there another name that I might use?"

That was a question not often asked in the little world he lived in. "You may call me …" Leonard paused, then asked, "Is everything I tell you kept in the strictest confidence?"

"Yes," she responded. "It is protected by law."

"Okay, you may call me Leonard."

"Thank you Leonard. Tell me, what rule did you break yesterday?"

"I bought a company that makes things."

"Your father did not approve of buying a company that makes things? Why?" Dr. Lilly asked.

"Building a business can be risky. It is much smarter to buy distressed real estate in good areas, make that property more attractive, get an ironclad lease and then let someone else take the risk of building a business."

"Was your father good at implementing his plan?" she asked.

"Oh yes," replied Leonard. "He started with a small farm and he was worth a quarter of a billion when he passed it on to me."

"And are you good at implementing your father's plan?"

"I, I have more than doubled the value of the holdings," he replied humbly, then added, "but I did it using my father's formula."

"Hmmm," murmured Dr. Carroll. "Would you call your actions yesterday, the buying of a company that makes something, an act of rebellion against your father?"

Leonard was quiet and thoughtful, then offered, "I don't know. I know I don't like the idea associated with the words you just used, but I did want to do something that was not according to his plan, something that I did on my own."

"Did you start running the company after your father's death?"

"No, I began running it three years before his death, because he had had a stroke that left him unable to easily communicate. So I became his voice."

"Was he happy with the way you ran things?"

Leonard smiled, as if remembering something. "He was always proud of me, except the one time. He gave me a piece of property and asked me to do my best with it. The property was adjacent to a rapidly growing high-tech company and they found I was the responsible party. They wanted that piece of property so badly that they offered almost twice what Mr. L, the original one, my father, paid for it. I knew he did not sell the properties he owned so I said, 'No.'

"Then," Leonard continued, "they made the same offer, but sweetened it by including two other pieces of property they already owned in a business park just outside of town. Each piece was as big as the one we had that they wanted. Anyway, I sold it to them."

"And your father thought, what?"

"He was madder than I have ever seen him since my mother went away. It was a very controlled anger, but very unmistakable. He said eleven words that I have never forgotten. My father said 'We don't sell property – we buy property. Don't ever forget it.' I haven't."

"How do you feel about the way that deal worked out?" inquired Dr. Carroll.

Leonard smiled again, but it was a much bigger smile. "The hi-tech company went under, their building is still empty. However, the business park, where they gave us the two pieces to sweeten the deal, we now own the entire business park. Not only that, but we are fully leased at above market."

After a short moment, Leonard added, "I finally made my father happy when I bought back the still undeveloped lot we sold to the hi-tech plant for less than what my father originally paid for it." Then Leonard grew quiet and somewhat grim. "But it was the wrong thing to do."

"If someone would have asked your father what he did, do you know what he'd say?"

"Yes, he always had the same answer. 'I am a buyer'."

"What kind of work do you do Leonard?"

He did not hesitate. "I am a buyer."

The two talked for almost an hour.

At this point, Trisha, the receptionist, buzzed the doctor on the intercom. "Sorry to interrupt doctor, but your daughter is here for your luncheon appointment."

Fascination

LEAVING her inner office Dr. Carroll greeted her daughter with a hug, then brought Leonard over to Trisha and asked the receptionist to accommodate Mr. L. with a 7:45 AM appointment on a day within the next week.

Trisha was a tiger when it came to keeping the doctor's schedule full and collecting for services.

"Yes, Mr. L," she said with a grin. "Let's see if we can find a day to make the next appointment. What does your schedule look like?"

"Mr. L." Trisha repeated, but he was far, far away. He was lost in the eyes of Doctor Carroll's daughter – and what was even more strange, she was caught up with a peculiar attraction for him.

Doctor Carroll had been busy gathering her purse, but now her attention was drawn to the bizarre pair. *Leonard and her daughter?*

The awkwardness of just drawing her daughter away by pulling her arm was out, so the doctor introduced them quickly and then she pulled her daughter away by the arm.

Meanwhile, the ever-persistent Trisha was virtually tugging at Mr. L's sleeve until the doctor/daughter duo was out of sight. He returned his attention to the persistent pest who was Trisha.

"When," she said again, "would you like to come back?"

"Tomorrow," Mr. L answered with finality.

"Tomorrow? Well okay. Dr. Carroll will have to come in an hour early and you will have to be here by 7:45. That will be $335.00 for your first appointment."

The Buyer

Leonard looked at her blankly. "Well, uh, I don't usually carry a wallet. Can you bill me?"

Trisha sighed at the very difficult Mr. L and said, "Okay, what is your billing information?"

Leonard LaFrance was not about to put this information in the hands of the clerk of a psychiatrist.

"Never mind," Leonard said. "I will bring cash tomorrow."

Chapter 3

IT OCCURRED TO LEONARD THAT HE HADN'T had an occasion to think of the word, 'Wow!' since he was a very young man. But there it was on the screen of his mind as plain as day. 'Wow!'

First, he had worn a sport shirt and slacks instead of a dress shirt, suit and tie. Then, he'd left the house without shaving or showering, and walked, yes he'd actually walked, to a meeting without security. He'd actually talked to a human being about personal issues. She was a nice person and reminded Leonard of his mother. She also smelled nice. Then he'd met her daughter. She had both mesmerized and confused him. *Wow!*

There was that word again.

THE offices of the Advantage Corporation were about two and a half miles from Dr. Carroll's office. Leonard did not know that. He only knew it was a beautiful day and that he had a song in his heart. Well, not really. He wanted a song in his heart, but he couldn't think of one so he rather tonelessly hummed something, as if it was a song in his heart.

While he mangled a tune, that had yet to be written, he also thought of the absolute vision that was Sharon, the Doctor's daughter, but he shook it off. There was no way he could carry on a conversation with a woman like her, let alone persuade her to allow him to take her to dinner or the like.

It occurred to Leonard that he'd never developed any social skills. As long as he was acting as a buyer he had few peers, but move the same set of people into a social setting and Leonard was speechless … literally.

Leonard had not done much walking in years. After a quick calculation he realized it was forty years. He also realized his unaccustomed feet were starting to feel a bit uncomfortable. Just about that time he heard someone call out.

"On your left!"

Leonard turned to his left and sure enough there was this fellow running right there.

Whumpf, another unfamiliar sound along with a major intrusion into his personal space, and the impact sent Leonard and the runner both sprawling.

The runner was clearly put out by being reduced to a sprawling heap. He invested tremendous energy in springing back up to a more dignified posture.

"What's wrong with you?" shouted the runner. "Didn't you hear me yell 'On your left?'"

Being out of his element and caught off guard, forced an admission, "Why, yes I did," said Leonard. "But I didn't know what that meant."

"It means the same thing on the street as it means on the ski slope." The now bewildered and disgusted runner said as he brushed grit from his hands and knees. Then looking down at the somewhat slim, but obviously unaerobicized pedestrian, he offered his hand.

Leonard accepted it and stood up. Before the runner jumped off to regain his exercise mode, Leonard took his arm and asked, "How can you run like that without hurting your feet?"

More confused than ever Leonard's collision mate looked at Leonard anew with an intense curiosity.

Clearing his head the runner asked, "Do your feet hurt?"

"Why, yes, they do."

The runner looked at Leonard's shoes. They were obviously expensive as were his slacks and sports shirt, but there seemed, to the close observer, an awkwardness of life in the man before him.

"You don't get out much, do you?" the runner asked gently.

The question and its sincerity caused Leonard to pause, then he answered thoughtfully.

"Well the answer to that would be both yes and no. I do get out every day, but only out in a car. It is very unusual to walk anywhere. Why do you ask?"

The runner brushed that question aside and returned to Leonard's earlier question.

"My feet don't hurt for two reasons. I walk at least two miles everyday and run six miles three times a week. The other reason is I wear the proper shoes for the exercise. Your shoes are expensive, but they're meant for riding in cars and sitting behind a desk. If you change those two things – get regular exercise and wear proper shoes – your feet won't hurt either."

The runner waited for the recognition of what he had said to show on Leonard's face. As soon as it did he turned to finish his run. But he didn't get far.

"Please wait," pleaded Leonard. "Will you work for me?"

The runner was kind. "It is clear you need help, but I have as much work as I care to have, so – no, I am not available for hire. However, if you have a card I will call you and help you find the right shoes."

Leonard desperately needed the man's help, but he had no card. He did not even know his phone number. The only number he ever needed was that of Shawn Davis, his assistant. In fact that was the only number catalogued in his cell phone. He explained this to the now somewhat incredulous man he had run into.

"I could give you my assistants cell phone and he always knows where I am – except for right now – no one knows." Saying this simple fact made Leonard feel almost giddy.

"I am jogging," said the runner. "I have no pockets and I like my hands to be free when I run."

Thinking quickly, Leonard offered, "Or if you know where the Advantage Corporation building is you could come by there and ask for me." There was such a subtle cry for help in Leonard's tone that the runner's heart softened even more.

"Okay," said the runner. "Who do I ask for?"

"Just ask for Mr. L. They all know me. I can leave your name at the reception desk and they can get you right up."

With a bemused smile on his handsome young face the runner stuck out his hand and said, "I'm Theodore Webb. Can you remember that?"

"Yes of course, Theodore Webb," responded Leonard.

The runner turned and jogged away.

Leonard walked on his freshly tender feet toward his office.

The spinning of Webb

THEODORE Webb never knew his father.

His mother was an artist of uncommon talent and beauty combined with a very keen mind that, like most true artists, saw the world differently than just about everyone else on the planet. She was also a born-again Christian.

His grandfather, Red, was a fisherman who had an engineer-like mind and capable hands. Red, could do just about anything – except make money.

Red's life had been one of immense hardship. Orphaned at age 14 and left to raise two younger siblings, he'd watched as his buddies had died in World War One. Then he'd suffered through the depression, and, just when he was starting to build a good life, his wife had died leaving him with four small children. Red had longed for a life with guarantees. He embraced Communism.

Red thought Theo was an angel and had spent lots of time talking to him and teaching Theo, that which could be taught.

On the other hand, Theo had an uncle, his mother's brother, William. Uncle William had few of the mechanical skills that his father, Red, had possessed, but he loved an entrepreneurial challenge. Having witnessed firsthand what it's like to live in a family without financial resources, he endeavored to correct that by completely throwing himself into his projects with great and unstoppable passion.

Theo's grandfather was not keen on how his son, William, had chosen to make a living. "It's just ideas and talk, you do no work with your hands; there is no tangible product." His derogatory nickname for his only son was simply, "Make a million."

The predictable result of this environmental mélange was Theo, the man. A person of outrageous artistic and entrepreneurial energy who found he liked it best when he made good money while helping the less wise, less driven, less blessed, to make money they never knew they could. All this coupled with a willingness to risk all on the next roll of the dice – as long as he was passionate about the cause or idea – made Theo, the amazing man that he was.

He already had many learning experiences in his young life. Some were successful, others, not so much. Regardless of the outcome, Theo greeted each experience with the same, 'Okay, we're richer for the experience; now what can we do with what we just learned.'

There is rarely a regular job for a man like Theo, so he created a fitting niche for himself; turning uninhabitable slums into thriving neighborhoods.

In 1997 the politicians either tried to do good or buy votes. Perhaps both. However, as usual they did a number of things wrong. This list of errors started with a very consistent flaw in the thinking of those who would be masterminds for the common man. They did not take into consideration human nature with all of its frailties and how it reacted to incentives. They did not consider what future legislatures might do to alter the original intent let alone what the program might become when it got into the hands of the non-elected bureaucrats. The politicians obviously forgot all about the Law of Unintended Consequences.

As Theo saw it, economists like Adam Smith, F.A. Hayek. Milton Friedman and Thomas Sowell had it right. The solutions to society's needs lie in the industry and innovation of the individual. Sometimes working alone, but usually in cooperation with others. They do this, not because they are forced to, but because they have sufficient incentive.

He firmly believed there are some things that a government can do better than the individual, but there are many more problems that are better, more efficiently, solved, and with less coercion, by individuals who freely choose to work together.

Some people fear the power of corporations and there is some justification for this fear. Theo's grandfather had taught him this.

Theo's Uncle William had agreed, but pointed out that both corporations and government were run by humans. Some humans seek power over other humans and these are the ones who generally wind up in positions of authority.

Some corporate leaders may be greedy power seekers, but as Uncle William pointed out, entering government service does not change human nature. So we find the same elements at work in both places. The difference is a citizen can choose to quit doing business with a corporation, but cannot ignore the power of government.

Corporations have advertising dollars and lobbyists as their chief weapons. Governments have the force of law backed by the force of arms.

In Theo's mind the nightmare scenario would be a marriage of government and private business. Because the government then chooses who wins and who loses. This crony capitalism will inevitably lead to corruption. The winners are the political elite and the heads of private entities that support them and keep them in power. The losers are everyone not in on the scheme. Once this corruption is in place it is almost impossible to root it out.

Theo learned to look for two things: follow the money and follow the power. Who got big bucks and who wound up with unjust power? He saw that in the wake of this abuse of power there was always a way to help others and make a profit.

In the case of the financial 2007 meltdown, which was caused by the Sub Prime Mortgage fiasco, tens of thousands of hard-working people lost their homes. Theo saw whole swaths of some cities with houses vacant and boarded up. He knew he could not save the world all at once, but block by block – this is something he could tackle.

Theo saw this as an opportunity to serve his God, his fellow man and his bank account. What's more his life's work to this time had prepared him for just such an opportunity. With lessons learned by observing his mother's artistry, his grandfather's mechanical skills and his uncle's entrepreneurship he got passionate and got busy.

He spent his time moving between the elite and those in defeat. Getting investment monies from the first while encouraging the latter toward a Carpe Diem –'seize the day' attitude.

It became his mission to explain to those who had money (both white and black), and therefore assumed they were smart, that they could buy an entire block of houses and completely rehab them for amounts ranging from $400,000 to three quarters of a million. These beautiful newly remodeled homes would be sold for a modest profit to members of that community, Theo would handle all of it and the investors would make a return of 12% on their investment.

Of course that was only half of his mission. The other half was to get the leadership in the community, usually African-American, to see he was for real. Theo's goal was to get the leaders to urge the people to imitate the behavior of those people of all colors who had built successful lives. It stood to reason that these people had successful lives because they imitated others who had already imitated others and so on.

Using the ratcheting system to pull an area up by the bootstraps, Theo would get a large portion of the community involved. He did this by recruiting and training, wherever possible, workers from within the community. He found that it was consistent with human nature that, if they were invested in, and monetarily rewarded for, building their own neighborhood, they became protective of it. In case after case he witnessed an amazing civilizing effect even in neighborhoods that had previously resorted to the most self-destructive behavior.

Even though successful, Theo was small fry compared to the Advantage Corporation. Being tuned into the real estate market as he was, Theo also clearly understood the nature and scope of the Advantage Corporation. He had no idea who Mr. L was, almost no one did, but he had to think the man had influence at this real estate giant.

While little was known about this company it was obvious there was a lot of capital and real estate moxie. So Theo planned to keep his word and take Mr. L shopping, but not just for shoes.

Chapter 4

ALMOST BACK TO NORMAL

THE WARM CALIFORNIA SUN COMBINED with the unusual exertion brought on a copious amount of sweat. Leonard's feet were quite tender now and somewhat painful. He even detected another first – his own body odor. All this made him feel a little dirty and a little pained … yet … he loved it all.

Looking up at the Advantage Corporation building gave Leonard a perspective he had not really seen. He always arrived in his limo with its limited visibility, entered through his own security gate into a secure private, basement parking garage, before entering into his private elevator to be swept up to the 27th floor that housed his offices.

He realized he had never come in through the front door of his own building.

Leonard said to himself, "First time for everything" and walked in.

Walking with purpose, albeit on tender feet, he approached the desk where two employees waited. Behind the attractive young woman, there stood a man in uniform. His name tag read 'McDougal'. He looked like a policeman to Leonard. In fact, he was ex-secret service and was the Chief Security Officer for the Advantage Corporation Building.

"Hi," said Leonard. "I would like to leave a pass for a Mr. Theodore Webb to come right up to the 27th floor upon arrival."

The security officer gave the rather rumpled figure before him the once over, made some assumptions and said,

"The 27th floor is a secured area, sir. We do not have the authority at this level to make any exceptions."

The words 'Don't you know who I am' began to form on Leonard's tongue when it occurred to him this man would have no reason to have any idea as to who he was. They had never met. Leonard had never even been in this area. There was a bust of the founder, his father, in the lobby, but Leonard was such a private man there were only a few people who had a clue as to who he was.

Instead Leonard said, "I see," and turned away. On the other side of the room Leonard pulled out his cell phone and hit the automatic dial button. Before the second ring the familiar voice of Shawn Davis said, "Yes Mr. L?"

"I am in the lobby, would you please come and collect me?"

Obviously confused, Shawn Davis, asked, "Which lobby would that be, sir?"

"The main lobby of the Advantage Corporation," replied Leonard.

"Yes Mr. L. I'll be right down."

As the elevator doors closed behind Leonard and Shawn Davis, the Security Chief took note. He saw what he saw, no doubt, but he could not be sure he saw what he saw.

Once in his own office the usual demands for Leonard's attention became apparent and his newfound reality began to fade.

Getting up was easy

AFTER a great night's sleep and two hours of office time Leonard pocketed the $3,000 he had Shawn bring him, and they made their way to the limo waiting in its usual place.

In another unusual act, instead of the driver taking them to a prede-termined destination, he found himself taking directions from Shawn, as Shawn received directions from Mr. L. They all arrived at Dr. Car-roll's office and Mr. L dismissed them with the instruction to go around the block or find a parking place within a block or two. He would call when he was ready for them.

"Good morning, Mr. L," chirped Trisha.

Leonard found her cheerfulness uplifting and he actually smiled back at her.

"Good morning. Am I right to think your name is Trisha?"

"It is," she beamed. "Please have a seat and Dr. Carroll will be with you shortly."

Leonard was completely inexperienced at waiting, but he tried to do it well. He took a seat, looked at the table next to him and found a newspaper. As he mindlessly thumbed through it he eventually came to a social page and what a shock it was to see Dr. Carroll and her daughter, Sharon, as the focal point of one of the most highly featured pieces.

Mother Passes the Baton to Daughter read the headline. As are all society page entries the piece was short and Leonard read on.

"Dr. Lillian Carroll, founder of 'Brian's Better Tomorrow Foundation' has decided to enlist the assistance of her daughter, Sharon Carroll, to head up the fund raising gala this year. As a prominent psychiatrist Dr. Carroll is keenly aware of the damage, often lifelong in its persistence, of brain trauma. The foundation assists patients in the prolonged rehabilitation process through grants and other funding mechanisms. The goal this year is $50,000 and young Sharon, a student at U.C. Berkeley, says she is ready and up to the challenge."

Leonard's father did not believe in charity. "That's why I'm a Democrat and don't complain about taxes" was his standard answer when asked to contribute to any cause.

Leonard had of course, followed suit. But this was different. He was smitten by the lovely Sharon and while he did not want to 'buy' her, money was the only way he knew to communicate affection.

Leonard had something in his pocket that he almost never had. Cash. Reaching into his pocket he counted out twenty crisp one hundred dollar bills and walked over and laid it on Trisha's desk speaking these words while he did so.

"This is a $1,000.00 contribution to the Brian's Better Tomorrow Foundation and another $1,000.00 dollars to hold on account for doctor's fees."

Trisha was unused to people paying in cash and she was not typically part of the foundation's money stream. However, before she could mumble anything about that her phone rang, she answered it, then, saved by the bell, Trisha announced, "Dr. Carroll will see you now."

"Good morning, Mr. L." The doctor's greeting was feminine, proper, and crisp.

Boy, thought Leonard, does she look, sound and smell like my mother.

"Good morning, Dr. Lilly, and won't you please call me Leonard?"

"Well of course I will, Leonard. How do you feel today as compared to yesterday?"

"Oh, so much better."

"Hmmm, I must be better than I thought," she quipped.

"Well, you know, it just felt good to actually talk to someone. I'd like to do it every day for a while."

This was quite a different Leonard than she had seen in this room yesterday. "Also," he continued, "would it be possible for you to come by my office instead of here?"

"I'm sorry, Leonard, I don't do house calls and I don't know how seeing you daily will be possible as I have a fully booked schedule for months to come. I saw you early this morning as an accommodation. This is usually my time to prepare for the day and clean up the last of yesterday's work."

"Do you eat lunch?" asked Leonard.

"Sometimes, but I can't count on being free on a regular basis, and frankly, it is not appropriate to see a patient outside of the office. However, I can recommend a colleague who is extremely competent."

Although he had no idea of how to be facile in a social setting, he was always fast on his feet when negotiating business. Leonard countered,

"That won't happen. I simply am not about to talk to anyone else. I am amazed that I want to talk with you. How about we make it lunch once a week, strictly professional, and I will buy the lunch and pay your fee?"

Leonard did not mention his contribution to her Brian's Better Tomorrow Foundation. Intrinsically, he seemed to know it would be a violation of her ethics, but he also knew she would know soon enough.

"Leonard, do you always have to be the exception? Very well, we will have lunch once a week until an opening occurs in my regular schedule. That said, we would not have the same privacy as we will have in my office and it may inhibit your ability to speak openly. If that becomes a problem we will have to find another solution. Can we agree on that?"

"Yes."

Dr. Carroll continued. "When you drove up this morning I was on the phone and looking out the window. That was you who came in the limo, was it not?"

"Yes."

"It also looked like," said the doctor, "you had a couple of body-guards. Is that also correct?"

"Why, yes it is."

"Are you involved with crime in any way, Leonard?"

Leonard looked suddenly downcast and answered with almost a pout, "How could you think such a thing? I have never broken a law in my life."

He paused, thinking about offering money for sex, then added, "Well almost never." Then Leonard rose to his feet and repeated, this time with some angst, "How could you think such a thing?"

"Please sit down, Leonard," demanded Dr. Carroll. "I asked for the simple reason that while I know many wealthy people, and with the exception of politicians and celebrities, I know of no person, in this country at least, who has a body guard."

Leonard sat.

Dr. Carroll then lowered her voice and asked plainly, "Why do you feel the need to have body guards?"

Leonard sought to control his injury and after a few seconds told her the story.

"My father's uncle had no children and left his small farm to my father. My father was able to mortgage it. He took some of the money and a lot of personal labor and fixed it up, then leased out the farm. He took the rest of the mortgage money and bought six small houses in Watts. When he bought them they were in a solid, middle-class neigh-borhood of mostly African-Americans, but by the time I was almost 40 it had degenerated and about half of them became crack houses. The tenants stopped paying rent. When our collection department stopped having any success, my father and I went down and threatened them with eviction and they threatened us with a gun. My father left and went to the sheriff and asked them to come and support him. They laughed.

"He hired an athlete, a big fellow, to go with him. He told me to stay in the office. The athlete and my father were shot before they even got out of the car, but they managed to get away. The athlete died in the hospital. My father almost died. At this point he bought a bullet proof limousine and hired an ex-government agent as his body guard. About three months later he still hadn't fully recovered and his weakened condition contributed to a massive stroke."

Dr. Carroll rearranged herself and took a deep breath.

"Do you blame yourself for not being with him when he got shot?" she asked.

"No, Doctor, he told me to remain in the office and I did."

"Did you always do what your father told you to do?"

Leonard did not hesitate. "Absolutely – always. He was a very strong man. He never argued. Whatever he said – everyone did. It was certainly my habit to obey him."

"Leonard, do you ever try anything outside of these comfortable behavior patterns?"

"I have never thought about it," he said in a tone that was pure puzzlement.

"I see. Are you now a very strong man, Leonard?"

"Hmmm," he said quietly, "I don't know. I used to think I was, but I have come to believe I am only imitating my father."

"How does that feel?"

"I'm confused."

"In what way?"

"I have no idea who I am."

"Do you," the doctor pressed on, "think other people feel that way about themselves?"

"I don't know any other people," was his sad reply.

Lilly paused, then asked, "Were you and your father always close?"

"Ever since my eleventh birthday."

"How about when you were a little boy?"

"I never saw him much before that."

"Why did it change on your eleventh birthday?"

Leonard grew very quiet.

Again she asked, and he was still quiet.

Finally Leonard began to speak and his words almost drifted. "My mother gave me two books of poetry for my eleventh birthday. One was a very small book by Omar Kyam. It was called the *Rubaiyat*. She read it to me that morning. We both sat on the sofa. It was a cool and cloudy day and everything was quiet. Her voice was quiet. The turning of the pages were quiet. I was quiet. I liked the way she smelled. You smell like her." Leonard stopped, he did not mean to say that – but it was out and that was that.

"We were almost finished with that book when my father came home. He took one look at what we were reading and flew into a rage. He grabbed the book out of her hand as well as the one that lay next to me on the sofa and hurled them across the room screaming for the housekeeper as he did. She came immediately and he instructed her to burn them.

"Then my father addressed my mother in a most ungentle way. 'Don't you ever try to fill his mind with this useless crap again! It will never make him a nickel and that's the only thing that really matters. Now, get out of my sight!' She ran to her room crying.

"Then my father turned his attention to me. His voice quieted and if I remember correctly, he almost pleaded with me to understand that the only thing that really mattered in this world was making money. Money, lots of it, was the only insurance in life. With money you could buy anything – without it you can buy nothing. He stressed the importance of being the buyer, because buyers held the power."

Leonard continued to remember that day.

"My mother was a Southern romantic; my father was all business. He sat down where my mother had been sitting and I could see he was deeply troubled. He put his hand on my shoulder and made me a promise. 'I have not been spending enough time with you, but that will change as of now. I must teach you what I have learned. You will be with me every waking minute of the day from now on and I'll show you the most important thing: how to make money. With money you can buy anything or anybody.'

"For some reason, even though I was afraid, I felt I could ask him a question. 'What about school?' His face changed, he looked pleased with me – like somehow I had asked a good question.

" 'I'll get you the very best tutors!' And he did."

Dr. Carroll's face was softer than usual. "How much did you see your mother after that."

"I didn't really see her hardly at all." Leonard's reply came from a vacant and distant place. "She spent most of her time in her room when my father and I were home. Even when I would knock on her door she didn't answer very often. She looked very, very sad when she did. I asked my father if she could come with us sometimes, but he just scoffed and said 'Business is business.' Then one day she just went away."

"Where did she go?"

"I never knew. My father became very grim whenever I would ask about her. I missed her so much, but I knew better than to show it."

"Leonard, you have had a most unusual life so far, but we are out of time today. What is your lunch schedule like for next week, do you know?"

Without any pride and with more than a touch of sadness Leonard said, "It is whatever I want it to be."

"Good. I'm glad it is flexible. Can we say Tuesday next? We will meet here."

"That will be fine." Leonard rose and left the room.

He took the stairs and called Shawn Davis.

Chapter 5

L EON HARDING, SEEING THE CALL WAS
,from Mr. L, picked up his phone immediately. "Yes, Mr. L?"
"Leon," began Leonard, "I want you to get the very best and most
discrete private detective who specializes in missing persons here
ASAP. Let me know as soon as you have set it up."

"Of course," was the only response Leon Harding knew to offer. For
the next 90 minutes Leonard poured over the 27-page report submitted
by Bruce Saunders, the bright, young accountant who had been sent
over to ensure the smooth running of Leonard's risky investment, La
Crosse Instruments. It was surprisingly detailed and comprehensive,
considering the amount of time Bruce had been active on the project.

What Bruce Saunders made clear was that La Crosse Instruments
had two problems that kept them from being the successful company
they could be. The first was that they were great at developing and
manufacturing exceptional products, but had no concept of how to get
them efficiently into the market.

The second was, that even though it was a young company, it had
already established impermeable silos between the companies divisions
that restricted information flow from one fiefdom to another. Each department head had jealously guarded their ownership of critical data,
both positive and negative.

Without timely exposure to this information, the other departments made moves and developed processes that were counterproductive. This wasted time, energy and momentum, not to mention money. The young company had assumed the same sort of rigor mortis that many much older and larger companies have to contend with. Not having deep pockets or major revenues, they ran out of money before they could bring their new product to market and had to sell themselves to Leonard for a fraction of their worth.

Bruce, in his report, stated he had ordered a copy of a book called *Dr. Deming* for each of the department heads. In his report Bruce noted that during the time of General Douglas McArthur's stint as governor of Japan the country had gone from infamously producing "Cheap Crap" to becoming famous for producing the highest quality products in the world.

Who was responsible for this miracle? The answer is Dr. W. Edwards Deming. In the late 1940's and early 50's this Dr. Deming was one of the world's preeminent statisticians.

He was summoned to Japan to organize a census. While doing that he noticed a major disparity as to how the Japanese people lived and the quality of their manufactured product. They, for the most part, lived modestly, but with great quality. Conversely, their manufacturing produced "Cheap Crap."

Dr. Deming proceeded to explain his theory about the importance of always pursuing that which would increase quality. He insisted that increased quality would result in increased productivity and less waste. These factors would in turn result in greater demand, efficiency and ultimately, profits.

Japan followed it closely, especially companies like Sony and Toyota. The U.S. manufacturing entities rejected Deming while the Japanese embraced him. It was not long before Japanese quality in many product lines was preferred to U.S. made products. To this day Dr. Deming is well known in Japan and a prize offered in his name and for his honor is the apex of quality awards for that nation.

Leonard stopped long enough to have Shawn Davis order him a copy of that book.

The Saunders report on La Crosse was dense enough in information that Leonard promised himself another look at it before day's end.

The Buyer

Shawn Davis rang Leonard and informed him that Leon Harding was there with one John Thompkins. However, explained Shawn, he had no such person on Mr. L's schedule for today.

Mr. L assured Shawn that it was okay, and that he had invited Leon Harding to bring the man by.

John Thompkins was about five feet, nine inches tall and weighed close to 170 pounds, had brown hair and eyes, or, in other words, he fit the description of average. The characteristics that differentiated him were his hair and eyes. His hair was somewhat curly and seemed to sit atop his head as a monastery might perch atop a hill. His eyes were slightly crossed and there was one other thing – he was fidgety.

Leon Harding introduced him and started to take a seat. Leonard waved Mr. Harding off and thanked him for his prompt response and asked him to wait in the outer office.

Once Mr. Harding was gone, Leonard looked at John Thompkins for a full minute without a word, Thompkins becoming steadily more fidgety until finally he started to say, "How exac –"

Mr. L cut him off with two quick questions. "How good are you at finding missing persons, and to what degree can I depend on your absolute discretion?"

Relieved that the uncomfortable silence had been broken John Thompkins spoke in a rush. "I'm the best in Southern California, the second best in the state and one of the top five in the country," he blurted.

"Why should I engage your services – why not the number one guy in California?"

"Because he is the best because he is ruthless, but he is not at all discrete. His reputation is based on his own leaks."

Leonard liked this guy and he especially liked the way he cut to the point.

"Okay. Here is what I want from you. In August of 1969 a Sarah LaFrance, wife of Fred LaFrance, left Beverly Hills, on her own, and I believe she went to New Orleans. Don't know for sure, but it is a place to start. I have never heard from her since. Her maiden name was Peachtree. She was my mother. Other than that I can't be of much help."

John Thompkins was busy addressing his note pad. He looked up when Leonard stopped speaking. Now Thompkins asked his first and only question. "Why do you want to find her?"

Leonard's initial response was forthright and simple. "I would like to know how she is doing now." He paused. "I also want to know everything about her. Not just since she went away, but about her whole life. I would like any information as soon as you are aware of it. Can you do that?"

"That is what I do," Thompkins shot back in a way that showed both irritation and self-control.

"Shawn," speaking to his assistant by phone, "Mr. Tompkins will be leaving now. Please have Leon work out the details with him."

"Yes Mr. L."

Chapter 6

NEW SHOES - NEW VISION

WHILE LEONARD WAS GOING OVER A MYRiad of data with his chief accountant, Samuel Levine, Shawn Davis interrupted. He seemed once again caught off guard. "Pardon me again, Mr. L, but did you want to see a Mr. Theo Webb? He is in the lobby and said something about having run into you recently."

"By all means, please go down and escort Mr. Webb up." Then Leonard turned to his chief accountant and said with a smile, "Thank you, Mr. Levine. I think we have a good start on this month's numbers. I'll let you know when I can meet again."

Mr. Levine gathered his papers, folded his laptop and went to his office.

As Shawn Davis opened the door into Mr. L's office, Theo Webb walked right past him and headed across the expansive room toward Leonard. Shawn was not a trained bodyguard, but still the sudden move readied him to protect his boss.

Leonard, who never rose from his desk to welcome anyone, sprang up like a kid who was just given his first bike and thus relieved any anxiety Shawn Davis may have had.

"Theo! Thanks for coming!"

Theo held up his hand with palm forward in the universal signal to stop.

Leonard did.

Theo, with an exaggerated look of concern and speaking with a cowboy accent said, "Now hold on partner, I know that calling you Mr. L got me past the lobby, but it is hard to carry on a meaningful conversation with a man known only as Mr. L."

"Call me Leonard," said the exuberant executive as he thrust his hand toward his guest.

"Okay, Leonard, let's go find you some shoes."

"Okay, Theo. Why not." As Leonard said these words it occurred to him it was the first time he had ever spoken them. *Why not* – hmmm, what a liberating thought.

Leonard had never ridden in a pick-up. If you can call a Ford F-350 dually, diesel flat-bed a pick-up. Getting into it was certainly more of a manly act than climbing into his Mercedes-Benz S 600 limousine.

Riding in the front seat was a new experience and being up high was a bit of a rush. It was clear that Theo was comfortable behind the wheel of the vehicle even before they pulled out of the parking garage.

"Where are we going?" Leonard asked.

"First," said Theo, "we'll go to my favorite shoe store over in Marina Del Rey. Then I want to show you something."

All of this was out of the realm of his normal reality. Yet he was somehow not only comfortable with it, but held the experience out in front of him and greeted it with an excited and hopeful anticipation.

The thought crossed Leonard's mind he had never been out running around town with another guy in a pickup. He knew from movies, especially *American Graffiti*, that this kind of behavior was the norm for young guys.

For a brief moment a dark cloud came over his mind. He realized he just now tasted what every other young man took for granted, but he was no young man.

The cloud lifted with the sound of Theo's voice announcing, "Here we are."

Leonard looked up to see a storefront that defined itself as Starting Line Shoes.

Theo was a good guide. The sales clerk seemed to know him personally and paid strict attention to Theo's suggestions.

It took about an hour with all the measuring, fitting and trying on, but when they left Leonard had a nifty pair of shoes that made his feet think they were walking on little pillows. Leonard still had almost a thousand left in his pocket and was proud to be able to pay for them himself. It was good to have cash.

"Are you happy with your shoes, Leonard?" Theo inquired.

"Oh yes, they will do just fine," he answered with a very large smile.

"Now, would you mind doing something for me?"

Leonard was unused to that question and his answer had a guarded tone.

"What would that be?"

"I would like you to look at some real estate."

Real estate was certainly something Leonard had expertise in.

However, his staff would always begin with in-depth research as to where, geographically speaking, an investment would be wise, then his accountants and lawyers would look for building code problems, restrictions, flaws and opportunities, the construction head would give him the numbers for a suitable rehab, and finally his leasing department would examine the feasibility of getting solid leases on such a property. Then and only then would Mr. L be called in to make the final decision.

"We have a process for that sort of thing, and it doesn't usually start with me," said Leonard honestly.

Theo was undeterred. "Good, I get the feeling that you are sort of burned out on routine so let's rock the Casbah."

Leonard did not know what that meant, but he didn't want to look ignorant so he rode on in silence.

After about 30 minutes of fighting the stop-and-go traffic on the San Diego Freeway, Theo swung East on the 105.

Leonard immediately sensed that something was wrong – very wrong. His voice rose measurably in pitch as he asked, "Isn't this the way to Watts?"

"Yes, you can get to Watts off of 105, but we are not going there, we are going to Compton."

"No, no, no, no, NO!" screamed Leonard. "I can't go there!"

Theo was silent, but continued to drive in the same direction. Then Theo pointed out their circumstance. "If we pull off here we will be in the heart of Watts. If we go a little further we can go South into Compton." Finally, Theo offered, "Leonard I know the people in the neighborhood where we are going. They will not harm either of us. I promise."

Leonard had calmed considerably. The panic that had been evident a few moments before was now under control, but there was no comfort when he said,

"Theo, I do not know you. I am out of my element and I am not in control. I will go with you on the condition that if I say 'let's go,' you will not hesitate, but will get me out of there immediately. Do I have your word on this?"

Theo spoke plainly. "Yes, Leonard, you have my absolute word that if you want to leave we will do so immediately."

"Against every instinct I am going to trust you. Do not let me down," said Leonard coldly.

Theo immediately and completely understood that the man next to him was riddled with genuine fear. He proceeded accordingly. As Theo turned onto the blighted street that he wanted Leonard to see, Leonard's angst increased again.

Theo said, in his most reassuring voice, "Leonard, this is a dangerous neighborhood, but I have been working in this area for the last 7 months and we have many friends here."

As if on cue, when the big black and loud Ford F-350 pulled to the curb three people emerged from seemingly out of nowhere and headed their direction. All wearing welcoming smiles.

There were two men and a woman; the most formidable in appearance was the woman. She stood close to 6 feet tall and weighed in at about 350 pounds. To say she was thick set would be a massive understatement. Her hair was close-cropped and she dressed very much like a man.

The two men were slender, one in his twenties the other looked either to be the eyes of age or he had lived a very hard life.

"Wasup, Theo, my man, and who you got wich you?" said the large woman.

"Latisha, my little flower," replied Theo. "Wasup is, I am here trying to do some business. This is my friend, Leonard, and Leonard this is Latisha and these two gentlemen are Doug and Leroy."

Doug and Leroy both responded simultaneously with, "Wasup Theo?" followed by, "Wasup Leonard?"

When all three of the locals put their fists up to receive bumps, Leonard froze thinking it might be an attack until he saw Theo bump their fists with his. Then Leonard hid his fear and followed suit.

Theo spoke first. "My friends, I want to show Leonard the possibilities that we have here for making money. He is pretty good at that already and I think he may see what we are doing here as valuable in more ways than one. You want to show us around?"

"If he be here to help, we be glad to show him what it is," said Latisha with authority.

"You know better than that," said Theo. "Leonard has no idea what we want to do, have already done; or where we're going with this. He may or may not want to play. It is our job to sell him. Is that clear?"

"Of course it is, Theo, baby. I don't mean to be pushy."

"Latisha, from what I've seen of you there are only two gears, pushy and more pushy, but that is not how we win friends and influence people, is it?"

"We all know that, but now look who's being the pushy one." She raised one eyebrow, a mean/furrowed look, and her ham-sized hands rested on her ample hips.

There was just a slight breeze of tension that floated over the small gathering that dispelled as soon as Latisha laughed.

For the next 25 minutes they went into or looked in every house on the street. They were all trashed and everything of value ripped out and taken away. Leonard did not like the place, was uncomfortable around the locals and was about to play his ace in the hole and ask to leave, now.

Theo sensing the timing proclaimed, "Now let's show him what we can do." They turned the corner and on the other side of the same block they just inspected lay an entirely different scene. There were three kids on bikes, a mother with a baby stroller and a half dozen people working in their yards.

Each house had been revamped and the yards were all landscaped. It was as normal as any neighborhood, anywhere.

Leonard could not believe it. "What …?" He hesitated. "What is the difference between what we just saw and what we are now looking at?"

Theo promptly replied "$437,212.00."

"What do you mean?"

"For $437,212.00 we bought every house, the materials, brought in one construction foreman for every four houses and paid them scale, taught every wannabe home owner how to swing a hammer, pour concrete, run wire, lay pipe and install plumbing, then how to paint. They got paid both with some cash and sweat equity in the house. We used the FUBU method to get it done."

Leonard was puzzled. "I don't understand. FUBU method?"

This time it was Doug who answered. "For Us By Us. It means we are making good things happen for ourselves. That makes it more important. That gives us pride. That gives reason to want to take care of it."

At last Leonard began to get a glimpse of what the goal was and the method by which it might be accomplished.

"Who oversees the construction foreman, the materials, the finances, the quality of the whole?" asked Leonard.

Now Theo took the ball. "That is what my staff and I do. Last year we were part of a private enterprise that rehabbed over 3,500 homes in California alone. Our investors will make about 12% on their money and we help people lift themselves without becoming dependent on the government or anyone else. They learn what they never were taught in school; how to stand on their own. After all that is the American way."

The dark side of bright

THE quintet continued to talk even as Leonard continued to marvel at the giant leap he had just witnessed from one block to the next.

Leonard's father had taught him to look behind the façade, because it is a lot easier and cheaper to make just the face look better than to do a thorough rehab job. Leonard, had in turn, taught his field staff to dig into the structure and determine just how far the beauty – or the rot – might actually go.

He was about to ask for a closer look at the interiors and the foundations when everyone turned to look at a conspicuous, shiny black, Cadillac Escalade with a powerful engine and ultra-loud exhaust come around the corner.

Even from a block away the slow-moving vehicle was ominous. Latisha looked at Leonard and found him staring at the car.

"Look away," she said with a commanding urgency.

Doug echoed her. "Don't be lookin' at 'em."

Latisha was already hitting the direct dial number of the local police dispatcher. When they promptly answered Latisha lost no time. "We are on the rehabbed block and some trouble is heading our way." She immediately hit the off button and shoved the phone in her back pants pocket.

Whoever that was on the other end of the call seemed to need no other explanation.

As the large SUV approached, the heavily tinted front and rear side windows quietly slid down revealing unsmiling faces with large gold chains. Not liking what they saw, they accelerated to the end of the block and flipped a 'U' turn.

The hair on the back of Leonard's neck was standing at attention and his stomach was turning over at about the same time his head began to spin.

The Escalade was now only 50 feet away and closing quickly, but Leonard, try as he may, could not move. He was quite literally frozen in place.

Suddenly, the Escalade stopped short. After a brief pause the car started to move again in what could only be called exaggerated nonchalance.

Now all five had lost discipline and followed the car with their eyes. The reason for the change of behavior on the part of the Escalade driver was quickly evident.

An equally large, if not larger, vehicle had entered the street from the other end. The hardware and paint design on that van erased any doubt as to its purpose and intent. They were there to enforce the peace.

As the two vehicles exchanged places in front of the five pedestrians, Leonard saw that which had just occurred as surreal. The experience was so utterly inconsistent with his normal existence as to make him feel that he was merely an observer and had in no way participated in the tableau.

"Hi Latisha. Mr. Webb, did you just give us a call?" asked the driver of the police van, a very muscular African-American with a smile that did not fool anyone into thinking he could be messed with.

"I did, you know I did," replied the large woman. "But how'djou get here so quick?"

"It is a new policy to have a van in the neighborhood. The man downtown seems to have had a long talk with Mr. Webb here and the powers that be like what you are doing. You know us, Latisha, we are here to protect and serve."

Latisha cocked her head, raised an eyebrow and only responded with a drawn out "Uh huh." Then she added. "You are good. How come you din't use to show up so fast?"

"Hey, if you who live here don't care, why should we?"

Latisha repeated her "Uh huh," then added, "I know thas right."

Theo interrupted at this point and said, "Officer Johnson, thanks for responding so fast. It could have gotten a little hairy." He extended his hand in the direction of Leonard. "By the way I would like you to meet Leonard LaFrance. He may be joining us in our effort. Leonard, this is officer Johnson. He has been a real ally in helping us keep the peace here."

The two men nodded towards each other before the police radio interrupted. What was said was largely gibberish to Leonard, but Officer Johnson responded with, "Copy that."

Officer Johnson saw the lack of comprehension and volunteered, "That was my partner, he just escorted Lamar the Big and his friends back on to the freeway."

Everyone knew what he was saying.

DRIVING back toward Beverly Hills both Theo and Leonard were quiet. Leonard was thinking of himself and realizing that he was not a very interesting man. Having never had that thought before he asked himself why he was thinking that now. It was because, he concluded, he was comparing himself to Theo.

For Theo the thoughts were directed toward the question of how much more could be done with the inclusion of the power of the purse, the experience and the staff of Leonard and his Advantage Corporation.

As they approached Leonard's building it occurred to Leonard that he did not have the electronic pass key required to get into his own garage.

"Why don't you just let me out in front?"

"That's easy to do," replied Theo.

As they pulled up to the curb Leonard spent a moment trying to find the pick-ups door handle. *This is ridiculous*, thought Leonard. *I don't even know how to open my own door.*

Theo interrupted Leonard's self-condemnation by asking, "By the way, what did you think?"

Without hesitating Leonard responded. "Come by tomorrow with an agreement at 2 PM and ask to see my assistant, Shawn Davis. He will coordinate the following two hours for you. I will want you to meet with my Directors of Finance, and Legal. Also I would like you to give our Director of Construction a tour. If they find what I did, my attorney will give you a check for $437,212.00 and we'll do another block."

Exiting the big truck, Leonard pictured himself as he walked. *I want to look purposeful as I walk into my building* - he thought to himself – *and by extension the world.'*

Chapter 7

BREATHING DEEPER

HE MOMENT LEONARD ENTERED THE large revolving door, Brian McDougal, Chief Security Officer for the Advantage Corporation Building, saw him and moved with amazing speed for a man of his size.

"Greetings Mr. L, is there anyone I can call for you or would you like to go directly to the 27th floor, sir?"

He knows who I am, thought Leonard. *I like that.*

"I am going right to my office, thank you."

Without another word except, "Very good, sir," Brian McDougal fetched the elevator and swiped his security card, entered the code for the 27th floor (activation required both the card and the code), then stepped back.

Shawn Davis looked relieved to see Mr. L and told him so.

After assuring Shawn it was good to see him as well he asked his assistant to contact Irvin Syrisst, the head of operations for Advantage Corporation, to give 'McDougal' at the front desk a hundred dollar a month pay increase.

"Yes, Mr. L, anything else sir?"

"Yes, get Leon Harding in here at his earliest convenience and make an appointment with him, Bill Vuchovich, and Samuel Levine for tomorrow starting at 2:00 PM with Theo Webb. I want their hard-core assessments of this man, his ideas, his history and his work. I will need it immediately."

Shawn Davis became aware of a difference in Mr. L, but could not put his finger on it. Rather than try to think it through on the spot he simply asked again if there was anything else Mr. L wanted, to which Leonard responded,

"Not at this time."

SITTING at his desk Leonard activated his computer and brought up "Holdings." In this folder he found all of the real estate that Advantage Corporation owned. This time he was seeing it with different eyes. By looking at the acquisition dates he could see a precise timeline of how his father had started and built the company and how he, himself had added to it.

In a very real way the transaction he just agreed to with Theo was going back to the beginning of the cycle – buying property in less than a desirable area. Leonard was not kidding himself. His last two acquisitions were far from the safe formula that had amassed the vast fortune. Both had broken his father's tried and true formula of buying distressed properties in very desirable locations.

That said, he liked the two risks he had taken. Together, the two investments were equal to about 2% of the corporation's assets, a substantial, but not a debilitating, amount should it be lost. However, he knew he must exercise prudence now and make sure the entire puzzle was working well.

In many ways the Advantage Corporation had become self-running. The formula was well fixed. His staff had very little turn over. At every level they knew their jobs well and were highly efficient.

Leonard watched the numbers just as his father had tutored him to do. If a property showed signs of falling off its traditional earning levels he knew George Koch, director of property management, would also watch the numbers and find the reasons for it. The cause was usually that the wear and tear of normal use was making it a less desirable property in comparison to other properties in the area. Usually, that was corrected with a simple facelift on the portions that had become vacant. Leonard's approval was almost perfunctory at this point.

On occasion, rare as they may be, properties around the Advantage properties became worn down making the neighborhood property less desirable. On three of the times this came to pass they had bought up the neighboring properties, re-habbed them and wound up actually being able to increase the value and the rents of their original property. On other occasions the rot was too wide spread to try to buy it all up and reverse the trend. In that case they decided to simply milk the property for what they could and when others began a gentrification of the surrounding properties then Advantage Corp would make theirs a jewel among jewels – in many cases they were still waiting.

This self-healing was integral within the Advantage Corporation. There was rarely a lot of stress.

Tomorrow the head of each department would come together in the boardroom and give their quarterly "State of their Departments" report. Then he would have an up-to-date picture. For now, Leonard instinctively knew he must be very careful. A small tear could rip open a wide gash if there were not the resources at hand to stop it.

The day was almost over. He knew that Shawn Davis was standing by to alert Simpson and Shook, his bodyguards/chauffeur, to ready everything for Leonard's trip home. But Leonard was restless.

Standing up he began to pace his office. Doing so made him aware of the comfort he felt in his new walking shoes. *Darn*, he thought, *I forgot to get my old shoes out of Theo's truck.* It would be an interesting test of Theo's character to see if he was thoughtful enough to return his shoes.

Leonard walked to the window and saw once again what a lovely Southern California day it was. He walked to his desk, then returned to the window. After thirty seconds or so he walked back to his desk, picked up his phone and informed Shawn that he, as well as Simpson and Shook, could have the rest of the day off. He would be walking home.

Realizing he was not all that familiar with the way home he decided to take the same walk he had taken the other day after leaving Dr. Lilly's office. It was a little out of the way, but once there, getting home was nothing.

Walking, he found was both tiring and invigorating. Walking was also a good vehicle for thinking. While depression was just beneath the surface, hope was moving toward the fore. His thoughts were all about possibilities. Some of them … quite daring.

He had dared to break some of his father's most stringent rules. He bought a company that made something. He invested in property in the most undesirable part of town. He had dared to seek out and speak to a psychiatrist. He had dared to walk to her office and then walk on to his own office. He had dared to try and find his mother. He had dared ride with someone he did not know to a part of town he was deathly afraid of. He had dared to look at his business from a different perspective. And now … he was now daring to walk home on his own.

To think, he did all of this and the world had not ended. What other dream or doubt was he capable of challenging?

His mind went right to his greatest fantasy. That of loving and being loved. It zeroed in on Sharon Carroll, the Dr.'s daughter.

As he walked Leonard questioned himself as to just how daring he really wanted to be. If he were to have a real relationship with a woman – not just a "reward," but a one-on-one, heart-to-heart, mind-to-mind, soul-to-soul relationship – how and where would it start?

Well, he thought, it would have to start with a conversation, right? Leonard had not seen much in the way of television or movies. His father had made it clear that make-believe was a waste of time. The few he had seen usually involved a boy meets girl, boy gets girl, boy loses girl, boy gets girl back sort of theme. Sometimes the boy never realized how much he loved the girl until she was gone. The constant theme, regardless of the twists and turns usually depicted the boy as the initiator.

Leonard had a most disturbing thought. He stopped walking. Standing still it became even more apparent. *He had missed life.*

He was not a boy, but a 51-year-old man. It was one thing to send his assistant out to fetch an attractive and financially disadvantaged woman off the street by offering her $10,000 in exchange for a no-questions-asked night of sex while he sat safely in his car. He had absolutely no risk of embarrassment or rejection.

When he allowed himself a reward he almost never had verbal conversations with the woman. If they did occur it was so superficial as to have no meaning whatsoever.

As Leonard started walking again he had a choice to make. The easiest one was to accept his condition, remain in his uncomfortable comfort zone, and slip back into depression. He rejected that with a shiver that shook his entire body. He was barely hanging on as it was. If he were to lose this infinitesimally small grip he would plunge forevermore into an unforgiving and eternal abyss. Leonard was certain of this.

Okay, he said to himself, *what is the other choice*? Was it not to continue to do daring things? If this was the alternative did he go about it with complete abandon as he had these past few days, or did he attempt to achieve it incrementally?

His mind exploded when the one word answer appeared in his thoughts. *Both.* Leonard nearly screamed. *Everyday carefully attempt to expand his horizons and every once in a while be absolutely impetuous!*

Leonard liked it.

Where to start? I know, instead of having the bistro bring me food at home I will go eat there. There is a bit of risk in the social setting, but I certainly know the food.

Now that he had purpose his pace quickened. His heart, unaccustomed to this much exercise began to beat more aggressively. Leonard liked that too. Not many people are so un-aerobicized that merely walking will bring on an adrenalin rush, but there it was and he felt wonderful.

As he moved his confidence moved with him. *Could I*, Leonard asked himself, *talk to a woman that I am interested in*? Could I talk to Sharon Carroll? What would I say? Where would I begin? How could I get her off on her own so we could have a personal conversation?

Sharon Leonard spoke in his mind, *How good to see you again.*
Good, he thought.
Now what?
Whoa, this is tough.
No it is not, he argued with himself.
First you have to separate her from the herd. His father used to say that. *Hmmm, how do I do that?*
You must have a reason to take her off. *So*, he mused, *you need a reason.*

What reason would I have to talk with her?

Her charity – that's it! Brian's Better Tomorrow Foundation. Oh, that is good! Leonard congratulated himself.

Where would I take her? Where do people who want to sell me their property try to take me? Out to dinner. I never go, but if they use this as a common tool it must usually work.

Leonard was moving fast and had almost completed his walk as he continued to go over and over his imaginary conversation with Sharon.

The streets of the shopping district around Rodeo Drive were bustling with tourists and late shoppers. Leonard found it necessary to weave in and out of the pedestrians he was passing. He bumped into a couple of people, nothing serious, not like the event where he met Theo, but a mere shoulder rub here or there. Some looked perturbed while others extended their apologies. Leonard liked the interaction and intentionally bumped into a few more just so he could offer apologies. It was not conversation, but it was a start.

Leonard ran into Sharon Carroll. Literally.

Both of them lost in their own thoughts had a dim recollection that the other was familiar, so it took a second to realize from where they knew each other.

Leonard spoke first. "Sharon, how good it is to see you again."

Her smile was amazing. Her voice like that of a Mourning Dove. "Why, Yes, you are Mr. L, right?"

"Oh, please, call me Leonard."

"Okay, Leonard. Good, I've been wanting to thank you for the generous contribution you made to my dad's charity. That was so nice."

"And I have been wanting to talk to you about your foundation." And before Leonard knew what he was going to say he asked, "Do you have plans for supper?"

Sharon hesitated only briefly. "Not really."

"Excellent. Would you consider eating with me? There is a bistro just around the corner and their food is quite good."

"Sure, why not? "Sharon replied.

As they moved toward the bistro Leonard was smiling as he tried to weigh what had just happened. There was that delightful phrase again. One that would become his mantra. Sharon had just said, "Why not."

"We may have trouble getting a table this time of night," Sharon suggested.

Leonard's mind, which was once very agile had, over the past few years become rather dull, but it was alive right now. Reaching into his pocket Leonard retrieved his cell phone and hit one key. Shawn Davis immediately responded. "Yes, Mr. L."

"I need a table for two at the bistro where we usually get my supper for about three minutes from now." Then Leonard spoke with a new level of intensity, "And Shawn, this is very important."

Shawn was becoming accustomed to the unaccustomed from Mr. L, as of late, and got on it.

When they entered the bistro the Maitre D' rushed over with the assumption that this was the mysterious Mr. L that they catered supper to almost every evening. He had never met the man, but according to Shawn Davis, a man he knew well, at least by phone, every courtesy should be extended and if done well the Maitre D' could expect a $1,000.00 tip that Shawn would bring by before Mr. L and his guest would finish dining.

"I believe," began Leonard, "that you recently received a call for a reservation."

The words had barely exited Leonard's mouth before the Maitre D' gushed, "Of course, Mr. L, right this way."

Following the Maître D' through the very crowded restaurant brought them to a private dining room that was held in reserve for just such a VIP occasion.

This was, after all, Beverly Hills.

Sharon was impressed.

Hell, Leonard was impressed.

After a bit more obsequiousness in presenting the menu and wine list the Maître D' suggested that if they would be so kind as to guide him as to their choice of beef, fish, pork, poultry or lamb he would be pleased, if they would allow him, to order for them.

"Excellent," said Leonard. And then he thought, *after all he does that for me every night. I think I can trust him with that chore.* Leonard made a mental note that he needed to learn about menus and especially wine lists, as he had no idea how to order.

The Buyer

Sharon looked at Leonard with new eyes. She saw in him a person who had a blend of characteristics that appealed to her. She had lost her father at a vulnerable age and had missed the guiding and protective hand of a father figure that could only be found in an older man.

Leonard looked back at the past ten minutes and froze. It was not clear to him how he got to this time and place with this woman. What he did know was that most of what had just taken place was a result of a rehearsed plan, but that was all used up. In a near panic, Leonard just smiled at the beauty across from him and said nothing.

He is, thought Sharon, so pleasant, so confident. He has no need to prattle on about his achievements and philosophies as the men of her age always seemed to engage in. He is just sitting there, smiling at me and confident enough to allow space in the conversation and allow me to set the topic.

Fortunately for Leonard the more he looked at the young beauty of Sharon, the more his mind puddled and he relaxed. He did not know why. He just relaxed.

It was Sharon who spoke first.

"It was my mother who started the foundation. My father had a life insurance policy, but we did not need the money so she directed it toward the cause that was so very important to her." Sharon grew quiet before continuing. "My father died in a fall that, had he survived, would have left him with such brain trauma that he would have likely been a vegetable. She has worked with many patients whose lives have been totally disrupted by brain trauma and very few have the resources to get any real help. This foundation only helps a little, but it means a lot to their families. It means a lot to us. So again I thank you for your generosity."

Lubricated with her presence and her praise, Leonard's fine mind started spinning out possible ways to help. But he said nothing. He simply allowed his smile to get warmer.

The waiter was ushered in personally by the Maitre D' and brought them a lovely array of small bite appetizers. For Leonard this was a welcome intervention.

As the wait people withdrew Leonard responded to Sharon's gratitude and asked a question.

"You're welcome, but if you don't mind my asking, why is your goal only $50,000 for the year?"

"My mother works long hours, I am a full time student, we have no paid staff, only volunteers, and that is about all the energy we can devote to it. Do you think it is a waste of time?" Sharon's tone was almost defensive.

"If you raised $10.00 and it was a help to someone at the right time it would not be a waste of time. I guess I am just used to thinking in larger numbers. What are the services you provide and what would you do if you had twice the money or even ten times the money?"

This question brought new eagerness to Sharon's voice.

"Right now we use the money to give a stipend so a family member can stay in a hotel near the treatment center, hook people up with the right doctor or clinic for the injury and sometimes we contribute to the costs of the pharmaceuticals. It is pretty low-level stuff. If we had more we would do more and I know my mother would like to direct some monies to research that she deems to hold promise."

"Hmmm," said Leonard, "I don't know much about this brain trauma, but I have been studying Alzheimer's disease for business reasons as of late. I wonder if your mother ever deals with that."

"I know she is very interested in it, but our foundation has only dealt with brain trauma due to injury." As Sharon finished speaking another course appeared and the conversation turned to the delightful nature of the food and wine and how well it all went together.

They rose to leave and the Maitre D' arrived to ask if everything was satisfactory. Leonard and Sharon both agreed it had been spectacular.

Sharon quietly asked Leonard if they had been given the bill yet.

Leonard's eyebrows shot up and he said, "I don't know." Turning to the Maitre D' he asked the same question.

"Please do not concern yourself, Mr. L. Everything is taken care of."

"Excellent," said Leonard and they walked to the door.

The thing about California is that once the sun goes down the cool air coming off the ocean drops the temperature rather quickly. The contrast between the warmth of the restaurant and chill of the evening caused Sharon to yield to a brief shiver.

Leonard noticed and at once pulled off his suit coat and draped it across Sharon's shoulders. The fast-paced walk that Leonard enjoyed this afternoon left a hint of body odor that Sharon found to be most pleasant.

Leonard smiled as he thought that his mother would have been proud of his chivalrous act. Wow! That is the first time in memory that Leonard thought about the parental pride coming from mother rather than father. It was a milestone and it, too, was liberating.

Realizing he was a short walk from home, but he had no idea where Sharon lived he inquired as to her wanting a ride home. He could, Leonard assured her, have his car there in a matter of minutes.

"Oh no, I drove here. My car is just on the next block. I will be fine from here."

Leonard would not hear of it. "Fine, but I will walk you to your car." Again, he thought, Mother would be proud.

When they said good night, Sharon gave him a spontaneous hug. Leonard grew dizzy for a moment. Then he recovered enough to volunteer that he had, in the back of his mind, a thought that might help her foundation.

"I want to think it through, but I will likely have my answers by tomorrow evening. Would you consider dining with me again?"

Sharon was thrilled. "Yes," she said, with no uncertainty.

As her car pulled away Leonard was speechless. That was okay, because, as usual, there was no one to talk to but himself.

So he ran. He ran all the way home. Theo would have been proud. Leonard *was* proud. He did not know what his father would think as the subject of running never came up. He knew his mother would be proud of the way he brought this evening together.

He yelled at the top of his voice. "Yay Leonard!" Then thought, *I am beginning to like you.*

He followed that with an equally loud, "Sharon, I love you!" though he was not quite sure of what that meant and there was no one there to hear.

Chapter 8

WHAT'S A MOTHER TO DO?

SHARON FAIRLY FLOATED IN THE FRONT door of her home, kissed her mother who was reading a book and headed up the stairs.

"Just one moment young lady," Lillian began. "Where have you been? I have been worried about you. I have been calling your cell and you didn't answer and now you traipse in here as if nothing were amiss. What's going on?"

Yanked abruptly from her own fantasies, Sharon came back down from the stairs as if she were climbing off of a cloud and back on to the dreary Earth.

"Oh, nothing, mom. I'm fine. Nothing is wrong. I left my cell in the car. In fact it's still there. I should get it and put it on the charger."

"Wait! Where have you been and why are you acting so goofy?"

"Okay, mom, I went out to dinner with someone who wants to help me with the fund drive."

"And who might that be?" queried the concerned mother.

"Leonard," Sharon answered with a simple sigh.

It did not register at first. Leonard? Not a common name. Leonard. Suddenly it hit her like a body blow. LEONARD! Oh no, oh no, oh no. Then the further realization that the two of them had made eyes at each other in her office, and now her daughter was behaving in the way of the moonstruck.

Lilly wanted to rave, 'don't you know he is a raging lunatic?' But that is so against HIPPA laws. Instead, and in very measured tones, Lilly said to her daughter, "I don't think that you should be seeing one of my patients socially, dear."

"Oh mother, please, I'm not some silly little girl anymore, I can see whom ever I want. Don't you agree?"

"Are you planning on seeing him again?"

"Yes I am. In fact we are having dinner again tomorrow night," said Sharon with unaccustomed strength in her voice.

Lilly knew the human mind too well not to understand what was unfolding before her eyes. She knew her strong-willed and independent daughter well enough to know she would not be bullied or intimidated by parental control. She knew she could not reveal what she knew about the unstable state of Leonard's mind. She knew her beloved daughter was in trouble. Hopefully it would be quick in passing.

"Well, you are a smart girl, and you will choose carefully before making any important decisions. I wish I could tell you what I know about the man, but that is impossible and unethical. I will just say I love you, good night and beware."

Sharon came over to the chair where her mother and the book she was reading were in residence. She leaned over, gave her mom a big hug and said, "I love you too. Remember, mother, you did not raise any fools."

They both knew there was truth in Sharon's statement. Lilly also knew she had put Sharon on the strongest notice she felt she could. It would have to do for now.

Falling in love with love

SLEEP is impossible, thought Leonard as his exhilarated state evened out a bit. His lungs and heart were still laboring from his run, but he did not at all feel like sitting down or resting.

About this time of night he would ordinarily be donning his pajamas and brushing his teeth in preparation for bed. So he went ahead and changed then brushed.

Aware that something was causing a discomfort he took his PJs off

62

again. He needed a shower. Showers were, of course a morning ritual, but he had been sweating heavily.

It felt so good. It all felt so good. His shaky legs, whether from running or falling in love, felt wonderful. The hot, needle-sharp shower peppered his skin and was marvelous. His heart was dancing. His mind was flying in a thousand directions and every sensation was better than he had ever felt ... at least since he was a small boy playing with neighborhood kids.

Putting on a clean pair of PJs rounded out the parade of sensations. Climbing into bed Leonard knew he could not possibly sleep. The next thing he knew his alarm was going off.

Shawn Davis rang the doorbell at precisely 5:15 and almost before he could step back Leonard bounded out the door.

"Good morning, Shawn! That was a fine job you did last night. Everything was perfect. What did you say to the Maître D' and what did it cost me?"

Shawn was a bit embarrassed by the compliment and by the fact that he had given such a heavy tip – actually it was more than a tip, it was a bribe. He knew Mr. L was a very thrifty soul; a man who rarely spent money unless it was an investment or a "reward." Still, there was a definite expectation in the bosses' voice last night when he told Shawn that "It is important" so he moved out of his own comfort zone to make sure it would be a great experience.

"Ahem," was Shawn's first sound as he cleared his suddenly dry throat. Then he blurted, "Mr. L it cost you a thousand dollars plus the cost of the meal and a standard 20% gratuity." Choked as he was, Shawn managed to get that out. Then he waited for Mr. L's reaction.

"Good job, man. Best money I ever spent. Now, let's go make a pile of money so we can have some more fun." Then catching another thought Leonard said, "Have Samuel Levine call me as soon as we get to the office."

Leonard was barely settled at his desk when Samuel Levine (he did not want to be called 'Sam' by anyone) head of finance rang Leonard's line.

"Yes, Mr. L?"

"Samuel, I would like for you to do a few things for me this morning."

"Of course, sir," said Levine.

"First," began Leonard, "Cut a check for a thousand, no, make that $5,000.00 as a bonus for Shawn Davis. Second, I would like to have some cash to carry around. How much would you suggest?"

"Well, I don't carry much in the way of cash myself, sir. I usually use a credit card – most people do anymore."

"Fine, get me one of those, but I also want some pocket money. How about $10,000.00?"

"Whatever you want, but in all honesty sir that would mean you are carrying a minimum of one hundred bills and that would be, shall we say, bulky."

"Of course you are right," said Leonard, "I had $3,000.00 in my pocket the other day and that was a bit awkward, but money can go so quickly."

Samuel Levin chuckled, then said, "Mr. L, do you carry a wallet?"

"Why no, Sam, I don't, never have. Why do you ask?"

Samuel was amazed, someone had just called him Sam instead of Samuel and he almost felt it to be a compliment.

"Sir, when I travel I carry a wallet, one thousand in cash, five travelers checks each worth one thousand, an ATM card on a personal account, and a credit card. I have yet to find a situation that the plan could not handle. If you had a wallet ..."

"Brilliant, Sam! I'll get Shawn to get me the wallet if you'll take care of the rest. And I guess I will need a personal account – put $50,000.00 in that account, would you? How soon can we get that done, do you think."

"By the end of the day, sir." Sam said with assurance.

"Good," remarked Leonard. "Very, very good."

One of the first items Leonard spotted in his email was a memo from Bruce Saunders, the young accountant that he had sent to La Crosse Instruments to oversee the finances.

"Dear Mr. L,

I would rather be sitting in front of you instead of telling you by email, because the news is so good.

Mr. Blake and his team have been working almost without stopping. The results are, they have had a surge of improvements and now feel the product will stand up to very rigorous testing.

As you know the trials required to bring this to market can easily run into the tens, possibly, hundreds of millions. We will need to finalize our strategy to raise the capital soon.

The excitement around here is so thick you can cut it with a knife. There is very little doubt about the instrument's ability to detect Alzheimer's in it earliest stages, thus, allowing for drugs that will delay it, possibly until a true cure is discovered.

As we discussed before you purchased La Crosse Instruments there are various options to fund these trials. You may wish to have Advantage Corporation fund the entire process. We also discussed bringing in Venture capitalists and ultimately an IPO.

However, one of the members of Blake's team has a brother who is a senior V.P. with Cronkite Pharmaceuticals, the leading company working on treatments for Alzheimer's. He would like permission for our legal department to draw up the necessary protection to allow him to share some of our findings with his brother.

The purpose is to explore a partnership with a company that has the entire marketing infrastructure in place and the capital to fund the testing. It might just be a marriage made in commercial heaven.

We will absolutely not do anything until we hear from you.

Bruce Saunders
Acting CFO
La Crosse Instruments

It is amazing how productive people are when you combine genius with capital and hope, mused Leonard.

Shawn Davis knocked and Leonard told him to come in.

"Your department heads are here for your quarterly meeting, Mr. L."

"Good", said Leonard. "By the way, Shawn, pick me up a nice wallet today, would you?"

As Shawn stood expectantly holding the door Leonard had one more instruction for him. "Please tell everyone I'll join them in the boardroom in just a few moments."

Leonard needed a few minutes to center himself. For every morning since he was about 13 he had meditated, while showering, about the most important thing to be accomplished that day – just as his father had insisted – that is until this morning.

Leonard knew he should have focused on this quarterly meeting as the most important thing of the day. He had showered before going to bed and felt no need to do so again when he arose. Even if he had followed his usual routine, Leonard justified, his mind would have been on the lofty condition of his heart and spirit, and not on the business of the day.

He realized he loved being in love. He certainly attributed his current euphoria to Sharon, yet his focus was not really on her, but on how he himself felt about how he himself felt. Then he wondered if that was what love was. He then further wondered if these thoughts made any sense at all.

Roping his mind back in, Leonard picked up the small stack of papers from his desk that dealt with the forth-coming meeting. He knew the material well and it took but a moment to get on track.

With unusual briskness Mr. L. entered the Board Room precisely at 9 AM. – not a minute late – which was not his custom.

"Gentlemen and lady," he began. "Let's take a look at where we are and figure out how to make it better."

Leon Harding, lead attorney and the man who usually opened these meetings was a bit surprised that Mr. L had taken the lead, but of course, he said nothing.

As the boss surveyed the room he became more excited about the business at hand. Over the years, between him and his father, Advantage Corporation had assembled what his father would have called a "Cracker Jack" team. This morning Leonard surveyed each man or woman as they presented and was thrilled by the expertise and professionalism of every one of them.

Leon Harding from legal, Amanda Epstein of Acquisition Research, George Koch who headed the property management division – each and every one of them were first rate.

Their presentations were followed by Samuel Levine who headed Finance and Accounting, Robert Vucovich, the Construction wizard, and Ervin Syrisst who oversaw Operations. They were as good a team at what they did as anyone in the business.

The overall report was good, in fact very good with the net value of the Advantage Corp totaling something over 787 million and net revenues topping 150 million.

Leonard rose from his seat and all eyes were upon him. He walked to the window. He was keenly aware of what the people in the room would see. It was this time of day the sun would stream through that window for the maximum visual effect. It made a person seem to almost disappear even as it cast the impression of a halo surrounding him.

There were two things on Leonard's mind. First, he was seeing afresh the quality of his team. Secondly, he wanted their help in determining the path for the Compton project.

"You," began Leonard, "all of you, are amazing."

This was a first. These people know the LaFrance's to be ethical and smart, but they did not know them to be quick with praise. Usually it was more like quick to criticize and slow to praise. Now, here was Mr. L telling them they are amazing. They were amazed.

"Further, although my father before me, and now myself, have always been guided by the philosophy of setting compensation for department heads at a level a shade above fair as the best way to keep good people, I believe that philosophy needs to be revisited."

The universal thought in the room was, *Oh no, he gave us the compliment to ease the pain of a pay cut.*

"I say that because what we have just heard is a report that proves costs are down and revenues are up."

Leonard paused. Everyone held his or her breath.

"That says to me we need to reward everyone with a bonus. Mr. Levine, would you be so kind as to draw up a check for $50,000.00 for each and every person here. The Advantage Corporation would also like to give each department a like amount for you to award to your people. All I ask is that you reward on merit and don't play personal favorites."

Now, each and every department head was truly amazed. Shocked, might be a more appropriate term.

Turning toward Leon Harding and Samuel Levine, who were the

heads of Legal and Finance, Leonard threw out a bizarre request.

"Leon and Samuel, I am going to ask you to look into the ramifications of turning our La Crosse holdings into a charitable foundation. I have just heard from Bruce Saunders that they are quickly arriving at the point where they are ready to undergo trials. This may be a big one. Get back to me on that ASAP.

"There is one last thing I want everyone to think about," said Leonard. "I have just bought a block of properties in the worst part of our city. They are houses, all empty, mostly boarded up, many are illegally occupied by crack dealers and gangsters. That said, I have seen, just one block over, the same houses after rehab and an effort to organize the community and the police. The difference is astounding.

"This is," admitted Leonard, "a complete departure from our business model. The fellow behind all this is Theodore Webb – he goes by Theo – and is coming by here today at 2 PM to meet with certain of you and you know who you are."

He turned to Robert Vuchovich. "Bob I need for you to go down there personally. Tomorrow if possible, but no matter what ASAP. I will arrange a tour for anyone who wants to go down there. I hope that will be all of you. I can see both danger and rewards here. Regardless of how far we want to take this I have committed to the first block, but I want your coordinated input as to whether we should devote part of our assets to more of this kind of community redevelopment.

"Thank you. You've done a great job and I, for one, am looking forward to a bright future." Leonard left the room, but he was certainly not forgotten.

Chapter 9

L EONARD HAD BARELY TAKEN HIS SEAT BE-
hind his desk when Shawn Davis asked if he might have a
moment for Samuel Levine.

"Send him in."

As Samuel Levine entered Leonard stood up. Samuel had been in
this office 500 times, but Mr. L had never stood on the occasion of his
arrival and this threw Samuel off a bit.

"Yes, Samuel."

Samuel paused, still somewhat off balance. Then to his own surprise he offered, "Please call me Sam."

"Very well, Sam. Please call me Leonard."

Samuel's state of mind was now in even more disarray. "Thank
you, Leonard. Sir, I mean no disrespect, but I am observing some rather
vast departures from your normal behavior and I'm wondering if you
are okay."

Leonard chuckled. "Thank you for noticing, Sam. You are right. I
am behaving differently, and what's more ... I like it."

A quietness filled the room for 4 or 5 seconds. Then Sam asked,
"Sir, do you think some of this behavior is irrational?"

"Sam, you are right again. I might be going overboard a bit and if it
gets to be too bad let me know so I may check myself. However, Sam,
I have been too rational for too long. I am searching for balance in my

life and I know you are a very rational man and that I can count on you for counsel if you see any destructive behavior on my part. Anything else?"

"Er, no sir. Thank you Mr. L."

As Sam Levine exited, Shawn Davis entered with a reminder that Mr. L had a lunch appointment with a Dr. Carroll.

"Thank you, Shawn." Leonard needed no reminder of this event. "Please bring the car around."

As the car pulled to the curb in front of the restaurant, Leonard instructed his team to stay put and let the doorman open the car door. "Shawn, why don't you take the three of you out to lunch. Charge it to me. Please be back here in one and a half hours."

Leonard was, by his own design, 5 minutes early. When Dr. Lilly was ushered into the private dining room by the Maître D' Leonard was ready. Light from the doorway surrounded her and it was quite evident where Sharon got her beauty.

He stood as she approached the table. He was smiling.

She was not.

His greeting was warm.

Hers was chilly.

Still smiling, Leonard said, "You look very nice today."

Lilly had already decided not to play the offended mother role today, but to only play therapist. She had decided that interfering with her daughter's business at this point was not a good idea.

"Leonard, I do not have any preconceived ideas as to how effective this arrangement will be, but let us give it our best shot and see where it goes."

"Thank you, Dr. Lilly, that suits me fine. Where do you want to start?"

As they talked and ate the conversation wound through much more of Leonard's childhood and transition from a mother-centric to father-centric life. Lilly started to see the innocence of Leonard and the great harm done to him by a well-meaning, but warped father.

It became clearer that Leonard had experienced very little interaction with the world outside of a strict business regimen. His social skills were close to nil, but somehow Lilly found that endearing. She even began to see what attracted her daughter to the man, though she could not be comfortable about this developing inter-generational relationship. If she had not been as sure of her daughter's common sense as she was it would have been a lot more difficult for her.

For whatever reason, neither party brought up Sharon and the relationship that was beginning to develop between her and Leonard.

The good doctor believed this lunch arrangement with Leonard could be both helpful to her patient and within the bounds of her own professional ethics; as long as he did nothing to harm her daughter in any way.

As for Leonard, he was quite impressed with himself. He was carrying on a conversation with a woman and felt at ease in doing so. He even injected a bit of humor on two occasions. Not really all that funny, but it did display a more relaxed self than he had known before. He wistfully thought how nice it would be if everyone were as easy for him to talk with as Dr. Lilly.

They agreed Leonard would not try to see Dr. Lilly beforehand, but they were to meet the following week. They shook hands and parted.

BACK at the Advantage building Leonard found he had two visitors waiting for him. The first was Theo. Their greeting was mutually positive and Leonard wasted no time in getting Theo with Shawn Davis for the preplanned series of meetings with key department heads. Leonard was also pleased that Theo had remembered to bring him his shoes.

The second was John Thompkins, the private investigator he had hired to look into the whereabouts and living conditions of his mother. As the pair went into Leonard's office, Shawn handed Mr. L a memo from Leon Harding and Samuel Levine stating there would be no major problem moving the La Crosse Instruments Corporation into a charitable trust.

"Well," began Leonard, "that was pretty quick. What have you found out so far?"

John Thompkins mood was somber. "Mr. L, the news is not good. I am afraid your mother is no longer living." The detective paused to let the enormity of his disclosure settle in.

Strangely, Leonard was not finding the news to be unexpected. He had somehow known that this was the case since he was a young teen.

"How did she die?"

"Our investigation shows that when she left Los Angeles she went to New Orleans and took her life with an overdose of sleeping pills."

"Phew," breathed Leonard. "Where in New Orleans did this happen?"

"She checked into the Sunset Motel. It happened there."

"Do you have any other information about her?" asked Leonard.

"Not much. I thought you might want to have this before we spent anymore of your money."

"Appreciate your concern, but I would like as complete a reconstruction of her life, warts and all, that you can put together on her. Let me know if and when the costs reach $20,000. That will be all for now."

When he was alone again, Leonard quietly wept. The overwhelming darkness that made her take her own life was an indictment of his father's treatment of his mother and of his own inability to reach her as a good son would have. Leonard wished he could go see Lilly. He did not even know for sure, at this moment, whether he wanted to see Sharon, the object of his newfound affection, tonight.

After pulling himself together he called Leon Harding and instructed him to put together the charitable trust they had been discussing and that the name of it should be the Sarah Peachtree LaFrance Foundation.

In turn, Leon Harding reported that Theo's contract had been spot on and needed few revisions. He also gave an uncharacteristically enthusiastic endorsement by adding the young man truly knew the law in regards to real estate. Leon had sent him over to see Samuel Levine, who would send him over to Robert Vuchovich, and they would soon be on their way to tour the project.

Further, a bus had been arranged to take all of the other department heads to the neighborhood and have Theo give them the tour.

"Thank you, Leon," said Leonard.

This would be a good day to walk home, thought Leonard.

He instructed Shawn accordingly, followed by a request for the team to pick him up at 6:45 for his dinner appointment. Then Leonard asked, "Did you get that wallet for me?"

"Yes, Mr. L. I'll bring it right in. Also, Samuel Levine stuffed it with the goodies you requested of him."

As Shawn delivered the wallet and its contents he added that Samuel Levine said to remind Mr. L that he must sign the first line of the travelers checks now and the second line in the presence of the recipient at the time of purchase.

"Good to know," remarked Leonard.

"Mr. L, are you alright, sir?"

"Um, yeah – I'm okay. Thanks for asking."

It was a slow and long walk home until the last three blocks. These Leonard ran with all of his might.

Love can lift

LEONARD was not looking forward to the dinner. He was drained by the day and the tragic news. Nevertheless he went.

The Maitre D' had again reserved the private dining room and ushered Mr. L into it with considerable fanfare, which for Leonard, tonight, was out of place.

A few minutes later Sharon arrived. With her was air, fresh as a spring day. She was an immediate elixir for Leonard. As he rose to greet her, she melted into his arms with the warmest of hugs.

Everything changed. Even when part of him said he must return to his state of remorse and guilt, he could not go there. He was here and now. The here and now was a good place to be.

It would be of little value to go over every detail of the dinner, as it is the same dance that all people who are falling in love go through. The only appreciable difference was due to the revelation by Leonard that he had assigned the profits of the La Crosse Instrument Corp into a trust that would go toward assisting worthy charities such as the Brian's Better Tomorrow Foundation. It would take a couple of years for that move to begin paying dividends, but until that time Leonard would personally guarantee $100,000.00 annually for the next three years.

Leonard walked Sharon to her car once again. Sharon, usually most cautious and conservative with men asked if she might see Leonard's home.

He did not know what she meant by that. His only experience with having a beautiful, young woman in his home was the "reward" aspect. He did not fully understand why, but he knew it was not yet time. He knew he must protect her from this moment of weakness if, indeed, that is what she meant.

Instead of moving her in that direction and taking advantage of her, Leonard gathered her in his arms and told her with sweet sincerity that there would be a time for that, but that he was in no hurry.

He wanted so badly to at least kiss her – but he did not know how. He had never kissed a woman – not even one of his rewards. Rather than embarrass himself by showing his ineptness in the art, he closed his eyes and kissed her long and gently on her forehead. They both reeled. They were both giddy.

It took a while for Leonard to digest the events of the day, but when sleep finally came it was deep and uninterrupted.

AT 5:15 the next morning he was greeted by Shawn wishing him a happy birthday.

Leonard had completely lost track of the days. Fifty-two years old today – just now beginning to experience life. He thought he may very well be the world's oldest living teenager. He almost expected an outbreak of acne.

While in his morning shower he realized two horrible things. One, he had not made another date with Sharon. Two, he did not have Sharon's phone number. *What an idiot*, he thought. He decided that getting that corrected would be his number one priority for the day.

Since Lilly did not have a public listing for her home or cell phone, and neither did Sharon, the only way he could get this done was to call her mother's office and leave a message for Sharon. He was pretty sure she would call back.

Leonard settled into the busy work that was usually on his desk, but interrupted it to get Robert Vucovich on the line. Vucovich was the only department head that had a perpetual tan. As the leader of the construction team that rehabbed all of the Advantage Corporation properties he believed in a hands-on style of oversight.

"Bob," began Leonard, "I know you went down to inspect the Compton project yesterday. Don't need you to get involved with the actual construction unless the work is not up to the quality that we need it to be, but I am very interested to get your take on our Theo Webb."

Bob chuckled. "That Theo is a pistol. He knows his stuff and his crews respect him like few contractors I've ever seen. Mr. L, the best part is, his work is first rate. It is very efficient and cost effective, but he does not cut a single corner that should not be cut. I say go with this guy."

"Thanks, Bob. Coming from a guy who is first rate himself that is an impressive recommendation," said Leonard as he hung up.

Shawn Davis rang in shortly thereafter.

"Mr. L, sorry to interrupt, but Calvin Frost is standing here and he says he has an appointment with you. I don't have it on my calendar, but he said you should check yours."

Leonard checked his computer calendar and sure enough – there it was – an appointment with Calvin Frost. Leonard was certain that he had not entered the appointment. *What the hell' thought Leonard.* "Send him in Shawn."

It had been three years since Leonard had seen or even heard from Calvin Frost. Calvin and Leonard had a strained relationship or so Leonard had judged. It was not to be unexpected, as Calvin had been to Fred, Leonard's father, what Shawn Davis was now to Leonard.

The changing of the guard began when Fred was crippled by his stroke. The stroke became more and more debilitating until, when three years after it hit, Fred died. Calvin stayed on for three more years during the transition as Leonard became more and more comfortable in his role as not only the CEO, but the absolute owner of the Advantage Corporation.

He was more than anxious to leave, thought Leonard. *I wonder what brings him here now?*

Calvin entered. Thin, straight, perfect gray hair, though now beginning to thin just a bit. Everyone was taken by his straight as a stick posture. He could have easily been a general, if the way one carried himself was the only criteria. But Calvin was not a general. He was a lawyer by training who had elected to spend his working years as a well-paid lackey.

"Good morning, Leonard. Thank you for seeing me." said Calvin as he extended his hand.

With a slight smile Leonard pointed toward his computer screen and said, "I could not avoid it. It seems I had the appointment already booked." Leonard was immediately pleased that he had already injected humor into this conversation with a man he had once feared almost as much as his father.

"I hope you will forgive my being so presumptuous, but I had one more piece of business to conclude for your father and I took the liberty of entering myself into your schedule before I left the employ of Advantage three years ago."

The corners of Leonard's mouth drew downward, not in disapproval, but as the prelude to a question.

"One more piece of business?" noted Leonard, his voice rising in pitch, not volume, on the word 'business.' "What might that business be, Calvin?"

"I have a letter from your father that I was asked to deliver to you on your 52nd birthday. Today is that day. I do not have any idea of the contents of the letter. If the envelope is any indication of its contents the letter was likely handwritten by your father when he was no longer able to speak."

Calvin continued at a determined pace. "I have something I very much need to say. When I look back at my life, I am far from pleased at my choice in a career. I might also add that I came to work here as a fairly young man. I readily admit I was taken by your father's single-minded brilliance and the money he paid me for the service I provided him and the company."

The two men were still standing. Realizing this Leonard pointed Calvin toward one of the sumptuous, but slightly lower guest chairs even as he took his own, rather elegant and slightly taller, chair.

"I get the feeling there is something more you want to say. Please feel free."

"Yes, well, the years I was in service here did not set well with me over time. As I say, at first I really did not see all there was to see about your father. As I began to see him for what he was I began to dislike him. And may I say, you were a carbon copy. Somehow working for you was even worse."

Leonard was experiencing a growing tumult in his innards and did not like the course of this conversation.

"Calvin, if you did not face my father with your criticisms when he was paying you, I do not feel it is appropriate for you to criticize him now that he is not here to defend himself."

"Very well, and you have an excellent argument, but I think you should know I left here sickened after serving for a total of 27 years. Three years with you while your father was ill, three after your father passed, and 21 one years of serving your father before that. I will not further address your father, except, to say again, that you are a carbon copy. You even carried on the same disgusting practice of buying girls, decent girls, right off the street by offering enough money to corrupt all but the most moral of young women."

Leonard was taken aback. Calvin was just getting going.

"Like your father you never cared about anything, but making money. Nothing wrong in making money, but as I have come to understand, if that is all you value you will never be a happy man. I did not want to retire. I'm not good at retirement, but I could no longer be around such low behavior.

"You may not ever be happy, however, you will succeed in making many miserable. In your mother's case, miserable enough to take her own life."

Leonard rose. "Calvin, I might want to take this up again. But right now I will ask you to deliver my father's letter and leave my office."

Calvin complied and left by saying, "I have been choking on this for a long time. I have said what I came to say." With that Calvin left the office.

Chapter 10

THE LETTER

LEONARD BOWED HIS HEAD. **H**E WANTED SO badly to talk to someone who would understand. He could not think of anyone. Perhaps, Dr. Lilly, but she made it clear that could happen only once a week. That 'once' was yesterday.

His only other possible escape routes were Theo or Sharon.

Theo was now a business relationship and therefore not an appropriate outlet.

Sharon ... Sharon was too sweet, too dear, to take such an ugly burden to at this stage.

There was no one.

Leonard lifted the 'letter from the grave.' He fingered the edges as he wondered why, and what, his father had written.

This was so strange. His father had given him plenty of oral communication, but Leonard could not recall a single time his father had ever written him. Even some of the instructions that could have easily been delivered by memo were always conducted either face-to-face or by phone. Leonard understood that his father wanted to make sure he understood. He wanted to make sure to imprint the father's ways upon the son in an indelible fashion.

The outside of the envelope read, 'Confidential' in large letters. Obviously written by an unsure hand.

Just below that it read, "From Fred LaFrance to Leonard LaFrance on the occasion of his 52nd birthday."

Leonard opened the third drawer on the right side of his desk and extracted a pair of scissors. Firmly tapping the envelope on one end to assure the contents were ensconced to just that side of the envelope, Leonard used the scissors carefully to cut off the other end. He then blew into the cut end allowing the pressure of his breath to force open an avenue from which he could retrieve the letter. His father had taught him to do that.

Yes, it was all handwritten. The letter had been crafted, with great effort and was decidedly legible even though the handwriting was unsure. Each large letter showed great concentration.

Leonard did not begin to read his father's words immediately. Instead he saw the overall importance his father had given the epistle by the effort required to write it. Leonard knew beyond a shadow of a doubt how difficult each and every pen stroke had been for the man.

When he began to read, Leonard entered into a new level of understanding; an entirely new way of seeing, that which was around him and where he had come from.

Dear son,

Happy 52nd Birthday.

By now you have either succeeded or failed in your role as pilot of the Advantage Corporation.

I cannot tell you how much I wanted you to know what I am about to say, but I guess it was more important to me to not interrupt the process of managing the empire I built until you were either safely through the transition or you had failed and there would be nothing to interrupt.

Leonard, I taught you many valuable things. I made sure you had the best teachers in the disciplines of English, Science, accounting and Math. Of course, I personally taught you business. I did everything I could think of to ensure you would succeed in the material world. Though I cannot know as I write this whether or not you have excelled in business, I cannot help but think you have done just that.

This letter is not about business. It is about life. What I did not teach you is as important, no, it is more important, than business. I have learned too late. I hope you take what I write to you now as seriously as you took all of the instruction I brought to you while I was there.

Sitting in this wheelchair for three years, not being able to talk, having to be lifted to the toilet, into bed, have someone dress me, has been sobering. It has made me reflect on my life, for in my current condition I have nowhere to hide from my thoughts.

I will start with your mother for it is the most difficult part of my story to tell. It is also the best lesson as to how not to live.

When I met her she was just 16 years old. Her father, Bobby Peachtree, had a gas station. Her mother, Marie, was sickly.

The State of California was in the process of building a major freeway. I had seen the states construction plans and knew her father's station was adjacent to what would become a major on/off ramp. After asking around, I found out about his wife's illness and the financial bind it was putting them in. This was made even worse by the construction work that literally cut his station off from all but a trickle of traffic. He decided to close it and go be with his wife. He was so broken he did not even look to sell the business. After all who would want to buy a place that could not open for business for 8 months or more.

I was able to get in front of him at his home before anyone else was aware of the future importance of this piece of property. When I asked if he could use some cash in exchange for the property, he wanted to know if I would be interested in also buying the four adjacent lots as well. He had bought all the land from a farmer when he first came to California, but had only developed the corner where his gas station was.

I was prepared to pay him $100,000.00 for the corner lot that held the station. The offer was predicated on the knowledge that I could weather the financial storm of no income for 8 months and even use the down time to renovate the building. When the traffic returned it would far and away exceed anything that corner had ever seen and I could then lease the more valuable gas station for an excellent return.

When I asked what he wanted for the property as a whole he said he had paid $25,000 an acre for it 15 years earlier and there was a total of three acres. He was not a businessman at all, but surmised the property had probably gone up in value.

"What if I double your money, would that be fair?" I asked. Mr. Peachtree shook his head and said, "All I wanna to do is get Mrs.

Peachtree back to Louisiana so she can die surrounded by family. I can do that with the $150,000.00 you are talkin about."

That, Leonard, is how we bought the land for what is now, the New Century Plaza.

As we closed the deal I met his wife and daughter. They were both quiet and their daughter was soft-spoken and shy. She was also the prettiest girl I had ever seen.

I asked her father if I could take her to dinner. He allowed that would be okay if I had her home by 9:00. I honored that condition.

When the family moved back to Louisiana they had a clear understanding that I would be coming down to marry her in their hometown and then bring her back to California.

Your mother lived in a dream world Leonard. The home I had purchased in Beverly Hills strengthened her perception that life is a fantasy.

I was just the opposite. We never quite saw eye-to-eye; never really bonded. I was afraid she would lead you into a fairytale view of life.

On your eleventh Birthday I came home and she was reading poetry to you. I decided then and there I had to take you under my wing and teach you the way the world really was.

I separated you from her in every way. She became more and more morose and depressed. One day we came home and she was gone. She took only one suitcase. She did not take her jewelry and only a small amount of her household fund.

I was notified less than a week later that she had gone back to Louisiana and there in a cheap New Orleans hotel, she had killed herself.

I never told you. I am sorry. Perhaps you have figured it out by now on your own.

I did not come from a healthy family. My father was a drunk and my mother was promiscuous. My Uncle Ted raised me most of the time and he left me his farm. I did not know what family was. I did not know how to love. I did not even know how to respect other people.

Somehow, you were the lone exception. It was clear to me that I needed to give you the best of what I knew. And I believe I did. The problem was I did not see, until I was so physically and mentally crushed, the importance of anything besides chasing and capturing the almighty dollar.

Trapped as I have been in this chair I have concluded the most important thing is not money; it is love. Not necessarily the romantic kind, although I believe the importance of that cannot be overstated, but love as a general condition of the heart.

Knowing that the end of my days is quickly approaching has also started to make me question the importance of ourselves in relationship to the importance of our relationship with God. I know nothing specifically to share with you regarding this except to advise you to look into it.

Should you find a woman that you regard highly enough to marry (I hope that has already happened) do not put her in a house, no matter how magnificent, and leave her there alone. Walk with her in every way you can. This will bring her joy and I now think it will make the husband a better man.

I am tired, son. Not the kind of tired that I will bounce back from. This is my last and maybe my most important lesson for you. I hope it is clear, as I have no energy for additional explanation.

Forgive me for keeping this from you for so long, but ego's die hard. I needed to be sure you were not distracted from the work at hand until you had completely mastered it.

The Advantage Corporation and you are my only legacies. Forgive me for my shortcomings and above all know that I truly love you. That love is the best of what I have done.

Love and Respect,

Your Father.

The explosive burning rush began in Leonard's groin and proceeded like an unstoppable train into his gut and through his chest. By the time it reached his throat it became a blood curdling scream. Tears were streaming down his face. Mucous poured from his nose. Drool slid from his mouth.

Shawn Davis rushed in. He could not begin to grasp what was going on, but somehow he knew he could not be part of, or a solution to it.

This was an utter meltdown. He quietly closed the door and stood outside listening for an opportunity to help.

The timing of this message from his father could not have come at a time more perfectly targeted for maximum penetration. A large comet hitting the Earth at an unthinkable velocity could have not impacted Leonard with greater force.

Shawn stood dutifully by the door listening to an unending stream of sobs, chokes and occasional shrieks.

Chapter 11

UNDONE

As LEONARD SLOWLY GATHERED HIMSELF THE best he could, the rest of the day disappeared.

Shawn had held all calls and delivered no messages while the extreme angst made itself known through the thick office door. However, at 5:30 it had been quiet for over an hour. Shawn knocked softly. An exhausted Leonard muttered, "Come in."

"Is there anything I can do for you, sir?"

"No. Thank you, Shawn."

"Would you like your messages?"

Leonard was quiet for a moment and then said, "Sure, why not."

The message on top was from Sharon. Shawn had arranged it thus. Although he had never met the young lady, he thought it might be a good thing, as he knew Leonard had a special place for this woman.

After putting the stack on Mr. L's desk, Shawn quietly withdrew and waited. He called the security team and had them stand by.

Leonard picked up the first phone message, saw who it was from, turned it face down and went on to the next. That one was from Theo. He methodically looked at each piece. He did the same with the correspondence, but did not read past the letterhead.

Taking the stack of phone messages once again he turned them over and looked at Sharon's name.

How could he call her?

If he did not call her of what value did he place on her? For that matter, what value did she place on him? With the act of a man placing his last dollar on the red to win, he instructed himself, *Let's find out what's real ... and what is not.*

He had to know.

When Sharon answered her cell Leonard found that he was either emboldened or had given up completely.

"Hello."

"Hello."

"Leonard?"

"Yes."

"What is wrong?" she asked.

"I am falling apart," said Leonard in naked honesty.

"Is there something I can do?"

"I don't know"

"Well. I do. Where are you?"

"In my office."

"Where is that?"

"Do you know where the Advantage Corporation building is?"

"Yes, I do. I can be there in ten minutes."

"I'll be out in front." Leonard then hung up.

TRUE to her word a concerned looking Sharon pulled her Honda up to the curb and gathered Leonard. After getting directions to his home she drove there and ushered him inside.

To this point there had been no discussion of his state of mind.

Leonard went silently to his bedroom, closed the door, put on his pajamas. Opened the door and Sharon came in. She took him by the hand and together they lay on top of the comforter and she held him as he wept. For the next 24 hours this was their life.

When Leonard awoke, Sharon was there with a tray of coffee and food that she had delivered.

Leonard stood. With clear eyes he looked at Sharon and asked, "How can I ever repay you?"

"I have not given it a moment's thought and what's more I don't want you to waste a millisecond thinking about it either." replied Sharon.

"I feel like a baby."

"Oh, don't worry about it. Everyone cries at some point."

"No, I mean I feel like a baby. Newborn, clueless, helpless."

"Can you tell me what happened?" asked Sharon.

"It was very strange. I received a letter from my father."

"But I thought," she said, "your father had passed away?"

"Yes. He died 8 years ago," said Leonard clearly, but then under his breath Leonard mused, "however, he may never actually leave the scene.

"What I mean is that he wrote a letter before he died that he had arranged to be delivered to me ... on my 52nd Birthday."

"The letter was that disturbing?" asked Sharon.

"Taken by itself it was not. Joined together with the emotional tumult of the past couple of weeks and ... you, it undid me. Thank you so much for what you did. Are you in trouble with your mom or anywhere else?"

"My mother was very concerned for both of us. But I have kept in touch with her. She knows I am okay and that you are resting."

"Please extend my apologies for this mess I've caused." Leonard paused and with such conviction as to make it unarguable he said, "No one has ever been so kind, so giving as you have been. I am in awe. Do you love me?"

Sharon was taken aback as anyone in her place would have been. The word had never been mentioned between them. She lowered her eyes and then brought them up to meet his. "Of course I love you and what's more I believe I am falling in love with you."

Leonard was frank. "Sharon, I have never felt like this for anyone, but I must not mislead you – I do not know what love is – or is not. I have never been exposed to it – at least not since my mother went away."

"Wow, you are wonderfully honest. That is one of the things I love about you. Thank you for the blunt truth. I will keep a check on my heart until you know how you feel. Fair enough?"

A very slight smile crept across Leonard's now relaxed and handsome face. He put his arms around her and brought her very close.

As he did this, a warmth started to spread in his loins. Unwantingly, he slowly released her and backed away.

Even as Sharon left his arms he knew what he must do.

Chapter 12

SIX WEEKS LATER LEONARD WAS BEGINNING TO MAKE SENSE OF things. It is not that he thought he had arrived. In fact he knew he had not. That, however, did not bother him.

His father always told him not to be as concerned about where he was as much as he should be concerned about his direction. Leonard was far from stable and nowhere near complete, but he was sure the direction was sound.

There were many moving parts; some in business, some with his personal struggle and some in his new love life.

He had spoken to Sharon, and she agreed, about slowing down their relationship. It was all for the best anyhow as she was back in classes at Berkeley for the Fall Semester and would only come down on the occasional weekend.

Also, Leonard was feeling a pent-up sexual need and did not want to venture there with Sharon yet. Of course he did want to go precisely there. But out of love he held back.

Theo was helpful in this regard. Theo was an old-fashioned Christian and shared with Leonard that "Love will wait when lust will not." Leonard was not a Christian, but he knew the difference and wanted to wait.

Part of Leonard's self-imposed therapy was exercise in the form of running. He could only manage a few blocks at first, and then, bent over, gasping for air, he would vow to make it a longer run tomorrow. It took only three weeks to make it to work in one continuous run. The executive suite his father had built into his office contained a private shower that, until now, had never been used. Leonard was thankful for its convenience.

Robert Vucovich, the head of the Advantage Corporation construction division, had been monitoring Theo's progress very carefully and was duly impressed at every turn. The Legal and Finance departments in the persons of Leon Harding and Samuel Levine were also praising the judgment, efficiency and transparency of Theo's project.

Leonard had met with Theo on a weekly basis and became more inclined to trust him. The thing that spoke most strongly to Leonard was the quality of the product, especially when coupled with how fast it was moving toward completion. Before the homes were even finished being built Theo already had willing buyers who passed the credit checks.

In the shower this morning the leading thought was once again the most important item of the day. It was indeed important. Bruce Saunders, the young man that Leonard had made Acting CFO of the La Crosse Instruments Corporation was coming in today with Barry Blake, CEO of that company and a Mr. Marvin Quinn, V.P. of Mergers and Acquisitions of Cronkite Pharmaceuticals.

If indeed, as Bruce Saunders purposed, there could be a merger with Cronkite Pharmaceuticals, the La Crosse Instruments project would be almost assured of success.

The profits, if there were to be any, were already placed in a trust named for Leonard's mother and would go to help charities that he felt were deserving. Leonard was strangely more protective of those profits than he was of the ones he kept.

All was going well and very smoothly. This gave Leonard the space to begin thinking about what he must do in the grander scheme of things.

The Cronkite Pharmaceuticals deal was scheduled for 11 AM. At a quarter after 10:00 Theo called and asked to see Leonard in the afternoon. This was not unusual; they would often schedule same day meetings, but for a variety of reasons Leonard put Theo off till tomorrow. He asked Theo to come in at 10:00 AM sharp.

After Theo agreed, Leonard called Shawn Davis and told him that he wanted all department heads to meet in the boardroom at 11:00 AM tomorrow and also requested that lunch be catered.

Leonard had done his homework. Cronkite Pharmaceuticals had

only one serious competitor: Virta Pharmaceuticals, and they were also rumored to be close to finalizing their own treatment for the dreaded and fatal disease. Again, the critical part, if there was to be a positive outcome, was the detection of the disease in its earliest stage. This made the La Crosse Instruments early detection system even more valuable.

In the unusual act of being the first to arrive in the large Board Room, Leonard took his seat and looked at travel brochures while he waited. Everyone was on time. Leonard's people were surprised to see that Mr. L was already there and not making his usual late, but grand, appearance.

Marvin Quinn arrived with a small army of seven colleagues. Quinn was considerably quicker and more observant than most of the people who sat on his side of the table. He noticed almost immediately that the chairs for his group were ever so slightly lower than those of the Advantage Corporation people.

Marvin Quinn was also unusual as compared to those who generally sat in this room in that he frequently sat in boardrooms, some more opulent than this. He was not intimidated by any of it.

Leon Harding was unsure of himself for a moment, not knowing what to expect from Mr. L, but when there was no effort on Mr. L's part to take the leadership role, Mr. Harding did.

After Leon Harding started the meeting Mr. Quinn, of Cronkite, asked if he might have the floor. Indeed, when he took it he held the room spellbound as he openly laid out what his company was willing to do.

He said such things as Cronkite Pharmaceuticals Corporation, which he referred to as CPC, had absolute faith in the La Crosse Instruments tool to be able to deliver a means of early diagnosis that would perfectly layer with the progress that CPC was making with a revolutionary drug for the treatment of Alzheimer's. However, Quinn acknowledged, the drug was completely dependent on diagnosing the disease in the earliest stages possible.

After 45 minutes of laying out the deal that CPC was willing to make, and a good offer it was, Leonard spoke for the first time.

"Thank you Mr. Quinn for what, I'm sure, most of the men and women in this room will consider to be a generous offer. However, it cannot be accepted in its current form."

Mr. Quinn rose to his full 6-feet 3 inches and used a method of aggressive posture that had effectively cowered many opponents.

"Fine, we will take our offer and go home!" said Quinn with an utter finality. His team rose with him and, as if choreographed, they moved toward the door.

Leonard said nothing, nor did he move. His employees did not move either – more out of shock than anything else. As per the choreography consistently and effectively applied on so many other occasions, Quinn, and his underlings, paused with his hand on the doorknob.

This is the part where the opponent usually said whatever words would translate into "Wait."

Mr. L sat, unmoving, unspeaking. His team, frozen in time and space, did the same.

After a long and uncomfortable silence, Quinn opened the door for his people and they filed out. Quinn, however, hung back.

It was at this point Leonard said very quietly, "Marvin, sit down."

"I will not sit down," replied Marvin Quinn, although his voice was considerably more hollow than he would have wanted it to be.

Before his own staff could break the tension, by moving or speaking, Leonard said with a gentleness that, at first, seemed otherworldly and out of place.

"Mr. Quinn, you have two choices at this point and we have three. You can sit back down and hear our plan, which I believe you will find quite agreeable, or you can return to your board empty handed. CPC needs this alignment as much or more than La Crosse.

"Our three choices are begging you to stay and taking your offer – which is definitely not going to happen. Option 2, would be working out a plan that fits our needs as well as those of CPC. Or", after a long pause, Leonard continued, "Or option 3, we will call Virta. We'll allow you to choose first."

Seizing on the positive, Quinn responded with as much authority as he could muster, "What is so agreeable about your plan?"

"Please, Marvin, have your people take their seats and I will lay it out."

Leonard LaFrance was clearly in control. This was not unusual, but he was far afield from the deals he had been trained to make. Nevertheless he had done his homework on his own and was ready to proceed.

"Gentlemen, the deal you offered was fair, perhaps more than fair. It simply does not meet our needs, nor is it in the best long-term interest of the La Crosse Corporation.

"You have offered a hundred million in cash for 49% of La Crosse. Certainly you know that is significantly more than we have invested; therefore, it is generous. However, the Advantage Corporation wholly owns La Crosse and we don't need cash. We need long-term success."

Looking around at his crew, especially the people directly involved in La Crosse who undoubtedly had high expectations of strong bonuses, and with a reassuring voice he said, "I know this deal would have earned those responsible for its success a handsome bonus. I want to assure them that they will receive what may be a much larger payday if we can put this to bed in a proper format."

Directing his attention back to Quinn he continued.

"Your company has devoted a disproportionately large percentage of its assets into developing your Alzheimer's med. In fact, it would be enormously destructive to your company if any competitor held the control of what Barry Blake and his team have developed. Interestingly, Virta is in the same boat. We could easily start a bidding war, but frankly I know what I want and I know your company will give it to me.

"I want stock in CPC. Lots of stock in CPC." Looking toward Blake and Saunders, Leonard added, "Some of that stock will go to the team that created this along with some additional cash from Advantage Corporation."

The smiles from that sector were very rewarding to Leonard.

"Further, we will trade not 49%, but 100% of the La Crosse stock to you, but again, we want lots and lots of CPC stock, because we believe in the value and efficacy of our two teams.

"Then, we want to bring your management expertise into play and have you provide a slate of at least three prospective CEOs, because we have no experience in that area and we want to win – win big.

"Finally, we want three seats on your board. You have 16 seats currently. This would be an expansion to 19 board members. These seats are to remain for a period of 20 years minimum. Initially they will be held by Mr. Barry Blake, the lead inventor, Mr. Bruce Saunders, the acting CFO now and who will become the official CFO of La Crosse, and myself. If I am unavailable I will be allowed a proxy. Future appointments will be made by this office with CPC board's approval, which will not be unreasonably withheld.

"Mr. Quinn, these are the rules by which we will play. You and CPC have until 10 AM on Monday to make us happy. Please, don't waste time or energy in posturing. That to me will be contrary to the spirit of cooperation that I am looking for. Give us your best possible deal on the stock and meet our needs on the other issues and we can get to work. Fool with it and we can say goodbye."

Leonard took the unusual step of shaking every hand of the men and women in the room. No one left their position until he had cleared the room.

Leonard did not know what CPC would do with his offer. He did not specify how much stock would be required. He put the onus on CPC, without any wiggle room for bargaining. He could only wait.

The funny thing was, he was happy. He had gone well beyond the rules laid down by Fred LaFrance and Leonard appeared to be winning. He did not know if his father would approve or not. He hoped he would, but he didn't care.

A quick survey of his situation told him three important things.

1. Running to the office every morning for the last month gave him energy and clarity of thought he had never had before (Mental note: Thank Theo again for the inspiration and the shoes).

2. Between the exercise, better diet and new purposeful force in business, his Testosterone and libido had risen to ridiculous heights. Right now for example he had to fight hard to take his mind off of sex.

3. The Advantage Corporation was all but self-running and he was ready to start a life.

Monday would be the day we will know about the CPC deal, thought Leonard. But that was not to be the case.

At 4:17 PM that same day Shawn asked if Mr. L would like to speak to Marvin Quinn.

"Hello Marvin, did you have a question?" asked Leonard as it was far too soon for Marvin to have an answer.

"No, Mr. LaFrance, I have an offer."

"Proceed!"

"You correctly assumed this was a big and important merger for CPC. I did not mention it, but our board was standing by waiting for my report.

"Mr. LaFrance, I am very good at what I do, but again, you were right – I was posturing – it is usually pretty effective.

"Further," continued Marvin, "you were blatantly open and honest. I was not prepared for that. We thought there would be the usual posturing – the usual give and take. You would have none of that."

"In my report to the board I told them what I found. I found a well prepared and utterly honest man who was a visionary and thought in the big picture and the long term.

"Our CEO, Brian McCroskey, is that kind of man as well, and he recognized a kindred spirit in you. His comment was, 'That is the kind of man we want to partner with.'

"We will meet the board and CEO requirements as you laid out. As regards to the stock, even I am surprised at what the board has come up with. We will have to dilute the stock, but when all is said and done you will have 10% of the total stock in CPC.

"Tell me, Mr. LaFrance – did we pass your test?"

"Mr. Quinn, you and CPC have exceeded expectations. If we both maintain this level of respect and cooperation there will be a better world for many people. I believe you know Leon Harding – he will be our point man. When would you like to meet with him?"

"How about if we let the dust settle until Wednesday afternoon at 1 PM Mr. LaFrance?"

"Done." And the call was over.

Leonard had Shawn call the department heads, and the La Crosse people, who were still in the building, together and he shared the good news. Mr. Blake, the creative soul who was the inspirational and intellectual leader of La Crosse, but a mediocre businessman, was especially moved by the 4% of the CPC stock that was to be distributed among the founders of La Crosse, to include now, Bruce Saunders. Mr. L's only stipulation was that he approve the distribution of the stock prior to taking effect.

Chapter 13

IT WAS CLEAR TO LEONARD THAT TOMORROW'S meeting with Theo was going to be a long and important one.

The problem with that was, tomorrow was also his lunchtime therapy session with Dr. Lilly.

Leonard placed a call to Lilly Carroll's cell phone. He had been upgraded and now had her personal number.

"Hello Leonard," answered a voice that acknowledged she was glad to get a call from this person.

"Hello yourself and see how you like it." *That was a silly thing to say*, thought Leonard, although he was becoming fonder of being silly.

"Did you call to remind me of our lunch tomorrow," asked Lilly?

"No, sadly I need to reschedule; any chance of a Saturday lunch?"

"Hmmm, no. I'm afraid not. I guess we will have to skip a week," said Lilly.

"Oh that is too bad. I have so much to tell you. Wait! How about meeting tonight for dinner?"

"I don't know about that, Leonard. That seems a bit out of bounds."

"No way. You know my favorite place not far from your office and we can meet there at five – be out of there by 6:30 or 7 and still consider that part of the workday. Come on – it's not that big a deal."

"Leonard, you have changed. Okay, but make it 5:15. And I'm guessing it is the same place where we usually have lunch?"

"Right you are, Doctor. I guess I need to start expanding my culinary experience, but we'll leave that for another day. See you there, Doc."

"See you there, you lunatic, – oops – psychiatrists can't say that. Bye."

ONCE again Shawn Davis and the Maitre D' were able to accommodate Leonard and Dr. Carroll. The two were obviously glad to see each other. Over the past few weeks, since Leonard's complete breakdown, Lilly had watched a new Leonard emerge. It was happing so rapidly she could only compare it to a butterfly emerging from its cocoon.

Sharon had told her mother of the conversation she'd had with Leonard about "Love." Being a good mother, and good doctor, Lilly was very respectful of his honest and protective answer.

In addition, the way he held off any intimacy was again protective of her daughter. She was particularly grateful for this last point, as Sharon had made it clear she was ready to proceed.

Leonard did not look the same, act the same nor even sound the same as the deranged man who pushed his way into her office just a few months ago. He seemed confident, taller, straighter, more angular and even a little tan. Lilly realized that she was beginning to find him more attractive than she ought and for several important reasons. Not the least of which were professional ethics and the fact her daughter already had a claim on him.

They discussed a series of issues, including the harmonizing effect Sharon had had on him during his meltdown and how grateful he was to both the doctor and her daughter.

Then Leonard unleashed his big news.

"Dr. Lilly, I know how important the Brian's Better Day Foundation is to you. I also understand that you are not a natural-born fundraiser; it is not in your character to strong-arm people into giving. That leaves the question of how much time can you give to the actual running of the charity if the revenue was not the deciding issue?"

Lilly laughed. Not out of any sense of the subject matter being unimportant, but amusement at her predicament. Her practice and public speaking invitations were consuming so much time there was none left for a life of any kind outside of that practice.

"Not much time at all," replied Lilly. "The fact that it is important does not give the day any more hours than God gave it. I have, as you already know, turned over the major fundraiser event this year to Sharon. And thanks to your generosity it's already funded beyond expectations.

"I have spoken to friends, but no one really has the time or the passion. It's not as though there was enough money to hire someone of quality. I don't know how much longer it will be able to continue," lamented Lilly.

"I somehow thought that was the case. I have a suggestion. There are people who are passionate about doing something that is bigger than themselves. The problem is they must make a living at it.

"Even with the $100,000 per year that the foundation now has, it can't afford to pay both a CEO and do any good for the people who need assistance. As I believe Sharon has told you I have set aside the profits from a startup for charitable purposes. I have named it in honor of my mother, just as you have named your charity in honor of your departed husband.

"I anticipated that it would take 3 or 4 years for it to produce any profits whatsoever. That all changed today.

"I traded the stock in that company for stock in a much larger company. I am assigning 100% of the stock that I will retain to The Sarah Peachtree LaFrance Foundation. At least 25% of that will go to Brian's Better Tomorrow Foundation. In plain English that means, starting immediately, your trust will be receiving contributions twice a year. This next year the funding should amount to about 2 to 3 million. After that I believe it will yield a minimum of 10 million a year, probably much more.

"Let's start looking for the right person to take the burden of running it off of your shoulders. You of course will be Chairman, or Chairwoman, if you prefer. You can direct it, but you don't have to run it. Then Brian can have the memorial you have always wanted. What do you say?"

Lilly of course said nothing. She was truly speechless. Her emotions were flooded in remembrance of Brian and now mixed with a deep feeling for this man who had changed his life so much and was now changing her world as well.

Finally, Lilly said, "I don't know anyone that I would trust enough to do that job at the level it would require. It would take a selfless person who had a strong business background. I would only feel comfortable with someone either you or I have strong personal knowledge of. Someone either you or I have watched as they conducted business. Someone we can trust with a lot of money."

Leonard, after a moment, said, "I know of one. It would be a great personal sacrifice. His name is Shawn Davis. He has been my personal assistant for three years. I know him well. I could not ask for a better one, but I have been thinking lately that he deserves a more rewarding role in life."

Lilly countered with, "I don't want to sound doubtful, Leonard, but a personal assistant to be the CEO of a trust with millions of dollars passing through ... I, ... I don't know."

Leonard smiled, "Don't let the personal assistant title put you off. The man has an MBA from USC where his focus was the non-profit sector. I don't mind telling you that focus put me off at first, but that bent may be why he is who he is. As far as handling large amounts of money, he has handled some pretty significant amounts of money for me and he is absolutely trustworthy and unbelievably loyal. The only question in my mind is would he be willing to take a cut in pay?"

Then Leonard offered, "He is waiting for me now. Why don't we have him join us for dessert and let you get a sense of him."

Shawn did join them for the next two hours. Lilly and Shawn bonded immediately. Shawn rose like a mighty trout after a May fly, took the bait and laid out scenario after scenario of how he would build what Sharon wanted. He was quick to say he would not hesitate to call on Lilly or Mr. L if there was anything he was unsure about. A deal was struck. Shawn Davis would start a week from Monday, making half as much money, but a whole new world would open.

From assistant to CEO

SHAWN Davis felt like he had died and gone to heaven.

He liked working for Mr. L, most of the time. His bosses' strange behavior lately was a little unnerving, but it was the duty of approaching and corrupting young women that really had started to sour him on the role he played. It was only four times in 3 years; yet, it was to the point where he did not think he could ever do it again. The timing for this change was perfect.

As he was thinking of women it became painfully clear that he had never had a serious relationship. *Man, what kind of guy is almost 27 and has never had a serious relationship?* Even in high school, college and post-graduate days he had 'friends' but never a serious girlfriend.

Working for Mr. L certainly had benefits, but he was always on call. His weekday schedule called for him rising at 4 AM in order to meet with the security team and pick up Mr. L at 5:15. This left no time for dating other than an occasional weekend break and even that was subject to interruption.

He liked the money, and for three years he had made unthinkable money for a guy right out of college. Plus he'd received some nice, fat bonuses lately and there was no time to spend any of it, so the cut in pay was of no immediate concern to him.

Opportunity and challenge had been in the back of his mind for many months and lately they had been pushing to the fore.

Shawn loved serving others. It surprised him how quickly he became animated and creative once the Brian's Better Tomorrow possibility opened. He could see his rush of energy at the restaurant overwhelmed Dr. Carroll and even Mr. L.

Good!

The greatest challenge would be to keep his mind on his current position as he unwound his work for Mr. L. The man certainly deserved that.

The only troubling part was, what was Mr. L going to do for an assistant? Calvin Frost had shepherded Shawn for six full months before he'd taken over. *Mr. L always has a plan*, thought Shawn Davis. I have to get through this week with flying colors, do my job as well or better than I've ever done it, and then, move on.

Shawn Davis – the new CEO of Brian's Better Tomorrow Foundation. His smile was sweet when he considered tomorrow would be better – for him as well.

The Buyer

SHARON hung up the phone in a partial delirium. Her mother had just told her of the dinner with Leonard and his generosity. *Leonard,* squealed Sharon inwardly, *is the most beautiful man on the planet. A true Prince Charming.* In her mind she ticked off the ways in which he had proven himself to be a one of a kind, and gentle man.

Friday was a light day for her as she had only one class at 8 AM and a lab at 1:15. Sharon quickly decided that blowing off the lab and heading south right after her morning class was a no-brainier. *Let's surprise Leonard by coming in tonight,* Sharon thought. That will give me one more day to encourage this man. She was determined to override Leonard's sexual timidity and give him her virginity.

She did not have time to wash her hair this morning; it took so long to dry. Sharon was burnt out on trying to keep her long hair coiffed. Many of her friends at school had opted for rather short hair and they loved the low maintenance. They also seemed to think that guys thought it was sexier.

Funny, thought Sharon, it was never important for her to lean toward promoting her sexiness in the past. Since her earliest teenage years she was attractive enough to get more attention from boys than she wanted. Leonard however was not a boy, he was boyish, but he was a man. The man she wanted.

Driving fast and using a cell phone was dangerous at best, and her mother had asked her not to do it. Today, however, there was an air of invulnerability. Besides, Sharon wanted to try out her new hands-free, voice-activated cell phone. So she called her favorite hairdresser, who just happened to be in her contact list.

"Call Lindsey," she said, and, as if by technological magic, a voice announced, "This is Lindsey."

"Hi, girl. This is Sharon Carroll. Could you fit me in for a wash and cut this afternoon after 3?"

"You must be psychic!" squealed Lindsey. "I just hung up from a call that cancelled her 3:30. Come on in girl."

Chapter 14

THE TROUBLE WITH DOING GOOD

HE NEIGHBORHOOD WAS NOW BEAUTIFUL TO behold. The landscape subcontractors had performed near miracles, and they were just pulling out for the last time.

Theo had an assistant, who had been through hell and was still finding his way out of it. His name was Maximilian, but no one dared call him that. It was Max – plain and simple – or, if you'd rather, you could call him Maximilian and he would beat the crap out of you.

Theo had hired Max when there were no other jobs being offered to him. In Theo's employ he made good money, but that was not the reason for his protective nature toward his boss. No, it was not the money Theo paid him; it was the respect. Max had never known a person that could look at him and see the man Max wanted to be.

The two had never had a fist fight, but both were tough and had no objections to backing up verbiage with brute force. Both were passionate and a bit hot-headed. They both instinctively knew a fight between them would not end well for either man. Both men also recognized that Max could now run his own company. Theo had taught him well, but for reasons known only to Max, he was willing to humble himself and remain an employee when he could have almost surely been a success on his own.

Max approached Theo. He had a paint brush and paint can in hand.

"That's the last of the touch up. What can I do now?"

Good question, but there was an answer and Theo gave it after he went through a short checklist.

"Max, this whole place looks great. Every house is sold, and some folks will start moving in tomorrow after the final inspection. We're just waiting for the city inspector. He's late as usual."

"I tell you what let's do," said Theo. "Let's give our homeowners one last gift. Having a garden hose front and back for each house along with a note to remind these people, most of whom have never owned a home before, that frequent watering will go a long way in keeping the outside of their home, and the entire neighborhood, looking more like Beverly Hills than Compton. Would you mind accepting that challenge?"

"Gosh, gee, that's a lot to remember, but I'll do my very best, boss," responded Max.

Theo played along by shaking his head and muttering, "You are incorrigible, Max – I like that."

Max gave a big grin and jumped into his pick-up just as the city building inspector and his assistant, who looked more like a thug, and probably was, pulled up.

Theo followed the city building inspector as he made his final rounds. The inspector did not say anything, but he made a lot of notes. *Odd*, thought Theo. In Theo's mind there was nothing to write about. Quietly, Theo activated the record app on his cell phone.

"I am afraid we have some real problems here, Mr. Webb."

"Such as?"

"Well sir, there is just no way I can approve these structures as they stand. I see foundation problems, some dangerous electrical work and the drainage on the lots will take a great deal of reworking."

Theo knew better. He had more experience building than this guy had inspecting. It was a blatant attempt to make Theo offer him a bribe.

So, in a way Theo did.

"Isn't there some way we can make this all go away?" Theo asked.

Coyly, yet with clear intent, the inspector asked, "What did you have in mind?"

"I was going to offer to kick the crap out of your ass for trying to get me to bribe you." Reaching into his shirt pocket Theo retrieved his smart phone. The inspector could see the record light was on.

"I captured this all on this recorder and even if you tear up that crap you were planning to blackmail me with I am making copies of this recording and turning them over to several authorities with whom I have long-standing and respectful relations."

Theo clearly saw the scam, but he did not see the inspector's assistant swing the sap that caught him perfectly on the temple and rendered him an unconscious and crumpled man.

The Inspector bent down, took Theo's cell phone and mockingly said, "I tol you and tol you to always wear your hard hat on the construction site – asshole. By the way, your buildings did pass inspection, but you don't want me to see you around city hall with any accusations."

Turning to his assistant he handed him the bogus inspection report and said, "Shred these when we get back to the office. Don't forget. If we are found out – you are that guy what hit him."

The perfect plan

THEO had a shiner that was ghastly. The thug had done his work well. Theo also had a rather persistent headache. Yet, resolutely, he sat before Leonard LaFrance at 10 AM as scheduled.

Leonard did not take much time in dealing with Theo's event except to say he had chosen to work in a dangerous area and should consider personal security.

Theo was not amused. His question was, now that the first inner city rehab was over, was Leonard up for another one?

Leonard had other plans and got down to the business he cared about.

"Theo, I consider you my friend. I don't know if that should be considered a compliment since you are probably my only friend. I also respect your business acumen and that is what I want to talk to you about."

"Sure, Leonard." Half in jest he added. "I always like talking about me."

Both men smiled.

"You know a little about my background, Theo; I have hired investigators to find out all about yours. I had no idea you were such a feisty guy. If we work out the deal I want to talk to you about, you will no longer be able to be remotely connected to any violence no matter what the provocation. I cannot make that point too strongly."

Theo sobered.

"The truth is, Theo, I know a lot about everything business and nothing about life. I have given myself a two-year assignment that I hope will help me catch up. It will take me away from this office and most of my duties. I want you to take my place and become president of the Advantage Corporation. Interested?"

"Hold on Jackson!" said Theo. "What are you talking about. I make good money. I do good work. I understand construction, people, accounting, cost control, real estate, but you are talking about running a half a billion dollar business. Why me?"

"Well it is actually more like three quarters of a billion dollar business, but the main reason I want you is because, as you just admitted, you understand construction, people, accounting, cost control and real estate. Add a few zeroes and that is what we do here. And the real reason I want you is that I have faith in you in a way that no other man enjoys. You will not be alone. Not only will I carry a cell phone so you can reach me if there is a truly important matter that you would like my input on, but the Advantage Corporation has the best people you can imagine. Over the next week I will walk you through it, starting with meeting all the department heads in about 15 minutes. I repeat. Are you interested?"

Theo was not overcome, but pensive. There was something in the way that Leonard had faith that gave Theo reason to believe he could actually do this.

"Okay, of course I am interested, but there are some conditions."

Leonard agreed in principle, "We will both have conditions and I believe we can rely on the other to earnestly comply."

Theo plunged right in, "I want to see good housing for those who will step up and take responsibility. That is how I have been making a living, but it is more than that to me. I have an assistant who is almost as skilled at that as I am. I would like him to continue to run my company in my absence just as I am running yours in your absence. Don't discount his value just because he is now an assistant."

Leonard shook his head knowingly and said simply, "We are on the same page. I will put 5% of our liquid assets in a pool that you, in agreement with the department heads, will allocate on these projects. Anything else?"

After a brief pause, Theo said. "I will want to know your precise expectation of what you want to find when you return."

"Theo, you tell me you are a solid Christian, a subject I might want to pursue at some point, but as I understand it, Christians put great importance on stewardship. Be a good steward of what I entrust you with. I believe I heard somewhere that 'to those much has been given, much will be expected'. I can't be anymore precise than that. Anything else?"

"We haven't discussed money."

"How much would you want?"

"How much will you offer?"

"I will offer you one million per year with substantial bonuses that will be at my discretion and 40% of what net profits are realized in your rehab company. You will also inherit my limo, and as my father would have said, a 'Cracker Jack' security team at no cost to you."

"I'll accept!" said Theo with a huge smile.

Leonard stood, walked around his desk, shook Theo's hand and said, "Wear that smile in the board room. It will help cover up that shiner. Our people are in for a shock and anything we can do to assure them will be to your advantage."

After re-introducing Theo, whom they had already met on earlier occasions, Leonard told them of his decision. In a very real way the team had been prepared for this by virtue of the absolute change in their employer over the past few months.

Theo was already well liked and had the respect of some of the leading department heads. Three of them stood and spoke positive things about Theo. They testified as to what they had already witnessed and said they were looking forward to working with him.

Leaving the new president to meet with the staff Leonard returned to his office. Here he told Shawn about the changes and asked if he could find a way to expedite a passport for Leonard.

In turn Shawn informed him that John Thompkins was waiting to see him.

The private detective was no more jovial than he had been on the other two occasions. He handed Leonard a rather thick file and informed him he was able to find some of his mother's family in Lafayette, Louisiana.

Thompkins also said that, while not withdrawing from the case, the bulk of his research had been accomplished and he would no longer be on the clock, but would be available if needed. Leonard was grateful and told John Thompkins so.

After the detective left, Leonard placed a phone call to Calvin Frost and asked for a meeting. He offered the choice of where and when to meet to Calvin. Calvin said he would be happy to come to Leonard's office and he could be there in 30 minutes.

"If that works for you it's great for me," answered Leonard.

Picking up and opening the file given to him by the private investigator led Leonard to discover details about his mother and her family that he had been completely unaware of.

"Mr. L," were the words from Shawn Davis that pulled him out of reverie.

"Yes, Shawn?"

"The answer to your last question is two business days to get a new passport. We will need a certified birth certificate and I see we have one on file. Should I proceed?"

"By all means, and by the way, not bad efficiency for a fledgling CEO."

Leonard loved it when he was funny. More and more often did he find the things he said to be funny. His poor father never said anything funny. Until recently, neither did Leonard. Hmmm?

Bill Bishop had been his father's, and subsequently, his barber, since his earliest recollections. He always came to the office once a week, cut their hair in the same style and left without ever saying a word. He had retired except for this singular client. Once a month Bill would receive a check in the mail for $100.00 for each haircut rendered. Before Bill Bishop left, Leonard took out his new checkbook and wrote a check, signed and folded it and came around to where Bill was standing.

"Bill, began Leonard, "you have been of great service to us over the years and I appreciate the integrity with which you have done it. I am going away for a while and don't know when I'll be back. Chances are you will be fully retired when I return. I apologize for the short notice, but here is a bit of severance. Thank you again and enjoy your retirement."

Bill the barber did not look at the check until he was in his car. He was not upset and didn't mind not dragging himself to any more haircuts. His arthritic fingers had been complaining for over a year. Yet his savings had not grown as much as he had hoped and the $400 to $500 a month Mr. L paid was a big help. As he began to unfold the check he was afraid to see the amount. They had never tipped him, but at a $100.00 per, it was not really expected. It took him a minute to grasp what he was looking at and then he did the math.

Mr. L had just paid him enough for two years of haircuts. Bill did not understand, but there was quiet gratitude in his heart as he headed back to the Valley.

AFTER a quick call to Sam Levine to move 5 million dollars into his personal account, and, to make note of it for tax reasons, he returned to his mother's file only to be interrupted a few minutes later by the arrival of Calvin Frost.

"Hello, Calvin. I want to thank you for your blunt honesty at our last meeting. There was much truth in what you said. Painful, to be sure, but truth nonetheless. I wanted you to read the letter you brought me."

With those words Leonard handed Calvin his father's letter and sat back silently allowing Calvin to absorb every nuance of the letter.

Calvin took his time.

Then he stood and said, "Thank you, Mr. L. I don't know if anyone can grasp the great leap this gives me toward a peaceful mind about the way I invested my life. This means a lot to me."

"Me too," was Leonard's simple answer.

Without invitation, Calvin retook his seat. The two men sat quietly for a few moments. Then Leonard asked, "How do you like retirement, Calvin."

"I am no good at it."

"Why is that?"

"Well, I have never married, so I'm lonely. I have never had any hobbies or sports that attract me. I don't like to travel, so I am bored to death."

"Want a job?"

"What kind of job?" asked Calvin displaying great interest.

"The kind we both know you are good at."

"Do you mean like an assistant to the CEO? Return as your assistant?"

"Almost, but not quite." Then Leonard explained that he was about to go on a two-year hiatus to see if he could catch up on matters of the world that he was totally unfamiliar with.

"That said," continued Leonard, "I have brought on a young man, a very moral young man from all I can find, to take my place. He will need you. Interested?"

Calvin Frost was at temporary loss of words. Then he decided there was no downside. So he said, "I would like to meet the man."

Without hesitation Leonard called Shawn. "Would you please get Theo. He's in the board room I believe, and ask him if he would mind coming directly to my office."

"Certainly, Mr. L."

While they waited for Theo, Leonard assured Calvin that the Advantage Corporation team that he knew was still intact. When Calvin inquired as to what Shawn Davis's role would be, Leonard told him of the move that would take place next Monday.

Calvin found that news to be of his liking. Nothing against young Shawn, it would simply be easier to have no a hint of conflict. In fact he was a bit envious that Shawn had found a way out and up at such an early age. Yet, that was not for Calvin. At his age, this job was perfect.

Theo was ushered in by Shawn.

"Theo, I have a great gift for you. How would you like to have an encyclopedic understanding of the way my father, and then I, conduct the business of the Advantage Corporation right at your fingers every day?"

"Awesome," was Theo's quick reply.

"In that case, Theo Webb, meet your assistant, Calvin Frost, that is if he likes you."

Calvin spoke, "I already know I will like him."

"That's funny," remarked Theo, "I already know I like you."

With that last piece of the complex puzzle in place, Leonard ushered Theo to the chair behind his desk – the chair that Theo would occupy full time very soon, and said, "You two get acquainted for a while. Then, Mr. Webb, if I might suggest, take Calvin around and re-introduce him to his many old friends and tell them of your relationship. That will be a significant brick in building the utmost trust in the Advantage Corporation's future under your leadership."

Theo took the seat offered, then rose and said, "Thank you, Mr. L. I understand the importance of well-placed bricks in any building."

All three men smiled and Leonard left the room, collected Shawn, who alerted the security team, and they headed home. It was a quarter to 6 on a Friday and this had been a most productive day.

"Let's go home."

Up until now this day had been just how Leonard had planned it.. However, it has been said, "If you want to make God laugh, make a plan."

Chapter 15

BEFORE LEONARD EVEN FULLY SETTLED IN the limo, he was becoming painfully aware of what a powerful force his libido was becoming. He did not want to be so easily tipped by his urges when Sharon was around. She would be down tomorrow evening. They had agreed to meet.

I have to protect her from me, Leonard reasoned.

Riding in the back seat of a chauffeur-driven, top-of-the-line Mercedes limo, and knowing you can buy almost anything you want can be intoxicating, especially when one's hormones are revved up. Looking out at the pedestrians on Rodeo Drive he saw many comely girls. Almost any one of them would do to take the edge off.

There was one in particular, a girl with short, blond hair and a wonderful, feminine, movement in her walk that caught his eye. She was not looking in their direction so Leonard could not get a clear view of her face, but he decided that the face, for his needs right now, was unimportant.

Leonard turned to Shawn and said, "Do you see the girl right there, the one in plain jeans and a gray sweater?"

Shawn Davis's stomach turned. *No, no, no, he did not want to do this again. Not ever.* This was his last day of being vulnerable to such a request and he did not want to do it. Neither did he want to fail Mr. L, the man who was making so much possible for him.

Shawn swallowed his conscience. When the car stopped he made himself walk briskly back to the short-haired blonde with the gray sweater. She was, as it turned out, so beautiful. This made his stomach turn over even more. It was not that pretty people are worth more than un-pretty people, yet it all became more sickening.

Shawn had no way of knowing this lovely creature happened to be Sharon Carroll.

"Excuse me miss."

Sharon looked at the young man. Perfectly dressed, very good look-ing, but her mind was on Leonard and she did not feel like dealing with a pick-up attempt at this juncture. So, she ignored him and kept walking.

Shawn was ready to accept the rebuke, but then reconsidered. He caught up with her, tapped her on the shoulder and said, "This is not what you think."

"Oh really," said an exasperated Sharon, "then what is it?"

Shawn swallowed hard. As he looked at this absolutely beautiful girl he wished to God this was not his lot today. Again, however, he proceeded to fulfill his last dirty deed.

"I represent a man of great means who finds you attractive. The arrangement is simple. You ask no questions, pleasure him and he will give you $10,000.00 in cash for the service. Will you come with me?"

Incredulous, yet intrigued, Sharon did not walk away. She was not interested in the money, but she was interested in knowing who this pervert was. What kind of man could believe he could turn a normal woman, minding her own business, just walking down the street, into an instant prostitute?

Shawn was very disappointed when the lovely young lady asked, "Can I meet him?"

Sadly, Shawn imagined how he would feel if this female were his daughter, his girlfriend, fiancée or even an acquaintance, and she was approached like this. He would want to do bodily harm to the one ask-ing. He answered with a sigh. "Yes, he will be pulling up in a moment."

Sharon almost felt sorry for this young man as he was obviously not enthusiastic at all about his job, but at the same time he took the job. Creep!

As was the custom in these situations, Leonard was on the far side of the bench seat. The plan was to invite the lady in, then Shawn would take the seat by the door; then off they would go.

This time would be different.

Shawn opened the door, but the girl did not get in. Instead she bent over to get a good look at the would be "Buyer."

She was shocked and crushed to see the face of the man she thought she knew and loved.

Leonard's jaw dropped. He said nothing.

Sharon regained her composure. She quickly figured out that the new short haircut had disguised her enough that someone going by in a car would not recognize her. This realization empowered her and she said in even tones.

"I just wanted to see what kind of jerk would think they could buy a woman that easily. I am so sad to see that you are that jerk." Sharon paused and in a prayerful way she uttered, "Thank you God for letting me know so early."

Sharon stood up straight, looked at Shawn with open disgust, moved him out of her way with the slightest effort, and exited their presence as quickly as she could. She barely made it to her car before she collapsed into heaving sobs.

Shawn stood there, door still open, and then, without a word, he closed the door and walked away.

The security team drove Leonard to his house. As Leonard left the car he had one piece of unfinished business. Turning to Simpson and Shook, his bodyguards, he said, "I will have no more use for your services for the present. I may call on one or both of you in the future, but you are to report to my old office on Monday. Your new charge is the safety of one Theo Webb. Thank you both, and goodbye."

With the heaviest heart he had ever known Leonard trudged up the porch steps to his empty home.

Oh Mother, sob

THERE was no hiding her crushed nature. Her mother immediately saw that Sharon was shattered.

Even her degree in the field, nor her years of experience could make a dent in the emotional distress Lilly's daughter was feeling at this moment. Only time could do that.

Lilly waited.

"Oh, mother, how could I have been so stupid?" were Sharon's first words when the heaving caused by sobbing began to lighten.

"About what, dear?"

"About thinking I knew a man I did not know at all," answered Sharon.

As the girl unfolded her experience the mother could see quite quickly that what she had feared had come to pass.

Rather than say, "I tried to tell you", or "I told you so" as many a parent might, she just held her until Sharon was cried out. At which time the mother fixed her a light supper, a glass of white wine, and, when Sharon was finished, Lilly asked, "Would you like to go and lay down for a while?"

"Yes, I think that would be best, mother."

After going in to say good night, Lilly began to look in her own mind for any signs that her new patient was a major pervert. Lilly was simultaneously angry for the hurt caused her daughter and more than a little sad for Leonard.

Of, course, she thought. *Leonard's behavior makes some kind of sense for a man who was so sheltered from normal civil behavior and molded by a father like Fred LaFrance.*

She hoped that Leonard would not even attempt to arrange another appointment; She was not at all sure she could ever treat him again. "God Knows he needs it – just not from me."

One of the shortest jobs on record

SHAWN Davis walked home. It was a very long way and he went right past his house and continued walking all the way to the ocean. He was more than disgusted with himself and Mr. L.

His heart hurt for that young girl who was brutally insulted and then had the horror of realizing someone she knew, and obviously cared for, was a man who would solicit young girls who had set out that day with no intention to prostitute herself. This was not the way Shawn had wanted to meet Sharon Carroll.

He also realized that he had been replaced by Calvin Frost and no longer had a job at Advantage Corporation. That was good, but although he had not known Sharon by sight, he did know that she was Dr. Carroll's daughter. Dr. Carroll would not be pleased with his participation in the perverse behavior and would certainly not be prone to keep him on in his new role. Not at all good.

He would contact Dr. Carroll in person. She would no doubt be aghast at his temerity and throw him out on his ear. It was, however, such a vile act that he had committed that she deserved the right to do just that.

Sadly, thought Shawn, *I deserve whatever it is she wants to throw at me.* Shawn considered his role once more and found a hedge to vomit behind.

An unwelcome caller

Trisha had been at the office for only about five minutes. She was just getting ready for the day when she looked out of her security booth and found a very attractive, yet extremely nervous, young man standing before her.

"Hello. How can I help you?"

"I would like, if possible, to see, Dr. Carroll."

My, thought Trisha, *He is nervous.* She automatically looked at the appointment book, but saw no new name and so made inquiry.

"Do you have an appointment?" she asked politely, but briskly.

"Ah …no. My name is Shawn Davis. Will you ask the doctor if she will see me?"

Trisha considered his request, then answered by saying, "Please take a seat and I will ask the doctor."

Shawn sat very near the door. He may not be able to go through with this after all.

When the doctor answered Trisha's call she had to think for a moment as to whom Shawn Davis was. A name familiar …, but – "Oh, no," said Lilly. She assumed that Leonard had sent him over to test the waters.

"No, tell him that I am not here or busy or whatever." Then she quickly reconsidered. "No – wait, ask him what it is about?"

"Okay," said Trisha.

Then speaking loudly enough for Shawn, who had taken the seat nearest the doorway, and, therefore, the furthest from her post, to hear her.

"Mr. Davis, may I ask what this is about?"

Shawn was not expecting this question for some reason. He thought he might be rejected out of hand, but did not even contemplate as to what he might say if he was asked this.

So he just said the obvious. "Tell her it is about my position with the Brian's Better Tomorrow Foundation."

Trisha repeated Shawn's answer to the doctor.

"Very well, send him in."

A very surprised Shawn Davis rose from his chair and went in to see the doctor.

After an awkward exchange of courtesy the doctor said, "Mr. Davis, I do not know if Mr. LaFrance is still planning on funding the foundation. Your salary is, of course, completely dependent on that funding."

"I can find that information for you, Dr. Carroll, but there is something else I must tell you before you can decide whether or not you want me in that role."

Here comes the plea for Leonard, thought Lilly.

"Just what might that be?" she asked.

It was clear that Dr. Carroll was not aware of Shawn's involvement, but by her tone and demeanor Shawn knew she was aware of the perverse event itself. So he said,

"I am sure that you have heard from your daughter that Mr. L, not knowing it was your daughter, tried to proposition her off the street last night."

"I am very aware of that Mr. Davis. Why do you bring it up?"

"Doctor, Mr. L, and evidently his father before him, used this method to satisfy their needs when needs arose. So this is not his first time. It has happened four times in the three years that I have worked for him. What you do not know is that both Mr. L and his father used their assistants to procure the girls."

Shawn let this sink in through the doctor's obviously heightened defense mechanism. Then he completed the picture.

"I must tell you that I am the one who actually accosted your daughter. I have never been as ashamed as I am now or as I was yesterday when we insulted your daughter. I can't imagine that you would still want me to administer the Brian's Better Tomorrow Foundation after this, but I would still be honored to have the post and I would live my life trying to bring honor to your late husband's memory and the work you intend to accomplish. I do not expect an answer, but here is my contact information for whatever purpose that may suit you."

Shawn paused, then added, "I am profoundly sorry, Doctor Carroll, and, if I could, I would say the same thing to your daughter. Please try to forgive me."

Laying the card on her desk he left with no other verbal communication.

Chapter 16

A LETTER FROM LAFAYETTE

10 days later

THE LETTER FROM LEONARD BEGAN,

Dear Dr. Lilly,

By now you have heard the terrible news and are as completely disgusted with me as I am with myself. I have no excuse. It is a cowardly act. It shows no respect for anyone. Not myself, not my staff, not for women in general and certainly not for the two people I care the most about, you and Sharon.

I am off. I have left the company in the hands of others. I am traveling. I do not know to where or for how long. As you will understand more than any other soul, I must decide who I am. I must define what I know.

The promises I made for funding Brian's Better Tomorrow Foundation are good. The foundation will receive the first monies within the week. There are no strings attached. You may speak to Theo Webb, Leon Harding or Samuel Levine. They are all aware of our arrangement and will assist you in every way possible.

You may want to replace Shawn Davis, but I would offer that would be a mistake. He is talented, honest, loyal and better suited for non-profit work more than anyone I know. He is known and respected by all of the senior executives at Advantage Corp and can navigate the waters there like no one else you can find. It may also be of value to know he despised the role I forced on him.

I know you must feel that I can no longer be your patient. I am okay with that. I do, however, have a plea. Thanks to you I am doing better, thinking clearer and much less depressed. That said, I would ask that you take the occasional phone call from me. I have found no one that I can converse with that brings me hope as you do.

If you cannot, so be it. If you will, I cannot tell you how grateful I would be.

You will also find in this envelope a farewell letter written to me by my father just before his death. It was delivered to me not long ago. It may give you clarity. You may not care and I could only say thank you for what you have already done.

My trip is starting in Lafayette, Louisiana. This is where my mother was from. She came back to this state to end her life, but there are a few relatives that I will try to reach.

Learning about life is probably hard at any age and always carries a heavy price tag. At my age it seems almost hopeless, but I don't believe that to be absolutely true. I also sense that I am not alone - there are probably many others who do not grow up until their life is nearly spent.

The take away from my disastrous interaction with Sharon is a good one. I have always been led to believe you can buy anything you want if you have enough money. What a sad way to learn a lifelong belief is so very, very false.

With unspeakable regret,

Leonard LaFrance

Dr. Lillian Carroll read the accompanying letter as well. She saw what his father left the world believing. His father learned too late, but Leonard, may just make it.

She did not know why she felt a soft place in her heart for a man with such despicable behavior. But she did and did not have time to dwell on it as Trisha called in to say her first patient was waiting.

Changing of the guard

THEO Webb felt at home in his new chair within 10 minutes of taking his seat. He called Calvin Frost and asked him to call a meeting of all department heads and asked Calvin to be sure to attend. "Calvin, you know these waters well and I will need for you to be my navigator."

Calvin liked the sound of that. If it were true he would be more than a highly educated gopher, his job would be closer to that of a Chief of Staff. He was ready.

The department heads were all more than willing to sit with Theo, because Theo listened intently. Most of the senior people had worked for both Fred and Leonard. They were both kings. Theo was a leader.

After the group meeting he asked Calvin to set up individual meetings with each department head.

Calvin suggested that each one be invited to bring any key people they thought might benefit Theo's understanding of the way Advantage Corporation functioned.

"Capitol idea!" exclaimed Theo, sounding more and more like a titan of the old school – and loving the role.

Soon the Advantage Corporation was breathing in a different rhythm. The heartbeat of the organization sped up just a little and there was new urgency to things.

Calvin immediately recognized Theo's management style as one that would change nothing, but the new blood would unleash some previously untapped energy. Any worry Calvin had about the future of the company without Fred or Leonard soon began to fade. The Advantage Corporation was moving forward and he finally had a job he could be proud of and genuinely love.

Dr. Lilly gets going

LEAVING immediately after her last appointment of the morning Lilly headed for the same bistro that Leonard had used.

It had been two weeks and many conversations with Sharon since Shawn had come in to confess his role in the sordid event.

The doctor, in her wisdom gained from her education and her practice, was able to sort out the layers of emotion and had decided to go forward with Shawn.

Leonard's letter probably had more to do with her decision than any other single thing. Although Shawn's coming to her office in person to admit his complicity demonstrated a courage that was more consistent with a man of character than that of a sleaze ball.

Her decision was made and yet she was open to drop him in a heartbeat if the man that showed up for this lunch was any less than the man who had come to her office. If he did pass this challenge, there would be one more. Lilly accepted the role of gatekeeper for her daughter, but the very last word on the subject had to be Sharon's.

Shawn was waiting, just inside the door. The Maitre D' led them to the private dining room even though Shawn had explained that the days of extravagant tipping were over.

Their meeting went well for both of them.

Doctor Carroll found it to be a very positive sign that Shawn had spent the first ten minutes trying to determine what affect the trauma he and Leonard had perpetrated upon her daughter had caused.

Dr. Carroll shared that Sharon was firm in that she would forever hold Leonard LaFrance in contempt. However, she was willing to move past Shawn's involvement. Sharon even considered Shawn a bit of a victim himself.

Only when he had the assurance that his involvement would not be salt in the wounds Sharon had already suffered did he move toward his own future prospects.

Shawn had not been idle. Reaching into the briefcase he brought forth nearly a ream of paper that held the fruit of his labor since the visit to her office.

It was not just voluminous, even at first glance it showed a plethora of ideas and approaches to build the Brian's Better Tomorrow Foundation, both as an organization and a brand.

Once he was satisfied that Sharon and the doctor were okay his excitement for the project took over and Lilly was quickly caught up in it. The one problem was that Sharon would be the person most involved in much of this. That was the reason for the multitude of conversations with her daughter. When all was said and done, both had to be okay with working with the man who had spearheaded the most indecent and insulting proposal.

For that reason Dr. Carroll decided the three of them needed to meet and determine if they could in fact work together.

When told this, a sudden shadow, as if a cloud had cut his face off from the sun, came over Shawn.

"Okay, but to be honest with you, Dr. Carroll, that may be the most difficult task I have ever undertaken," looking into her eyes "after what I did ..."

"Yes, Shawn, it will not be easy for any of us. Perhaps we should just let it go –" offered Lilly.

Shawn's response was immediate, "Sharon deserves to look at me and express anything she feels. I deserve anything she wishes to lay on me."

"Okay. Saturday Sharon is coming home. Do you mind meeting on a Saturday?"

"No ma'am. Name the time and the place."

Chapter 17

IMON PEACHTREE HAD HAD A HARD week. His old Lincoln welder had finally and completely bitten the dust.

The timing could not have been worse. Eight months out of work and then they give him a contract to do work on the new pipeline going right through his neck of the woods – and his damn welder goes out. He considered himself to be a grade 'C' Christian, but one could only wonder, *What kind of God would treat an honest man like this*?

His home was a very modest one, but he did have a pretty nice computer right there in the living room. He bought it for the grandkids, but they had one at their home and didn't come by grandma and grandpa's to use it very often. His wife, Sally, had no use for it and wanted it out of the living room.

Simon had asked her, "In a house this small, where ya gonna put it? The bedroom's so small you don't have room to change your mind, let alone your pants, let alone place for a damn computer."

"I don't know," said Sally. "All I know is it jest ain't right to put a computer in the livin' room."

Little by little, during the time there was no work, Simon had been teaching himself, with the help of the grand kids, how to use this computer.

That was how he'd found out that experienced welders were wanted for a pipeline they were building. The company specified they wanted local welders as while the money was good, there was no per diem.

Hell, I don't need no per diem, I just need a good payin' job.

But now Simon also needed a new Lincoln Welder.

Opening the window that Google brought him to, he saw exactly what he would love to have.

The ad said,

ONLY 60 HOURS!!!

3 YEAR WARRANTY!!!!
Used Lincoln SAE-300 Welder w/ Perkins
Diesel Engine 3000 Watts Auxiliary Power.
All Copper Windings. Great for Pipeline Welding.
Welds 50-390 Amps DC.
$13,750.00

He had the money in the bank, but there was no way Sally was gonna let him spend any of it.

She may have been contrary when it came to having a computer in the living room, but she was adamant about not touching their retirement account.

"It's not gonna happen – so don't you even think about it." That's what Sally had said.

Simon knew Sally was serious, but he also knew he could make enough in six weeks to pay for that welder. They told him it was a seven-month job, and if he did good work he'd get to work the full period.

He also knew he was 63 and starting to feel it. It would be nice to have a great welding machine like the one in the ad, but he, too, had a hard time with taking any money out of that retirement account. *Lord knows the guvmint been fooling around with the books at that Social Security office.*

The knock on the door caught Simon off guard. He wasn't expecting anyone.

The stranger standing on his porch had a familiar look, but Simon could not place it, so he just said, "Yeah."

The stranger asked, "Are you Simon Peachtree?"

"Who's askin?"

"My name is Leonard LaFrance."

Hmmm, thought Simon, that sounds a little familiar too, but like the face Simon could not quite put it into context. So he asked, "Do I know you?"

"Probably not," replied Leonard, "but I believe you knew Sarah Peachtree. In fact I believe you were cousins."

A slow smile spread across Simon's face, but it quickly faded and was replaced by a most unfriendly darkness.

"You the man that married her and took her out west?" asked Simon.

"No," said Leonard quietly. "I am her son."

"Well of course. You are too young to be that man what married her and took her out west. I didn't know your mama well. Her daddy was my uncle and he lived out west for a while and didn't come back here till her mama was real sick and ready to die.

"Your and her mother lived by themselves for a few years when Uncle Bobby first went out West. I attended the wedding when Sarah and that LaFrance fella got married, but I was only bout ten years old back then."

After a short pause Simon continued by asking, "Is that sonuvabitch of a husband she had still alive?"

"No sir," replied Leonard. "He's been gone about 8 years."

"Glad to hear it. He treated her something awful. Well, what in the world am I doing making you stand out on the porch. Come on in. Your mama was my cousin, so I guess that makes us second cousins, or somethin like that."

"Not sure exactly how that works either, but it sounds right."

"Wait right here and I'll tell Sally you're here and have her rustle up some coffee. You like chicory or plain?"

Leonard started to say plain, then realized he had never had Chicory and asked for the latter.

Simon grinned and left the room.

Leonard could not help but notice the computer sitting right there in the living room or the ad for the Lincoln Welder that was still on the screen.

124

When Simon returned he brought Sally. Like Simon she was thin, almost gaunt, but had the sweetest smile.

"I'm sorry, but I've already forgotten your first name," said Simon.

"Hi Sally. It's Leonard, Leonard LaFrance."

"Oh my word," gushed Sally. "You are Sarah Peachtree's boy. My older sister, Maybelle, and your mama were the best of friends. Sarah wrote Maybelle a lot in those days. Maybelle shared many of her letters with me. That was before we got the TV."

Then Sally's tone got much quieter, "Your mama sure was sad before the end. Well – let me go get everyone some coffee – you say you like it with chicory?"

"I don't know," said Leonard. "Don't believe I've ever had it, but I remember Mama" (he had never called his mother Mama before – but all of a sudden it seemed right) "used to drink her coffee that way."

Sally dashed back into the kitchen to prepare her brew. Leonard took the occasion to ask Simon a question.

"Are you a welder, Simon?"

"I am," replied Simon with an unmistakable air of pride. "At least I am if I can get another welding machine."

"Like the one on the screen?" asked Leonard as he pointed to the now black monitor.

Simon walked over and hit the space bar and the picture came back. They both took a close look at the screen.

Simon, with a hint of disgust said, "Not like the one on the screen, I want the one that is on the screen. But I ain't gonna get it."

"Why not?" queried Leonard.

"Look at the price and you'll know why not," answered Simon dejectedly.

"I see," said Leonard.

"I got the money in the bank, but it's for retirement and Sally won't let me touch it. And, damn it, she's right, I'm too old to be makin investments in big expensive tools."

It was quiet for a while, then Sally came in carrying a black TV tray painted with multicolored flowers and three cups of coffee with Chicory in it.

"I sure hope you like it this way. We've been drinkin' it jes like this for generations," she said.

Leonard turned his focus on Sally.

"Were you friends with my mama too?"

Sally quickly understood that Leonard was trying to get to know his mother through others who had known her.

"I'm so sorry," Sally said. "I was a lot younger than Maybelle and Sarah and jest wasn't able to go with them much. Your mama was born here and she and her mama stayed while uncle Bobby went out to California to make his fortune. She only went to school around here till about the 8th grade, then her daddy came and took the whole family out west. But my sister is still alive and would love to talk with you about her. In fact there are a lot of people here abouts that knew your mama. Many of them were kin to her and they all know a little something about her." She paused and then added, "I bet you never knew that much about your mama and would love to get to know more about her, isn't that right, Leonard?"

Leonard was choking up a bit. It was a good feeling. So was the empathy emitting from Sally, so he answered, "I sure would."

"Well," said Sally, "she was from a right nice family. Her mama, Marie, was a sweetheart to everyone."

"An her daddy was one smart cookie. My daddy use to brag on his big brother all the time, at least until Marie got so sick. Then it seemed he forgot how to think," offered Simon.

"After the funeral Uncle Bobby just sat in that house he'd rented for her to die in," continued Sally. "He didn't work, he didn't go out, he didn't even watch TV. He just sat in that chair."

Again Simon chimed in. "He didn't even cook. Hell he didn't even hardly eat. Sally took him supper every night, but he rarely ate any of it."

Leonard looked at Sally and in near disbelief asked, "Did you really make him supper and take it over every night?"

"Well, ya know, it seemed liked it twas the least I could do. You never saw a sadder man. He loved Marie so much. Then one evening I took him over the supper; it was pot roast, but he didn't answer the door. It wasn't locked. It never was. There he sat in that chair. His head was on his chest. He coulda been jes nappin, but I knew he had gone to be with Marie."

There was a strong silence while the three of them gathered themselves. Sally broke the silence. "Well if you'll be here Friday night
I will put together a nice social. It is about time we all got together
anyhow. Course it'll be a little crowded in here. Maybe we can get one
of the kinfolk with a bigger house to hold it."

"Do you find your house to be too small?" asked Leonard.

Simon stiffened a bit, but Sally answered. "This house is just fine.
We raised three kids here, two boys and a girl. It just seems that houses
are bigger these days. We got an acre and a half and used to think about
adding on one of them family rooms – you know they're kind of big
and open and hold a ton of people.

"The problem has been my sinkin' spells. Never had a doctor smart
enough to tell me what causes them, but they seem to hit around sun-
down and Simon likes to be home by then to watch over me. There is
not a lot of work close by for Simon so we just never got around to
building it. We sure don't want to touch our retirement money, do we
Simon?"

With a touch of sadness, Simon agreed. "No Hon, we sure don't."

"Well how about you let us throw you a party come Friday night
so's you could meet some of your kin and folks that knew your mama?"

Leonard was very moved. "Yes, I will certainly stay till then. Thank
you for doing this for me. It is more important than you know. May I do
something for you in return?"

"Oh, pshaw, Leonard, we don't need nothin'."

"Well let me suggest this. There are two things I can do for you. And
it would require less effort on my part than you will expend making
this party happen on Friday. And by the way, let me cover whatever
expenses that arise out of this party if I may."

Leonard took a breath and continued. "Simon, are you a pretty good
welder?"

Sally answered for Simon, "He is the best around here. He is a Master Welder and everyone admits there is no one like him."

Simon blushed beneath his sun-browned skin and put his head very
low.

"Simon," said Leonard, "I admire a man who can work with his hands. I think we need to invest in people with know-how, so they can do what they do, and teach others. My father was a pretty sad character in many ways, but he did teach me most everything I know. Maybe you can teach a few people, maybe even your sons, about what you know. You can't do that without a good welding machine and I would like to invest in Simon Peachtree, Master Welder.

"Here is the deal, take it or leave it. I will invest $50,000.00 in your company providing you buy that Lincoln welder we were looking at and hire an apprentice. If the pipeline people will pay his salary, good, if not, you pay him out of the investment. Also, sounds like you can use some good health insurance – do you have any?"

"No," said Simon with embarrassment.

"Well, getting health insurance is another requirement for the investment. Have a good doctor figure out why Sally is having those sinkin' spells. Simon, you commented you were too old to be investing in tools, but I bet you will have a lot more working years if you have a young apprentice to help you with the heavy stuff."

"Leonard," said Simon, in a slightly agitated, but polite manner, "I don't have no such company for you to invest in."

"I am investing in you, Simon. I won't interfere. The only thing I want is if you make over a million a year after expenses I want 10% of the profits, do we have a deal?"

"Can I read the contract first, before I agree?" asked Simon.

"Simon, there won't be a contract. We don't need one, we're kin. All I want is a handshake. Does that work for you?"

"Yes sir, Mr. LaFrance, that works just fine," said Simon smiling ear to ear.

"Damn it, cousin, we just agreed we are kin. Besides, Mr. LaFrance has been buried for eight years."

"Now Sally, you have a decision to make. I can either send down an expert crew that we use to rehab all kinds of property or I can deposit $100,000.00 in an account. The only catch is it MUST be spent on a very large family room. A woman has to have a place big enough for kith and kin."

"You have to agree that all the money will be spent on the family room. If any is left over you must do something that is totally for fun –

maybe a trip or something. I also believe Simon will be putting plenty of money in that retirement account."

Both Simon and Sally were nothing short of being, what they like to call, flabbergasted. But they did manage to agree.

Before he left, they used his credit card to buy the Lincoln welder before someone else did and Leonard gave them two checks to meet the balance of his promise.

Sally got on the phone and arranged for a bigger place and drew Leonard a map. They agreed on a time on Friday, hugged and said goodbye.

The Party

IT was too late to be good to his mama, but he could be good to her family. He was, however, about to see a different side of family. The side that looked a lot like the same greed he saw in business.

Leonard saw that man's nature is consistent.

Most everyone there knew his mother and as he was introduced around the room Leonard learned many endearing things about her. All of this information dealt with what a sweet child she was, for that is the only part of her life that she lived among them except for the short span just before her mother died.

The exception was Sally's sister, Maybelle, who was particularly warm and helpful. Her sadness about his mother's ending was about as profound as his own.

"Your mother was my dearest friend, Leonard. Even though she was only 14 years old when she left, we stayed closely in touch by mail. There was not a week that went by that we did not write to one another, even after she was married.

"Your mother really loved you, Leonard. I have no idea why your father was so mean to her at the end. She went from writing me letters that spoke of her beautiful home, and then her beautiful son. Your mother was a wonderful poet and she put a lot of her poems in the letters she wrote me. Then it all started to change. Her letters carried stories about how Fred, your daddy, became so domineering and tyrannical, so dark I could barely read them. I have since read them all many times. I have them all in two boxes. I've read them so many times I don't need them anymore. I brought them for you if you want them."

The news and the sincere delivery by Maybelle staggered Leonard. He told her he definitely wanted the letters. Her husband volunteered to take them to Leonard's car. Leonard thanked them both, but felt the need to move away from Maybelle's sorrowful eyes, so he continued around the room in shallow conversations.

He also saw that the story of his generosity had made the rounds and the hints were less than subtle. Leonard had always been a shrewd judge of people and was able to size up the individuals in the room quite quickly.

A few of the people were embarrassed by the blatant efforts of the majority to win favor and get goodies. After learning what was to be learned about his mother, he asked to speak privately with Simon, another man named Jeff and the woman, Marie, who had opened her home for the occasion. She had a small study off to the side and they retired to that room.

Leonard wasted no time. "It is clear," he said, "there are many needs in that room out there. I am going to ask the three of you to be a board of directors and take a one hundred thousand dollar contribution and spread it wisely amongst the family where it will do the most good. Will you do that for me?"

There was a chorus with three-part harmony insisting that it was unnecessary and that they were embarrassed by those who were attempting to enrich themselves.

"I knew you would say that and that is why I am asking you to perform this thankless task and to do it in the name of Sarah Peachtree. Will you do it?"

It was Marie who took an unexpected stand.

"Leonard, I know you mean well. I do not know how the people of Los Angeles would be affected by your generosity, but I am afraid this family and the others out there would find themselves at war over the money. It is very hard to turn down $100,000.00, but I do not want to turn folks against folks. I hope you can understand that, and I hope Simon and Jeff see it the same way."

"That is the way I see it," volunteered Jeff.

"I can see Marie's point too," said Simon. "But it is easy for me, I already got a welder and family room. I don't feel right about me being singled out."

"Don't give it another thought", said Jeff. "No one would deny you that. And you are the only close relative anyway."

Marie said, "I agree."

Leonard did not really understand. His experience had never shown him that money was not the answer, but the sincerity of Marie's rejection made him stop and say, "Alright. But I will ask the three of you to be my eyes and ears. If there is ever a need within the family, my offer of $100,000.00 is there for the asking."

Finally they all agreed. Leonard waded through the small crowd saying thank you's and good byes and went back to the motel to read his mother's letters and poems.

Chapter 18

SECOND MEETING

L ILLY HAD CHOSEN HER OFFICE FOR THE second meeting. This occasion would be the final determination as to whether she and her daughter were going to be able to work effectively with Shawn Davis after Sharon's disastrous first meeting.

Saturdays frequently found Lilly at her office cleaning up the mountain of paper work that she could not get to during the workweek. This Saturday would be longer for her, because of the extra time needed to make this decision.

Lilly was tired. Perhaps it was time to shut down the charity named for her late husband, return the money already received and refuse the rest that Leonard had set up for the foundation's use. The good doctor was pretty close to being burnt out.

Because she had arrived earlier than usual, by almost two hours, she had already made a significant dent in the stacks of work that awaited her.

Her concentration was broken by a loud knock on the outer door. *That must be Shawn; it had too much force to be Sharon's knock*, Lilly thought, as she walked in that direction.

The good doctor was wrong. It was Sharon. Her daughter's face told her the young woman was there for business. It was immediately clear that this person was not going to be intimidated by any man today – in fact she would be a force to be reckoned with.

"Good morning, mother," said Sharon in a brisk, business like manner. "Is he here yet?"

"No," answered Lilly, "but you are seven minutes early."

"Let's hope he is not late," said Sharon.

"Are you looking for a reason not to work with this man?" asked the mother. "For, if you are, let's save ourselves a lot of grief and just close it down and try to get through life without it."

"Mother, you always tell me I am level headed, but I did let romantic notions blind me. Absolutely blind me. I did not even see that a life with a man 32 years older than I, would not have a happy ending. Now that is blind.

"So, yes, I am looking for every possible reason not to work with this man, but I also want to keep and grow Brian's Better Tomorrow Foundation. My father was such a special man, and it is very important to me to help people in his name."

Lilly could not stop the small smile that replaced her overworked and worried look that was her standard fare these days.

"I believe," said Lilly, "you have just made my point. You are a very level-headed girl – no, that's no longer true – you are a very level-headed … woman."

At which point a much gentler knock on the door interrupted.

SHAWN Davis stood just outside the door. In a suit and tie, brief case in hand, and a very resolute look on his face. When, however, he saw Sharon, his entire demeanor softened.

"Come in Shawn," said Lilly, in a businesslike manner.

Before any pleasantries were exchanged, Shawn looked at Sharon and with pain written large in his eyes he apologized. He made it clear that he wanted the opportunity to set good things in motion for the Brian's Better Tomorrow Foundation, but if it were to be too difficult for her, because of his actions, he would turn over his ideas and work and leave them to their own path.

"You do have a lot to overcome," Sharon answered, "but my personal feelings will take a back seat to getting on with the work to honor my father by helping people in his name.

"I believe you, Shawn, when you say you're sorry. I believe that you understand that what you did is indefensible and, therefore, I am willing to listen with an open, but suspicious, mind. I have looked over the ideas you left with my mother and I must admit they are sound and exciting. But are you the person to implement them?"

"I honestly believe," said Shawn, quietly, "there is no one you can find who has the heart, or will for this project, that I have. I don't know why, but I think you know I am the right person. Perhaps it is because we are all aware of how much good I must do to make up for my willingness to be a creep just because it was part of my job description."

"With that said," interrupted a very tired Lilly, "let's take a seat and see where we are."

A quiet Sunday

LILLY had slept late, missed church, and was now having her second cup of coffee. She could not have asked for a better resolution than that which came out of yesterday's meeting. She had quickly discovered she could sit back and watch as Sharon took the lead.

Shawn and Sharon were very much in sync. Shawn completed Sharon's thoughts, and she completed his. Rarely had the doctor witnessed such organic teamwork. It was a terrific load off Lilly, both psychologically and in terms of workload.

The development of the foundation named for her late husband would be possible only because of Leonard's generosity and his introduction of Shawn. It was to Lilly an inescapable conclusion that the same man who had traumatized their lives had also brought them much good.

Leonard was a strange and unquestionably poorly developed human being, yet his instincts and nature were some of the kindest and least egocentric she had come across. She worried about him, but was glad he had removed himself from the everyday. As soon as she was glad of this, she simultaneously wondered when he would return.

It was providence that her phone rang right at that moment.

"Hello," said Lilly without looking to see who was calling.

"Hello," said the unmistakable voice of Leonard LaFrance.

The conversation lasted but a few minutes. It starred with apologies, a commitment to never repeat such behavior. An explanation that it was part of his father's life lessons, but that was no excuse. It happened because he was unaware of so much of life and was now off on a pilgrimage to find the missing parts.

Leonard repeated the request that he had laid out in his goodbye letter, that Lilly be kind enough to take the occasional call. She agreed and the call ended.

Her heart was always above, not in, the doctor-patient relationship. It played no part in it at all. It took so much out of her just on the professional level, and she was never tempted to let emotion play a part in her work.

There was, without question, something about Leonard that escaped this boundary. There was an empathy that she could not completely escape. In so many ways he was like an innocent child and it touched her heart in spite of herself.

Lilly climbed back into bed. For a moment she tried to make sense of it all, but blessed sleep came over her and she spent most of the day healing.

Chapter 19

IT TOOK TWO AND A HALF DAYS TO CAREFULLY go through the two boxes of his mother's letters. He now knew more about the heart of her than he would ever know about his father. She was so soft. She exclaimed her amazement at the joy she found in her son. As the marriage crumbled and became more and more ugly, she clung more to her little boy.

Everything she knew, or imagined to do, to encourage Fred to be a good father to Leonard and a good husband to her, she tried. They discussed having another child, perhaps a daughter. It all failed.

Some of her poetry was more than Leonard could stand. She spoke to Maybelle of a poem she had written to Fred and left it on his desk. She latter found it crumpled in his wastebasket.

His mother had included the rumpled poem in a letter. It read.

Show me a Man
Show me a man who teaches his son
And I'll show you a boy
Who will know how to run
His own life
Even as he helps others

Show me a man who plays with his son
And I'll show you a boy who has already begun
To understand he can do more
When he tries harder

Show me a man who prays with his son
And I'll show you a boy
Who will not be undone
For he knows how to live as God intended

Show me a man who stewards his daughter
And I'll show you a girl who won't be led to her slaughter
by some fast talking boy
Who would destroy her

Show me a man who encourages his daughter
And I'll show you a girl who can more than tread water
But swim well the most turbulent
Of life's rivers

Show me a man who prays with his daughter
And I'll show you a girl who knows God is her Potter
And will fill her vessel
With a heart that pleases Him

Show me a man who loves his wife
And I will show you a woman who brings beauty to life
On every level
And in every phase

Show me a man who honors his wife
And I'll show you a woman who levels the strife
That is sure to come
No matter what

Show me a man that prays with his wife
And I will show you a couple that even the sharpest knife
Cannot severe
Nor ever separate

Show me a man who masters these things
And I'll show you a man whose heart sings
And I'll show you a man
Yes, I'll show you a man

When he finished reading the letters, he sent them FedEx to Leon Harding with instruction that the boxes were to be held, but not to be opened.

Then Leonard checked out of the motel and caught a plane.

Closing his eyes, Leonard sank back in the luxury of his 1st Class Air France seat.

The Buyer

Before takeoff a young woman took the aisle seat, but Leonard did not take note of her presence. At least, not at first, as he was in a twilight that is found between wakefulness and deep sleep.

But after they were in the air an awareness of a vague, but highly sensuous, fragrance overcame his sleep. Opening one eye Leonard surveyed the lovely creature in the seat next to him. She was very, very pretty. He then noticed her wedding band and large diamond engagement ring.

She, Leonard concluded, *was not available*. He reclosed the one eye. But the fragrance alerted his newly inquiring mind to questions about what a woman wants in a man and out of life. He decided that in order to learn one must be an enthusiastic, truth-seeking student.

Sitting up in his chair Leonard said, "Excuse me ma'am, may I ask you some questions?"

The woman gave him a lovely and gentle smile that emboldened Leonard, then answered with a rather thick French accent, "But of course."

"I can see," said Leonard, "that you are a lovely woman who could undoubtedly have almost any man. I see by your left hand that you are married. How did you decide on that particular man?"

"What an unusual and wonderful question," answered the woman.

"He was, of course, very handsome, much like yourself. He was successful and I come from a family in which success is a major factor in choosing a mate; this was important to not only myself, but also my family. He was kind, funny and smart. He seemed, more than any other man, to want to know who I was. I do not know how to express this well in English, but he knew my heart and he loved what he knew."

She did not stop there, but added, "He pursued me. Not in an ugly aggressive way, but in a very considerate way. He was willing, really almost eager, to hear my thoughts. Most men like to talk about themselves. This is entertaining, but not as endearing as a man who tries to find out about who the woman is."

Leonard was quiet. He understood how far from that kind of man his father was and how, again, he had imitated him.

Turning to face the woman, Leonard said, "Thank you very, very much."

She was not through with Leonard. "Is this your first trip to Paris?"

"It is," he answered.

"Where are you staying?"

"I don't know. I am just traveling – no agenda. No reservations. Can you suggest a good hotel?"

"Oh yes," she said. "There are many, many wonderful hotels in Paris, but have you thought about an apartment?"

"An apartment, no, I am just staying for a short period."

"But of course, however, many tourists now choose to stay in apartments as they are less expensive and they allow a person to cook. Restaurants in Paris are wonderful, but very expensive."

Leonard blushed slightly and admitted, "I don't know how to cook."

The way she said "But that is terrible," was so endearing. He loved the accent.

"Why is it terrible?" Leonard asked.

"Because," she said, a bit flustered, "oh, there are so many reasons. For health, for joy, and it is a good way to win a woman. It is good for a woman to know she will not be the only one in the family to know how to make the kitchen sing."

She did not hesitate, but persisted. "You will be in Paris – the French know food and how to prepare it. We invented the fork. We know food well and some of the best cooking schools in the world are in our city."

"Do they bother with people who do not know how to boil water?" Leonard asked.

For a moment she forgot to speak English and answered, "Mais oui bien sûr." Correcting herself, she said, "But of course. In fact, many who think they know how to cook actually learned the wrong way to boil water and then the teacher has two jobs. The first is to unteach and the second is to reteach. I know the perfect school for you. Do you want to know?"

"I do," said Leonard. "I absolutely do."

"Tre' bon. I will arrange it for you, but you should know it is not cheap, about a thousand Euro a week and it will take three weeks at least. Ce va?"

"Okay by me. I can give you my cell number and when I get settled in my hotel you can call me and tell me what to do next."

"Oh," she exclaimed, "you are terrible and do not listen. If you go to a hotel how will you practice what you learn – there will be no kitchen?"

Leonard smiled broadly at her delightfully French frustration.

She continued. "My husband and I have three apartments that we rent to tourists. They are all very nice. My husband will pick me up at the airport and he will know if there is a vacancy."

Leonard was truly happy with his good luck in being seated next to such an enlightening person – and a beautiful one at that.

"I have a good feeling about this," Leonard said. "I think I am going to like Paris."

"OOH!" she said as she punched him in the arm. "You are impossible. Of course you will love Paris. Everyone loves Paris."

Her husband embraced her and glared for a moment at Leonard, but his wife soon made it clear what had transpired and what was to come. Leonard just stood there as the barrage of French exploded around him.

When satisfied that Leonard was not an interloper, her husband shook his hand and welcomed him to Paris. It was at his point that the young woman and Leonard realized they did not even know each other's name. They all thought this funny.

"My name is Leonard LaFrance," offered Leonard.

"With a name like that you can't be all bad," said the husband, but he was not through. "However," he continued in nearly perfect English, "being a husband who is aware of how very beautiful his wife is, I still cast a suspicious eye on any man that I might find in her company, especially when she has been away and he arrives with her."

Leonard blushed.

His name was Jean Fontaine. Her name was Lillian. A pang hit Leonard's heart when he heard her name.

Turning to Jean, Leonard said, "How do you spell your first name?"

Jean spelled his name "J E A N" and then explained all Leonard need do is call him as if his name were John.

As it turned out there was one vacancy. It was their most prestigious rental property.

"Tre Bon," she said; "it is right on the Champs Elyse and within walking distance of the cooking school I was telling you about. It is perfect."

Jean said, "Perfect, yes, but I must warn you the rent is 300 Euro per day – that is about $450.00 a day in U.S. dollars."

"But," his wife objected, "Mon cheri, surely we can give him a discount, he will likely be here for three weeks."

"But of course," said Jean with a less than enthusiastic tone. "We could do 1500 Euro per week."

Smiling, Leonard said, "Let's compromise, how about 2,000 Euro per week?"

"Mais qui, I like this compromise, but are you sure, we could cut deeper," Jean offered.

"I am very sure," answered Leonard.

"In that case", said Jean, "you must join us for dinner. I have made a welcome-home feast for my beautiful wife, and it would be good if you joined us. Then we can take you to your new apartment."

"Bon," said Leonard with a purely American accent, and they all laughed.

The homemade dinner was beyond anything Leonard had ever experienced, and it created a deeper enthusiasm to immerse himself in cooking school.

As Jean and Lillian gave him a tour of the apartment he would be living in, Leonard knew he would feel right at home. He thanked his new friends and invited them to choose their favorite restaurant and be his guest in return for their hospitality. They agreed, set a date and time and offered to pick him up and departed.

Leonard unpacked, took a shower and went to sleep imagining the worlds that were about to open for him. He slept well.

Lillian Fontaine called Leonard's cell phone just before midday and gave him the information for the cooking school. After giving him directions, which were easy, she announced she had also taken the liberty of enrolling him. He should be there no later than 9:15 the next day.

Leonard spent the rest of the day in a very pleasant way. He went for a run, a habit that he was beginning to not only enjoy, but to actually need. Then he walked to a local market that Jean had told him about and shopped till he could not carry anymore. For dinner he made some fresh fish and a salad. The fish was inedible, and the salad had very little flavor. He dined out.

THE cooking school, which Lillian had signed him up in, commenced classes at 10 AM. Leonard's lifelong habit of rising early gave him a few hours to run and see some of this amazing city. At one point he asked a Parisian what that beautiful white building sitting atop a prominent hill was.

"Ohhhh, Missuer, that is the Sac le Couer, a most beautiful cathedral, non? Have you not been?"

"No," admitted Leonard. "How would I get there?"

"If you do not have a car you will need a taxi."

"What if I am running?"

"Sacre bleu, that is a long way and up a steep hill. If, however, you think you can do it, please try. Go down this street, you will see much of Momarte then head up the hill and there is a beautiful view of all of Paris from there."

Leonard thanked him and started his trek. The Frenchman was right. It was a struggle, but Leonard felt like Rocky Balboa as he ran up the final steps. He did, however, take a taxi back home where he showered and headed to the first day of learning the illusive art of cooking.

As it turned out all of the years he had spent as a student of his father and his tutors had made him an excellent listener. By applying that skill he discovered a talent and a new passion.

At the end of his three weeks in Paris, Leonard had become a remarkably competent cook, not yet a chef, but he could put a meal on the table that would make a woman he wanted to impress sit up and take notice.

He did not want to leave this magical city. Among other reasons there were a couple of women that he felt a mutual attraction with. But, as strong as this yearning had become, this was not a time to get comfortable; this was a time to learn and get ready for life in full measure.

Chapter 20

THAT IS THE DIFFERENCE IN POPULATION between Paris, France and Vernazza, a tiny town on one of five peninsulas of Cinque Terre, in the Ligurian region of Italy.

His new friends, Jean and Lillian, had recommended Italy as his next stop. They further recommended that he go by train – the bullet train from Paris' Gare de Lyon to Milano's Porta Garibaldi – then a normal train from Milano to Genoa, a city which reminded Leonard more of San Pedro, California, an industrial port where they owned some real estate, than of the quaint home of Christopher Columbus. The last leg would be not on a bullet or even a normal train, but a milk run.

It was not a fast nor a particularly elegant train. It was simply that winding down the coast of the Ligurian Sea to the clickety clack of the wheels on rails was hypnotizing to Leonard. At one point, looking out to the west, he could see the peninsula that was home to Portofino. Even the sheltered Leonard knew this town was the playground of the rich and famous, the jewel of the Italian Riviera, and he knew he wanted no part of it.

There were places where the tracks ran so close to the cliffs he could look right down into the sea. There were tunnels so numerous he lost track of them. The booklet he had picked up on the area said the railroad was built in 1874. Before that, the only way to get there was to walk or come by boat.

During the train ride Leonard found more time to reflect on the letters that Maybelle had given him. The most depressing aspect of her writings came toward the end of her life. Within her there was a battle that raged between her not having the will to live any longer and the tenant that God would forgive anything except taking your own life. She had taken her own life. Leonard did not know where to go from there.

After an hour and forty minutes he heard the conductor call out, "Vernazza!"

Leonard grabbed his one bag and a newly acquired backpack and walked out into the sea-refreshed air. The sun was bright. The colors were amazing. He immediately felt that this was home away from home.

Jean and Lillian had told him this was the place to go to get a sense of what Italy was about. True, it had been "discovered" and there were many tourists in the summer, but at this time a year there was little evidence of that. There were no taxis. In fact there were no cars at all. So Leonard followed the small band of travelers as they headed down the hill from the depot. After a long block he came to an open square, what he would later learn the Italians call a piazza.

As he told Lillian Fontaine on the plane, he had no agenda and no reservations. He looked around the Piazza and saw a sidewalk cafe and bar called the Blue Marlin. He took a seat in the sun.

A fine looking fellow, around his own age, came out and said something in Italian. Leonard asked him if he spoke English.

"No, me dispiace," said the man, then offered, "Habla Espanol?"

"Si, pero muy poquito."

It was funny that these two men of different backgrounds, different socio-economic standings and not even a common language, would soon become friends at a rather remarkable depth.

His name was Massimo. He did speak some English. It was soon clear his mother tongue was Italian. However, he had lived in Barcelona for a few years and was also fluent in Spanish.

When he told Massimo his name was Leonard, Massimo shook his head vigorously, and in a torrent of broken English and a touch of Italian insisted, "No, no, no! Not leonard, ma Leonardo. A greata nama for a you."

Leonard knew no Italian, but as a boy he had overheard and learned enough Spanish to be conversant with the gardeners who cared for his yard.

Somehow, they muddled through.

Leonard was ready to get a shower and take a nap after the long train rides so getting a hotel was his priority. After Massimo brought him a cappuccino and a roll, Leonard asked Massimo if he could recommend a hotel.

Massimo shook his head and told him that Vernazza had no hotels, per se. Then, without waiting for a response from Leonard, he put two fingers in his mouth and whistled. The half dozen people sitting around the square looked up. Massimo pointed at one of them and motioned for him to come over.

"Si," said the man who had been summoned. Massimo rattled off a few lines in the local language. The man nodded his head in an affirmative way.

"Molto buono," said Massimo. He then introduced Leonard to Pino. Pino spoke no English, nor did he speak Spanish, but in a matter of a few words Massimo had arranged for Pino to show Leonard an apartment.

Leonard quickly finished his roll and coffee and followed Pino down the main street toward the harbor; then, after just a few yards, they went left into a winding walk that led to a few steps made of stone that had probably been laid nearly a thousand years ago. The climb was not limited to the first set of steps; it continued. More steps and more winding until finally Pino opened a door that led into a small apartment.

There was no kitchen. In the past that would have meant nothing, but now cooking was to be considered a critical and basic part of life. After several futile attempts to communicate the importance of a kitchen, Pino finally understood. His face lit up and he led Leonard outside and a bit further up the path to another apartment, above the first, but in the same house.

This one had a kitchen. Unlike the small sleeping area downstairs, this had a view that was magnificent. From one of its two bedrooms you could look down on much of the town and catch a glimpse of the Ligurian Sea. From the second, smaller bedroom, one could look straight down the cliff into waters off the south side of the little peninsula on which Veranazza was built.

"Ma," said Pino, "molto caro." While saying this he rubbed two fingers together in the international sign that meant 'expensive'. Reaching into his shirt pocket Pino extracted a pen and a small notebook. He took a clean page and wrote '80 Euro.'

After Paris, Leonard knew the value of the Euro in relation to the dollar, and he also knew that, while the owner thought it was expensive, Leonard thought it was a steal. Reaching into his wallet, Leonard extracted ten $100 bills and put them into Pino's waiting hand. Pino again took up the note pad and wrote '7 giorni.'

Leonard, with a smile, took the pen and correctly assuming that 'giorni' meant 'days' he wrote '8 giorni.'

"Okay," said Pino, which was likely his longest sentence in English. They shook hands, Pinot gave him a key and Leonard settled in.

Vernazza had about 900 residents during the summer and possibly another 500 tourists, but now there were barely 500 in the town. That was fine with Leonard.

After a shower and a nap, Leonard found his way back down the winding path to Massimo's bar where he thanked the man for the introduction to Pino and the wonderful apartment. Then he asked Massimo what he would recommend that he have this time of day.

Massimo looked at his watch and said with assurance, "Vino." He did not ask Leonard whether he wanted white or red. Leonard would have said red. He'd had very little wine in his life, almost no alcohol at all really. His time in Paris had softened him up, and he was ready to try almost anything.

Massimo brought him a glass of chilled white wine. It was wonderful. Leonard asked, "Where did the wine come from?"

Massimo said, "Come" and led Leonard down to the harbor. When they reached the other open piazza area by the harbor, Massimo pointed to the hillsides above the Catholic Church. The hillsides were more like cliffs, but somehow men with nothing but shovels and baskets had turned them into narrow terraces, clinging desperately to the walls of the cliffs.

"Da vino isa from dere – also our olives," Massimo explained.

After returning to the bar and finishing his wine, Leonard asked Massimo what he should order for dinner. He had found this to be a good tactic in Paris. The waiters loved to show off their expertise, especially when they became aware of the fact that Leonard could be a generous tipper when he was pleased with the meal.

To Leonard's surprise, rather than bring him a menu, Massimo had him stand, turned Leonard around and pointed him toward a restaurant directly across the small square. Massimo had Leonard learn the word 'Pesto,' and then explained that it was a dish invented right here in Cinqua Terre.

Leonard thanked Massimo and asked one more favor. Massimo was happy to oblige, because Leonard wanted him to find a tutor that could help him learn some conversational Italian.

"Domani ata 10 AM and I will have a tutor fora you," instructed Massimo.

The dinner, in the small restaurant that Massimo recommended, was better than good, especially with a carafe of the local wine. It was a fraction of the cost of a dinner of similar quality in Paris, and the atmosphere was so soft and without a commercial tint. Leonard imagined this was more like a family gathering would feel, but having never had a family he could not know for sure. The closest to having a family was that gathering in Louisiana, and that had left him with an unsavory taste in his mouth.

Later, as he settled into bed, he was certain Vernazza would be a nice, albeit short, stay.

EARLY the next morning Leonard walked the town. It did not take long. While standing on the jetty that gave protection to the harbor, he saw a very small boat equipped with an outboard motor moving gracefully toward the entrance of the tiny town's harbor.

As the fisherman drew nearer, Leonard could see his face quite clearly. At first he could not identify the expression. Then, ever so slowly, it dawned on Leonard that what he saw was the look of complete contentment on the man's face.

Pulling his small boat up on the gravel, the man brought forth two large buckets of freshly caught fish, and, with a bit of effort, trudged up the cobblestone roadway to a place where an older woman was standing beside a wooden cart.

"Buon giorno mama," the fisherman called out.

"Buon giorno, Luigi," answered his mother.

Leonard moved off the jetty toward the cart. He bought one of the smaller fish that looked something like a mini sea monster. He made motions that indicated he would like the fish cleaned.

The fish woman wore a slight scowl. This was not a usual service and the fish the tourist had just selected was a sculpin. The fish was sometimes called a scorpion fish, because of all of the thorny spines that could be painful if they stuck you.

Leonard offered her a $20.00 dollar bill. She took it and with the skill of a surgeon filleted the fish in a matter of moments and offered him 5 Euro in change. Leonard waved it off. The fishwife smiled and turned to the next customer.

Leonard immediately went into a small grocery and delicatessen shop where he bought the accruements the French cooking school suggested when cooking super fresh fish. And fresh it was, though it was now filleted, it had been moving just moments ago.

There he bought a bottle of olive oil, a single lemon and some fresh Rosemary along with small containers of salt and pepper and straight away climbed back up the path to his apartment.

The fresh fish cooked quickly in the sauté pan, and, in the blink of an eye, he wound his way up the spiral staircase that led to the terrace on the roof of his apartment. Here, he ate the sweetest breakfast he could remember. After all, if you start with very fresh fish, cook it yourself, and eat it in a beautiful atmosphere, how can you go wrong?

From here Leonard could see the whole town. Right in front of him was as ancient stone tower, a place where the villagers used to seek refuge when the Muslim raiders would come to pillage their town. Off the coast was an island of some size. Then there was the sea that went all the way to Spain. Most of all, Leonard could see a much bigger future for his life than he ever could see from the back of a limo.

At 9:45 AM Leonard arrived at the Blue Marlin, well fed but looking for some caffeine. Massimo had not yet shown up when Leonard had ordered his Cappuccino. Though he did not order a pastry the waitress brought him one.

I must learn this language, thought Leonard.

As he sipped the coffee and leaned back in his chair, the sleep-tasseled Massimo arrived, still rubbing the night's gunk from his eyes.

"Good morning," greeted Leonard.

"Buon giorno," croaked Massimo.

That was all that Leonard got out of his new friend until Massimo had downed a cup of very dark, extremely strong coffee. Even then all Massimo could offer were two words that Leonard did not yet understand, "Troppo Vino."

Suddenly, Massimo jumped up as if someone had plugged him in to a 220-volt circuit.

That must be some coffee, thought Leonard.

Then Leonard followed Massimo's unflinching stare and saw the reason for his friend's sudden animation. It was not the coffee.

She moved with a fluid grace that defied physics. The fabric in her flower-print dress flowed around her like cloud, and her face, surrounded by heaven sent hair, was angelic.

"Angelica," exploded Massimo moving toward her.

"Ciao, Massimo," the voice of the vision responded.

After several excited exchanges in a language that seemed unknowable to Leonard, they both turned their attention to Leonard.

Angelica, upon being introduced to Leonard, quickly switched to English.

"So," she asked, "you are to be my student?"

Leonard, in a shy moment said, "If you'll have me."

"What has Massimo told you about me?" asked Angelica.

"He has told me nothing about you, only that he would arrange for a tutor to meet me this morning at 10 AM. Nothing more."

"Allow me, please, to introduce you to myself more fully. My name is Angelica Porta. I am a teacher of the Italian language to people who speak English, French, German or Spanish. My fee is 30 Euro per hour. I will not tolerate any lateness or laziness from a student. You will be given words and phrases in Italian to study on your own. The first time a student fails to do those lessons to my satisfaction, I will no longer be willing to teach that student. I will teach only to people who are serious about learning. Have I said anything so far that displeases you or that you will have difficulty with?"

While Leonard was at first shy he was now a bit riled. No one, save his father, had ever spoken to him that way. Even the private tutors his father had bought him treated him as if he were a prince to be taught, but never offended. Certainly he never entertained such abusive behavior from an employee – which, regardless of her beauty, is exactly what she would be.

Although a little unsure of where to go with this, Leonard decided to rely on his well-honed business instincts and make a stand. If she walked – she walked.

"I will not pay you 30 Euro per hour, but 100. And I will be as late or as lazy as I choose to be. However, I will likely be neither. I will be here for at least one week and will want a minimum of three hours of tutoring per day. Have I said anything so far that displeases you or that you will have difficulty with?"

Leonard did not speak.

Angelica did not speak.

Massimo, who had been standing off to the side, but within hearing distance, hurried to their table.

In a mixture of Italian, Spanish and English, he demanded to know why they were fighting.

Leonard did not speak.

Angelica did not speak.

Massimo, in frustration, threw his hands up and out to the side with his open palms up and walked back into the Blue Marlin.

Angelica had been defended by her truly spectacular beauty since she was a child. No one ever spoke to her with such an imperial tone except, of course, her mother.

She was ready to call him a stupid American and stomp off, but it was, after all, winter. Her business model depended on tourists who wanted a crash course in conversational Italian and were willing to pay between 15 and 30 Euro per hour. She did tutor a few local students who were slow to capture the Italian grammar in school, but they were willing to pay only an average of 7 Euro per hour. Even if there were many of these kids, it would not produce enough income to support her in a decent fashion and allow her to help her mother.

This man was challenging her in a way she was not used to, but she was also not used to making 100 Euro per hour. And this was winter and tourists were few.

She chose a different line of attack.

"Why are you eating a pastry in the morning. Don't you know you need protein to start the day?"

Leonard had won. He was both pleased that he had read her correctly, as he always seemed to do while closing a business deal, and confused and curious about this nutritional advice.

"I am interested in what you might have to say about nutrition, but only after you have assured me that my terms are agreeable to you. What do you say?"

"I say ... I agree. But if you are not a serious student I will still fire you."

"Deal. When do we start?"

"Right now!" answered Angelica.

"No, wait," said Leonard.

"Wait for what?" she demanded.

"Until I'm ready to start."

"When will that be, Mr. LaFrance?"

Very quietly and with a great deal of confidence he said, "Now."

Chapter 21

WHAT ABOUT ANGELICA?

THE FIRST THREE HOURS WENT WELL. Leonard was not a natural linguist, but he was persistent. Angelica liked and admired his tenacity. Leonard ate up her admiration. They had sat at a table under an umbrella at the Blue Marlin for the first hour.

During this time, there was an unmistakable second-tier drama involving a growing realization that Massimo regretted that he had put the two together. He'd brought her in as a tutor, primarily, because he wanted to have a shot at her himself.

Simultaneously, his attraction to Angelica became obvious to Laura, his long-time, live-in girlfriend who was also his business partner.

As the tension became palatable, Angelica and Leonard took a walking tour of the town, using the various shops and their merchandise to further teach him in a tangible way.

By the end of the day, they felt quite comfortable with each other with just a touch of sexual tension. Leonard was hungry and invited Angelica to show him food that she believed to be more nutritious than pastry. She agreed to have a late lunch, but only if it was 'off the clock.'

Lunch over, they set the meeting time and place for tomorrow at 10:00 AM and again at the Blue Marlin. Leonard had a long list of words and phrases to work on and no mention was made of homework assignments.

Angelica's beauty and feminine softness made Leonard yearn. She had awakened a powerful hunger, but he was holding himself in check. This is one who would not be bought, and Leonard did not have the vaguest idea as to how he might move this relationship from one of teacher/student to that of lovers.

With the 10-hour difference between Vernazza and L.A. he realized that he still had 2 hours until it would be 8 AM and permissible to call Dr. Lilly.

At 6 PM Vernazza time he made that call to the one person he could really talk with. Leonard had called her only once since he had been in Europe. In this call he brought the doctor up to speed by giving her a quick version of the events that had taken place in Paris and now in Italy.

He spoke of the train ride, the village of Vernazza, his friendship with Massimo, his Italian lessons and … his attraction for Angelica.

"How old is she?" inquired Dr. Lilly.

After a pause, Leonard answered truthfully. "I don't know. I would guess early twenties."

"How old are you, Leonard?"

After another substantial pause, Leonard said, "I guess about 30 years older than the girl."

"Do you see a problem with that?" she asked.

"I've never thought about it," he said honestly.

"Let me give you one thing to consider and one last question to think about, and then I'll let you go as I have a patient waiting. Find someone who is desperately in need and has nothing to offer you and give yourself, not your money, but yourself to helping them. The last question is this: Leonard, do you see a pattern in behavior that keeps you from finding a woman near your own age attractive? Bye for now."

Leonard dismissed the thought of giving service to a needy person as rather silly, but he tucked it away. He pondered Dr. Lilly's question until sleep overcame him.

THE next morning Leonard had plenty of time to take his run, and grab a shower before arriving at the Blue Marlin at 9:45. The run was a particularly challenging one.

Leonard was told by another early riser, a German tourist, that the most magnificent run would be along the ancient footpath between Vernazza and the next village to the south, Corniglia.

The German had spoken the truth, but not the whole truth. The trail that had been the only land passage between the two storybook small towns for centuries, and, while unimaginably picturesque, was more fitting for a mountain goat than the semi-fit Los Angelian, especially one who was on the trot.

That said, Leonard tackled the task with a bulldog persistence that he knew would please his father. He knew it would please his father, because it pleased him. Leonard was beginning to understand that he and his father were basically one in the same man. He hated this, but that hatred drove him to add dimension to the monolithic man that his father had carved out of a compliant young boy.

The rugged trail was cut into the cliff far above the sea and filled with abrupt ups and downs that made it more tiring and more dangerous. Leonard was tired enough from running that he willingly took the milk train from Corniglia back north to Vernazza.

Stepping off the train, Leonard got a fresh view of the contented village of Vernazza. It was, he decided, the most idyllic place he had ever seen. The town was coming to life at this hour, and, after a quick shower, he arrived for his meeting with Angelica.

Strange as it may seem he was surprised at her beauty. Even after spending 3 hours or more yesterday looking at her, nearly memorizing every contour of her face, her exquisite Mediterranean complexion, her dark brown and inviting eyes, the slender neck and glorious hair – it was all brand new this morning. He felt both joy and discomfort.

Angelica bounced right into her teacher role with a sassy "Buon Giorno, Leonardo, Como stai?"

"Molto Bene, Anglica, a le?"

Thus began day two of the lessons.

By day six, Leonard was totally infatuated.

Angelica was warming to him in a way she had never allowed her feelings to develop for any other student. She had learned early in life that a girl who possesses physical beauty must be careful. The slightest hint that she finds a man attractive to any degree could lead to the unleashing of passion on the part of the man that was, to say the least, very unsettling and most unwelcome.

On this particular day they had met at the Blue Marlin, taken a walking tour of a different part of the village and wound up back at Leonard's place to get down to some serious drill.

Massimo was extremely unhappy with this pattern, because he could only imagine what he would do in Leonard's place. Had it not been for the brotherly affection he felt for the mild-mannered Leonard, he might have gotten violent.

Leonard never touched Angelica. Never – in any way – did Leonard lay a hand on her. Not her hand, her shoulder, her painfully beautiful face. Leonard bottled up his feelings. He was so controlled that the actual closeness to this woman was surreal. He wanted. Oh how he wanted, but he gave no external sign.

It had become customary for them to have something to eat together after their lessons. Sometimes at the Blue Marlin or one of the other eateries, and sometimes Leonard would display some of his newly acquired cooking skills, but not without the aid of Angelica's Italian culinary input.

"My mother is a wonderful cook. She taught me," said Angelica.

"You and your mother are very close, aren't you?" asked Leonard.

"Oh yes, yes. She is a single mother who gave up everything to raise me."

"What happened to your father?" he asked.

"I never knew him. He came to Vernazza on holiday from Roma, and he swept my mother off her feet. They made love only once, and he went back to Roma, promising he would be back to ask her parents for the right to marry her. But she never heard from him again.

"Her burdens were heavy, but she put all of the money she could into educating me so I would have opportunity. Now, she wants me to get married and leave Vernazza. But how can I do that with her poor health and little money. She was ostracized by the people of the village, especially the women. The men all thought she was an easy target and treated her shamelessly. Even though she has never known another man, she was considered a whore, and so the men chose to treat her coarsely and the woman were jealous of the things she was accused of, but never did.

"Those days are gone, but she grew used to being alone or with me and though she could have friends, she is a loner. Except for me. I love her and I will protect her as she has protected me."

Leonard was quiet.

"What about you and your mother?" asked Angelica. "Are you close?"

A pained expression passed over Leonard's face which Angelica did not miss.

Finally Leonard spoke. "My mother is dead. She went away when I was 11 and I never saw her again. My father drove her away. He raised me to be the man he wanted me to be, but I cannot be that man."

Neither of them moved for a moment, then Angelica came and kissed his cheek. It was not a kiss of sympathy or any one of a number of reasons that one person may kiss another's cheek. It was a kiss that was more intended for the lips. One that was made with soft lips and that lingered too long to belong on the cheek.

What happened next was sad.

Leonard lost control. His lips found hers, and his right hand found her left breast. From warm and soft to striking his face with her open hand chilled the moment like an avalanche. Angelica, now with tears streaming down her face, left without a word.

Stunned, Leonard stood there. His arms full just a moment ago were now embarrassingly empty. His heart full, just a moment before, now horribly empty. He stood in the same place for what seemed like an eternity. Reliving the week he had been around her, the joy she had brought. Now he had injured her. Once again, his lack of knowing life had crushed a woman he cared for so much - even as it had also crushed him.

Hours later he went down to the village. He dared not go to the Blue Marlin. It must surely be written large across his person that he is one to do great damage to women who trust him.

He walked into the little delicatessen he had frequented. No purpose in mind, just roaming. It was now dark early as are the days of midwinter. The store was empty other than the clerk and a woman shopper who was about his age, but seemingly so much older. He picked up a tin of sardines. He had never had one, didn't know if he would ever eat it, but got it just the same. He moved toward the cash register.

The other woman was already there, but seeing he only had one item told him in Italian that he should go first.

Leonard was anything, but in a hurry.

"No," he told her. "I am not in a hurry. Please, you go first."

She obliged. Her stack of items was formidable. When the clerk was through tallying it up it came to 127 Euro. The woman opened her purse and swore. She told the woman she had forgotten her wallet. The clerk gave her a disgusted look that said she had never cared for her small town neighbor in the first place.

It was closing time, and the clerk did not want to wait for her to go home and get her money. It was easy to tell the cashier was an employee and the store did not belong to her. The shopper was embarrassed and promised to come back tomorrow with the money. Despite that, the clerk escalated the scene by raising her voice and almost spitting at the woman.

Leonard was already in a most uneasy style of mind and could not bear the acrimony. Stepping forward and seeing the amount on the cash register he held out two one hundred Euro bills.

The clerk scowled and reached for it.

The proud, but embarrassed shopper grabbed Leonard's hand and stopped the transaction. Leonard shifted his attention to the old woman. Her eyes were incredibly sad.

"Per favore," said Leonard in a very soft and compassionate voice, "mi piacerebbe molto fare questo."

The shopper looked into Leonard's eyes and there saw kindness. She also saw a hurt she could not describe and intuitively knew his gesture was more for him than for her. She blinked back tears and said a gentle, "Grazia."

When she asked how she could get the money back to him, he told her it was not important and that all was even.

Leonard walked out on to the jetty. It was much different here tonight than it had been on the first morning he was in Vernazza.

The Buyer

The inviting blue-green of morning on the Ligurian Sea was gone. In its place were the dark wind-swept waves that crashed mockingly against the rocks and proffered a different invitation. It said, "Leave the dark empty life that you do not know how to live and lose yourself by slipping below the waves into the serenity of the deep."

It seemed almost like a good idea, but Leonard did not buy it. He had bought a lot of things. That is what he was – a buyer. But he was not ready to buy this … yet.

The path and stairs going back to his apartment seemed longer and steeper than he could remember. On his mind was the thought that he was a buyer – little more than that. A buyer of things – that is what he does, but is that who he is – or just what he does?

Entering into his apartment there was just enough light to find a chair. Leonard took a seat. If someone were to ask him how long he sat there in the dark, he could not even give a rough estimate. Perhaps he had fallen asleep in the chair. He did not know. The only thing that brought him back was a knock on his door.

He knew he should answer it, but he just sat there.

The knock was repeated and this time it was followed by a voice. A concerned and beautiful voice. It was Angelica's voice.

"Leonardo." A pause. Then the call was repeated, only this time she used his Anglican name, "Leonard."

Rising from a stupor Leonard shuffled toward the door. It was still dark out. He turned the latch and pulled open the door.

"I have a question for you. Do you know my mother? Have you ever seen her?"

Leonard, lost in confusion, shook his head in an effort to say 'No.'

"Did you shop at the delicatessen on the piazza tonight?"

Again, Leonard shook his head 'no,' but then remembered he had, and corrected himself by saying, "Well, yes I did."

"Did you pay for a woman's groceries?"

The events of the night coming back to him now, he acknowledged that he had.

"Yes – ehh, there was woman who forgot her money. Why?"

"Are you sure you do not know my mother?"

Starting to come fully around, Leonard spoke as clearly as possible and said firmly, "No, I do not know your mother."

Angelica's voice grew very soft. "That woman is my mother."

"Oh," said Leonard, not showing much surprise or interest.

"That was a very nice thing you did."

"The clerk was being disrespectful, after my disrespectful behavior today with you I simply could not abide being around it."

As Leonard gained cognizance, it caused him to feel more ashamed. He put his head down and said, "I am so sorry."

"Why did you do that, Leonard?" It was almost a cry as it emerged from Angelica's mouth.

Leonard was honest. "I do not know how to be with a woman in any personal way."

"What does that mean? Are you saying you have never been married or had a girlfriend?"

"Yes, that is what I am saying."

"How could that be? You are tall, very good looking, and when you're not being arrogant with your teacher you are the kindest man I have ever known."

Leonard gave a short, soft laugh. Then he told her his whole story, his mother, his father and the way he had been raised.

They both were still standing just inside the open door. Mild as Italy's winters are, it still made the room uncomfortably chilly. Angelica turned, closed the door, then turned back to Leonard, who had yet to move at all. She took him by the hand and led him to the bed. She climbed up on it and brought Leonard with her. He buried his head in her breasts and began to cry. She rocked him as if he were a small child.

They both, exhausted as they were, dozed off. Leonard awoke first. It took only seconds for him to realize where he was. Who it was that lay with him and who the softness that cradled his face belonged to.

Leonard stiffened. Angelica awoke and began to rock him gently again. Soon they were both awake and her rocking encouraged his rocking. Angelica brought her face up to his and she said, "Come, let me show you how to be as gentle a lover as you are a gentle man."

As dedicated a student as he was for the Lingua le Italiano, he was a much more ardent student for this life lesson. By midday she had tamed the wild beast and taught him to channel his passion.

The Buyer

For a moment Leonard was not sure whether or not he should feel guilty about not giving Angelica $10,000.00 in exchange. Then it dawned on him like sunrise – *No! This is how it should be!* He was grateful, but he wasn't quite sure to whom.

A LITTLE after noon, Leonard found Pino and paid him for two more weeks of rent. Winter in a summer resort allows for such last-minute luxuries.

Over the next week they were inseparable. One warm afternoon as they took their coffee outside at the Blue Marlin an older couple was seated at the next table. The man was in a wheel chair, his much younger wife was dealing with everything and was not happy about it. During their entire meal the couple did not exchange a kind word. Bitterness was written large across both of their faces.

Angelica and Leonard could not help but take note. It was a sobering moment. They may well be seeing their own future. The other couple left. The coffee gave way to some local wine.

Over the next few days their eyes cleared. Both of them knew theirs was a love more of compassion, appreciation, and friendship than of enduring romance. They were disappointed to be sure, but grateful for the clarity as well.

Angelica took him to meet her mother. Their apartment was on the outskirts of town in a very modest community of the village. Though it was extraordinarily small, the home was clean and bright and Leonard felt comfortable there. During the course of their visit, Mona, Angelica's mother, thanked him for his generosity and offered to return the money now. Leonard still would not hear of it.

The language for the entire visit was Italian. Leonard was pleased, as was his teacher.

Mona revisited the night of his generosity and told Leonard that when she described the very kind man with the heavy American accent to Angelica, her daughter knew immediately of whom her mother spoke.

"She told me," said Mona, "about how you changed from a very shy and totally gentle man into a sex-crazed monster." They all laughed, although Leonard's was more of an embarrassed laugh than a belly laugh.

160

"I told Angelica that your eyes told me that you were not that kind of man. I told her to go find you and find out why you were so awkward with women. I did not tell her to take you to bed though – that was her idea."

This time when they laughed both Leonard and Angelica's laughs were primarily due to embarrassment.

They had a wonderful supper that Mona had made, it featured a pesto that was even better than the one served in the little restaurant across from the Blue Marlin.

Leonard asked what seemed to be a whimsical question.

"What would you change if you had money?"

"Oh, that is easy," said Mona. "We would have a larger apartment in town so the store was not so far away."

"I agree," echoed Angelica, "and I would finish at the university, and with my degree I'd be a teacher instead of being a tutor."

"Those," said Leonard, "are very modest requests. Is that all you would want?"

To that, Mona answered, "We do not want to buy a good life. We want to be blessed with a good life. If we are pleasing to God, all will be fine. I was excommunicated, because I had a baby out of wedlock. I cannot go to the church, but that does not mean that I cannot be with God here in my home. I spend all of my time talking with Him."

"You," said Mona to Leonard, "will not be staying, will you?"

Angelica answered, "It is okay, Mother; it is not too be."

THE next morning Leonard got busy. He found and bought in the names of Angelica and her mother a beautiful home right off the piazza. It was very large by local standards and gave them not only wonderful living quarters but three apartments to let out for income. He made arrangements with his office in L.A. to pay the taxes annually for five years.

After finding out where Angelica would go to college if she could and how much time it would take to finish her degree, he paid her tuition and the rent on a very nice, though modest, apartment near the university for the duration.

The Buyer

Lastly, he opened a savings account for Angelica and her mother with enough euro to fill in the blanks for at least a few years. He did not tell them about it, but put it in a letter for them with his contact information and instructions to call if they ever wanted his help. When they met for their last breakfast at the Blue Marlin, he gave Angelica the letter with instructions not to open it for two days.

Massimo liked Leonard, but was secretly glad he was leaving, because – who knows. Laura, Massimo's longtime significant other, was sad that Leonard was leaving.

Not as sad as either Leonard or Angelica.

They both acknowledged that a 30-year disparity in their ages would soon show up. That did not mean that the other would ever be forgotten – more than ships passing in the night, less than a lifetime of sharing bliss – both were better for the meeting.

Leonard hefted his backpack on his shoulders and locked on to his suitcase. Angelica walked him to the train station and they waved goodbye through the train window.

Angelica kept her promise not to open his letter, at least until his train was out of sight.

Chapter 22

WHEN IN ROME

T HE MILK TRAIN TOOK HIM TO LA SPEZIA
and then on to Pisa. He took a break and walked this sea-
side town famous for its leaning tower.

After a night's rest he proceeded to Rome, or, as the Italians call
their ancient capitol, Roma. When considering a place to stay, Leonard
rejected an apartment. Rome was too large for him right now. He just
wanted a taste of 'When in Rome' and a hotel would do just fine.

The taxi driver responded warmly to Leonard's effort to carry the
conversation in Italian. When he asked Leonard, "Dove?" Leonard
asked if he knew a good hotel near the Spanish Steps.

"Si Signori, le Regina Hotel Baglioni e' perfetto."

"Va Bene, andiamo."

Leonard had never been in a palace, *but this must be what it is like*,
he thought. There was a grand sweeping staircase. Even in his room
the stonework in the floors and the walls were of such impact that he
decided to send his top interior designers here to get ideas for some of
the upscale remodels.

He dropped off his bags, took a shower and went into the bar of the
hotel for a glass of wine. He had gone his entire life with very, very
little alcohol, but was now accustomed to having a glass of wine before,
during and after dinner.

The room was quite full of interesting looking people and quite short on available seating. He went to the long, curved bar and ordered a Brunello di Montalcino, a wine he had become most fond of after Massimo introduced him to it. He was told that it was available only by the bottle, so Leonard said, "Fine."

Shortly after the expensive bottle of wine arrived a very attractive young woman came and tapped him on the shoulder. She had dark eyes that were almost black and seemed to dance when she smiled. She was smiling when she invited Leonard to join her family at a nearby table.

Her family was a man and a woman of the approximate age one would expect them to be if they were this woman's parents and another young woman who looked to be this woman's younger sister.

"How nice of you to ask," said Leonard, and gladly went to her table.

They talked, had some food, which Leonard insisted on buying and then the parents asked to be excused. When they started to leave the young woman who had initially extended the invitation to Leonard protested that she was not yet ready to retire. They accepted that and her father came to Leonard's chair, shook his hand and gave him the kind of look that said, 'do not seduce my daughter,' and left.

The young woman had given Leonard her name as well as the names of the rest of her family, but he couldn't recall any one of their names. They were all unusual, and seemed to be unusually long.

Though Leonard was far from proficient with Italian, he seemed to detect a bit of an accent. So he asked her where they were from. Her face grew guarded. Finally she offered, "Romania."

She asked him more questions about where he was from and what kind of work he did. She seemed particularly interested in his holdings. Soon Leonard lost interest in her and the banal conversation and decided to take a walking tour of Rome near the hotel.

When he asked to excuse himself the woman pouted and pleaded for one more round. The Brunello was gone and he did not want another bottle and she suggested he try her favorite cocktail. Leonard agreed though he was unfamiliar with the drink.

No waiter was nearby so she volunteered to go up to the bar.

"Oh no," said Leonard, "I will be happy to go."

"But you do not know the drink, or how I like it made," was her firm, but whiney answer.

While she was gone Leonard looked about the room. It was a strange mixture and it was obvious, even to Leonard, that these people were from many different countries and many different cultures.

The waiter came by and Leonard pointed to the young woman at the bar and explained that she was getting the drinks, but that he would appreciate the bill as soon as possible. The waiter brought it right away.

The young woman with the forgettable name returned and with a gleam in her eye told Leonard how glad she was to have met him. During their conversation, which had very little meat, but a lot of oohs and aahs from the young lady, she began touching Leonard's arm and even his thigh.

She toasted to him having a happy and fun holiday. The drink reminded Leonard why he did not drink more hard alcohol in the past. He did not like the taste.

When it was gone, Leonard, tired of her shallowness and the meaningless touches wanted to go for his walk. He was not the least bit caught up in her physical charms.

However, she was determined to take the walk with him. He deferred and said he needed to go to his room to put on his walking shoes.

"I will go to your room with you. They have such beautiful rooms here," she said touching his leg in a most seductive manner.

Even so Leonard was not very enthusiastic about the direction this seemed to be going.

When they got to his room she insisted on a tour. She said she loved it all, but when she saw the bathroom with its big cast-iron bathtub, surrounded by marble walls, she flipped. Coming very close to him, putting her forearms on his chest and using a voice more suited to a 10-year-old than a grown woman she asked a question that Leonard had not heard since he was a small child.

"May I give you a bath?"

Leonard was not really tempted. He thought he wanted to go for a walk, but now he felt that he was strangely tired and in need of a nap.

The girl, whose name he could not remember, was talking about how great and restful he would feel if he would just let her give him a bath. As she said this she unbuttoned his shirt and took it off. She did the same with his pants. When he had lost all of his clothes and slipped into the warm water of the bath she had drawn it seemed that the young woman was right. It felt so good.

HOURS later he awoke with a pounding headache in a tub full of cold water. Unlike when he had fallen asleep with Angelica this time when he opened his eyes this woman was gone. So was his money, his Travelers' checks, ATM card and his American Express card leaving him only his checkbook and passport.

Leonard had room service bring him eggs and coffee and two Tylenol. It was far too early to call Samuel Levine and get his help canceling and renewing his American Express and ATM cards, so he called the concierge and explained the events of the night before.

The concierge was highly apologetic and offered to get the police involved. Leonard started to say no, but then felt it was his civic duty and asked them to go ahead.

Within the hour there was a knock on the door.

When opened, the door revealed a tall, muscular looking man holding forth his badge. His accomplice was not nearly as formidable looking and was taking a subservient role even before they entered Leonard's room.

They exchanged Buon Giornos, the lead officer offered Leonard his card and introduced himself in Italian.

"Io sono Ispettore Capo, Pepi Luca."

Leonard clearly understood that the man was chief inspector, but was not yet comfortable enough with this language to carry on a formal conversation and so he inquired, "Do you speak English?"

"Of course," responded the officer. "I studied it at university and played soccer in America for two years. I know the language pretty well."

"Oh good, thank you," said Leonard. "I am learning Italian, but that has only been going on for about three weeks."

"We have a report that you have had things of value taken. Can you tell me about it?"

Leonard proceeded to relate the events of the night before. When

166

he had completed the story, the detective began to question him as to whether there had been any sexual activity between he and the girl. Even after Leonard gave him a complete answer, the inspector asked the same question in different ways until finally Leonard asked him why he persisted in this line of questioning.

"Because, you woke up naked in the bath tub," said Ispettore Luca.

Leonard gave an embarrassed laugh and acknowledged that would cause one to think that there was sex involved, but he assured the policeman there wasn't.

When Leonard had difficulty in pronouncing ispettore, the officer told him to call him Pepi. Then Pepi continued by making it clear to Leonard that he did not usually come himself in a common theft of this kind, but because what seemed to be an extraordinary amount of cash and travelers checks involved, over $20,000.00, he was curious as to why Leonard was carrying so much money.

The casual manner of the officer caused Leonard to be more honest than he might be ordinarily. He explained that in the past he had not handled money himself and now that it was his responsibility he wanted to be sure there was always more than enough.

Pepi had cause for disbelief, but accepted that answer for now.

His next question seemed innocent enough. "Are you in Italy for business or pleasure?"

Leonard smiled. He liked Pepi.

"Good question, but if I am to be completely honest I must say – I don't know why I am here. In fact I don't know why I *am*. Does that make sense?"

Pepe frowned. His assistant fidgeted. Leonard regretted his openness.

"Signori La France." Pepe used not the French nor the English pronunciation of Leonard's last name, rather, he slipped back into Italian mode; sounding more like La Franchay. "You have taken a simple question that is best answered in one word and have given me some kind of philosophical answer. Do you have something you are hiding?"

Leonard started to go into an even deeper philosophical answer, but swerved into a more common, yet complicated answer.

"I am not in Europe to do business, yet if I see something that interests me I might buy it. The one word answer is 'pleasure,' the modifier is 'so far'."

With a change of posture he looked right at the chief inspector and said, "Pepi, I am trying to find myself."

A smile of understanding spread across Ispettore Capo Pepi Luca's face.

"You are soooo American. Let me guess, you are either from the north east U.S. or the west coast, si?"

Leonard laughed, "Si, Io sono da Los Angeles."

"Va bene e' perfetto! So tell me Leonard," the chief inspector gravitated toward the same informality that Leonard had opened the door to when he called him 'Pepi', "how much cash and other valuables were taken?"

"I believe I had about $3,000.00 American, 4.000 Euro in cash and 15.000 Euro in Travelers checks. I have a little more than 4 million U.S. in my checking account and though they did not take my checks they did take my ATM card related to that account. The credit card had no limit as far as I know, but I can check with my office this evening."

Pepi raised one eyebrow at the amount, but putting aside his inherent mistrust that is the gift of all good policemen he asked, was there anything of value they did not take?"

"Well," said Leonard thinking aloud, "I have no jewelry and they did not take my checkbook."

"What about your passport?" asked Pepi.

"They left that."

"Can you describe them?" inquired the chief inspector.

"Hmmm," responded Leonard, "they looked like a family. Mother, father and two daughters. The girl, who was the one I believed drugged me, and was the most aggressive, was very attractive, dark, almost black eyes, black hair. She was about five-seven and slender ..."

At this point the detective interrupted to give a translation of her height from imperial to metric measurement to his assistant.

"Serabbe 170 centimeters," said the inspector and his assistant dutifully entered that into his laptop.

Leonard continued, "The father and mother were both portly."

Again the inspector interrupted, "Che cosa, portly?"

"Portly is a nice word for fat."

"Ah, si, grazia." Then the inspector changed to a different gear. "Would you mind looking at a few photos?"

Leonard did not mind, but asked if he might get them a coffee. The Inspector agreed and Leonard phoned it in.

Minutes later they were going through an online mug shot book and having little luck. The coffee arrived. The bellman served, had Leonard sign the bill and was about to leave when he suddenly stopped and said to the chief inspector, "Sei Pepi Luca?"

"Si," answered the detective with a touch of modesty.

While Leonard did not understand every word, especially at the speed the bellman was speaking, he did get an overall picture. It seemed the bellman recognized the inspector from his soccer playing days and was indeed a major fan. He said something about being heartbroken when Pepi left Hellas Verona and came to play for A.S. Roma, and, above all, he wanted to know why Pepi had forsaken Italy and had gone to play in the U.S.

Instead of answering the bellman's question the inspector asked one of him.

"If you could go to America, what would you do?"

There was a short silence and then the bellman admitted, "vorrei andare."

The bellman took his tray and went to the door, turned and said something that Leonard could clearly understand. It translated to, "But I am not a hero to so many. Ciao."

After an awkward moment they engaged themselves in their coffee and page after page of mug shots – about 15 photos per page. After turning to a new page Leonard asked Pepi's assistant to go back to the previous page. There in a photo was a man that looked somewhat familiar. Leonard asked if the photo could be enlarged and with one click the face filled the entire page.

"This man is much younger and thinner, but when was this picture taken?" asked Leonard.

Pepi's assistant manipulated the computer and a rap sheet on the fellow came up. The assistant offered, "Undici anni fa."

Leonard had mastered numbers in Italian and knew he was saying the photo was taken 11 years ago. *That would be about right,* he thought.

"This man has been in prison up until 3 months ago," said Pepi. Then he instructed his assistant to go back to the office and run a check on the man's recent whereabouts and see if there was any information on his family.

Turning his attention to Leonard he said, "Why don't you and I go to lunch. I have missed conversations with Americans. Do you have time?"

"Yes, and I would like that. Can we go somewhere that is not too touristy?"

"Si," answered Pepi, and then to his assistant he asked him to drop the two off at Sabatini's in the Trastevere district. At a most pleasant outdoor restaurant right on the Via Veneto, the two men, strangers before today, exchanged glimpses of their life.

Leonard asked Pepi, "Why did you leave the A.S. Roma for the U.S.? Was it just for money?"

"Money is very important, but there was much more. Like our fattorino, or, as you say in America, bellman, I am from Verona. When I played there for Hellas Verona it was so much fun. We were only second tier and we never won championships, but Verona is a great city and there I was a star among stars. Everyone in the city would call me by name. I felt cherished.

"I could walk through a piazza and twenty people would call my name. Coffees and even meals were gratis out of respect. The women loved me and the men were my friends.

"When I finished at the university, I was encouraged to leave home and accept an offer from A.S. Roma – a great team in the first tier who had won many trophys and championships. But there I was just another player. Hardly anyone in this big city recognized me. I made more money than in Verona, but it cost more to live in Roma.

"When an American team, the Seattle Sounders, came to me and offered five times what I was making in Rome and with the promise that I would be the face of the team, how could I resist.

"Seattle is a great city – beautiful city. The people were all very nice. The women were amazing. They loved my Italian accent and confidence. Back home I was just another freakin' Italian, but to the women there I was a king. Why, because they were crazy about the way I talked.

"However, I discovered a most unfortunate thing about America, some like soccer or as we say football, but they are not crazy for it. They think of football as American football. They don't think about soccer hardly at all. I did get to travel and see most every city in the U.S., but after two years I wanted to come home."

"Do you still play," asked Leonard, "or are you too old?"

"Why do you trouble me with such questions?" asked Pepi, a bit irritated. "Of course I still play. I also coach."

"Whom do you coach?" Leonard asked.

"Kids," answered Pepi. "Very, how do you say, ah yes, poor – kids. In Verona my family was not rich, and I could never have gone to university without soccer. In Roma the very poor are much poorer than we were."

It was easy to tell that the subject was one that Pepi was passionate about.

"The problema," moaned Pepi "is that in the neighborhood these kids live in there is no public soccer field that is close. These kids have no way of getting to the soccer field that we can use for free. There is a field, a good one, in their neighborhood, but it is private. Outside people can schedule, but it is 7.000 Euro a year.

"I have some savings, but do you have any idea what it costs to live a decent life in Roma? I tell you. 200.000 Euro. I don't live that well, but I still have to use savings sometimes if I want something nice."

"What is the name of this club and can you get some sponsors to pay for that?" inquired Leonard.

"Ahh, Piccolo Leone is the name – the little lions. In truth, I was not that big a soccer star in Roma. The big stars can get that money easy. And besides – the ones here who do know me think I sold out to America for money," answered Pepi.

"How did you go from being a soccer star to being a policeman?"

"My university focus was in, what you call in America, Criminal Justice. When I tried to get a position in Verona I found that the municipal police were only involved in traffic and the like. So at the next level, Polizia Stato, I could not find an opening in Verona. The only choices with a future were Roma and Napoli. I am sorry, but the people from Napoli are crazy. I chose Roma and here I am."

"Where would you rather be?" inquired Leonard.

"In Verona. If you ever go there you will know. In fact, if you have no itinerary, you should do this. On the way to Verona go through Siena and Firenze. Two magnificent cities. Spend only a day or two in each, then on to Verona. Spend a week, no better, spend at least two weeks. It is not that there is so much to do there, though there is a lot, it is that it is a good-sized city that feels like a small town, and it will capture your heart.

"In Roma things are bigger. Like the Coliseum here is very big, but it is a ruin. In Verona, in the summer they still use the Arena, almost every night in the summer. There is great opera there. When they do Aida, they have elephants and camels on the stage. When they bring in some super good rock and roll bands, they always choose the ones who are melodious. You can hear it echo all throughout the city, it is fantastico!"

The food was excellent and they enjoyed each other's company. Pepi promised he would put a rush on their investigation, but asked Leonard not to leave town for a couple of days.

Two days later Pepi called Leonard and asked him to come to the station and identify the suspects. He would send a car for Leonard.

It was them. When they saw Leonard it did not take long for them to tearfully confess. They had Leonard's ATM and credit card on them, plus a large amount of dollars and Euro. That would be held for evidence until after the trial. Leonard was fine with that.

Sam Levine, back in the office, had arranged for the issuance of new cards, a new checking account number along with new checks, and 15.000 Euro in travelers checks.

"What will happen to them?" asked Leonard.

The mother and younger daughter will probably spend six months. The girl who drugged you will get around five years. The father will not be back – he is a career criminal."

Leonard felt sad for them, but he knew justice must be served. He thanked Pepi and his team.

"Will you be leaving Roma now?" inquired Pepi.

"Si."

"Where will you go to find yourself next il mio amico?"

"I will find myself in Verona," Leonard said, with a hopeful smile. "And you, Pepi, will find yourself and your Piccolo Leone soccer club on that nice field for the next five years, if you will accept this check. Oh – it's not a bribe – it is made out to the football club."

Chapter 23

IF IT'S GOOD ENOUGH FOR ROMEO AND JULIET ...

THE DAYS SPENT IN SIENNA AND THEN FIrenze were wonderful. It did get a bit rainy and cold the first day in Florence, but even sunny Italy has its winter.

Stepping off of the train in Verona, the first thing Leonard noticed were the clouds. They were not fearsome, but they were awesome. He set his bags down and took a photo with his phone just as a clearing allowed the sun to send a shaft of light that illuminated the square in front of the station where he was standing.

Leonard did not have much faith in signs, but could not help but feel a bit cheerful about being in Verona. His mother had read Shakespeare's *Romeo and Juliet* to him when he was around 10 years old. He could tell that it had stirred her. He still could feel it now. Verona was the city where the *Romeo and Juliet* story takes place. The balcony is still there – or so they say.

As the taxi driver took his bags and placed them in the trunk, he asked his passenger "Dove?"

In Italian Leonard said, "I don't really know." Then he laughed. "Do you know a small hotel, one that has a kitchen?"

"Si!" exclaimed the cabdriver, suddenly animated. "Arena House Verona." Before Leonard could ask another question the driver, who spoke decent English, rattled off a list of reasons why a traveler would have to be a fool not to stay there.

Leonard had it right. The guy definitely had a relative involved in some way. However, as it turned out, the place was perfect. The kitchen was large and the owners, Andrea and Mayumi, anticipated a lot of little things that most large places do not have the flexibility to provide. Stuff for breakfast and snacks already populated the cabinets and a map that showed the markets in the area with notes of recommendation.

The train ride from Florence was not particularly long or tiring and Leonard had heard such raves about Verona he had to see for himself.

One of the reasons that Italians and other European peoples are not obese is because they walk a great deal. Leonard was more and more into walking and or running; he liked those endorphins.

The first item on his agenda was to walk to Piazza Bra and see the Roman Arena. Pepi had lavished such praise that not to go would indicate a complete absence of curiosity.

The directions given by the desk clerk were both simple and confusing. After simple directions to the nearby bridge called Ponte Nuovo, the clerk then instructed Leonard to, "Firsta, go across the bridgea. You wanna taka Via Nizza, buta don't geta confused, the street is gonna changea names. Firsta to Via Stella, and thena change names again to … never minda – justa go straita and you will runa right into it."

Florence is an excellent example of Renaissance architecture. Verona, like Sienna, is of the Medieval period. Both forms of architecture are magnificent, and through great effort have been remarkably well preserved. Most tourists probably prefer Florence, but Leonard was quickly enamored with Verona.

Like Vernazza, he felt at home here almost immediately.

By the time he reached Piazza Bra he also felt a bit hungry. On this warm and sunny winter's day he found himself attracted to a sidewalk cafe that was open and taking advantage of the weather.

Italian menus were becoming easier to read for Leonard, yet the dishes here were different than the ones he had become accustomed to in Vernazza, Rome and to some degree even Sienna and Florence.

As he struggled with his order, at a nearby table a petite and comely woman, probably slightly older than himself, found his flawed effort amusing. Leonard smiled and shrugged his shoulders. His shrug gave her another reason for amusement.

The Buyer

The waiter brought Leonard some fresh bread and a dish of warm olive oil with garlic, parsley and red pepper flakes. On the same pass the waiter brought the main course for the amused woman.

Leonard dug right into taking the bread and dipping it into the fragrant, spicy oil. He found it really pleasing to his palate.

He could not help but notice that as heartily as he attacked his food his neighbor was merely pushing hers around with her fork. She looked sad, but Leonard kept on eating, and, before he knew it, his main course of Risotto e Agnello terra con Fungi (a rice dish with ground lamb and mushrooms) was put before him. Now he got down to some serious eating and enjoying every bite.

He was paying attention to nothing but his flavorful food when a cacophony exploded just a few feet away. It was the amused woman. Not so amused now as she lay crumpled like a thrown-away note. Leonard being so close was the first to her side. She opened her eyes and looked vacantly about.

"Do you speak English?" asked Leonard, trying to find out what was wrong.

"My English," said the woman with a most pronounced British accent, "is certainly better than your Northern Italian." She then gave a weak smile and attempted to sit up. It was obvious she needed assistance. Leonard gathered her protectively and held her in a semi-upright position.

The waiter and the manager arrived simultaneously. They were not as hyper as the Italians he had seen in Rome, but were nonetheless short on answers as to what to do.

The manager offered to call an ambulance.

The woman, gaining strength, waived off the invitation saying, "I have a condition and this is not unusual. I will be fine."

Leonard helped her to her feet.

"I will see you home," said Leonard with authority.

Again she waived of the offer.

"It won't be necessary."

Looking at her, pale and shaking, Leonard took control. "I have no ulterior motive, ma'am, and I will see you home."

The waiter started to say something about the bill and Leonard gave him a 50 Euro note. Both he and the woman had ordered sparingly and that amount would more than cover their combined bill and provide a generous tip.

The manager had, at Leonard's request, summoned a cab. Leonard assisted her into the vehicle.

"Dove?" asked the driver. She gave him an address.

"May I ask what caused you to fall?"

"O really, it is nothing of immediate concern. I simply do not have an appetite and I get weak." She said guardedly.

"Oh," said Leonard. "Do you not like Italian food?"

"Typically I do, but right now it seems to be too heavy and the smells that I usually love are making me nauseous."

Always a problem solver, Leonard had a question. "What do you think would be appetizing to you?"

Almost perturbed the woman sighed, "I don't really know. Perhaps some chicken broth with a few vegetables. The Italians make wonderful soup, but it is all so rich to me right now."

Though he did not recognize the name of the street she had given the driver, it turned out to be very near to where he was staying. As he walked her to her door, over her protestations, he asked a strange question. "Do you have a kitchen?"

"No," she said. "This is a pensione. They serve a breakfast and an afternoon tea, but I have no kitchen. If I did I would try some of that broth I described," she weakly joked.

"My name is Leonard LaFrance. I am staying about one block from here and I have a kitchen. I am not yet a great cook, but I can do broth with vegetables. I would be honored if I could prepare some for your lunch tomorrow."

"Oh no, Mr. La France, it is so very nice of you to offer, but I will be fine. And, by the way, my name is Samantha Bradford. You have been so kind. Thank you."

Leonard was not through. He could see this person needed someone to intervene. "Here is what I will do. Tomorrow, I will rise early, as usual. I will find a place that sells very fresh and organic chicken. I will bring it home and make a broth of it and I will knock on your door at precisely 12 noon. If you are willing, you will have broth with me, and, if not, then I suppose I will be eating broth for a couple of days. Good night Samantha Bradley."

Another faint smile and "Thank you again, Mr. La France" and he was on his way home and asking himself, "Now why did I do that?"

AT 6 PM, his time, Leonard called Dr. Lilly and told her where he was. She seemed glad to hear from him and she suggested he call her over the weekend so that they might have a more leisurely conversation. Leonard liked that invitation a lot.

Early morning found Leonard at one of the shops recommended by the hotel. According to the recommendation sheet this one was noted for excellent fowl, and he bought one large chicken. He then went across to a vegetable market, picked up a small onion, a clove of garlic, a small amount of broccoli and some spinach; all fresh picked and full of life.

There was already salt and pepper at his apartment per the courtesy of the hotel, but he stopped into a spice shop and picked up some ground white pepper.

At the J'adore culinary school Leonard had attended in Paris, broth was Basic 101 stuff. Still, he was nervous. Leonard was lucky, the batch turned out even better than he had hoped.

He was nearly dancing around the kitchen. "Why," he asked himself, "do I feel so excited? Sure she was pretty, but not nearly as pretty as either Sharon or Angelica. She was not at all personable. She was not youthful. She did absolutely nothing to encourage me, and on top of all that she is sick. Very sick."

Then Leonard knew. He had answered his own question. He had to provide her with more than a passing word or writing someone a check. Not for her, but for himself.

He sensed she had little or no family support. If he was wrong, then there was not much he could do for her. If, however, his hunch was right, this woman was alone in the loneliest place known to man; at death's door.

Leonard was once again surprised to find he had so much to learn that most 'normal kids' learn while growing up. One important thing they learn is that sometimes you are a giver and sometimes you are a receiver. Either way, it is not always pleasurable, it is not always kind.

Leonard had never known – never learned. Perhaps that is why Dr. Lilly had suggested he try it.

So now, he told himself, "If I want a shallow life I don't need to know. If I want every drop of life there is to be had, I believe I will need to know.

"She may be the one who helps me understand how important it is to be a person capable of giving myself to the caring of one who has nothing to offer and who has no hope."

What did I just say? thought Leonard. *I mean, really, where did I come up with that?*

Yet, he kept up his momentum as he went downstairs and got in the taxi. When they reached Samantha Bradford's hotel, Leonard had the driver wait while he went to knock, as promised, on the door of Samantha Bradley.

If it were possible, the diminutive woman looked even smaller today than she had when he'd brought her home.

"I have come to invite you to broth with me."

She had not yet dressed for the day. The look in her eyes said thank you, but she was not up to it. Then her voice simply said, "No."

Leonard was not to be so easily dissuaded.

"Okay, wait here and I will bring it to you."

She stood there in a state of non-comprehension and then slipped noiselessly to the floor. Leonard saw a blanket on the couch. He grabbed it and quickly wrapped Samantha in it. As he lifted her the wig she was wearing fell off and there was not a hair on her head. Somehow, he managed to pick up the wig, shove it in his pocket and then close the door.

Even as thin and light as she was, Leonard was out of breath and his muscles were very tired by the time he reached the taxi. The driver looked shocked, but quickly regained his composure and opened the rear door.

"Emergenza ospedale," wheezed Leonard.

"Si," said the driver, and then in near perfect English said "University Hospital of Verona is just across the river and is very good."

"Buono. Andiamo," said Leonard as he began to recover.

The reception area was not crowded and a young resident physician saw her right away.

Leonard sat and paced for over an hour and then was called to the recovery room by a nurse. The young physician asked Leonard what his relationship to her was. Leonard already knew the answer to that. "I am her caretaker."

The resident then began by telling Leonard, in a combination of English and Italian that Señora Bradley had given permission to discuss her condition with Leonard.

"As you know," began the doctor, "She has terminal cancer. She has a little time, ma no troppo." He then went on to describe today's problem, "Oggi il problema es disidratati – or how do you say – dehydrated. You may take her home inna bout uno ora - one hour. She also needs nourishmenta. Buona fortuna," the resident added as he went on with his busy schedule.

Entering the room where Samantha lay, with an IV fluids running in her arm, Leonard could already see color returning to her face. Samantha smiled weakly, and, before any other conversation could take place, she asked in a small voice, "Would you happen to know where my wig is?"

Reaching into his pocket he brought forth an item that looked like a very small dog. He assessed which end was the front and then slid it on her head.

"Thank you. I feel ever so much more presentable." They both smiled.

A serious look came over her face. "Who are you, Mr. La France, and why are you here? And why are you doing this?"

Leonard, honest as usual, said, "I don't know why I am here exactly – the only thing I do know is that I am here for the duration."

They both knew the finite meaning of 'duration.'

"But why would you take such a stand for a total stranger?"

He sat on the edge of her bed and took the hand that was not hooked up to the saline solution and said, "Above all, I believe, we need to be completely open and honest with each other."

Leonard got a bit more comfortable on the edge of the narrow bed and continued.

"The reason I am here to take care of you is as much for me as it is for you. You are going to need someone to stay with you. Do you have anyone in your life who is willing and or able to do that?"

Closing her eyes, Samantha quietly said, "No, I do not." She started to inquire about his gain, but Leonard put one finger to his lips in the international sign for quiet.

"For me it is about learning not just to buy with dollars, but to learn the depths of life by giving of myself. I am almost completely ignorant of such things. You have looked at life's end and have had to face things that I can learn from. Will you teach me what you know in exchange for what I can give?"

Samantha did not answer. Instead, she closed her eyes, and Leonard could almost see her going to some distant place. After a few minutes she opened her eyes, which were brimming with tears.

"You cannot possibly know this, but I have been praying for someone to come and see me through this. I do not know how I could face it alone.

"I have had many variations on this prayer. They have ranged from coming across a crusty old Nun to having a handsome young prince to ride in, marry me and make everything right. Looking at you I see God has sent me my handsome, young prince."

"Samantha, I would like for you to move in with me. There is a foldout bed in the living room for me and you can have the bedroom."

"I don't know," she answered. "I am not one who believes in sex without marriage."

"Hmmm," he said. "Honestly I hadn't thought about that at all. I was focused on being close so I could keep a watchful eye on you."

"Now Leonard, you are a beautiful man. I know I look a fright right now, but all of my life, if you will forgive my lack of modesty – you did say we must be honest – I have always been among the very pretty."

"No," admitted Leonard, "I still find you beautiful and if you had energy I can see where temptation would be very likely. I will give you my word that nothing sexual will be initiated by me. Will you allow me to collect your things and bring them to my room?"

"Please, please, do not disappoint me on this matter."

"I won't."

"You will," asked Samantha, "forgive me if I am more grateful to God than to you, for He has sent you. However, I do not believe you will ever be in doubt as to my gratitude to you. And, of course, I will teach you whatever I may have learned."

Both were quiet.

"Can we go home now?" she asked.

"I'll go see."

Chapter 24

WHOLLY IN

WHEN LEONARD HAD FIRST CHECKED INTO the apartment at the Verona Arena House he had selected the Romeo and Juliette suite as a tribute to his mother.

The apartment was simple, but it had three things Leonard really liked. First, there was a nice kitchen. Then, there was a place in the living room where the 1200-year-old rock of the original building was exposed and ensconced in a frame of plaster; treating the ancient wall like a piece of art. And there was a balcony. What would Romeo and Juliette do without a balcony?

Now was not the time for a balcony. He simply helped the fragile Samantha into the apartment and fed her some of his freshly made broth.

For the first two days Samantha slept. Awakening only to take liquid nourishment, which more often than not was regurgitated, and for trips to the bathroom.

She then became disoriented, had a very dry mouth and skin. Leonard knew very little about health issues or medicine, but the hospital had warned him to look out for dehydration, and these were the signs.

Samantha was utterly exhausted, and, with that, Leonard had the front desk summon a taxi, and he took her back to the hospital for another round of hydration.

As often happens with medical residents, the same doctor was still on duty. Leonard asked him what he could do, as his ward could not keep anything down and had absolutely no appetite.

The young doctor pulled him aside and out of range of anyone's hearing.

"This is often the case after a tough round of chemo. She must get past this stage. I know what will help, but I cannot tell you – it is against the law in Italy."

After saying this, the doctor just looked at Leonard.

Leonard waited for him to go on, but the doctor remained silent.

"Please tell me how to help her."

"I cannot. If it was someone I loved I would get them marijuana, but I cannot tell you that. I must go."

And so he did.

After the hydration treatment was complete, and he had her back in the apartment, he got on the Internet and found evidence that the young doc knew of what he spoke. Medical Marijuana could help with nausea, but Leonard was helpless as to where to find some of the illegal plant.

If he were in L.A. he could go down to the area in Compton where Theo was doing their makeover and he was sure he could find it. But it would be dangerous to try to find and buy some in a foreign country. He did not want to get arrested.

Then it hit him. Ispettore Capo Pepi Luca! Who would know more about where to get an illegal substance than a policeman? Leonard fished the inspector's card from his backpack and dialed the number.

The phone rang but once and a formal voice said, "Ispettore Capo Luca."

"Pepi," it was evident that Leonard was happy to reach his police friend. "I need a favor, but I need to make sure our call is private."

"Sure," was the prompt response. "Give me your number to where I can phone."

After giving Pepe the number Leonard hung up. A few minutes later Leonard's phone rang and it was Pepi. A brief, but comprehensive description of his situation was followed by, "please, Pepi, help me find marijuana in Verona."

"Why do you ask these things of me?" muttered Pepi.

"Am I asking too much?"

"Not at all, my father always used that expression and I use it whenever I can, but what you ask is easy. Dangerous for both of us, but easy."

Pepi continued. "The safest way is to go to Turin; they have allowed it openly there – also in Roma and a few other places it is not too strict, but in Turin the Council has made it official. It is not very far from Verona to Turin."

"She could not handle a trip like that, and I don't want to leave her alone," responded Leonard.

"Oh, why do you ask these things of me?"

"Stop it." said Leonard.

"I know, I know, I said it for fun. Okay, my friend, you are a good man to help this woman – or she is very beautiful."

"Aspetta - uno momento, you almosta hada me fooled. You want the marijuana to seduce her, is true, no?"

"No, mio amico, I do not want to seduce her. I want to help her."

"But Leonard, she is a stranger, you are trying to find yourself, why do you stop to do this?"

"You are right. It is not like me. I wonder about it myself. Maybe, Pepi, by helping someone that cannot give me anything in return, I might just find myself faster."

"Va bene – either way I will help you. I will give you a phone number of a boyhood friend. Give me 10 minutes to talk to him first. I will call you back, let it ring only once, and then hang up and it will be okay to call him."

"Thank you, Pepi, I very much appreciate it."

The man Pepi had referred him to lived not far from the university. His home was modest, but well appointed. Not unlike someone who had money, but did not want to display wealth. His name was Roccia – the "Rock" in English. *The name fits*, thought Leonard, as the man had a very solid appearance.

"Pepi said you were okay and that I should treat you well," said Roccia as he welcomed his guest.

"Thank you for seeing me," said Leonard, "and may I say you speak English like someone from New York."

"That is because my father taught at Columbia University, and New York is where I spent a lot of time as I grew up."

"Small world," quipped Leonard. "Did Pepi explain my predicament?"

"Yes, and I am very familiar with the nausea problems that accompany cancer. Pot was used as a medicine thousands of years ago and it still does things for people like your friend, better than anything else. The biggest problem with it as a medicine is that it has to be heated to release the components that make it work. Smoking it is the easiest way, but there are over a thousand toxins in pot that make that an unattractive option."

Roccia offered Leonard a chair and inquired as to Leonard's interest in a coffee.

"I don't want to be gone for too long. She is very weak," responded Leonard. "You mention option. I'm sure she would not smoke anything, is there more than one way to ingest it?"

"Oh yeah, but for someone in her condition here is what I would do. There is a product called Marijuana wax. You set it in a bowl, put a towel over your head to catch the vapors, light it and breath deeply. Two minutes later your world changes, your nausea is gone and there is a definite increase in appetite."

"Do you have this wax?"

"Yes, and I recommend it to start with. You could also use a vaporizer, but it is a little more complicated."

"I'll go for the simplest way, but you used the phrase, 'at first'. What do you mean by that?"

"When her nausea passes to the point she can hold food down, she should advance to Cannabutter."

"Okay, now you are confusing me, Roccia."

"Not intentionally. I'll give you the recipe, it's simple to make. Once you have made the Cannabutter, just put a half of teaspoon of it on a cracker. Start with that amount and increase it if it is not enough to increase her appetite. It takes about an hour to reach its max, and it will sneak up on you."

"This is amazing, how do you know so much about pot and cancer?"

"Occupational side benefit," answered Roccia. "I managed a medical marijuana facility in LA and I saw a lot of it."

"It is probably not good of me to ask too many personal questions in a situation like this, but may I ask how you decided to make this your business?" inquired Leonard.

"If Pepi says you are okay – you are okay. However, this is not my business. I am actually a computer-programing consultant. I generally work from home.

"I don't even smoke that much – once or twice a week when I have no other business. Everyone is different, but for me the motto is 'If I don't abuse – I can use.' Yes, I have a few friends who are customers, but I am more of a connoisseur of Cannabis, like my father was with wine. In our circle when we come across something of particular interest we share it."

NOTHING much had changed back at the apartment. Samantha was still sleeping. He woke her and gently told her of his research and the help an unnamed individual had given him. Samantha was very weak, but her morals were still strong and she said no.

Without being pushy he explained this was not for recreational purposes, but that it was purely medicinal.

"That sounds surprisingly like 'me dear old dad'," she said with her British accent a bit exaggerated, "just before he took another nip from his bottle. He handled it okay, but I've seen many marriages and childhoods destroyed by such addictions."

Leonard was patient; she finally said, "yes."

Leonard prepared the small bowl with a portion of the wax. He had her sit up and draped the towel over her head as instructed and inhale the vapors coming off the burning wax.

Poor Samantha was weak and extremely tired and so she curled up on Leonard's lap and went to sleep. Leonard waited for an hour. While waiting he studied this person he did not know, but to whom he had committed an uncertain amount of time. She was very lovely.

There was no hair to frame her face. However, the more he studied the fine cheek bones, long lashes that had defied the chemo, deepset eyes, refined jawbone and slender neck, the more beauty he saw.

At one hour and five minutes he woke her. She appeared to be no different than the way he had seen her for the past two days. She was obviously disoriented.

Leonard helped her to her feet. He walked her to the small table and put her in a chair. Roccia had suggested some high-protein/ high-calorie supplement which Leonard now poured for her.

Samantha looked at the glass and then at Leonard. Then she looked at the glass again and for no apparent reason began to laugh. She then, as she continued to laugh, felt a need to explain her laughter and chose to point at the glass as if she could make Leonard, just by looking at the glass, also understand what was so funny. Alas it was all in vain.

Roccia had made Leonard aware that this behavior could be expected, but the dealer could not have prepared Leonard for the joy he would feel in seeing his ward giggle and squirm.

It was not instantaneous, but together they got all of the drink into her shrunken belly. Leonard saw how drowsy she was and walked her back to her bed.

She slept and did not get nauseous.

Leonard took the recipe for Cannabutter and began the multi-hour process. When completed he put it in the refrigerator to cool.

Samantha slept.

Chapter 25

VERY DAY FOR THE NEXT FOUR DAYS SAmantha was treated with the wax and the Cannabutter. The nausea did not return, but her appetite surely did and Leonard fed it with the most nutritious foods he could find.

Her body was naturally small and she had become emaciated. Now Samantha became stronger and stronger and stronger. She had emerging energy that turned her pale and sickly complexion into a vibrant and healthy one. Both Samantha and Leonard found their sexual attraction taking a firmer hold.

Wanting above all things to keep his word, when a moment of intimacy outside of the boundaries they had agreed to started to develop, it was Leonard who applied the brakes.

"You, young lady, need to get dressed," he said in a fatherly way. "We are going out to see Verona."

Both disappointment and elation struck Samantha simultaneously. She tamped down her emerging passion and with the heart made light as only a deep trust can, she readied herself for the outing.

They walked the cobbled streets of Verona for only a short while. The winter air held a cold moisture and, though warmly dressed, her still fragile body could not maintain warmth. Her energy did not last long. Samantha quickly looked wane and worn. Leonard hailed a passing taxi, and they went back to Arena House where he prepared a snack of crackers, Cannabutter and some more of his homemade broth.

The marijuana in the Cannabutter was an hour in coming, but when it hit, Samantha Bradford soon had three over-arching needs. One was best defined as the 'munchies'. The second best defined as 'thirsty' and the third was 'chatty.'

He decided to take advantage of her chatty drive by asking about her life. She graciously complied, hardly stopping to breathe. It was as if she had been waiting for years for someone to ask her about her life.

"Well, I was born to an academic mother, she was an archeologist, and an entrepreneurial father. They met when she was giving a lecture in order to raise money for her next project. My father was there with a woman he was dating at the time who literally had to drag him to the event. However, in short order he was totally taken by my mother.

"After her talk he approached the podium and handed her his card and said, 'I would like to contribute, would you please call me?'

"Well she did call, they got together and he did contribute a sizable amount of money to her effort. Then he asked her to dinner and swept her away."

Leonard laughed.

"Do you think that is so funny?" snapped a slightly paranoid Samantha.

"Uh, er, no, it just reminded me of a similar thing I did once – but it did not have a happy ending as it appears yours did."

Samantha continued, "Though my mother was passionate about working out in the far-off places where the interesting digs were located, my father proposed by mail and she accepted.

"She taught at Oxford and later, to make it easier on my father, she moved into London and taught in a much less prestigious school in the city. After I came along it dashed her thoughts of a career as a field archeologist, and she settled in to raise me. I don't think she ever forgave me. Being the only child of a frustrated academic is not as easy as it sounds."

Samantha was wound up and demonstrating a dramatic flair Leonard had not seen before.

"Excellent grades were not only expected, they were demanded. By the time I was ready for university I sailed right into Oxford.

"My father, on the other hand, was no academic – he was strictly business. He inherited a very small, but highly profitable store on the West End. By the time I was born he had seven such stores, and by the time he had to sell out for health reasons he had 5 more small stores and four large stores, two in London, one in Brussels and one in Amsterdam, for a total of 16.

"Funny though," mused Samantha, "he never sold any of his stores until he had no choice because of health."

Leonard laughed again.

Again, Samantha flared up. "And why do you think that funny?"

"I don't," said Leonard with a quiet smile. "Your father reminds me of my father."

After a brief bit of silence Samantha spoke again.

"His illness was the same cursed disease I have and our lives will be of similar length." Samantha grew grim and quiet, but only for a moment.

"He held on to his business for two years longer than he should have, and it lost quite a bit of value due to poor management. Still in all he left my mother and I well off."

Samantha stopped short as she looked at Leonard with suspicion. Everyone from her parents to her now-deceased husband had warned her to beware of fortune hunters. She decided, in her Marijuana haze, to be shrewd and therefore asked, "Leonard, do you have any money of your own?"

"I have some," he answered.

Samantha pressed on, "Would I be rude if I asked you to tell me how much?"

Admittedly, this question took Leonard aback. However, in a flash it came to him that Samantha had some money, and he was offering unending care with no obvious motivation for his doing so – he realized she wondered if he was after her money. At the same time, he felt he needed to be both honest and protective of himself.

Reaching into his back pocket he pulled out his checkbook. Leonard showed her the balance. Even though he did not disclose all of his holdings, he did reveal enough to win.

"Oh my, forgive me," said a humbled Samantha.

"I understand," replied Leonard. "One can't be too careful. Please go on with your story."

"Thank, you Leonard," offered Samantha. "Okay, where was I?"

"You had just said that you got into Oxford."

Snapping back into the conversation Samantha continued.

"I hope you don't see this as boring, but I have always been interested in history, and it would be difficult to find any university that is richer in the antiquities of this world than Oxford.

"As I was finishing my third year, Rebecca, my best chum, came and asked me to accompany her to the cricket field so she might come to the attention of a certain boy. I did not care to go. I know nothing of cricket and had no desire to change that, but when your best friend asks a favor – what is one to do?

"Although cricket is quite popular, I find it boring. The game goes on and on. If it is a test match it goes on for five days. The only saving grace was that the bowler, I think you call him a pitcher in your baseball, was quite cute.

"I was about to lose my mind in boredom when the game was called because of darkness. The boy Rebecca came to see went over to the bowler and congratulated him on an excellent game, then both of them walked in our direction.

"I can tell you that I went from bored to enthralled as the bowler came closer. The four of us decided to go to the pub, and, after that, Cecil, the bowler, and I were quite inseparable."

With a look of a fond remembrance in her eyes she went on with her story.

"Cecil, like me, was also a student of history, except he was doing post-graduate work with an eye on joining the Foreign Service. It was the proper thing for him to do. He was born a diplomat.

"Against my parents wishes, they did not want me globetrotting, we were married. Our first post was Riyadh, in Saudi Arabia. Very luxurious, but it was all about oil, tribal affairs and we had little in common with the people. We were only there for eight months then we were off to, of all places, Montevideo, Uruguay. Which, incidentally, became our standard for the most pleasant weather.

"Cecil had a remarkable facility for languages. In addition to English and French he was fluent in Spanish, Italian and even quite good in Arabic. Over the years he was able to employ them all. Our last post was in Tripoli, Libya. That is where Cecil had a massive heart attack and then a stroke. He died there. He is buried there."

Her voice grew softer. "It was not until his illness and passing that I realized I had no home. We had always been home to each other and now my home was gone. I considered going back to England, if for no other reason than to have more religious freedom, but I did not have enough motivation to do much of anything. So I simply stayed in Libya. For over two years I grieved and did little else.

"I have had annual physicals since I was forty, but somehow they missed my cancer until it had metastasized. I went back to London, I went to Mayo in the states, hell, I even went to Berlin, and I still don't like the Germans. They all said the same thing. Avoid this and that and enjoy every day.

"Well, as it turns out, the most enjoyable thing I have ever done was to holiday for a fortnight in Verona, Italy. That is why I chose to die here. It is sad to come to the end when one has no attachments, no family, not even a church family. Only acquaintances.

"Now, Mr. Leonard LaFrance, here you show up. Imagine that. We have not discussed your view of God or Christ or the like, all of which are core to my life. Nor have we discussed your story, but I'm afraid I've worn myself out. Will you tell me later?"

Leonard said nothing. He picked Samantha up from the couch and held her in his arms like a baby. He walked the length of the room and then back again.

She nestled her head securely into his shoulder as Leonard started to hum a non-distinct tune. She seemed as light as a marshmallow in his arms as he paced the floor and he did not tire. It was while he laid her in her bed and brought the covers up around her that he knew he was finding a facet of love that was deeper than any he had known.

AND SO ... each new day continued ... Leonard rising before dawn as had always been his practice. Samantha was not a morning person,

193

but she would arise for a while as a gesture of affection and respect and then fold back into bed for a good nap while Leonard took care of business.

He had been away from the environs of Los Angeles for 7 months, but had kept contact with the happenings through concise e-mails from Leon Harding from Legal, Samuel Levine from Finance and Theo for an overview.

The Advantage Corporation was, much to Leonard's delight, running as designed. He had no alternative than to acknowledge his father's business acumen even as he disdained the man as a man, and especially as a father and most especially as a husband.

Thanks to the communication skills of his staff, the catch-up process was efficient. There was rarely a hiccup. The holdings and profit margins were increasing due in large part to the new blood of Theo's leadership. Leonard was reminded of the surge in growth when he took the reins from his father. Even the skilled and talented can grow a bit jaded and then weary.

Leonard wisely told his key people what he expected, took his hands off and then inspected what he expected. It took very little of his time, rarely over a half hour a day.

He had made some accommodations to his new schedule. Instead of showering and dressing for the day as a first measure, he ran, then he read his emails, he had 3 papers delivered and he always had a good book on hand. By the time he had done all this and showered, Samantha was stretching and sitting up. He brought her tea and a cracker with Cannabutter.

She was slow to get moving. Even in her morning stupor, enhanced no doubt by the continuous ingestion of Cannabis, Leonard found her adorable. Staggering a bit as she began her day, giving weak and goofy smiles each time she passed him, until her cocoon of sleep gave way to an intense alertness. Samantha was bald as billiard no more. Her scalp was starting to be covered by fine, silver colored fuzz. No eyebrows yet, but her overall recovery from the chemo held promise that these too would be restored.

On warm and sunny days they would explore the shops, the back streets and small piazzas. Inevitably, they would wind up along the

Adige River. From the pontes, or bridges as we call them, the wide stream that was born in the Tyrolean Alps and its waters competed for the attention of the eye with stone walls, castles, and other ancient buildings – all properly interspersed, of course, with tall Italian Juniper and other vegetation that stood the rigors of winter.

Samantha continued to grow stronger. They continued to grow closer as only two lost souls finding perfect friendship can. There was never a word of criticism from either toward the other. He encouraged her to heal; she encouraged him out of affection. The only source of tension was sexual. They chose to sublimate that desire to the oath of chastity, but it was becoming ever so much more difficult.

In April an amazing spectacle took place. Verona, a small city of about 250,000 people exploded, and the population instantly grew by more than a million and a half people. Every hotel room, every pension, every B & B and many private homes absorbed the throng.

While this was a form of excitement, it also was a major inconvenience. Until Leonard and Samantha learned that the commotion was brought about by VinItaly, probably the most important wine festival in the world. Then they both wanted to play.

Roccia filled them in on the details of VinItaly when they went to replenish their supply of cannabis. Of course Leonard phoned ahead and asked if he could bring Samantha. She appreciated Roccia's contribution and wanted to meet him.

"By all means," responded his supplier.

Again Roccia was gracious. He complimented Samantha on her healthy look and then her beauty. So Italian.

Samantha made the comment that the city was busting its seams with all of the people in for VinItaly. "We would like to go," said Samantha. "Is it difficult to get in?"

"No, no, you must simply buy a ticket. Perhaps about 50 Euro, but …" said Roccia, looking at Samantha, "how are you feeling?"

"So much better, thank you."

"Yes, I am sure that is true," said Roccia, "but you must understand that going to VinItaly is like running a marathon on the most crowded avenue even as you consume a great deal of wine. I do not believe it is in your best interest … unless," he paused.

"Please go on," pleaded Samantha. "Unless what?"

Roccia seemed hesitant, but went ahead with his thought. "Unless you go today."

"And," asked Leonard, "why is today so different?"

"Today," explained Roccia, "is for the trade only. The wine makers come with their best, the buyers come from all over the world, importers, hotels, fine restaurants, you name it, they are all here. So still it is crowded, but not so much as when the public comes. The problem is you are not in the wine business."

Roccia cradled his chin on his hand and thought, then smiled. "My cousin Giuseppe makes great wine, he frequently attends VinItaly, and he may be able to get you in."

Thanks to the introduction Leonard and Samantha were treated like insiders. Giuseppe had lost his mother to cancer the year before, and he took it upon himself to have his daughter Alessandra escort them for the day.

The kindest and most honest assessment of the couple would be to say they got carried away. They had so much fun and drank so much wine, that the moment they arrived back at Arena House Samantha fell to her knees before the toilet and stayed there for over an hour.

Leonard used the kitchen sink.

The next morning found them back in the emergency room to get poor Samantha hydrated once again. After that experience Leonard was even more protective of Samantha. A week later she was stronger than ever. They were more sexually excited than ever. Something had to give.

That morning, during his run, Leonard made a decision. During the day he weighed that decision from every possible angle.

AT 6 PM Verona time he called Dr. Lilly and told her of his decision. She was unhappy with it and asked him, quite strongly, not to do it. "There is much to be considered, Leonard. Your lawyer will want you to have a Pre-nup. She may live another 30 years." The good doctor's list of reasons went on and on. Leonard listened carefully to all she had to say, as he always did. This time not even Lillian could persuade

Leonard to change his mind.

On his run the next morning he made sure to take his wallet. Leonard charted his run to include a small jewelry store he had often passed. After a consultation with a very sensitive jeweler he purchased an engagement ring and a simple band. Both were of white gold.

Samantha was the strongest she had been since their meeting. Now she loved to walk the city and jumped at Leonard's invitation to go to the restaurant in the Piazza Bra where they had first met.

The waiter was the same one who had been on hand when they met. Due to the trauma of that day he remembered them. Seeing them together, obviously very attracted to each other, he could not help but ask, in Italian.

"Did you know each other before that day?"

It was Leonard who spoke first. "No, we met right on the ground next to this table," he said with a smile. The waiter smiled even more and in less than a minute he was back with the manager. The couple could see the waiter excitedly telling his boss of the romantic miracle.

They considered ordering a modest bottle of a local Valpolicella from a wine maker by the name of Guiseppe Lonardi, but the manager took charge. In his best English he said,

"No, no no. The Valpolicella is a very gooda wine, and Giuseppe Lonardi makes the besta, but for this occasion you need Valpolicella's Big Brother – also made by Giuseppe. You want Amarone, for it is love in a bottle."

It was a wonderful wine and a wonderful meal. This time, Samantha did not push the food around on her plate. Instead, she ate each morsel like a child at a picnic.

They headed home. It had been a warm day and was now getting chilly. As they approached the Adige River, with lights dancing all over the water, Samantha sighed. She started to ask herself why must she die. However, before her lip could tremble she remembered that she was British. She steeled herself, took a deep breath, looked out over the fairyland that lay before them and decided to just be grateful.

On cue Leonard took his jacket off and draped it over Samantha's shoulders. Before she could adjust the jacket squarely, Leonard bent on one knee.

Before giving her the coat, he had removed a small, black box from its pocket. He now held the box open and offered its content up to Samantha.

"Samantha, will you marry me?"

She did not answer. The lower lids of her large eyes brimmed with tears and then she closed them. Thirty seconds later she said, "Amen" and opened them.

Smiling warmer than the Italian sun she said, "Please Leonard, forgive me for not answering sooner. Of course, the answer is yes darling, but first I had to thank God for this answer to prayer. Leonard, I was so close to just giving in to what I considered my sinful urges. I was convinced I could not go another night lying in my bed and not have your weight upon me. You are greater than a mere Prince Charming; you are a saint sent by God. I consider us married as of now – let's do rush home."

"No, Samantha, we have so little time. I do not want to rush anything."

Folding herself into his side she melted into him as he surrounded her with his arm. Their walking rhythm was in harmony. The fog was rolling in, and its light mist put halos around every light. Their walk was so ethereal and satisfying Leonard believed he could spend the rest of eternity doing nothing else.

"How does May 1st sound?" That was Leonard's first question of the day.

Cuddling closer, Samantha, still half asleep asked, "For what, Mr. LaFrance?"

"For you to become, Mrs. LaFrance," he said quietly.

She somehow cuddled even closer and murmured, "Perfect" and went back to sleep.

Finally it was May

THE first to hear of their plans were Andrea and Mayumi, the owners of the hotel. Italians are crazy about romance and among the more traditional nothing is more romantic than a wedding. They referred the eager couple to Villa Giona and a woman by the name of Marion, a wedding planner of no small repute.

Meeting over a glass of wine it was easy to discern the wedding planner would have liked for it to be a more lavish event, but she listened carefully and then provided everything as they wished.

Simple, but beautiful. A string quartet lifted the civil ceremony to a different level and the bride was at her peak of health and beauty. Leonard was outwardly calm, as usual, but inside he felt more excited and curiously responsible than he had ever before experienced.

Their honeymoon was to include Vienna, Paris, Amsterdam and London, but was cut short. In the beginning of their third week Samantha's health began to fail and reluctantly they did not journey on to London, but returned to their apartment hotel in Verona.

Everything was different now. The doctors made it clear the remission was over and it would not be back. There were no more walks. Leonard would carry her on to the small balcony when the sun warmed it.

They had drawn up a prenuptial that simply stated that each retained full ownership of their monies. Samantha had asked Leonard to donate all of her money to Cancer Research UK after her death. He did not wait. Leonard brought her checkbook and with the words, "You write it Samantha and we will post it today. I can cover whatever we will need."

Their conversations slowed. Samantha was more thoughtful than chatty, as was Leonard.

One unavoidable conversation was what to do with her remains. She mentioned that when she bought her late husband's gravesite she had also purchased the one alongside it, but her voice trailed off, never finishing the sentence.

Leonard swallowed hard. "It is only fitting, Samantha. You and I were brought together for reasons we may never fully understand. I am glad I was here for you, and I am so much richer for you coming into my life. But it has always seemed that our love was an island. Cecil was your husband for many years. I am your husband for a matter of weeks. When you are gone from that sweet body I will have no grief or jealousy that you will lie next to Cecil." Through moist eyes and a choked voice he repeated, "It is only fitting."

The Buyer

Samantha had one last request.

"Leonard, I am not afraid of what is to come, but I worry for you. I want you to promise you will look into God. He is real. You will have to face Him at some point. At that point you will want to have Jesus on and by your side. Will you promise me you will be open to the possibility?"

"I have never told you this, but I have greatly admired the person that you are. I know of a few others who are like you and they are all Christians. So it only makes sense to make that promise to you and myself."

It was virulent, the cancer. It seemed to be everywhere. It gave no quarter. It gave them only 26 days until Samantha was gone.

As he had promised her, Leonard took her body back to Libya to lay to rest next to her late husband.

Leonard had no reason to stay in Libya. And had no reason to go anywhere else. So he went back to Beverly Hills.

Chapter 26

CATCHING UP

ONCE THERE HE DID NOT CONTACT ANY-
one. His days were spent running or walking the streets or along the beach. He also acquired a new practice: writing everyday. After nearly a month he picked up the phone.

Looking at the screen of her smart phone made Lillian's heart jump. She had not spoken to Leonard since he told her he was going to marry a dying woman.

"Hello doctor, I'm back home, are you still speaking to me?"

Lillian cleared her throat, and in a most professional tone, she said "Of course." She paused then continued. "I have so many questions, I honestly don't know where to start."

"Today is Saturday, will you have time for lunch?"

"Oh," she said with obvious sincerity, "I am speaking at a psychiatric seminar luncheon today. I am sorry."

"Good," responded Leonard, "then dinner it is."

Lilly smiled. "That would be rather unprofessional. Dinner by its very nature is more intimate and less professional and, therefore, not consistent with a doctor-patient relationship."

"Okay, you're fired. Now, where may I pick you up?"

Lilly noticed that, while authoritative, Leonard's voice was soft and kind. Again she smiled as she answered, "The seminar is at the Beverly Wilshire. Why don't I meet you in the bar at 5:15."

"I will look forward to that."

After the call to his best friend, he called Theo.

"Hey Leonard, how's it going?" answered Theo.

The thought crossed Leonard's mind that the casual breeziness of his southern California friend was kind of refreshing. "It is going well Theo, and you?"

"Well, since I have the greatest job in the world, until you take it back, since I am healthy, until God has other plans and since I am in love, till death do us part, I'd say I am phenomenal!"

Leonard chuckled and said, "Good for you. By the way, are you open for lunch?"

"What! You're back in town? You said you'd be gone for two years. When did you get back? I mean, we have been exchanging e-mails on a three to five times a week basis. I had no idea you were coming home. Sure. I am not in the office today, but I can come to wherever you are."

"Good, how about my house about 11:30?"

"Give me the address and it is a done deal."

THEO had put on a little weight.

"Are you still running?" asked Leonard, as he reached out and patted a tummy that hadn't been there when he'd left.

"I just started again. When you gave me the job I put everything else aside, even running, but I started feeling like crap and got back into it a week ago. I am feeling so much better already. And look at you. You are not the same dude that threw yourself in front of me about a year ago. Are you running?"

"Yes, Theo, I am running and I have you to thank for it. Where do you want to eat or are you trying to cut down?" asked Leonard with a grin.

"No, I am good. Let's go to Santa Monica so we can look out at the beach, sitting in that office gets really old."

There was a light breeze coming off Santa Monica Bay, and it ruffled the large Mediterranean blue umbrellas that sheltered the tables from the sun.

After they ordered, Theo began talking, and, even if Leonard would have had something to say, it is doubtful he would have found a safe place to interrupt.

Leonard admired Theo's exuberance and passion for the mission of the Advantage Corporation, and, it was, in fact, contagious.

Other than the cursory exchanges in the e-mails, Leonard had been substantially removed from all aspects of company. Theo was laying out the changes and reinforcements that he saw as essential to the future profitability of the Advantage Corporation. Many had already been achieved; others were in the process of initiation, and some were still on the drawing board.

Finally, Theo slowed down. He also took on a worried look. He spoke with frankness.

"Leonard, I know this is your company. I know with the team you have you can run it from your hip pocket anywhere you can find internet access, but man the world is changing so fast. Some of these projects I am initiating will need me or someone like me to see them to fulfillment. The old business model will at some point be lethargic and inefficient. What are your plans now that you are back? Do they include me?"

Leonard smiled. He reached out and took Theo's arm, and, in as reassuring voice as was possible he said, "Theo, first, thank you for allowing me this opportunity to speak."

They both laughed. "I was afraid that I might have lost my voice due to atrophy during the deluge you just poured out."

Another smile was exchanged.

"The *Reader's Digest* version is this. You are now, and if you want, and if you maintain your enthusiasm you will continue to be, the president of The Advantage Corporation.

"I want to be very much involved as we go forward, but not only do I like what you are doing, but I don't want that job back. Together we can do great things. Do you believe that?"

"I seriously believe that, Leonard. In fact, I would like to raise a toast to that vision."

It was now time to go home and get ready to see Lillian.

Leonard told Theo he would be in the office on Monday at 10:00. While Theo drove him to Beverly Hills, he asked Leonard if he would like his office back.

"By no means," answered Leonard. "However, why don't you ask Robert Vuchovich to look into adding a story to our building. I might like to have the floor to myself and include an apartment. Let me know what he says."

Theo grinned and with respect answered, "You bet, Mr. L."

As they got into the giant pick-up, the same one Theo had driven on their first visit to Compton, a problem occurred to Leonard. He was no longer in a city where taxis were readily available. He had no car.

Leonard had given up his limo and his security detail to Theo when he left to travel. Theo obviously was a more employee-friendly boss to the security detail than he had been; here it was Saturday and it looked like Theo had given them the weekend off.

What to do? He had no car in which to pick up Dr. Lilly. Finding a taxi in LA is not dependable. He briefly considered asking Theo for the limo and a driver for the night, but rejected the thought as being too imperial and a step backwards.

"Theo, if you were to buy the best car you could think of today, what would it be?"

Not unsurprisingly Theo asked, "Do you want a car or a truck?"

Leonard chuckled. "I think a car would be best for now."

"That's easy. An Audi R8 Spyder 5.2. Can you drive a car that doesn't have an automatic transmission?"

"Good question, Theo. My father made me learn how, but that was 35 years ago."

"I think," said Theo, "it is like riding a bike; you never really forget. And the Audi manual is so smooth, and I believe it comes in a 7-gear automatic as well. Hey, the Santa Monica Audi dealer is right up here on this very street. Let's take a look."

"YES," said Larry the car salesman, "it does come with the DL800 automatic. We call it the S tronic – weighs about 45 more pounds than the manual transmission but provides lightning-quick shifts and it trims the quoted 0-to-60-mph time from 3.6 to 3.3 seconds."

"Wow!" said Theo.

"Hmmm," said Leonard.

"Yeah!" said Larry.

"How much is it?" asked Theo.

"This one, as equipped, is $198,642."

"Whoa Mama!"

"I'll take it." Leonard said.

"Can't have it," said Larry.

"Why not?" asked Leonard.

"Yeah, why not?" echoed Theo.

"Because somebody else ordered it."

"How long will it take to get one just like this?" asked Leonard.

"This is a rare car," said the salesman, thoughtfully, "and an even rarer color. So there is probably not another one like it in the country. Sooo, probably 2 to 3 months."

"If some else had not already bought this, could I drive it out of here right now?" asked Leonard.

"Yeah, that's not the problem; it is fully serviced," said Larry.

"Would you be so kind as to get the person on the phone and ask them if they will take $50,00.00 to wait and let me have this one?"

Larry jumped to get the sales manager. The two hustled back to the potential customers and, after introductions, the sales manager, Bob, asked Leonard how he would be paying for the car and the inconvenience money.

"By check," said Leonard.

"That would be a problem; this is Saturday afternoon and the banks are closed. There is simply no way to verify your check. If you are still making this offer on Monday we can process everything quite quickly," said Bob.

Theo stepped up to Bob and nearly whispered, "Would it help you to know he is the sole owner of the Advantage Corporation and that his company owns this building?"

"One moment please." said Bob, the sales manager.

It was more like ten minutes, and Leonard had much to do before picking up Dr. Lilly. The whole thing was looking less appealing. Then Bob returned.

"Do you have ID, sir?" asked Bob.

Leonard was still carrying his passport and he presented it.

"Thank you, Mr. LaFrance. One more moment, please?" asked Bob. This time his return was just about a minute.

"Mr. LaFrance, if you would like to conclude the deal you can write a check to Santa Monica Audi in the amount of $248,642 plus tax and I will give you a bill of sale and you can be on your way."

Larry, the salesman, could now see why Bob was the sales manager and he was the salesman.

Theo could see what it was like to be extremely rich.

THERE was no time to go back home, clean up and get to Dr. Lilly on time. Leonard pulled up in front of the Beverly Wilshire. The valet looked at the car and at Leonard and he wanted to be just like that.

Getting direction from the doorman Leonard quickly found the bar. He was early. So was Lillian.

It had been a year. She looked different, but he didn't know whether she had changed or if he was seeing her differently.

She looked at him and saw a new man. Much more self-assured, re-laxed and tan. His face, while it had always been rather handsome, now was not as fleshy. It had a firmness that speaks of character and ability.

Softly and respectfully he gave her a hug. It felt good. He'd had no physical contact with any woman since he'd carried Samantha down to the hearse.

Lilly was surprised at how muscular Leonard felt.

"Do you really want a drink?" he inquired.

"Not really, how about you?"

"Not really. Look, I didn't have any transportation and I had to buy a car today. That took a little longer than I thought and I haven't had a chance to clean up. Would you think me rude if we stopped by my home for a glass of wine while I do so?"

Lillian cocked her head. In a tone of voice, both unsure and uncom-fortable she answered. "I don't know, Leonard."

"Ok, you have had a long day too and may want to freshen up your-self. I can drop you by your place, go home clean up and come back for you. Or, we can just go to my place. I have learned to cook, so we can eat in and not worry about being properly dressed; your choice."

"It has," confessed Lilly, "been a complicated day already. I think your offer of a casual dinner and no fuss sounds quite attractive."

"Me too. Let's go."

After giving the valet the ticket, the two stood amidst a small crowd who were also waiting for their cars. They waited without exchanging a word. It seemed prudent to allow osmosis to merge the two from their diverse paths of the day, and for that matter, the year.

"Look at that car," remarked Lilly. "I wonder who that belongs to?"

As the valet respectfully placed the key in his hand, Leonard looked at Lilly and replied with a grin. "Evidently, it belongs to us."

Lilly, always one to admire subtle beauty, was as taken with the inside as she was the sleek exterior. The snug seats assured the passenger a never-before-experienced security even when standing still. There was so much rich leather in a color somewhere in between Amaretto and Cinnamon. The rest of the high-tech cockpit murmured only one refrain: 'this beast can fly.'

The pedal, even when lightly caressed with the foot, demonstrated unspeakable power. Leonard, unused to any car with this kind of response, learned quickly to respect the beast. He did not hot dog, but did his best to give the doctor, not a thrill, but a comfortable and impressive ride. He and his new super toy did both.

Lilly started to ask if Leonard was having a mid-life crises, but decided it was more of a cheap shot than high-level humor and she sank back to enjoy the experience.

Leonard's home was about 70 years old and had not been updated. However, it was Beverly Hills, and, while the kitchen was old, it was highly serviceable. The range was intended for a professional chef cooking for large dinner parties, and had always been cleaned and well cared for.

Vegetable broth and white wine were added as the Risotto sizzled in the olive oil. He sautéed the prawns separately in fresh garlic along with a bit of herbs. A salad and a simple Chianti Classico finished off the meal.

"Leonard! This is outstanding. Where did you learn to cook like this?"

The Buyer

"I met a Parisian woman on the plane to Europe. She was married and I asked her what a woman looks for when she is choosing a husband. One of her first thoughts was a man that could cook. She then directed me to a culinary school that I attended for three weeks, and I have been adding to that knowledge base ever since. Do you really like it?"

"Very much," she said. "By the way, I like that you asked her that question. You are eager to learn about how life works, aren't you?"

With a slight blush, Leonard answered, "Yes."

There was silence for a while as the two sat across from each other. They chose to sit across the breadth of the table as opposed to side by side or across the length of it. The latter would have required speaking in a very loud voice in order to be heard across the vast expanse. Still it was too formal a setting to really be comfortable.

Leonard rose from his chair, went over to his upstairs wine cabinet and fetched a bottle of Brunello di Montalcino, along with a pair of appropriate wine glasses and bid the good doctor to follow him.

She did.

They reached the top of the elegant staircase and headed south. There was no doubt in Lillian's mind they were headed toward a bedroom.

As he opened a door Lilly stopped short and asked, "Leonard, are you taking me to your bedroom?"

"No ma'am. I am taking you through my bedroom, and forgive the unmade bed, to the balcony. It is far too nice an evening to sit indoors."

"What a relief," sighed Lillian. "I was afraid you had not learned anything about seduction."

Leonard gave a short, soft laugh and admitted, "Well you would be right. I still don't have a clue."

They arranged themselves around a smaller table on the balcony and watched the twilight of southern California take over.

When relaxed, Lilly asked Leonard to tell her about the last year.

He began in Lafayette, Louisiana. He'd been a little shocked at the behavior of some of his relatives and very warmly impressed with others. He did not dwell on that part of the trip and said nothing of his largess.

Paris was a great place to start his exploration of life. The cooking school introduced him to the subtleties of the palate. Which, incidentally, led him to notice more subtlety in wine, which, in turn, led him to notice more subtlety in everything.

He loved the boulevards and the avenues, the monuments and the parks. He especially liked the lights. "Paris calls itself the City of Lights. I was told that before they joined the EU it was illegal to drive with your headlights on in Paris."

The bullet train to Milano was a treat, but he also liked the milk train that took him down the Italian coast to Vernazza. He loved Vernazza.

When he spoke of the youth, beauty and animal magnetism of Angelica, Lilly squirmed a little, but said nothing. As he described the small village and its glorious setting, Lilly could almost see it.

Rome was a hoot. The robbery was worth going through just for the experience, and, if that would not have been enough, just meeting Pepi would have justified it.

Then Leonard grew silent.

The two friends watched as the sun sank below the trees and just a hint of light remained. After what seemed several minutes, Lillian asked Leonard, "Would you tell me about the woman you were considering marrying?"

More silence.

Leonard had not been able to hold that time up in his mind to revisit it. He had not acknowledged any of the feelings he'd had since Tripoli. Now he had to articulate it – cold.

Lilly could see it was a struggle and she was patient. Finally, Leonard started by thanking Lilly for her good advice.

"Without your giving me the assignment of giving of myself, not just writing a check, but investing myself in someone who could give me nothing in return, I would have never gone there.

"I did not expect to do anything but to give of myself. That was my entire goal. As it turned out, she actually gave me a great deal. The most astounding thing though is that the experience itself gave me more than I have ever gotten from any source, ever."

Leonard once again withdrew into himself.

Lilly respected that.

The Buyer

Slowly Leonard rose from his chair. Looking down at Lilly he asked, "Are you going to charge me for this time?"

There was just a hint of humor in the question and Lillian responded in kind.

"No, you fired me, remember?"

"Now that you mention it, I do remember firing you. I guess that makes it okay to do THIS." Raising both his volume and his pitch on that last word he moved in on Lilly and tickled her. In shock, she began to giggle. He pursued it for another moment, much as a boy might, then stopped and said, "Now the tables are turned. You need to tell me of your life."

"Oh, no, I couldn't do that," responded Lilly, as she came down from her giggle.

"Okay," said Leonard in a mock maniacal voice "but that means you will be subjected to more of THIS." And again he began to tickle her.

"No, no," she cried. "Leonard, stop it. Leonard!"

"Then," said Leonard in the same maniacal voice, "you must begin with your childhood and tell me everything, or the tickling will increase and continue without mercy."

"Okay, okay. Please stop."

He did.

Tears of laughter had run down Lilly's face along with some eyeliner. It caused the good doctor's face to appear quite comical, though not unattractive.

Over the next hour she told him things that she had never told anyone else. She spoke of Brian and what a dear, dear man, husband and father he had been. She could not believe it when she began to cry as she related the day of his death and the agony of the months that followed. When she completed her catharsis, she shivered.

Leonard got out of his chair. "Let me get you a wrap."

Lillian rose as well and said, "I'd better be getting home. What time is it?"

Leonard, looking at his watch, said, "it's 1:10 AM."

"We have been talking for hours and hours and it seems like minutes – but I have got to get to bed – I have church in the morning." Then as an afterthought, she asked brightly, "Hey, would you like to go with me?"

"Is that an invitation to sleep with you between now and then?"

"OOOOOHHHH", Lilly growled as she punched him in the shoulder. "You are right, you do not have a clue when it comes to seduction, but how about church?"

"I've been thinking about it, but I'm not quite ready."

THE next day was Sunday and it was all Leonard could do to keep from calling Lilly for a reprise of last evening. *What a great friend*, thought Leonard.

Interestingly, Lilly had the same inner battle, but with slightly warmer thoughts.

Chapter 27

W HEN AT PROMPTLY **10 AM,** AS PROM-
ised, Leonard stepped off of the private elevator on the
27th floor, the place looked quite different than the way he'd left it. It
took a moment to adjust - then he liked it very much.

The new reception desk was manned by an official-looking receptionist and an official-looking security guard.

"Good morning, Mr. L," they said, almost in unison.

Leonard smiled and told them, "It's nice to be back. Looks like
you've done a lot with the old place."

"You can thank Mr. Webb, Mr. Koch, Mr. Vuchovich and all their
staff. They just completed the facelift about 6 weeks ago. I really like
it," she said.

"Me too," said Leonard. "I did not realize how tired the place looked
until I see all this. Could you please let Theo Webb know I'm here."

"Oh, I'm sorry, Mr. L," responded the receptionist, " Mr. Webb and
the division chiefs are down on the third floor in the convention room.
I believe they are hoping to see you."

Leonard didn't know whether to be sardonic or grateful. He was
not sure anyone really wanted to see him. However, ever open to new
experiences these days, he said, "I would not want to disappoint." Then
he re-boarded the elevator and pushed '3'.

He had no way of knowing the receptionist, whose name he could not remember, had, as previously instructed, phoned down to Theo the moment the elevator doors closed.

STEPPING off the lift, Leonard found the hallway eerily quiet. When he opened the convention room door, a chorus of "Welcome back Mr. L!" shattered the silence.

This was a shock. The greater shock was that they all seemed genuinely delighted to see him. Theo was the first of a long line of old-time friends, colleagues, and, yes, employees, to greet him with handshakes and smiles.

Hugs were not part of the menu. The esteem, with which this orderly band held him, was far too high for such familiarity. Leonard understood and was humbled.

When the commotion settled down at the request of Theo, Leonard became aware that he should say something. Leonard wanted to break the ice, so he began in with an uncharacteristic bit of humor. "As you may know I have been away." A ripple of unsure laughter wafted around the convention room.

"I cannot tell you all that I have seen and learned. There has been so much. I can tell you that things here will continue just as they have for the past year. Theo Webb will handle the day-to-day running of the company along with our tried-and-true division heads. And I hope to make some significant contributions myself along the way.

"More importantly, and above all, I cannot tell you how pleasing it is to know that you are such a superior breed, and that I never once felt the Advantage Corporation would crumble or even lose ground in my absence. I want to thank Theo Webb, Leon Hardin, Amanda Epstein, George Koch, Samuel Levine, Robert Vucovich, and Ervin Syrisst for their excellent leadership. I will be meeting with all of them as their schedules permit over the next few days."

There was a solid round of applause.

"I know they could not have done such an amazing job if it had not been for all the support, ingenuity, and enterprise that each and every one of you have provided. It will take me a while, but I will attempt to do something that shows my heartfelt appreciation."

In a manner that reminded the crowd of the majesty and the reason why they all called him Mr. L, Leonard, with head slightly bowed, left the room.

He was a full dozen paces out of the room before the applause started. As the elevator doors closed, the clamor rose to its zenith and his eyes filled with tears. Leonard stopped the elevator, sat on the floor and tried to comprehend what had just happened. He wanted to scream. He wanted to cry. He wanted to dance. He wished Lilly had seen this.

Then he wondered why he would wish for that. Was she that good a friend? Was she the replacement for his parents when it came to giving him the approval he longed for? He knew not which it was. He did know it deserved some considered thought.

The view from space

THE elevator buzz meant someone was trying to access the private elevator. It must have been Theo as no one else, except for Calvin Frost and security, had the code.

Leonard got up. He cleared the tears and his throat and went back down to gather Theo.

Surprised and delighted best described Theo's reaction to seeing his boss in the elevator.

"I was just coming down to get you," fibbed Leonard.

"I was hoping to find you," said Theo, as he entered the elevator. There was a brief and awkward silence. Then both men spoke at once. Theo immediately gave way.

Leonard, with great self-control, said, "Theo, that was very good of you to arrange such a wonderful homecoming. I really don't know what to say or how to react. It was completely unlike anything I have ever experienced."

"All I did was call the meeting," said Theo. "They were genuinely glad to see you. I have never seen anything like it either. They have responded well to my leadership, but you hold a different place in their minds. I think they feel more secure with you back."

"Oh, by the way," Theo continued, "I spoke to Bob Vukovich and he said when he designed the building with your father it was made specifically strong enough to add up to four more floors. So he will have plans for your new office within the week. In the meantime, we will have what has been our executive conference room ready for you by noon, so you will have a place to camp out till the addition is ready."

"Excellent," answered Leonard. "I knew you were good when I made you the offer, but I had no idea you would be this good."

"You know what, Mr. L, I didn't know all that I had in me, either. Thanks for the opportunity to surprise myself."

Leonard liked that. "Theo, I know you are busy, but would you mind accompanying me as I share a few thoughts with some key people. If everyone can sign on to these thoughts and make them their own, you will be the one charged with seeing the ideas become reality."

"Mind?" responded Theo. "Working alongside you is an opportunity. Besides, I have more to tell you. I couldn't put everything I want to talk to you about into those e-mails."

Their first stop was Samuel Levine's office. His inner door was closed and Leonard looked at Theo, shook his head and they started to walk away, but Samuel Levine's secretary stopped him when she said, "Oh Mr. L, Mr. Levine told me to send you right in if you came by," jumping up as she spoke and opening the door.

Inside the office Leonard and Theo saw Sam and three of the other division chiefs: Robert Vuchovich, George Koch and Amanda Epstein.

After a quick hello round, Leonard again praised the work Theo, Amanda, Sam, Bob, and George had done during his absence. Then Leonard launched into ideas that he had percolating.

"It is fortuitous that you are all here as you are just the ones I want to run a couple of thoughts by."

Amanda and all the men found chairs in Samuel Levine's spacious office as Leonard paced. As he spoke, Leonard was eyeball to eyeball with each one, as his or her division became the subject.

"There are two ways to keep your properties full," Leonard began. "One is filling the vacancies with fresh tenants, the other is retaining the tenants we already have.

"What I would like us to focus on is retention, keeping each tenant for as long as possible. We have done a great job of keeping our properties occupied. Our average vacancy is 7.2% compared to the national average of 13.4%. We are obviously doing some things right, wouldn't you say?"

Of course, everyone enthusiastically agreed.

"Do you think we could tweak it and make it better?"

The agreement was still there, but a bit less enthusiastic.

"After going over the spreadsheets you have been sending me, I am getting a better idea of how vast our holdings are."

Leonard chuckled, then continued.

"I know that sounds strange, but I have always kind of taken them for granted. Obviously, we have done very well, more importantly, we are positioned to grab a larger share of the market."

Leonard paused for effect, then said, "Iffff –" exaggerating the word to emphasize it, "we can reduce our turnover rate and keep our current tenants in place longer, even as we add new properties and new tenants.

"George, your leasing staff is very aggressive in replacing lost tenants with fresh new ones. That is why our vacancy rates are well below the national average, but I think we can do better."

George Koch accepted the first portion of the thought as a compliment, but then shifted his posture and looked uncomfortable.

"As I traveled I had to learn to see the world from a customer's point of view. I have come to understand that all businesses, to varying degrees, have one of two views. On one end of the spectrum they are there to make money from you – pure and simple.

"On the other, they are there to serve you, and whatever is best for you is very important to them. And it shows.

"Looking at Advantage Corp from a distance, almost as if I were seeing it from the Space Station. It occurred to me the Advantage Corporation has always acted in the way my father and I have wanted it to act. We have been a bit imperialistic and have always had the 'If we build it they will come', attitude. And it's worked well, but in today's world I see a flaw in our model."

The team unconsciously leaned in.

The name of our company is the Advantage Corporation. My father named it that because he always wanted some kind of advantage in every situation, and he was a master at finding or creating them. He taught me to do the same, and I have faithfully executed that philoso-

Chet Hanson

phy.

"However, as Theo recently pointed out to me, 'the times they are a changing.'" Leonard paused for a half second as he found it delightful that he was able to recall and use a lyric from a Bob Dylan song. "And," Leonard continued, "we must find ways of changing with them, if we want to keep and grow what we have.

"Here, we can learn from Henry Ford and the automobile industry. When Ford first started to mass-produce cars for the workingman you could buy any color you wanted, as long as it was black. That has changed. So must we.

"It is probably obvious to our tenants that the advantage in Advantage Corporation belongs to us. We want to change the way our tenants look at our name. We want them to see the advantage belonging to them.

"The best way for our *customers* to see our name differently is for *us* to see our name differently. Make no mistake; we are not going to become an eleemosynary institution. In fact we will likely become, over time, more profitable. However, it is my belief that we will be the best we can be when we are truly customer centric.

"We want the tenants to want to stay, because it is clear to them we are one of the few landlords that are on their side. That we see them as valued customers and not just cash cows. To whatever extent a tenant might feel like a cash cow now, that is my bad, but let's be the best we can be to the degree we can afford it.

"I suggest we have three obvious avenues to achieve that goal. One is price, one is the environment of our properties, and the other is proactive customer service.

"As for price we have always shot for a sweet spot, just below, but right up against, all the market would bear. I believe we refer to it as LRCC or Lease Rates Compared to Competition, right?"

All four-division heads nodded in affirmation.

Leonard was on a roll and more excited than his staff had seen him in a long time.

"So let's talk about lease pricing. I'm wondering if all of you are seeing what I am seeing.

"I've noticed that the closer we get to charging all the market will

217

bear, the higher the turnover rate. That is because if they are spending that much they have more choices. Of course that is especially true in times of economic contraction when businesses are scrambling to cut costs wherever possible.

"Let's lower our prices, just a bit. I think we should do it incrementally. Look at the landscape and strategically select about 20% of the properties that would most likely retain a larger percentage of our customers, if they got a price break. You all will decide what that price break will be. I'm thinking a drop of about 2%. My gut tells me our tenants will find our prices harder to beat, and they will be less likely to move. If that proves to be true, let's expand the process to every property. And when we drop those prices, consider tying their savings in with a new, extended, lease using the lower price as a carrot.

"That is our price ploy. The second leg of my proposed strategy is enhancing the working environment that we provide to our tenants."

Looking right at Robert Vuchovich, Leonard said, "Bob, I'd like you to run the numbers on a typical rehab after move-out as compared to what it costs us to do a facelift while the tenant is still in house."

Bob nodded. He was a true product of his construction craft. A big fellow, the only one in the room with a tan, hands that spoke of rough work, and a bit rough around the edges. Bob felt his engineering degree did not preclude him from being a hands-on type. Bob also had to restrain his course language in these settings, and, therefore, spoke as little as possible.

Leonard continued.

"I can't begin to tell you how invigorated I was by the changes you made in this building while I was away. It is inspiring and it leads me to think we might want to provide that same invigoration to the business productivity of our clients. Do you see a cause-and-effect factor at work here?"

The division heads were in cautious, thoughtful, agreement until Theo added, "Seems like simple logic, if the productivity of our tenants increases due to a more motivating work place, we have a greater shot at retaining that customer."

With that said, the enthusiasm of agreement came up a notch.

"By the way," asked Leonard, "who is responsible for the idea of updating our offices?"

Nearly in unison the three division heads said, "Theo."

"Well it's true that I brought it up," Theo humbly admitted, "but every one of our people, especially those in this room, are responsible for the great end result."

"Why am I not surprised," said, Leonard. "Good work. Very good work."

Coming back on target, Leonard went on.

"What I expect we'll find, Bob, while it will require more comprehensive planning and will be more difficult to do the upgrade while the tenants are in residence, without disrupting them, it will be no more expensive than the post-move-out re-hab, which is generally more extensive. The other bonus is we will not have the cost of the vacancy or the expense of re-leasing the property.

"The third leg of the strategy is customer service.

"George, because a lot of this falls into your court, I would like your group to look into how we can make the most contented tenants possible."

Reaching inside his suit-coat pocket Leonard extracted a single sheet and unfolded it. Before giving it to George, he read it aloud.

"First, I believe we should have an agent pay a courtesy call to every property every month just to see how the tenant thinks we're doing. If they are thinking of contracting or expanding their business, let our agents show so much interest in the welfare of their business that even if they have to move, they will WANT to have us as their landlord. We can use their needs as a sales opportunity to find them a home, of the right size and price, in that same building or one of our other properties.

"If they do decide to leave us, let's start getting an exit statement from every tenant that moves out – find out why they are leaving."

Leonard stopped at this point and asked, "Are we doing any of that now, George?"

"Not really, Mr. L. When they are gone, it is pretty much over."

"Okay, let's look into changing that. And while we're at it get a list of reasons why those who do renew their leases decided to stay. I would like you to work with Theo on this, especially the part that deals with motivating the agents that will drive the change."

George took out a pad and a pen and began to take a note, but Leonard stopped him.

"George, I will give you this sheet and e-mail it to the rest of the group. For now, George, I would like you to survey all of your field people, and mine from them whatever anecdotal data, good or bad, they have picked up in the past. Then translate that into an assessment that might assist us in getting even more of our tenants to stay with us longer.

"This will require a change in the way the agents are rewarded for their work. Now they are incentivized when they sign a new tenant. Since there are more spaces to rent as our older tenants leave, our current system is a disincentive to retention. Get with Theo and Sam and construct a pay formula that is more consistent with keeping the old, even as we add the new."

"Yes, Mr. L," said a subdued George Koch.

"Theo," continued Leonard, "if you and the team decide to execute these changes it will fall upon you to work with all your people and co-ordinate this into a seamless program."

"Got it, Mr. L," was Theo Webb's quick response.

"To wrap up this thought, I believe we are leaving money on the table by trying to get too close to top dollar. I think that by letting them keep a little bit more of their money, instead of spending it for rent, they will likely be more profitable.

"By keeping their working environment fresh it will help inspire our customers and their employees to be more successful in their business and remain with us.

"And the key to their understanding that the advantage in doing business with Advantage is to their advantage will be obvious to all because of our outstanding customer service.

"Under our current model we are forcing businesses that are marginally successful to look for a property that will lower their costs. I think you might find it would be more profitable for us to alter our business model to be as user-friendly and as flexible to their needs as possible.

"I know it's just gut instinct. Your job is to prove me right or wrong with hard numbers.

"Two more quick thoughts. I know we are keeping a 14% cash reserve. I have noted both in the IBD, the WSJ and almost every financial newsletter that a majority of the pundits think the good times will roll on. Others disagree. From my anecdotal, but firsthand look at the economies of Europe, I agree with those who think we are in for a rough ride. Let's cut back on property acquisition until we can reach 21% cash reserve, we may need it."

Turning directly towards Amanda, Leonard said, "You will have less money to buy new properties until we reach our new cash reserves goal. I would suggest you will want to focus on considering only very, very good properties at highly distressed prices in the near term. Use this quieter time to strategize how we can fine tune our acquisition process. Amanda, if you need to park some of your people in other divisions, let's all work with her so we don't lose any of our good people.

"The last item on my agenda is a little bit difficult. We have always been very loyal to our people and our properties. Those people who do not want to elevate the importance of pleasing our customers will have decided they do not want to work here.

"The same is true of some of our properties. I think it is time to let go of some of the properties that no longer fit into a profitable model. My father bought them in the very beginning and we have held them. Theo, I would like you to check them all out personally. I suggest you put those properties into one of three categories. Some might be candidates for a major rehab and we will keep them in our portfolio. Others might benefit from a complete, but cost-conscious upgrade, as you have done in your Compton model, and then sell them. The rest we will simply want to sell off. This will help Amanda by bringing in the cash to reach our reserve goal more quickly."

Amanda spoke for the first time. "Mr. L, I would like to work with Theo in evaluating the disposition of those older properties." Amanda then added, with a hint of defensiveness. "I do bring some expertise in that area."

Leonard looked at Amanda with new eyes. He realized instantly that neither his father nor he had given her or any woman the opportunity to demonstrate all that she might be able to contribute to Advantage Corporation. In a flash he combined the strength of the women he had gotten to know over the past year and realized that anyone who was really good at something can be a true force.

With a big smile, Leonard said, "Amanda Epstein, you are right. You are brilliant and probably under-utilized in relationship to your potential." Turning to Theo he added, "Theo you have a lot on your plate, rather than you micromanaging this project, how would you feel about letting Amanda run with it – in consultation with you?"

"Perfect," was Theo's one-word response.

"Amanda, I still want to see some thoughts on how to fine tune our acquisition process, do you feel like doing both?"

Amanda said, "To borrow a phrase from Robert Vuchovich, 'Hell yes!'"

The room relaxed in laughter.

"Dig into it my friends. I'm sure Sam and Theo will be interested in looking at your findings."

Leonard left and Theo followed.

George Koch was the first to speak after their departure.

"We are already doing some of those things, why is he driving us to do more?"

Robert, Amanda and Samuel were all quiet. After a full 30 seconds Samuel spoke.

"George, get your thinking straight. The world isn't standing still. This company is not standing still. I don't see Mr. L or Theo Webb as executives who are going to be satisfied with same-o- same-o. We have good jobs, but we need to see the future. Lazy leaders will not be part of it."

Robert simply agreed, "Well said, Sam. George, you are a good man – pull your head out of your butt."

Amanda had the biggest grin and could only say, "Isn't this wonderful?"

Outside, Leonard offered, apologetically, "Theo I should have discussed these thoughts with you first. I won't make a habit of going around you. It is counterproductive."

"I think," said Theo, "it is an excellent piece of fine tuning and thanks for protecting me. As big as the Advantage Corporation has grown, it is still not immune to market pressures, and besides, first rule of business is always, 'The customer is always right'."

As Leonard put his hand on the doorknob of his temporary office, Theo brought up a topic dear to his heart. "If you have some time I would love to show you the new project we took on in the Compton area."

"How about tomorrow at ten?" asked Leonard.

"That would be great, Mr. L."

"One more thing, Theo. I have never met your wife. When you speak of her I can see that she is the center of your universe. I'd like to meet her."

"Well actually, Christ is the center of my universe, but Kim is my greatest earthly treasure. I would love for the two of you to meet. When and where?"

"How about dinner at my place on Wednesday – I'll see if I can find a date. I only know one female that doesn't work for me who will still talk to me."

"No problem, Mr. L. I know of a couple of fine women that are friends of ours. I can bring one along."

"Good of you to offer, but I have one really good friend I'll try first. However, I may take you up on that at some point. Meeting women is not one of my better skill sets.

"I know I said one more thing, but if you will oblige me, there is one more thing. You used to call me Leonard, now you call me Mr. L. Why?"

"Actually, I used to call a guy that I saw as somewhat of a nerd, Leonard. Now that I have seen what you have built, and the awe that your employees hold you in, I feel more comfortable in joining with them and calling you, Mr. L."

Leonard blushed, nodded and went into his temporary office.

Chapter 28

SOME LIMITATIONS ARE NEEDED

ILLY FOUND THAT WHAT BEGAN AS A SMALL trickle had now become a constant stream of invitations to speak at medical seminars and community groups. At first she said yes to just about everything, booking herself up for months in advance.

Now the burden of fulfilling all of these hastily accepted obligations was beginning to not only weigh on her, but was interfering with other parts of her practice and her life. It was exhausting.

When she saw the incoming call was from Leonard, she did not let it roll over to voice mail.

"Hi, Leonard, good to hear from you."

Leonard smiled, "Well thank you Lillian, it is good to hear that it is good to hear from me."

They both released a small giggle.

"Any chance," asked Leonard, "that you might join me as I entertain Theo Webb, the young fellow who has been running Advantage Corp in my absence, and his wife, for dinner on Wednesday around seven?"

Lillian hesitated. Then said, "Honestly, I would love too, but that is the only night I don't have other obligations this entire week." Then she quickly asked, "What would it entail?"

"I was just going to cook. Nothing special – hey, I understand."

"Well, if you are going to cook, and it is a casual affair, and you don't mind if I bug out a little early, then I will come."

It was hard for Leonard to digest the rush of excitement he felt. "Oh, that's good. Can I pick you up?"

"Thanks, but no, I am booked right up to that time so I'll just drive. See you on Wednesday at seven, Leonard."

When she got off the phone she anticipated feeling burdened with one more hasty acceptance. That, however, was not the case. She was actually invigorated and a bit excited.

On Tuesday, at 10 AM, as agreed, Theo showed Leonard the new twist in his home rehab project in the Compton/Long Beach area.

"Mr. L, these people have either had no mentor at all, or worse, they were taught some disorganized way of life by some well-meaning, but misinformed person."

"As you know," Theo told Leonard, "I have been driven to get these people affordable housing in neighborhoods others have given up on. Now my vision is to teach them how to use money to make money and give them a better shot at the life they want. I am going about doing that by buying up what used to be grand old homes, places with 6, 7, even 8 or more bedrooms and dividing them into duplexes, triplexes and the like."

Theo wanted Leonard to get a good grasp of this vision, because he wanted the program to have his approval, and Theo wanted some of Leonard's approval for himself. People are funny that way.

Pulling onto the rehabbed street Leonard immediately got the picture. There were only ten houses on the entire block. They were once single-family mansions. Now they looked like mansions, except that the new owners, all who had proven themselves to be responsible, lived there in a very nice apartment and had other apartments to rent out.

Theo pulled into what appeared to be the largest home on the block. They got out of the car and headed toward the front door.

Leonard could not help but recall the run-in that he and his father had had just a few blocks from here. They were threatened with physical harm. Shortly thereafter his father went back with a big burly guy, but without Leonard, and the two were shot. The man who was supposed to protect his father died within hours. His father was also shot and never fully recovered.

Leonard was able to put that fear behind him. That was another time;

it was also quite a different neighborhood, he reasoned.

As they started to climb the steps the door opened before they even got to it. A very large black man wearing a police sergeant's uniform came out to greet them.

"Hello Mr. Webb. I got your messages and made sure I was home when you got here. Is this Mr. L?"

"It is, Sergeant. Mr. L, meet Sergeant Thomas of the Long Beach police department. And Sergeant Thomas, Meet Mr. L of the Advantage Corporation."

"This," said the sergeant, "is a real pleasure. Mr. Webb has told me so much about you. Thank you so much for making all this possible."

"I'd like to take credit for this, but it is all Theo Webb and people like yourself that make it possible. Tell me how it works for you?" asked Leonard.

"It is simple, really. Every one of my neighbors is a prior customer of Mr. Webb's. We all bought houses that were completely redone, but we followed his advice and continued to improve them. When it came time to get responsible people to buy these converted mansions, we were his first choice. To be honest, when I first looked at it I said 'Huh-uh' – not for me. Then Mr. Webb explained how I could actually pay less than I was paying for the mortgage on my little home. He helped me sell it at a pretty fair profit, and I bought one of these. Now I rent out a couple of apartments and apply that to my new mortgage. I actually don't pay a penny of this mortgage – my two tenants cover it all."

Leonard asked, "How much room do you have in your apartment?"

The sergeant's chest expanded perceptibly as he proudly told Leonard he had three bedrooms and two baths, a kitchen, dinning room, living room, a full basement, with a family room.

"Another plus," said the sergeant, "one of my rental units is two bedroom, two bath. That one is rented by a single mother who is a school teacher, and by the way, she is now engaged to a very fine young man that works for me. And the other is a three bedroom two bath and he works for the airline and she is a stay-at-home mom. Both of their kids have their own room." The sergeant looked very satisfied.

"If I am not being too nosy, may I ask how you pick your tenants?" inquired Leonard.

"No sir, not too nosy at all. You see Mr. Webb here made it clear to all of us who wanted to buy one of these properties that we would need to attend two days of schooling to be eligible. In that class we covered everything from how to select a responsible tenant, to what repairs you should do yourself and a list of good honest craftsman who could do what we were not capable of doing ourselves. He taught us how to set our prices, to keep track of revenues and expenses, you know, all of that stuff."

"How are you doing with all of that, Sergeant?" asked Leonard.

"We have no vacancies and Mr. Webb has sent accountants out at the end of two months to make sure our records are together. We all passed. My neighbors on either side will be absentee landlords by this time next year. Mr. Webb wouldn't sell to anyone who would not actually live in the house for a year, but after that, if we followed the rules and were successful, we could rent out all the apartments and go get something else for our personal use."

Sergeant Thomas continued to brag. "The guys who own the properties on either side are a surprise. One is a mailman, the other is a school janitor and they both are preachers at the same church. They not only own this place, but they each own about a dozen rent houses already."

Leonard had become very curious. "What do you think is the most important thing about this project, Sergeant Thomas?"

"That is a good question and it was raised at our monthly neighborhood meeting. I think, hell, we all think, the most important thing is not the money we are making, it is the example we are setting for our kids and some of the other people in our community that want a better life. Oh my word, I was so excited to see you that I left you standing here on the porch. Please come in and we'll have some coffee."

Now it was Theo who spoke up. "Thanks, my friend, but if I may I would like to take a rain check – got to get back to the grindstone."

"I understand. Thanks for the heads-up that you were coming. I'd better get back to work myself," responded Sergeant Thomas.

As the two drove back to the office, no words were exchanged. Theo wanted to ask what his boss thought, but with a significant amount of self-control he remained silent.

Leonard mulled over the project. *What was man here to do*, he asked himself; *what is his purpose? Was it only to be personally prosperous – was that enough?*

Leonard's own life answered that question.

Then Leonard asked himself, *how far should one venture out of the realm of personal prosperity?* He was not, in any way, yet prepared to answer that question.

Finally, Leonard turned toward Theo and let go a river of thoughts.

"In regards to your pet project, Theo, I want to say the following. You are giving people the opportunity to change their lives. Some will accept it eagerly and have the character to see it through; others will disappoint. I am seeing a possible financial meltdown in our country, and I don't want us to be caught with our pants down. Therefore, I am going to ask everyone to start cutting expenses wherever it makes sense. I am not going to ask that of this project, but I am going to ask that we redouble our efforts to thoroughly check out everyone you are thinking of selling to.

"I want you to find a teacher who can teach what you have been teaching. You are too valuable to do it yourself. Keep a tight rein on the expenses for that job. For the time being see if you can administer it on around 150k per year. Their job will be to teach and continuously inspect the status of compliance being demonstrated. Make sure the people we are investing in have the disciplines required to make this investment work for them and us. I want an ongoing accountability program that does not allow any of them to slip through the cracks.

"We are carrying the paper, and we can make that part of the deal. If a potential buyer has not proven they are responsible people, don't move them in. Raise the bar while continuing the project. I can see some self-appointed group or a bunch of bureaucrats trying to gain some power by taking it over. Guard against it. If that happens, sell the paper and we are out."

Leonard finished his monologue of thoughts by saying, "Can you do all of that and still run all of the day-to-day you are called upon to do?"

Theo was quick to answer. "I can."

Pulling into the garage of the Advantage Corporation, Theo asked Leonard if he would be going back into the office.

"No thanks, I have some grocery shopping to do for tomorrow."

Chapter 29

Kim, Theo's wife, was all that Theo said she was, and more. Solid, as a human being, pretty as a picture, and it was easy to see that she was a rock for Theo. Lillian also liked her and said as much.

The food, wine and conversation were all delightful and everyone was surprisingly open. Lilly left early with the blessings of Leonard who walked her to her car. Theo and Kim left not long after that.

The next day, Leonard decided he liked his new calling. Thinking about things, sharing his ideas with Theo in a respectful way and not worrying much about the day-to-day was something he was ready for.

Leonard had not seen Theo yet today, so he poked his head in. Theo could not wait. "Hi Mr. L. My wife really approved of you and she really liked Dr. Carroll. That's saying a lot. Kim rarely makes snap judgments."

"Well, I haven't spoken to Lillian since I walked her to her car, but she did say you both were good company. I must tell you though Theo, you are a very lucky man. I only hope I have someone to stand beside me one day in the loving way Kim stands beside you."

That was, of course, exactly what Theo wanted to hear. He did correct Leonard on a minor point.

"I would not say I was lucky or even shrewd, I would say I am blessed. And, by the way, what is wrong with Dr. Lilly, as you call her.

She is a jewel."

"Oh," opined Leonard, "I could not agree with you more, and I would not mind being with her always, but that is not our relationship. I was her patient, and now I am her friend, nothing more."

"Leonard, you are being a nerd again. That woman is crazy about you. Even Kim was talking about that."

"I'm afraid you are totally wrong, Theo. She feels nothing like that for me."

Reverting to a more respectful tone, Theo took one more shot. "Mr. L, you may be right, but I would at least encourage you to give her the opportunity to say no to the possibility, rather than just assuming it is a dead end. What have you got to lose?"

"That's easy. I could lose the best friend I have ever had."

"Okay, Mr. L. I guess you know best."

Leonard left. As he walked back to his temporary office he thought, *Hmmm, do I know best?* He was unsure. However, after handling a number of small things on his to-do list he noticed it was almost 6 PM. Lilly was usually through with patients and just cleaning up paperwork about this time, so he called her cell.

She always made him feel so glad he called. Her voice was light and cheerful and welcoming. Leonard always felt special when he answered.

I could never jeopardize that for some impossible fantasy, he decided.
"Hello, you!"

No, Leonard agreed with himself, *we are great friends, she is the most wonderful thing in my life. I will not jeopardize it. Period.*

"Hello yourself and see how you like it."

"What are you up to, Leonard?"

"I was calling to see if you might consider having dinner with me tomorrow night?"

Even as he said it he admonished himself for pushing too hard. She had already made herself available, as tired as she was, one night this week.

"Oh I can't. Sorry, but I have to speak at a seminar in Monterey on Saturday and it is a long drive, so I'll leave on Friday and get a good night's sleep. I'd much rather have dinner with you, but I am committed." Lilly sighed the sigh of the thoroughly tired. "I was planning on driving, but I think I'll take a plane."

Leonard wanted to get off the phone. He was disgusted with himself for being so pushy.

"Okay," he said, "maybe when you get back." He abruptly hung up. He had an uncomfortable feeling, similar to the one he'd had after pushing himself on Angelica in Vernazza.

Leonard got up from his chair at the desk and walked over to the chair by the window. As he sank into the cushion, he thought about how out of touch he was with so much that was important, and how little hope there was of ever changing that.

Lilly felt her face flush. Was Leonard just rude to her? Did he act like a spoiled boy that did not get his way? Was her life so out of control with external commitments that she would not be able to craft a meaningful personal life?

"This is crap," she said as she grabbed her purse and headed for her car.

Leonard realized he had been rude to a person he would go to the ends of the earth for before he would offend. He picked up his phone and dialed her cell. He quickly regretted his decision to call and hung up.

However, he did not hang up quickly enough, and her cell made a record of his call.

Driving into what was left of rush hour traffic, Lilly heard the phone, picked up and saw that it was Leonard. But there was no one there.

"That son of a bitch!" yelled Lilly at no one. "He hangs up on me – then calls back and hangs up on me again – that son of a bitch!"

In her anger she pushed the call back button. Leonard answered and Lilly lit into him with all the pent-up frustration she had from a thousand different cuts that life had endowed her with.

"You know, Leonard, I do not have time or patience for petty games and pouty boys. Lose my number!" and she hung up.

Leonard was stunned. What had he done? How could he have made such a mess? He had to try to salvage anything he could. Leaping into his new Audi and screeching out of the underground parking he raced to Lilly's office. He found a parking place right in front of her building and raced up the stairs. The door was locked. The lights were out. He ran back to his car and sped toward her house.

Lilly stormed into her home and threw her purse across the living room. She could not remember being so mad in all of her life. Then the thought hit her. What was she mad at, exactly? She could not find the cause. She had taken it all out on Leonard. Okay, he asked for some of it, because of his rudeness, but she thought, *I was way over the top.* Now she felt terrible, and reached for her phone to call Leonard.

Leonard was flying across Beverly Hills with the top down and he heard nothing.

Oh great! thought Lilly, *now he is playing hurt little boy again and not answering my calls.*

Looking around her living room made her feel claustrophobic. "I'm going for a walk!" she said with an air of finality. As she pulled the door open with some urgency she found Leonard standing there trying to decide whether or not he should knock. They both were shocked by the confrontation.

Leonard spoke first. "I'm so sorry."

"No," said Lilly. "I am the one who is sorry."

"I knew," began Leonard, "that I should not keep pressuring you to see me. I don't know why I couldn't wait till next week. You already saw me once this week."

Lilly looked up at Leonard with incredulity. "What are you talking about?" The fury that had subsided was beginning to rise again.

"I'm trying to say that if you will forgive me and still be my friend I promise I will only call once a week."

"Leonard! Are you mad? I like talking to you. It is one of the highlights of my day. But not when you act like a spoiled brat and hang-up on me just because I have over booked myself and have no time for the things I want to do. Then you call me and hang up before I can answer. Then when I call you back you do not answer and arrrgh."

Leonard's face became much softer, the anguish gone.

"A phone call from me is one of the highlights of your day? Really?"

Lilly could not help herself. The last thing she wanted to do was to laugh, but laugh she did.

"Leonard, you are so silly."

"I know. I'm a mess. But, you didn't answer my question. Do you really like talking to me? It's not a burden or you're not doing it just because you want to be polite?"

"Oh Leonard, every time I think I have you figured out you show me new depths of your innocence."

"So you really do have to go up to Monterey? That was not a made-up excuse?"

She took his hand, "No, dear friend, that was not an excuse. I'm sorry I lost it. That never happens, but I am tired. Very, very tired and I don't even want to go."

As Leonard shrugged, he pushed his other hand deep into his pocket out of sadness for Lilly, there he felt the bulk of his key.

"Hey! I have an idea! Why don't we take my new car? I'll drive. In fact I have been wanting to take a road trip in it. That way you can get some rest and it won't be so hard on you."

"You want to drive me all the way to Monterey?"

Leonard sang, "Do you know the way to Monterey dum dum dum te dum dum tee dum dum." Followed by, "Yes, yes, yes. What time do you want to leave?"

Before Lilly could answer Leonard offered, "Why not leave around 10:30 and then we can have lunch, take Highway 1, see some of the sights and have dinner by 7 in Monterey?"

"Have you driven there before?" Lillian asked.

"Only once, I drove my father up there after he had his stroke. I do remember this; it is as beautiful as anything I've seen in Europe."

Lilly let go of Leonard's hand and reached up and gave him a hug with the words, "10:30 it is."

Chapter 30

L EONARD WAS BUSY MAKING PLANS. ON the phone, on the Internet and in his mind. He had even programmed the route on his car's navigation system. He was busy.

By the time he rolled up to Lillian's he was confident he had done all he could think of to please this person he cared for so much. Excited as a child he stepped up to her door in a lively fashion. She was waiting only a few steps inside her home, bag packed and ready to go.

Door opened, hi's exchanged then stares. It was as if neither of them had considered in advance what the next move would be. So they each gave a giggle, Leonard grabbed her small bag and off they went.

His web search had led him to find that Brophy Brothers was an ideal place to have lunch. He had arranged for a table that was out of doors on the porch overlooking the Santa Barbara Harbor. Just below their vantage point was a vast array of every kind of small craft imaginable. From houseboats, to day sailors, simple fishing craft, luxury motor-driven yachts and sailboats capable of transoceanic adventure.

The steady, light breeze cooled the summer temps and made music as it spun through the nearby boat rigging – like oversized wind chimes, each with its own sound. In a high wind it could have been a cacophony, but in today's breeze it was a symphony complete with the vocals of a dozen Seagulls.

"Leonard, this is amazing. How did you find this place? Have you been here before?"

Leonard, somewhat shyly, admitted he'd found it on the Internet.

"Well you did excellent research, my dear."

They both ordered a seafood salad and a bowl of clam chowder, which, according to the internet, was among the very best chowder to be found. They consumed it, paid the bill, and it was so enjoyable they were reluctant to leave. However, new adventures waited.

In deference to Lilly's hair Leonard had kept the top up for the trip. The sports car was powerful and fast, but it was also comfortable and relatively quiet.

Just north of Santa Barbara the navigation system, in accordance with the route Leonard had preprogramed, instructed the driver to exit on to California Highway 1.

Once past Goleta, civilization seemed to dwindle and was replaced by a wilderness paradise that resembled what the mind might conceive if one had never personally witnessed the coastal beauty of California.

"Leonard, do you ever listen to music or the radio?"

"Not very often. Why? Do you like to listen to music or the radio?"

"Not always, but sometimes."

Leonard, sensing this may be one of those times, found the here-to-fore unused off-on knob and as the radio sprang to life, the announcer was saying, "Here is an old favorite of mine by Bob Bennett - entitled, *1951."*

The music began. Then a voice, almost ethereal, gave up the message and Leonard became lost in the lyrics. The singer told the story of how his father had married back in 1951. He didn't make much money, things were tight, and things were scarce. Their life was quite humble, yet he treated his mother like she was royalty.

As the singer watched his father and mother interact he came to realize that everything his father did was out of love and out of respect for his wife and for his family. No matter what the hard times were, they prayed, they stayed together, they saw it through. He stood strong and was so kind, and he loved her so much. When the song was over ...

The announcer returned to say, "and today's scripture is John 14:6. Jesus answered, 'I am the way and the truth and the life. No one comes to the Father except through me.'"

Leonard leaned in and switched the radio off.

"Did that offend you?" asked Lillian.

"What I just heard is too much to think about and still try to absorb any more," he answered softly.

Trying not to sound too much like a psychiatrist, Lillian asked, "What did you hear?"

"The song," began Leonard, "described what a real man is. As you know, better than anyone else, I have been trying to find meaning – find myself. I have been thinking the first step in understanding me is to understand what a human being is. The second step is to find what a man is, only then can I find who I am.

"That man in the song, that father, took his wife the same year my father married my mother. The year of their marriage is the only thing they have in common except for their genitals. That man was poor, my father was rich. That man lived a rich life, my father lived a poor one. That man gave all he had to his wife and his family, my father took everything. He took all that my mother had, even her life."

"What did he take from you Leonard?"

Thoughtful silence filled the car.

"My childhood. My sense of what is of value."

"I could not help, but notice," observed Lillian, "you turned off the radio after the announcer read a verse out of the Bible. Was that offensive?"

"No, but if what he said is true, then my theory as to how to find myself is flawed," said Leonard.

"In what way does that scripture, if true, undo your theory?"

"I believe the announcer said that Jesus claimed that he was, what? The way, the truth, the life – in other words – all the things I am looking for. After that he said Jesus said he was the only way to get to God. Put all that together and it means that before I can find the way, the truth, the life – in other words – find my place, I have to know who I am not just in relationships to other humans, but what my relationship is to God. That is a lot to absorb – so I turned the radio off."

Lilly had one last remark, "You are a very interesting man." Then she turned off her conversation and the two rode in absolute silence for thirty minutes.

Then Leonard threw some inner switch. "Enough about me, what would you like to hear or talk about. I'm ready to go on."

Lilly had been absolutely resting and was all the happier for it. She stretched and said, "Nothing, Leonard. I couldn't be happier ... except..." then she went silent.

"Come on, come on, out with it," urged Leonard.

"Well, it is such a beautiful day," declared Lilly, "wouldn't it be nice if this were a convertible?" She stretched again. Her stretching made Leonard tingle.

Leonard pulled over, pushed another button and with the words, "It is a convertible," the hard top of the car folded away.

That did it. That was the missing piece. They could not have had freer spirits if they were teenagers.

The miles evaporated beneath the wide tires of this formidable sports car. Soon there was a sign informing them they were in Big Sur, then Pt. Lobos, followed by Carmel-by-the Sea, and then they crested the hill and sailed down into Monterey. The Hilton Garden Inn was the venue at which Lilly would be a speaker, and that is where the navigation system directed them.

Leonard assisted Lillian with the check-in process, but did not register himself.

"Are you thinking you are going to sleep in my room?" asked Lillian, her right eyebrow raised.

With a strong sense of frustration and embarrassment, Leonard answered, "Of course not. I'm just not staying here."

"Oh," remarked Lilly, relieved and yet a little disappointed. "Where are you going to stay?"

More composed now, Leonard said, "Just down the road." Changing the subject, he asked, "What time do you speak tomorrow?"

"For some reason they made me the keynote speaker, and I have to fill an hour and 15 minutes from 10:30 to 11:45. Those poor people are going to be so bored. I don't even know for sure that I have enough material prepared to fill that much time."

"You could always talk about Brian's Better Tomorrow Foundation," offered Leonard.

"Hmmm," said Lilly, "I hadn't thought of that. Good to have that arrow in my quiver."

"Do you feel like dinner?" asked Leonard hopefully.

"Can I take a rain check on that? I need to go over the material for tomorrow. I'd like to just have room service bring me a tray." Then, seeing the disappointment in Leonard's eyes, she said. "But it is not fair to you for you to drive me all the way up here and then be put out on your own. You can get a tray in my room, too, if you promise not to talk to me while I'm preparing."

Leonard almost said, 'yes', but thought better of it and said "Tomorrow at noon, here at the hotel?"

She said, "Okay, it will be a short lunch. The seminar starts again at 1 PM."

They hugged and gave each other a kiss on the cheek. It was a warm and tender kiss. They said good night with words, and Leonard left her to her room service food.

Heading south, Leonard wound his way back to Carmel-by-the Sea. For his own evening meal he pulled into a shopping center and quickly found a place with an intriguing name: Sea Harvest.

Nothing fancy, but it was both a fresh-fish market and an eatery. Leonard felt reckless and ordered the Prawns and Chips with coleslaw. It was delicious and well worth the calories and the dangers of ingesting fried food. While there, he purchased a Dungeness crab, a couple of small octopi, a small piece of halibut, and some assorted produce and herbs.

The accommodations Leonard had arranged were here in Carmel. A three-bedroom cottage right on a cliff, overlooking the Carmel Bay, and beyond that, the Pacific Ocean. The cottage was like the Audi R8 Spyder in that someone else had prior claim, but he could see on the Internet it was just what he wanted. So, like with the Audi, he'd arranged a generous 'inconvenience fee' for both the dislocated renter and the agent, and now he drove into the residence that would change his life.

Arising early and taking his usual early morning run was a great way to start the day. Even better than usual because of where he was. Running the beach at low tide gave him an ideal surface and his body responded well to it. When he ran out of beach he climbed a bluff and found himself on one of the world's most famous and most beautiful golf courses: Pebble Beach.

He could hardly contain his appreciation of the beauty of it all. The Eucalyptus trees rose above the wind-shaped Monterey Pines, even as the pines rose above a plethora of other luxurious vegetation. All of this took on a surrealistic taint as a light morning fog established thin patches of mist that tied it all together.

A small golf cart sped toward him. The driver, an employee of the storied course, stopped his cart and got Leonard's attention.

"I'm afraid you are on private property," he said, not unkindly, "but I don't think you will have a problem if you are off well before the first foursome tees off at seven. Can you be out of here by then?"

Leonard smiled, "Of course, sir, thanks for the leeway."

"You're welcome. Have a nice day."

BACK at Lilly's hotel, he found the reception desk for the seminar and asked to buy a ticket.

"For both days or just one," said the comely young lady manning the desk.

"Just today, please."

Leonard was wearing one of his tailored suits. All of them were quite conservative, but this one spoke clearly of its birthplace: Italy. Those that took the trouble to analyze their fellow attendees probably thought him to be some big-shot medical person, maybe a psychiatrist, an ophthalmologist, dermatologist or perhaps a dentist, probably from the east coast. Undoubtedly, well off.

Leonard just wanted to fit in.

He did.

The event started at 8. For two and one half hours Leonard suffered through incomprehensible speaker after speaker.

Then Dr. Lillian Carroll was introduced. The reception was polite, but not enthusiastic; unless you count Leonard's.

She had been worried about not having enough content to fill the time. But she did include an overview of what the Brian's Better Tomorrow Foundation was beginning to do.

It was the first Leonard had heard about what had been going on in his absence. The audience had never even heard of the foundation and everyone in the room seemed fascinated. In fact, Lilly went 7 minutes over and not one person left or even squirmed in their seats.

Throughout her speech, no matter the topic, Leonard did not hear anything he could not, even as a layman, understand. The following applause held all of the enthusiasm the welcoming gesture had lacked.

Leonard held back afterward, and let all of the others congratulate and show their appreciation. Many gave her their card to stay in touch. One of those was a tall, good-looking German with a sizable accent. It was clear from where Leonard waited he had more than professional designs on the good doctor. Lilly was cool towards him, Leonard noticed, but not entirely disinterested.

When she finally set her attention on the last one to step forward, she said, "Good, you got here just in time. Lets grab a quick bite so I can be back by one."

Seeing another man move on this lovely person that had so captured him was the motivating factor that brought out an alpha male aspect that had been missing.

"Lilly, you are wrong about two things. One, I did not just get here. I watched every speaker. They were boring as hell and spoke in gobbledygook. You were brilliant and made it so easy to understand that even I got it.

"Two, you will not be coming back for the afternoon sessions. I have a rain check, given to me, by you, last evening. I am cashing it in. We are going for a leisurely lunch, a walk on the beach and maybe a swim. Let's go."

"Leonard, I can't do that. It would be rude to the other speakers," Lilly complained.

"Of course you can, darling. Come, let's not let this beautiful day go to waste in here." As Leonard said this he took her arm, gently, but with an undeniable determination and Lilly accepted it.

The valet, as previously directed, had the R8 front and center. A small crowd was standing around, asking what it was. As Leonard and Lilly arrived at the scene one nerdy fellow was exclaiming the virtues of this automobile.

Leonard waved the valet off and opened the door for Lilly, then went around and buckled himself in. He took exceptional pleasure in the defeated look of the would-be German suitor as they drove off in a car designed and built in the man's mother country.

As one might guess, a day that takes this kind of turn will not be a modest one. It will either be a disaster of Titanic proportions or victory of the ages. It was the latter.

The mighty 10-cylinder engine of the R8 5.2 swept them back to Carmel. When the subject of nothing to wear for the day that Leonard had planned came up, they went immediately into one of the lovely Carmel shops. If that one did not have everything needed – then on to the next. It was done with efficiency and the outfitting took little of the day.

He wanted everything to be perfect. The only things that did not go according to his design, worked out better than if it had proceeded as intended.

Lunch, a dash of shopping, a hike on the Pt. Lobos trail and then back to Leonard's cottage.

"What in the ...," said Lilly. "Where did you get this?"

"The internet and I are on a first-name basis," answered Leonard. "Come on girl, do not shilly shally nor dilly dally. Let's get changed and get to the beach."

A wonderful day. At its end, Leonard had Lilly take a short nap while he prepared a most savory and exotic dinner. Yes, some recipes were from the web. So what?

Dinner was served on the veranda above the ocean. The waves and breeze sang to those who could hear, and Leonard and Lilly could hear, see and smell every essence.

The Prosecco before dinner, the Verdicchio with the meal and the Sauterne as dessert, released all of the tensions of many days. Their conversation was rich and fluid.

"You have had quite a journey, Leonard. What have you learned and – what is the most important thing you have learned?"

"The most important thing I have learned is amazing. I have learned there is so much to be learned that no one ever has an excuse to be bored. I have learned to laugh. Especially I have learned to laugh at myself. I have learned that people are more important than money. I am not saying money is not important – it is very important. The fact that I have some has enabled me to do things that without it I could only stand by and watch people suffer or watch opportunities be lost.

"I believe it was your Jesus who said 'It is more blessed to give than to receive'. He is right. I have also found it is even more blessed, if that is the right word, to love. Love is what makes life worthwhile.

"I have learned that you, Dr. Lilly, have given me such a strong foundation to build my life on. Not only because of your professional help, but because I cannot help but think you believe in me. That is a terrible responsibility, to have someone of your quality see the best parts of you and make you live up to them."

This all slid out as an uninterrupted burst. Then he said something totally unplanned.

"I love you, Lilly."

She swallowed hard. "I know you think you do, Leonard. I also know that you lost your mother at a particularly sensitive age. The first time you came to my office you told me that I reminded you of her. I am afraid that what you think is love for me is really using me as a replacement for her. That is not a love you can build a strong relationship on."

Leonard had not touched her much during the day, but now he took her hand in both of his and said, "I have thought the same thing. In fact I thought that same thing for a long while. But, you know what I've decided? That my mother, what I knew of her, embodied every virtue a man would want in a woman; strong, intelligent, sensitive, vulnerable, funny, beautiful and caring. You embody those traits as well. Even beyond that, you are exciting. When I am in your presence, or even think about you, I am warmed and excited in a way I have never known."

Finding a source of bravery he did not know he had, he left himself open for utter destruction. "Lilly, do you love me in the same way?"

She laughed. "You know what's funny, Leonard?" She laughed again. "My Brian died a long time ago. He was such a sweet man. It was a sweetness that I thought I could not live without. If it had not been for Sharon and my work, I don't think I would have done well.

"I," she continued, "have had exactly six dates since he died. All of them were one-time events. There was never any intimate contact; there was not even a hint of a yearning. As I got to know the heart of you I saw that same innate sweetness. What is funny is that I feared my attraction for you was just a transference, an attempt, really, to get Brian back. Now here I am, the psychiatrist, learning from an ex-patient, that it is not the person, but the quality of that person that I need. I am weak that way.

"You asked me a question and you deserve an answer. I've loved you for a long time, Leonard. Longer even than I have realized. You are one of a kind. You are humble, soft, strong, proud, smart, very kind and you are developing a sense of humor."

This is what Leonard wanted more than he wanted air to breathe, but he was not prepared to hear it. Stuttering Leonard muttered "I, I, I'll get some more sauterne," he said as he stood and went inside.

Lilly followed. She came up behind him, put her arms around him, snuggled her breast into him and told him again.

"I love you."

She felt him tremble.

He turned, his face flushed with excitement. In defiance of the passion of that moment, Leonard was ever mindful of who Lilly was and what she believed. He could only protect her and the new and seemingly fragile relationship by asking; "I want to make love to you, Lilly. Do we need to get married first?"

She gave a gentle laugh that came from deep within, and asked, "Do you want to marry me?"

"Oh my word, yes. More than anything I have ever wanted," he blurted.

She burrowed deep within the protective enclave of his arms and chest and answered, "Then we will perform that part of the ceremony later, but we will make love tonight."

And so they did. And did. And did.

THE problem with pinnacles is that they are generally short lived.

LILLY and Leonard found their fall in a single cell phone call that came to Lilly somewhere around Oxnard.

Lilly's daughter, Sharon, called from Berkeley just to check in.

Lilly was ebullient. It was not a condition that could be obfuscated.

"Mom, what's up?" Sharon asked after detecting a manic happiness in her mother.

"Oh, nothing," chirped Lilly.

"Mom, cut the crap, are you on drugs?"

"Well, I guess you could say I was high."

"High on what, Mom?" Sharon's voice was showing a bit of panic. This was not her mother. Her mother did not get out of control like this. "You'd better tell me what's going on, right now!"

"Okay, okay, I am engaged."

"What are you talking about?" asked Sharon, her voice rising a near octave. "To who?"

"I think you mean 'to whom,'" answered Lilly, still in the afterglow of a wonderful breakthrough she'd never expected to find again.

Sharon had reached such a level of concern and frustration that she screamed at her mother. "Tell me right now what's going on. You're scaring me mom."

Lilly sobered her tone. "It's alright sweetheart. Leonard and I have just discovered we can't live without each other and we are going to get married. How about that."

Sharon's voice became steely. "When you say Leonard, do you mean Leonard LaFrance that creep who tried to buy my body?"

The ebullience evaporated like a teaspoon of water on a strip of Death Valley asphalt.

"Yes, I am speaking of Leonard LaFrance. Knowing him as well as I do I can assure you that is not his nature."

Sharon went ballistic. "Mom, I swear, if you do this, you will not ever see me again. How could you even think of such a despicable thing? I can't believe this happening."

Sharon was now in tears and everything that followed was gibberish until she hung up on her mother.

Leonard, having been in the fluffy clouds, just as Lilly had been, saw the cloud grow suddenly dark and heavy.

"What did she say?" asked Leonard.

There was no need to hide anything from each other at this point. Lillian was forthright. "She thinks you are a creep. She has only a limited knowledge of who you are, and from that perspective it is understandable that she is upset. She said I must choose between her and you."

Silence. Impenetrable, uninterruptible, silence. Only the deep hum of the engine and the whir of the tires.

Leonard felt the need to pull over.

He put the top back up.

Cars on the 101 raced by without caring.

Leonard cared. "Lilly, I have known love before, but I have never been in love before. Now I am. I really did not know there was such a vast difference. Yet, my love for you is big enough to know you cannot step away from your only child and ever find peace.

"I will drop you off. I will not be in touch with you again. I will not change my phone number, but please, please, do not call me unless Sharon can forgive me and bless our union. Under any other circumstances it will kill me to hear your voice."

He started the engine and they withdrew to their own corners of the car to mourn.

Chapter 31

WHERE DO YOU GO TO GET YOUR LIFE BACK?

PARIS. LEONARD ANSWERED HIS OWN QUEStion – but he knew it was an empty answer.

He had just gotten off the phone with Theo. He had apologized, but without explanation Leonard was firm that he had to go away again. He felt terrible admitting to himself and, in an oblique way, to Theo and the great people at Advantage Corporation, that he was too weak a person to face being in this town so close to Lilly without caving in and seeking her out.

He had offered Theo the use of his car. Theo said thanks, but would not feel comfortable enough to enjoy it. Leonard seriously considered selling it, but did not think he cared enough to even go through that. He put it in the garage.

Calling Jean and Lillian Fontaine to once again secure the apartment in Paris was more difficult to do than he had anticipated. He knew, that they knew, it was not a happy return.

THERE were many things that Leonard didn't know

Back in his native country other stories were unfolding that would directly or indirectly affect his life, but Leonard would not learn of them until much later.

For example:

Roland Pinion had always been a lucky man. He was lucky to be born, and not aborted. His mother had seriously considered it.

He was lucky to be born in America. His father had been born in Mexico and came to the U.S. for medical school.

Roland was lucky that both of his parents were highly intelligent and physically very attractive. He inherited a great deal of both.

He was lucky in that his father had become a world-class neurosurgeon and Roland was raised with a certain degree of affluence.

However, in Roland's opinion, the luckiest thing that had ever happened to him was to meet Sharon Carroll on the rebound after her catastrophic experience with Leonard LaFrance.

She was heartbroken and crushed like a flower's petal beneath a boot. She needed someone strong to lean on. On top of that, her hormones were absolutely raging. She had been completely prepared to surrender her extraordinary lovely self to Leonard. He was out and that is how Roland found his way in.

Roland, for the first time in his shallow life, was smitten.

Why, one may ask, why was he such a shallow man? His mother knew, because her grandfather had explained it to her when she was growing up.

His mother, Sabrina, had been born and raised on a vineyard across the San Francisco bay and a bit up to the north in Napa. Her grandfather and grandmother cleared the fields, planted every vine, dug up every stone they used to build their home, walls and wine cellar; they also raised six kids.

The wine they crafted was considered to be some of the best wine on Howell Mountain. Every year their entire production found willing buyers in some of the finest hotels and restaurants in San Francisco and the Bay Area.

However, what they had spent so much effort in building was not cherished by even one of those six kids. Their vision of a small family dynasty was doomed to die with them. Owning a vineyard sounds romantic, and it is, but none of them wanted to do the hard work that came with making wine.

Sabrina, Roland's mother, was the granddaughter of this couple. Her father was the youngest and he remained at home all through his schooling. He married, and brought home a wife and even raised their only child, Sabrina, there. However his passion was not farming. His call lay across the broad bay in San Francisco, in investment banking.

So Sabrina had some of the lessons that were taught by the earthy grandparents and some taught by 'only money matters' lessons from her dad.

Her mother was so quiet as to almost be invisible.

By the time Sabrina went to Berkeley she had become a full-blown hippy and was utterly disenchanted with the lifestyle of her parents. The one prerequisite for dad to pay for her college was that she must join a sorority. "Crap," said Sabrina, but went along.

Sabrina recognized, albeit too late, that her son, Roland, was a victim of what her grandfather called 'River bottom grapes syndrome'. Actually, Sabrina added the 'syndrome' part. However, the essence of the malady lie in the comparison of grapes that are grown in very rich soil with plenty of water down in the valley as opposed to those that grew in the poor, rocky soil, with meager water high up on the slope.

The conditions for the river bottom grapes were such, as her grandpa would say, that each vine yielded bountiful, large and beautiful bunches of fruit. They could not be any prettier, but they made wine without joy.

In grandpa's opinion the problem was that the lives of these grapes were too easy. Too much in the way of water and nutrients were readily available. The roots of these valley grape vines did not have to struggle down deep, past the surface soil, into the nutrient-starved gravel and even work their way into small cracks in the rock in order to find enough of those commodities to survive.

The parent plant of the river bottom grapes had so much energy that they produced voluptuous leaves and long, thick branches. These loving outgrowths shielded the grapes from the scorching sun of mid-summer.

By contrast, the mountain grapes were not planted in rich soil. No, not rich at all. Rather it was rocky, because the rich soil had long ago washed down the mountain.

The river was not nearby, and the gravely soil did not hold moisture for long. The roots had to dig and dig hard in order to reach water. However, as they did, they found new rock and that rock had to be penetrated. It was a struggle, but the search also yielded a source of minerality never experienced by the pampered plants of the river bottom.

A large part of the water for the mountain grape came from the early morning fog. It was meager and fleeting, but it was slurped up by the eager plants.

Like all living beings the mountainside plant, when threatened by the hostile environment, did not spend its energy on lavish adornment for themselves. Rather they grew fewer leaves and less voluminous vines and put their energy into the next generation, the grapes. It is as if they had an innate intelligence that ensured the survival of their progeny.

The result – fewer grapes – fewer leaves – deeper roots. The mountain grapes had a hard life, but it made them stronger; gave them a greater density of flavor and a marked amount of minerality that pleased the palate.

The sun can be brutal, especially on the south side of a mountain, but it can also fill each piece of fruit with the life force that comes from afar. With fewer leaves to shelter the grapes, they absorb more of this life. "If you look for that life in your mouth, you can taste it," Grandpa said.

When Roland was in his senior year of high school, taking honors courses, getting 'A's with ease, president of his class, countless girls calling, the idol of many of the guys, Sabrina suddenly realized she had raised a river bottom grape.

Everything came too easy for Roland. He had developed no deeper character, and, unless some hardships made him struggle, he was likely to remain a very pretty, very smart, very shallow man.

When Roland looked across the lobby of the sorority house that was hosting the mixer, he saw Sharon Carroll. He was immediately attracted, as he had been numerous times before. Yet somehow, even from this distance, there was something markedly different about this girl.

Grabbing the arm of one of the fellows who followed him around, simply because it was cool to be near him, Roland navigated the short distance between where they stood and where this attractive girl and the young lady she was in conversation with, were standing.

"You," said Roland to his wing man, "take the one on the right."

That girl was also attractive and it was an easy sell. However, when the wingman saw who his buddy was aiming for, he balked.

"Hey, no man, you don't want that," he said to Roland. "I know about that girl. She is strange. She never accepts a date from anyone, she won't hook up, she won't even return a call. Some of the guys think she is a lesbian."

The challenge only encouraged Roland as he had yet to be turned down if he was determined. Roland was smooth, very handsome and supremely confident. Those characteristics, at this precise moment, seemed to be the key that perfectly matched the lock that had held Sharon in a state of virginity till now.

In 30 seconds Sharon knew that she would be taking him to bed. Tonight.

Roland never knew what hit him. Days of daze followed. He could not focus on anything. He could not eat, he could not think. His conversations diminished to babel. It was confusing. She'd obviously been a virgin. He had known many.

Sharon, however, was much more passionate. So much so that it frightened Roland. Her appetite was fueled by a force that Roland could not recognize nor relate to. It was as if he were just along for the ride. Her passion forced him to deliver at unprecedented heights. She owned him.

After one encounter he told his parents about her and invited her home for dinner. His mother had had many young female candidates over. Women she considered to be made of the stuff that drives a man to greatness. Even she was unprepared for Sharon.

Roland's father, Arturo, was, in the vernacular, blown away. This girl was smart, beautiful, articulate, funny and exuberant. He knew why his son was so enamored. He could absolutely relate.

It reminded Arturo of a time a quarter of a century ago when he had met Roland's mother. Also at a mixer, in this case an intercollegiate mixer. He'd been attending Stanford and joined his fellow fraternity brothers along with another fraternity to take two charter buses to meet the girls at two U.C. Berkeley sororities.

Arturo had stood to the side and surveyed the room. However, his immediate fixation, though he did not yet know her name, was in the middle of a like-minded crowd of young men vying for her attention.

He did not want to be one of many, not one part of the throng. The only contact they had that night was when the party was breaking up and the men were about to board the bus, Arturo walked into the middle of the mass that surrounded his fascination and said, simply, "My Name is Arturo Pinion. You will be hearing from me."

All the other men standing around her, fellows who had used all of their best shtick over a considerable portion of the evening, did not understand. To them, Arturo looked a fool. Sabrina did understand. Her analysis of the man was distinctly more positive.

Knowing nothing more than what she looked like and the name of her sorority Arturo ventured forth. The very next morning found him driving his Porsche (his parents were from Mexico, but were not without money) across the old Dumbarton Bridge and up past Oakland to Berkeley.

He waited patiently outside of the sorority, and three hours later Sabrina returned from the library where she had been ensconced, studying.

When she approached the sorority house she saw him. Her walk slowed perceptively; she cast her eyes downward and took a deep breath. After a few steps she breathed again and looked up and into his large, brown eyes.

"I see," said Sabrina, "that Arturo Pinion is a man of his word."

"And I am humbled that you recall my name." He continued with a slight accent and perfect grammar, "You have me at a serious disadvantage, I do not know your name."

Arturo still remembered how she cocked her head, looked at him and then smiled as she offered, "I believe I am really going to like you." And she did.

Coming back to the present and the presence of his son's lovely friend, Arturo heard her say something about brain trauma and a foundation that she was passionate about.

Arturo was, as a brain surgeon, a man who was himself absorbed on a daily basis in the challenges associated with this debilitating event.

That dinner had been about a year ago. The parents had met. The match appeared to be perfect. The relationship on all sides and all levels was simpatico. As seen from the curb, no one could ask for more.

Sharon's mother flew to Roland's parent's home in San Francisco on four occasions. The last of those trips was about two months ago and it took place just four days after the heated phone call Sharon had with her mother while Lilly was driving home with Leonard.

Sharon's only comment regarding the phone call was that she could not imagine sharing a Thanksgiving dinner with Leonard at the head of the table, "Yuck."

Lilly had said nothing. The subject was too painful to approach and her relationship with her daughter too sacred to sacrifice.

Lilly had watched her daughter and Roland interact. Roland was a puppy. Sharon was more akin to a Mustang. There were not many places where their most passionate interests connected. Lilly noted this because she now had a new metric with which to measure: Sharon and Roland had nothing like the dynamic that she had with Leonard for those few beautiful hours before her daughter's phone call. She noticed, but remained quiet about it.

Chapter 32

ALL LIFE GOES ON TILL IT STOPS OR BEGINS IN EARNEST

MEANWHILE, BACK IN L.A, AT THE SMALL suite of offices that served as the modest headquarters for the Brian's Better Tomorrow Foundation, Shawn Davis was cranking it out. His plan was a good one, and as soon as Dr. Carroll and Sharon gave him the green light his energy was amazing.

He knew he was well prepared for this role. In his first few months of working as Mr. L's assistant he had, in a rare, unguarded moment, told his boss of his great dream of running a not-for-profit that really made a difference. That is why he worked so hard to get his MBA. The advanced degree was specifically targeted for the not-for-profit sector.

Over time the dream had begun to slip away. Now he not only had such a position, but more motivation than ever. Fueled by the twin desires to make his mark in the not-for-profit arena and the need to justify the faith the two women had placed in him he pulled out all the stops. In less than a year he had aligned the Foundation with over 60 of the best neurosurgeons in the nation. These men and women agreed that the Foundation would be the clearing-house for much of their pro bono work.

The hospitals were naturally a lot slower to make the same commitment, but five had already become an active part of his network, and another half dozen had taken it to their boards for consideration. Three others agreed to look at it on a case-by-case basis and would, in any

The Buyer

case, give his uninsured patients who were unable to pay a very steep cash discount.

In the past, the Foundation had given assistance in various ways. Primarily in assisting recipient's families with their relatively small personal expenses, like hotels and meals and perhaps plane fare. Medical care and medications were not often provided for. The Foundation now still did the former, just as it always had, but Shawn had dramatically widened the scope.

He used the surgeons themselves, along with other healthcare professionals, churches and social service entities, to funnel those who were in dire need into the Foundation's support system. This enabled the healthcare providers to exercise some of their own will and in return get help where they might need it from the Foundation. It was not just the Foundation asking for favors; it was highly reciprocal, a real partnership. There were now more pro bono offers from the healthcare sector, certain public monies found their way into the mix and churches and other civic groups had an opportunity to contribute as well.

This partnership expanded the ability of the Foundation to find and serve people in need. Equally important it multiplied the effective power of the Foundation's financial resources by having more association with those who would now willingly contribute medical services and other supportive donations.

In his effort to keep overhead low, Shawn was a one-man show. He had no staff except an answering service. His phone rang 24 hours a day. A usual workday ran between 15 to 17 hours and weekends were not sacred.

To be honest, he not only needed the next Cronkite dividend check for the patients, he needed to hire some staff. Shawn was exhausted. He also needed to get that dividend check so he could recoup some of the money he had lent the Foundation in order to limp through this period.

Thanks to the generosity of Leonard La France, the Foundation now had the ability to cover a portion of the actual costs of the surgical and rehab treatments. It also had resources to assist the patients and their families with a myriad of other expenses that crop up in these emergencies.

Shawn's recruitment of people needing help was titanic. Not one of the people involved when he took over the CEO position, not Dr. Carroll, not Sharon, certainly not Mr. L, nor Shawn himself had anticipated the overwhelming response. The problem was no longer finding the people to give aid to; the problem now was paying for it.

The only source of funds that the Foundation had control over was the dividends generated by the Cronkite Pharmaceutical stock. Even with CPC's gargantuan expenditures to roll out both the La Crosse technology and their new Alzheimer's drug, the Foundation would receive about two million dollars this year and promised a huge cash flow in the near future. That was the good news.

The bad news was that Shawn had expected 2.5 million this year based on the stock's past performance and the Foundation had incurred obligations of about 2.2 million. In the plan Shawn had a $300,000 cushion – in fact he had a $200,000 deficit.

It reminded Shawn of a joke cracked by a Jewish friend in college – "You want to make God laugh – make a plan."

Of course the amount of the dividends were never precisely known in advance and they were paid semi-annually. This made it tough to plan and it meant that sometimes income followed the Foundation's need for funding.

And now, as if to emphasize the over ambitiousness of Shawn Davis patient recruitment efforts, one of the most prestigious surgeons in the pantheon of doctors had brought him the Funderburke case.

Cassie Funderburke was a four-year-old girl who, while riding her trike in her driveway, lost control and went into the street. A car hit her trike and catapulted the child through the air and headfirst into a tree. There was hardly a visible mark, but her skull cracked and she was in a coma. Whatever modern medicine could do for her, had to be done soon.

This case came at a particularly awkward time. The Foundation bank accounts were all but empty. Shawn had to suspend assistance to any new cases pending the next dividend check, which would not arrive for about two months. Yet this one was so urgent, and how could he say no to a surgeon of this rank who was willing to work for free? Shawn had to ask himself what this interruption would do to the network he had built if the Foundation could not meet its promises.

The Buyer

The surgeon was ready to go, and the hospital agreed to charging only 10% of their stated costs. Yes, the surgery and care would be costly, but that was not the immediate problem as there was not to be a demand for immediate payment. Other expenses, however, needed to be covered now.

Not the least of which was an airlift to get her to that hospital, the anesthesiologist who was not yet on board with the Foundation, and the child's only parent had to leave her job and travel to the place where her daughter would be for the next four months for follow up and therapy – that is if, all went well during surgery. The Foundation's share would be in the neighborhood of $50,000.

Shawn did not tell the surgeon and the mother 'No', but he could not give her an absolute go until he found the needed money.

The mother was frantic. She learned that Dr. Carroll and Sharon Carroll were the heads of the Foundation. In an effort to secure the care her daughter needed she tried to reach them both. Strange as it seems, she was able to reach Sharon, a student, in a car en route between Berkeley and L.A. before she could reach the doctor.

Sharon and Dr. Carroll had both pretty well taken their hands off of the wheel after Shawn began to display competence. They got written reports weekly, and were impressed by the large number of people the Foundation was helping, but neither paid much attention to the metrics.

When Linda Funderburke, Cassie's terrified mother, unloaded on Sharon, Sharon tried to reach her own mother. At that time the good doctor was once again in the middle of a speech and had her phone turned off. Her only other resource was Shawn. She had elected to have little to do with him for personal reasons. Sharon was confident he was a good catch to run the organization, but she still had a visceral hatred of Leonard, and Shawn remained in the shadow of that hatred.

In her angst and frustration, Sharon was rude to Shawn.

After a three-minute tirade, loaded with "how could you's?" such as, "How could you leave a desperate mother hanging when her daughter's life and well-being are on the line" or "How could you besmirch the name of father, it's all done in his name, ya know." But the one that really got to Shawn was, "How could you have gone through all that money that Leonard gave us. You must really be living it up!"

Shawn shouted into the phone. "Where are you right now?"

Stunned by the exploding soul on the other end of the line Sharon just said, "I am driving down to LA."

Shawn, still shouting, which unnerved Sharon to the point she became relatively meek, "No, I mean where are you right now?"

"I am," Sharon said, "coming into Ventura."

"Are you going to your mother's home?" asked Shawn, still barely holding his temper.

"Yes, I'll be there in about an hour," said Sharon, anticipating Shawn's next question.

"I will meet you there in two hours," shouted Shawn emphatically.

"I can't reach my mother, she's not answering her phone."

"You drive. I'll find your mother. I will be there in two hours – we need to talk."

Click.

"Shawn? Are you there? Crap,"

SHAWN had taken the time to get to know Trisha, Dr. Carroll's receptionist. He even had her cell, and, after failing to reach Dr. Carroll directly, he called Trisha.

Trisha had Dr. Carroll's itinerary and knew she was just finishing a talk at the Santa Monica Miramar Hotel. Trisha thought the doctor would make herself available for 15 to 30 minutes after her talk to meet with colleagues.

The hotel was but only 10 to 15 minutes from Shawn's bungalow.

Jumping into his car and moving as quickly as possible through heavy traffic, he got to the hotel in less than 20 minutes. However, he just missed her.

In the meantime Lilly had turned on her cell phone and saw the messages from Sharon and Shawn. Her goal right now was to get to the supermarket and get something for her and Sharon for dinner. So she waited till she arrived in the store's parking lot to return the calls.

As she pulled into a convenient spot her phone rang and it was Shawn. She quickly learned he was extremely agitated, a persona she had never before witnessed in him.

When he told her that he needed a meeting in an hour and a half, it was not a request.

"Shawn, are you okay?"

"Not really, Dr. Carroll. I will be at your home in an hour and thirty minutes. Please be there. Sharon already knows."

AT the appointed time everyone was in the home of Dr. Carroll. There was an apprehension on the part of both women. In fact, Sharon even had her stun gun in her pocket.

However, Shawn arrived with a good-sized briefcase and he seemed to be cool calm and collected.

After a slightly strained round of hello's, Shawn spoke.

"May I have the use of your kitchen table?"

Lilly took a look at Shawn's briefcase and said, without a great deal of assurance or enthusiasm in her voice, "Yes, it's this way."

The small and tasteful kitchen could not afford space for a large table. Shawn looked at it and shook his head. "I'm afraid this won't work, can we use your dining room?"

A faint sigh of displeasure on Lilly's part passed quickly and the small band went into the adjoining room.

Shawn brought forth the papers from his brief case and systematically placed small stacks of papers around the table until it was completely covered.

Lilly, after a tiring day, asked, "What's going on Shawn?"

"Yeah," repeated Sharon, "What's going on?"

Very slowly, and with emphasis, Shawn said, "I am so glad you asked."

Then, moving to the stack with the earliest date, Shawn began his presentation.

"First, I want to thank you both for giving me the opportunity to serve as CEO of Brian's Better Day Foundation. That was no small thing. It took a lot of understanding for you to take that step.

"When you met me I was a lapdog, a sycophant, for Leonard La-France. And worse, when you met me Sharon, I was performing a despicable service. One I had performed on four earlier occasions and one I swore, as I left the car to approach you, that I would never repeat, even if it cost me my lucrative position. You could have, and maybe should have, dismissed me without another thought, but you chose to trust me. For that I thank you. I will always remember that kindness."

Both women saw the same gentleness Shawn had always shown, but now both also saw a man of strength. There was clearly an intent and purpose to everything about him.

Looking directly at Sharon, one who was always so sure of herself, but now not quite so sure, he said, "Sharon, you in particular had to make a difficult decision, for it was you that was injured by insult; an insult that I personally delivered. Again I am sorry and grateful.

"However in your phone call this afternoon you said something that puts our relationship in a precarious position. Before I continue let me ask you both this question. Do you recognize the papers laid out on this table?"

Both women did and nodded in ascent and murmured an acknowledgement.

Sharon said, "Those are your weekly reports."

"Have you," asked Shawn, "ever read them."

As he asked them he looked directly and deliberately at each.

It was Lilly who answered.

"Oh, the first couple of weeks I looked at them carefully, it was clear you were using the seed money appropriately, providing the same services the Foundation had always provided. After it was clear that you knew what you were doing I put my attention back onto what I was doing and thereafter only looked at the number of people being helped. And I must say the number was impressive, but I did not try to follow all of the numbers. That is why we brought you on board, neither of us had time to pay the proper attention."

"How about you Sharon?" Shawn asked.

"About the same. I did not pay much attention."

"I guess I can understand, but it is very disappointing to have worked this hard, given you detailed reports and no one is paying attention.

"Up until 10 minutes before you called, Sharon, we had brought in revenues from all outside sources that totaled $2,031,119.00. We had expenditures of $2,241,821.00.

"Some quick math will reveal we spent $210,702.00 more than we took in. You, Sharon, asked me point blank, 'What happened to the money,' indicating by tone and inference that you suspected I had used it for personal gain."

Shifting position, Shawn said, "If you had bothered to read the reports that I painstakingly prepared at the end of an 80-hour work week, you would have known that I have not yet hired a single person to my staff. There are three staff members in my original budget, but I elected to do the work myself until the finances were more predictable.

"You would have also noted that as of this date I have not drawn my salary, which by the way is a cut in pay from what Mr. L was paying me.

"Lastly, you would have noticed that the Foundation has borrowed more than $200,000 to meet its obligations to those we are trying to help. True, the reports do not say who the lender of those monies was, but to be clear, it was me."

Sharon, with eyes wide, said, "Are you telling us that you did not take a penny of your agreed upon salary, did all the work yourself, and lent the foundation $210,000.00 of your own money?"

"No," said Shawn in a very soft, strong voice. "I said that 10 minutes before you called I had lent the foundation a couple of hundred thousand dollars, but then, after hearing the plight of Cassie," Shawn paused as he drew out two last documents from his briefcase and handed one to Sharon, "I put in another $50,000.00 of my money so she could get the medical help she needed, now. When she needed it."

"Oh, no. Oh my God, I am so sorry, Shawn. I did. I did accuse you of misspending the money. I had no idea. I didn't read your reports. I acted like a child."

Shawn's remaining document was handed to Lilly. It was a letter of resignation.

Dr. Lillian Carroll read the letter. Her headache had begun about half way through her speech today. It started as a dull discomfort and as she read the letter of resignation it swelled to one of stabbing pain.

She looked to Sharon and handed her the paper. Her daughter had always been a source of pride and joy. She had given Lilly the strength to go on when all else was failing her. Now, however, that same daughter had destroyed the one relationship that could have brought her into life's fullness again and chased off a brilliant partner who lifted the burden of the foundation while continuing its work.

"Here Sharon, this is your mess. Get on it. I have a killer headache. No one wants to be around me right now and I don't want to be around anybody either." She paused, then added, "Except Leonard, and he is gone."

The two remaining figures watched Lilly disappear down the hall.

Sharon read the letter. She looked at Shawn, then back to the letter.

"Are you tired of it, Shawn? Do you want out? Is that what you want?"

Shawn's shoulders slumped. "Hell no. It's not what I want at all. I have loved the work. I have loved the challenges and I have certainly loved the gratitude that the recipients have shown."

Sharon crumpled the letter. "I refuse to accept this letter of resignation. Instead I offer you a sincere apology and I ask that you do as I did, as my mother did. Overlook our human frailties and give us the benefit of the doubt just as we gave you. If you will, I will give you my word that I will read every report, and if there is something I don't understand I will call you and get clarification. Fair enough?"

Shawn let out a long breath. One, it seemed, he had been holding since the phone conversation with Sharon this afternoon. He looked at her. He saw trust. Deep trust. He also saw, once again, the most beautiful woman he had ever seen.

Rather than answer, he asked, "Have you eaten?"

She sighed, "No, I haven't been hungry ... until right now."

"Can we," asked Shawn, "wrap this up over dinner?"

They both knew.

They did not discuss it verbally. They did not kiss or even touch. However, before Sharon went to sleep that night, she knew she would have some bad news for Roland come morning.

Chapter 33

Time to man up

As HE PACKED HIS BAGS IN HIS RENTED Parisian apartment he reflected on his journey to date. Leonard had noticed that he had been subconsciously praying lately. Wasn't too sure to whom. But little appeals to some higher power would creep into his thoughts. The most common thought was a request for guidance.

He had given the key events of the past a great deal of consideration as he walked the streets of Montparnasse, Saint-Germain-des-Prés and through the Bois de Boulogne.

There was one spot, however, that became his thinking place. He found it, as most treasured places are found, quite by accident.

The plush apartment he had rented from his two Parisian friends, Jean and Lillian Fontaine, was right on the Champs Elyse near the Avenue George V.

Anyone who had known Leonard previously would not have known him after his third week in Paris. He had always been somewhat slender. After he started running his body assumed a more athletic look. Now he was eating little and looked, not so much fit, as thin.

While he did bathe from time to time, his whole appearance could only be described as unkempt. His hair was longer than it had ever been. For the first time in his life he did not shave – not at all.

He tired of going to the cleaners, and had replaced his business and dressy sports clothes with jeans and turtlenecks.

He did not attempt to change his persona; there was nothing intentional about it at all. It was as organic as a metamorphosis can be. But it all fit well with the place and his state of mind. There were almost no distractions. He could think without the annoying responsibilities of maintaining an appearance consistent with his station in life.

Leonard would leave his apartment early. He would run or walk as the mood moved him. After several sorties around Paris, he found his favorite to be down the Champs to the southeast, all the way to the Place de la Concorde.

It is the largest Plaza in Paris, and right in the center of it is an astoundingly ornate fountain with gold leaf covering parts of the statuary. The streets were still made of individual rocks hewn to size and shape and put into place, all by human hands. There were large streetlight poles every few feet and the traffic was impressive.

But it was no place to think in peace.

Just beyond the Place de la Concorde he discovered Jardin de Tuileries or, in English, Tuileries Garden.

Sometimes he would linger in the garden. He loved its vast open plaza, huge pool with its fountains and the woods and flowers right in the middle of one of the world's foremost cities.

But even in the garden there were many distractions. When he decided it was not the kind of place he could go to be alone with his thoughts, he went back to a bridge that had caught his eye. It was part of the Place de la Concorde and offered an escape route across the Seine.

On the other side of the river it seemed more conducive to introspection. Leonard wandered through some of the back streets and out of nowhere he found his thinking place.

He did not enter in search of such a place, he went in to get a cup of coffee. The autumn was moving in and there was a slight chill in the air. A cup of coffee would be well tolerated.

THE room was rather long and equally narrow. As he looked about, he noticed a small group, mostly student-looking young people, sitting around an older gent.

The Buyer

Company is not what he sought and Leonard was thinking about leaving when he noticed a staircase in the back of the café. The stairs were a divider, of sorts, the larger part of the room was on the right where the old man and his intense listeners were holed up, and on the left was a small table all by itself. *That would be better*, thought Leonard, and he settled in.

He had been in Paris long enough and consumed a sufficient amount of coffee to order it with barely an accent. Beyond that, Leonard was very much an American.

"Café Au lait , s'il vous plait."

The waiter answered with a brusque and disinterested, "Oui."

While waiting, he tried to look at the gathering on the other side of the stairway, but made no attempt to move to a site with a better view. He could hear the melody and rhythm of questions and answers, but even if he were fluent in French there was no way he could have heard clearly enough.

Fishing into his right jacket pocket he pulled out a pair of reader glasses. He had never needed them, but age has a way of sneaking up on even the best of us. He put them on.

Leonard waited until the waiter brought the coffee before reaching into his left jacket, there retrieving a note book and a ball point pen. He began to write. In a random order he listed the items that were on his mind, both the good and the troubling. A list that the more he thought about it the longer it grew.

When he reached a point where the list seemed complete, he tore out the three pages and laid them side by side. Leonard wrote the first item at the top of the sheet. He drew a line underneath the item and another line, perpendicular to the first that came straight down the middle of the page.

Just as his father had taught him he wrote the word "Pro" to the left of the line and the word "Con" on the right. He listed all of the pros and cons that came to mind for that item, and went to the next clean sheet, where he repeated that process with a new item.

An hour or so later, Leonard was unsure how much time had passed, he heard a rise in the commotion level coming from the direction of the old man and what appeared to be his students.

The young people were all on the way out. They seemed to be in a good mood.

Leonard went back to his work, but there was new commotion, though not a disturbing one, as more people drew up chairs at the old man's table. Leonard pushed on.

He had not been eating well. The waiter came and with a strong hint of arrogance gave him a menu. *The waiter wants me to order if I am taking a table,* thought Leonard. He then looked around and saw that only the old man and his crew and himself were the only patrons.

"Ce va," said Leonard, then ordered some French onion soup and returned to his work.

And so the day went. Leonard saw a large crowd come by for the dinner hour. They smoke and drank wine as they ate. Almost everyone seemed to enjoy talking. The place grew louder and louder. Then the crowd drifted out, and the only ones left were the old man, two avid listeners, the waiter, and Leonard.

Leonard rose and stretched his lanky, and now somewhat gaunt, frame, collected his written materials and headed for the door.

The waiter, always presumptuous and now piqued, caught Leonard and handed him the bill. Leonard had genuinely forgotten. He handed the waiter the exact amount and then gave him a 200 Euro note for a tip.

The old man was still at his table and now alone for the first time. He caught Leonard's eye and called out in perfect English, "See you tomorrow."

What's he talking about? thought Leonard. Then realized the old man was right. He would be coming back tomorrow, and probably the day after as well.

Indeed, for many, many days this was his place to think, to work, to try to make sense of where he had been, where he was now and where he wanted to go. He took to the task like the morning sun takes to the noonday sky. Leonard's small notebook and ballpoint pen were replaced by a laptop computer. He could not have been more serious.

It was on the fourth day of the third week of his coming to the café that Leonard asked about the old man and all of the people who came to his table. The old fellow, like Leonard, was there every day. Even the waiter had a day off, but not those two.

The Buyer

The old man always had some kind of an audience.

Of course, Leonard did not always tip as grandly as he did on day one, but he was always generous, and the previously contemptuous waiter was now his new best friend. Yet, he and Leonard never spoke. It was certain that the man who greatly resembled a starving artist, but who was obviously only starving because he was not hungry, did not desire small talk.

That is why the waiter was taken aback when Leonard said, "Tell me about the old man."

Once the waiter regained his composure, he was a well font of knowledge, some of it useful.

"I," announced the waiter in English that was quite good, but with a distinct French accent, "have worked here for twelve years. He has been coming here long before I arrived. From what I have heard he used to be a priest. He is from a wealthy family and this is how he spends his time."

"Who," asked Leonard, "are all the people who sit at his table?"

"They come for advice." said the waiter. "He, as you might say in English, holds court here. The people just come. Sometimes the same people, sometimes they are different. He does not make appointments – he sits – they come."

"Have you ever talked to him?"

"Non."

Leonard could not help but ask, "Why not?"

The waiter threw up his hands and said, "I have never had a question."

Leonard nodded, indicating the conversation was over. He felt sorry for the waiter. He felt a little sorry for himself, because he had so many questions, but sorrier still for a man who had none.

As the weeks and days had gone by Leonard had thought of more things that troubled him. He treated them all the same. Examining the positives and the negatives of each issue. Finally it was clear what he wanted. What was not clear to Leonard is what he could actually have.

Leonard repositioned his chair, for the first time, to see the old man at work. He wondered, but he did not move toward the sage. There was a small gaggle keeping the man they called, "Papa" busy anyhow.

He ordered his last cup of the wonderful French Onion Soup and finished in little time. He then shut his laptop with finality that clearly stated he could do no more here. He closed his eyes and simply sat. For how long, he was not certain, but it was precisely at this time he became aware of a presence. Looking up he found he was looking into the bright blue, but ancient, eyes of the old man. Papa Chevalier. And a profound meeting it was.

As if it were the most natural thing in the world, Leonard asked for the man's story. Papa Chevalier gave him a *Readers Digest* version. When Leonard was comfortable that this meeting was providential, he told Papa Chevalier his entire life story.

Over the next several days Papa would give Leonard all the hours he could without hurting others who sought him out. Papa listened carefully to every word, and, as happened so often, he was amazed at the complexities of some people's lives.

More than a week later Leonard finished. He had told the sage everything in exchange for some words of wisdom. And he was surprised that he still had so much emotion invested in his past, including a lot of quiet anger.

"So," said Papa Chevalier, "I have seen you earnestly working over here. Do you have the answers you were looking for? Do you have it - figured out?"

Leonard opened his lap top and showed Papa his work and he gave no explanation. He did not need to, because Papa was familiar with the system.

"I know this. This is what you Americans call the Benjamin Franklin method for making decisions, oui?"

Leonard nodded.

Papa closed the laptop and folded his wrinkled hands.

"Leonard," he said, "there are many things you want to do, but there are only three things you must do. Forgive your father. He was wrong, absolutely wrong, but thought he was doing the right thing. If you hold on to that anger, it is like drinking poison and expecting your enemy to die. It will not happen.

"Simultaneously, you must seek God, now. There is a God and you are not Him. Let Him be God, not only is it proper, it also will take a lot of pressure off of you."

"Papa, all due respect, how do I know there even is a God?"

"The scriptures tell us that man is without excuse, because God has made Himself known through what He has made."

"What do you mean, by 'What He has made'?" inquired Leonard.

"I see you have a bit of technology in your laptop. I'm sure you've seen the tablets, like, what are they called, iPads?"

"Yes," answered Leonard.

"Let's say you are walking down the beach of a deserted island and you spot a black rectangular thing in the sand. You pick it up, touch the screen and it springs to life. You have never seen one and you know nothing about it except what you see before you.

"Are you going say, this device had a brilliant designer? Or are you going to say, 'I get it, the sea, the sand, the sun and time have melded together to make this complicated device'. Interestingly, the human eye that is looking at the iPad is probably 10,000 times more complicated than the iPad itself. Is there a God? I repeat, man is without excuse."

Papa Chevalier stood up, reached for Leonard's hand, which was promptly offered. "You will not be needing me anymore, at least for now." He turned, but Leonard grabbed the tail of Papa's coat.

"Wait a minute," complained Leonard, "you said there were three things I must do, but you only gave me two. What's the third one?"

Papa grinned. It was a setup. With the warmest of smiles he told Leonard, "I thought that one was obvious. The final thing you must do is to go back to L.A., find the Lilly person you kept talking about and find her daughter. Tell Lilly - you love her and want to marry her and spend the rest of your lives finding out how the two of you can make God smile."

Papa moved back a half a step and concluded with, "Tell the daughter that you were a fool, you probably still are a fool, but your penance will be assuming the responsibility of making her mother happy for the rest of her days. Au revoir, mon ami."

Leonard paid his bill, gave a generous tip and said he would not be back. He then gave the waiter a 500 Euro note that was to pay for any expenses Papa Chevalier or his guests might incur. The waiter was both elated and in grief.

Papa Chevalier already had three young boys huddled around him.

Leonard, clasping one hand on the shoulder of one of those young men said, "Pardon my interruption, but if you are smart, you will listen to, and follow the advice of this man. You are lucky, or perhaps, blessed, to find him. I know I was."

As Leonard closed the café door behind him, the three boys looked at each other and one said, "Qu'est-ce que c'est?" Another said, with a shrug "Je ne sais pas." Then looking to the old man for clarification they found him uncomfortable even with humble praise and so he also shrugged and said he did not know either.

LEONARD did not walk back to the apartment. He took a taxi. After he packed he called Jean and Lilly Fontaine and told them of his decision to go back home. He said he would leave two weeks rent since he had given no notice. They argued, but Leonard persevered.

The taxi that had brought him back from the café was still waiting, as promised, and that is how Leonard made it on to the overnighter to L.A.

Chapter 34

CLEAR INTENT

SHARON WAS TREMBLING AS SHE HUNG UP the phone. She had decided, and she had promised herself, that she would call Roland this morning and tell him what she now knew. It was an easy decision to make, because it was based on a true and undeniable reality. She did not love him in a way that would bond them for life.

Deciding was much easier than doing. Roland did not take the news well. It confused him. Life had never collided with him with such force before. He wept, he pleaded, but Sharon was too strong and she held her ground against Roland's forceful tide of emotion.

It was 11 AM. She had been up for five and a half hours, steeling herself for the call. Exhausted, she lay back on her bed, closed her eyes, but her mind was moving too rapidly to even begin to sleep. She covered her head with a pillow. Sharon wondered if she had misread Shawn Davis. Was she the only one who interpreted the signals as intense? It did not matter. She did not cut off her relationship with Roland because she thought Shawn was more her type. She cut it off because the relationship was not right.

The doorbell was startling. She was not asleep, but she was in a different world, and the shrill sound of the bell was intrusive.

Dragging herself from the bed, Sharon slothfully stumbled to the door.

Not expecting anyone, she peered out the peephole out of caution. His profile was strong and gentle. She let Shawn stand there while she appraised him. He did not seem to be perturbed to be waiting. Okay, she finally turned the latch, even as she continued to observe him through the peephole. The mechanical sound caught his attention and his focus was now on the door. In fact it was on the peephole.

Sharon smiled. She did not open the door right away. Instead she enjoyed looking at this man, full face, for a moment longer. He was becoming visibly apprehensive. She wanted to continue looking, but she also wanted to open the door and throw her long, lovely arms around his beautiful neck and hug him with all of her might.

She opened the door. Before she could do anything about giving him a welcoming hug Shawn blurted out his well-prepared speech.

"Sharon, I know about Roland. Your mother told me all about him, because of how his father and he were willing to help your father's foundation."

"I looked him up on Facebook. He is very handsome. I'm sure he will be a great surgeon someday, and he is a man any woman would love to have as a husband, but before you marry him I must tell you how I feel. I don't expect an answer from you today. I am only asking for the courtesy of hearing me out."

Sharon just stood there. A very silly grin plastered across her face. After a tense moment she spoke.

"Why don't I save you some time, Shawn Davis?" She paused. "Why don't I save both of us some time?"

Shawn grew tense.

"I know I am going to regret cutting you off. You undoubtedly have a wonderful speech prepared."

Shawn, now as desperate as a man who is watching his oxygen supply being severed, tried to speak, but he had nothing to say.

Sharon did. "Why don't you just ask me to marry you and then we can eat something."

It took a moment. Shawn was dealing with the concept of total defeat. It was a brutal thought. It gripped both his mind and his heart as he saw the hope of a good life going into the arms of another man.

Abruptly, she was now asking him to ask her to marry him. *What the ...*

Shawn was momentarily overcome, but he was not dense. Dropping to one knee, there on her mother's porch, he proposed marriage. She graciously accepted.

Later that same day they set a date and he gave her a ring.

Their days were then full of each other. There was only a week before Christmas break when she could be here in L.A. full time for nearly three weeks. They spoke of Shawn coming to Berkeley frequently and of meeting half way on other occasions.

The teeter-totter of life

LILLY left her physician's office. He had just officially informed her of that which she had already unofficially found for herself. She was pregnant. *Funny*, she thought, *I have become pregnant twice. I have only known two men sexually, but both times the pregnancy occurred out of wedlock.*

With Brian it had ended beautifully. This baby would not know their father, a most difficult realization. Almost as difficult was the strength it took to repress resentment for her daughter. It was Sharon who demanded she quit Leonard. Now it was Sharon who, in a dramatic example of obliviousness, had excitedly told her mother of her engagement to the man who was the messenger in the very act that had so offended.

Lilly had no place of refuge. Sharon was at home for Christmas break; she could not go there. Being pregnant, she could not go to a bar. So she drove to her office, cancelled all of her appointments and sent Trisha home. Knowing she could not lose herself in a bottle, in her daughter or in her work, Lilly locked her inner door and lay on the couch where she usually put those in need of counseling.

The eagle has landed

BEFORE boarding the plane in Paris, Leonard had made two calls. One to Theo to ask if he would be so kind as to arrange for someone to pick him up at the airport. Theo declined to get someone, he wanted to do it himself.

There was a great deal to talk about since Leonard had not followed his previous pattern of staying in touch with Theo and other company leaders while traveling. And Theo genuinely liked Leonard. It would be good to see him. All the people who knew Leonard well had been worried about him.

Leonard's second call had been to old Bill Bishop, the man who had been the barber for both he and his father.

"Bill, do you still have a pair of scissors?"

"Who is this?" snapped Bill. He had never spoken with Mr. L on the phone and did not recognize the voice.

"Leonard LaFrance."

Again Bill said, "Who?"

Leonard, with great patience and kindness said, "It's Mr. L, Bill. Can you cut my hair tomorrow?"

"Damn right. I'll just stay by the phone and you let me know when and where."

"Thanks, Bill, that's just what we'll do. I'll call you in the morning."

"Yes sir."

Leonard stood at the curb outside his terminal at LAX. Right where he was supposed to be. A big, dark-blue pick-up with dual tires on the rear pulled into the 'no parking' area. Theo rolled down the tinted window and looked for Leonard. Leonard laughed quietly. He knew his appearance was quite different than when Theo had last seen him.

After Theo had a chance to examine all of the faces, Leonard stuck his bearded face in the window and said, "Can I catch a ride with you?"

"No way," said Theo, as he eyed his boss with amazement.

"Way," said Leonard, as he threw his bags in the back seat and piled in.

"Where to Mr. L?" Theo knew full well that he could call him by his first name, knowing that, it made it all the more enjoyable to call him by the name all of the other employees knew him by.

"Hey, Theo, good to see you and very nice of you to come yourself. How about heading to my house. I want to change and get my car. I haven't driven since I left."

"Your house it is. Would you care for a business update?"

"By all means. Are we still in business?"

"Yeessss," said Theo in an exaggerated effort for the sake of humor.

"Revenues are growing at nearly 3% per month and for the last three months the actual book value of the company is increasing at a rate of 2.2% per month. The company I brought in is doing well, except that our model is being copied by others so the profit margins are shrinking, because we are paying more for the distressed properties. We are no longer the only buyer."

Handing Leonard a folder he said, "I brought you an extended P&L for the time you have been away."

Leonard was surprised at how quickly his mind was back on business after not giving it a lick of thought for the last couple of months. Theo drove and was silent as Leonard perused the reports. It took only a few minutes for Leonard to come up to date.

"Not only is the bottom line better," Leonard said, "but the internals are stronger. I sometimes amaze myself at how smart I am."

He skipped a beat. Then Leonard continued. "To bring on a guy like you was a stroke of genius." They both enjoyed the mutual compliment.

In the quietness of the cab with only the sounds of the engine and the road, Theo asked a personal question.

"How is Leonard doing?"

"He is, like the more fortunate part of humanity; on the mend."

Leonard went on. "He is decisive, he is determined, he is hopeful and a little less callow, a lot less shallow and ready to break into life at a full gallop. And how is Theo?"

"Theo is good. I still have my home in San Diego, but with my kids all grown my wife has moved up here and we are seeing more of each other than we have in a long, long time. When you first gave me the reins of the company I was working 16 to 18 hours a day, but I have finally gotten the rhythm. I work only a half a day now – 12 hours. I am very happy."

"Glad to hear it. You are a good man, a serious man. You deserve the fruits of a good life."

"Don't mean to be too personal, but was I right about my observation that Doctor Carroll had eyes for you."

"Yeah, Theo, you were right. Oh so right."

Leonard continued to talk about Lilly by changing the subject.

"I have finally come to peace with my father. He taught me many things. Most of them damn good, a few of them – pathetic.

"He had me start everyday by concentrating on what I most wanted to achieve that day. Today my goal is to stake my claim on Dr. Lillian Carroll. I do not know how all of the pieces will fit together. I know that behavior has its consequences, and my behavior had some serious potholes. One of them has done serious damage. I do not know how long it will take to mend that damage, but I am in for the struggle."

Leonard concluded by offering, "I know what I had with Lilly. I've known it for some time. I know it is rare. It is so easy to see. I know it is a treasure I would forever regret losing. And I will lose it if I do nothing. I knew all of that even before I found my mentor."

Theo could not hide his amazement. "You needed a mentor? You are a mentor."

"Every mentor needs a mentor," said Leonard.

Chapter 35

THINGS YOU DO NOT KNOW

HAWN TOOK SHARON TO LUNCH. THERE were only a few days left before their uninterrupted time together would halt. He took her to the same bistro where he had arranged for Mr. L to eat; sometimes with Dr. Carroll and even with Sharon. He was unclear as to his motivation to bring her here, yet it seemed like the right thing.

"Why," asked Sharon "did you bring me here?"

"Not sure, but I have learned over the past year to use my second brain: my gut."

"Why would your gut tell you to bring me to a place that reminded me of Leonard?"

"Good question," followed by a moment of thought, then, "maybe, because your memory of Leonard may be the only thing that stands in our way. Maybe we can't get to the heart of where we want to be with each other until we confront what Leonard" he paused and took a deep breath "and I – did to you that day."

"I don't want to talk about it. It makes me sick," said Sharon.

"Exactly," responded Shawn. "Let me say it was wrong. I performed that service less than a half dozen times and got sicker each time I did it. As you know, I vowed it would never happen again. I cannot tell you how angry I was with Mr. L for putting me in that situation. I have relived the whole thing many times in my head.

"You know what I finally figured out?" Shawn continued, "He did not understand that what his father trained him to do was wrong. It became clear how wrong when you stuck your head in the back of a limo and told him, – and me – off. And it goes without saying, you were right.

"Sharon, in a real way what I did was more despicable than what he did, because I *did* know better.

"The truth is Mr. L was like a big, dumb kid. Smart in some ways and utterly unconscious in others. But on the whole, the guy is one of the most decent and generous men I have ever known. I wish you could see that, but I understand why you can't," concluded Shawn.

"The important thing," said Sharon, "is that I have forgiven you, and I am ready to walk through life with you knowing what I know. I don't know that I will ever experience that sort of forgiveness with your Mr. L."

As if it were perfectly planned

LEONARD had run four miles. He had showered, Bill had cut his hair and had delighted in trimming Mr. L's new beard. Getting dressed in his usual L.A. garb made him a bit uneasy. He changed back into a fresh turtleneck and jeans.

The big sports car started right up.

It was now 6 PM. Leonard did not want to call. He wanted to tell Lilly in person that he was back and of his intentions. He first drove to her home. She was not there.

He then drove to her office and found a place right in front. Looking up at her window it was clear there were no lights on that could be seen from the street.

On the off chance Lilly might be there anyhow, Leonard knocked on the door. As he had feared, there was no answer. He turned, but then turned back and knocked hard enough to bring discomfort to his knuckles.

LILLY had dozed. But that was a distinct pounding on her outer door. In her groggy state, she did not go to the door, but to the window. She peaked through the blinds at the street below. There was no mistaking that car for any other. She was either dreaming, which was, in her mind, entirely possible, or, that was Leonard at her door.

As if sleepwalking, Lilly went to the door and opened it. A thin man with a beard, who looked a lot like Leonard, was standing there. Now she had a decision to make. Was this a cruel dream that let her think she was awake and would only snatch her back to the emptiness when she awoke – or – was this the real thing?

There was no way she would willingly interrupt this if it were but a dream. When he bent slightly to accommodate their difference in height and wrapped her in his arms, she was still not completely sure until he said, "Lilly, you have opened so many doors for me that had always been closed. I have learned how to love and I know I love you. I know I am in love with you. I may not be the quickest study, but once my lesson is learned I am tenacious, you know that. Also know that I'm not going away and I will meet Sharon's standards, whatever they may be. I know what we have. If you know it too, just hug me back."

Lilly did hug Leonard back with a hug that would stand the test of time.

His father never taught Leonard that.

Epilogue

Shawn and Sharon devoted their lives to each other, their three beautiful children and their foundation. The earnings from Leonard's gift, coupled with their ingenuity and hard work gave respite to thousands of families each year whose lives were interrupted by a brain injury.

Theo Webb kept a balance that enriched his family's life, the owner and employees of the Advantage Corporation, while he continued to assist those who needed a leg up.

Angelica Porta cared for her mother and her only husband Alberto. She became a full professor of English Literature at the University of Bologna. They had one child; a boy they both decided to call Leonardo.

Massimo lived every day as only a good looking, ponytailed Italian who owns a hip and prosperous coffee bar in one of the most beautiful places on earth, could. However, even a good-looking Italian knows when he has the right woman, so he married Laura.

Samuel Levine called Mr. L to inform him that the Simon Peachtree & Sons Master Welders Company had just sent them a check in the amount of $183,412.18 for his 10% as per agreement, but Sam could find no such agreement. Did Mr. L know what it was about? Mr. L responded to Sam by saying, "That is great news, Sam. It was a personal investment. Earmark that check and all future payments from the Peachtree investment to go directly into the Sarah Peachtree Foundation. Leonard then called Simon to congratulate him and his family on the roaring successes and told him where the profits would go. Simon liked that. Sally got on the line and said her big family room and her retirement fund were both "Lookin' good."

Leonard and Lilly were married in a church that became their home away from home and a place through which they could perform many a selfless and generous act; he also donated his Audi R8 to an auction to benefit Brian's Better Tomorrow Foundation. Leonard bought a pick-up.

At Leonard's encouragement Lillian wrote a book based on her commonsense approach to life and overcoming its problems that stayed on the NY Times best seller list for two and a half years. Her opportunities to speak became bigger and more important. Leonard made it his job, in addition to feeding great money-making ideas back to Theo, to go along on Lilly's trips and play babysitter to their twins, Samuel and Sarah. Leonard never again bought anything of importance without Lilly's input.

Were they happy? Think about it.

About the Author

If one-word descriptions are permissible, Chet Hanson is a man who feels he is best described as Grateful. His family believes he is best described by the word Creative. God Himself may well describe him as Problematical. He is 5th generation Californian and has now taken refuge in Prairie Village, Kansas. He has been a singer, a soldier, creative consultant and a founder of several businesses. His only major grief was that when he finished this novel he loved the characters so much, he suffered post partum.

Special Thanks from the Author

This book would never have had the richness without the wonderful people who came to mind as I built the characters. It would never have had the finished quality without the help of a good, knowledgeable and talented man by the name of Skip Coryell of White Feather Press. It would never have had the cover artwork that pleases my heart and has so perfectly captured Leonard La-France without the artistry of Steven Graber with valuable input from Roxann Graber. And many thanks to Ron Bell for tying the cover all together.

And to the following I offer my heartiest of thanks:

- to Kurt Brungardt and Tracy Marx for their insights and wonderful selves

- to Nathan Rightenhour for guiding me to the right recording equipment and teaching me the basics

- to John "Chris" Morris for cleaning up my messes and his friendship

- to Scott Garen for his creative spirit and loyal friendship

- to David Lawrence XVII - a generous mentor

Get the Audiobook now!

The Buyer, in audio book form, has been narrated by the author and may be found at Audible.com. You may find other narrations by Chet Hanson at PapaChet-StoryTeller.com or White Feather Press.com.